'Lisa Wingate takes an almost unthinkable
chapter in our nation's history and
weaves a tale of enduring power'
Paula McLain, author of *The Paris Wife*

'Heartfelt, honest, and entirely entertaining . . . this
poignant story will touch your heart from
the first page to the last'
Kristin Hannah, author of *The Nightingale*

'One of the year's best books . . . It is impossible
not to get swept up in this near-perfect novel. It
invades your heart from the very first pages and
stays there long after the book is finished'
Huffington Post

'A poignant, engrossing tale about sibling
love and the toll of secrets'
People Magazine

'Wingate roots her tender tale in hope,
redemption, and family'
Publishers Weekly

'Wingate sheds light on the toll that aging and
disease take on families as she launches a
new series with broad appeal'
Booklist

Lisa Wingate is a former journalist, an inspirational speaker, and the bestselling author of more than twenty novels. Her work has won or been nominated for many awards, including the Pat Conroy Southern Book Prize, the Oklahoma Book Award, the Carol Award, the Christy Award, and the RT Reviewers' Choice Award. Wingate lives in the Ouachita Mountains of southwest Arkansas.

Also by Lisa Wingate

Before We Were Yours
A Month of Summer
The Summer Kitchen
Beyond Summer
The Book of Lost Friends

Dandelion Summer

LISA WINGATE

Quercus

First published in the USA in 2011 by NAL Accent,
now Berkley, an imprint of Penguin Publishing Group,
a division of Penguin Random House LLC

First published in Great Britain in 2020 by

Quercus Editions Ltd
Carmelite House
50 Victoria Embankment
London EC4Y 0DZ

An Hachette UK company

A CIP catalogue record for this book is available
from the British Library

PB ISBN 978 1 52940 251 3
EB ISBN 978 1 52940 250 6

10 9 8 7 6 5 4 3 2 1

Typeset by Jouve (UK), Milton Keynes

Printed and bound in Great Britain by Clays Ltd, Elcograf S.p.A.

Papers used by Quercus are from well-managed forests and
other responsible sources.

To Samuel, Halley, Jarrett, and Shane,
May you find the paths
To your own Camelots
And recognize them when you get there.
To my dad, the guy with the punch cards and printouts –
Thanks for not panicking
When I quit computer school to study writing.
And to my grandfather, Norman,
Thanks for letting me borrow your name
And for that great line about old age and treachery.

CHAPTER 1

J. Norman Alvord

A single drop of water changes the ocean. A noted colleague of mine once asserted this as we dawdled over lunch at a restaurant near Cape Canaveral. 'How can it not?' he demanded. 'Some amount of matter is displaced. There's transference of energy. Nothing is as it was before.' We were young then, certain of our own importance. Convinced that our presence in the world, that our work, was destined to change it. 'I discussed it with Einstein, you know,' he said, and went on to share a story of having accompanied the physicist on a fishing trip, of all things. They'd considered the drop-of-water theory while Einstein reclined on the deck of a sailboat, trails of pipe smoke drifting lazily into the air. Less than a year after their conversation, Einstein's sudden demise sent a ripple around the world.

There are those men whose deaths displace water in the far parts of the sea, and then there are those for whom the pool seems to have dried up long ago. So much of a life can pass without a thought of where the journey might end. A young man's days grow full and his nights become short, and his mind is crowded with all that must be done, and all that has been done, and all that waits to be done. Hours come and go, a rush of time that seems limitless as it passes.

Looking back through the haze of years, you wish to whisper in the young father's ear, tell him to put away his books and his calculations, go out into the yard and play a game of kickball, stop worrying about engineering the best tree house on the block and just climb the tree. Sit quietly in its branches with a son or a daughter and watch the minutes drift by in glorious splendor, as aimless as the cloud ships in a summer sky.

There comes a time when the opportunity for sailing cloud ships is gone, when time is not just passing, but speeding toward something. You attempt to communicate this truth to the young people now, but to them you're just an old man growing uncomfortably sentimental.

You remember, of course, when you stood where they are. There were mountains to be scaled, bridges to be built, bills to be paid, work to be done. A man's work defines him when he is young. Time flows as water through an estuary, accomplishments collecting like leaves in the brackish tide pools against the shore. The water hides beneath them, moving yet invisible, placid on the surface. Accolades amass in tidy black frames and hang on a wall to be dusted and polished, straightened now and again if tipped askew by a child visiting the office, or a cleaning woman brushing by with a feather duster, or a colleague leaning casually against the paneling, stroking his chin.

'Good heavens,' the visitor might say, if the frame jarred

loose. 'I didn't see that hanging there. My word, man! You were in on *Apollo* 13? That must have been some experience.'

On occasion, such a question fades into the background. A missing frame yields a gap in the covering of leaves, through which the rush of water is obvious. *How long ago was that? Twenty years? Twenty-five? Thirty? No . . . even longer. Longer than I'd care to admit.*

'Tense times,' I'd say, when recalling those days, for the benefit of conversation. Deborah was just a girl then. Thirteen years old. Thirteen, the same as the mission number. An odd coincidence. Otherwise, I wouldn't have remembered her age at the time. 'A four-day nail-biter, getting the Command Module back. Could have heard a pin drop in the control center when it went through radio blackout during reentry.'

On occasion, I considered telling the rest of that story – there was so much more. Those were glorious days. Exciting hours. What words could describe the moment when the Mission Control Center became impossibly quiet, every man in the room hanging on edge, waiting as the crew of the crippled *Apollo* 13 plunged through the atmosphere in a hail of fire? The void lay so heavily, I heard my heart pumping that day, each beat individual, distinct, separated by the silence that sucked the air from the room at Mission Control. Over four minutes waiting for a radio response, the difference between success and failure, between life and death. The heartbeats slowed inside my chest, my body hoarding oxygen as if I were in the *Odyssey* capsule, time stretching and bending as the pilot of an ARIA support aircraft hailed the crew of *Apollo* 13. 'Odyssey, Houston standing by, over.' Already, we were one minute and twenty-seven seconds beyond the expected end of radio blackout.

We waited, the moment one of breathless hope, consuming fear.

And then came the rush of adrenaline when a voice broke through in response: 'Okay, Joe.' Swigert, letting us know the crew had survived against all odds.

What words could encapsulate such a moment? How beautiful to have lived it, to have felt the suffocation of fear followed by the rush of joy. I'd often thought that the journey from this life to the next would be like that instant – fear, a struggle for breath, a grasping at what is familiar, a clinging to one's own understanding, and then surrender, joy, freedom, air abundant, and finally peace.

But it was a hypothesis that remained unproven. I considered it as I lay on the floor of my study, my eyes opening, then falling closed, then opening again, my heart struggling in my chest, the beats erratic, weak then strong, like a peg-legged dancer doing a clumsy jig on a wooden floor. There was a searing pain, a dim awareness that my body was twisted into a strange shape, then another stab, sharper this time, radiating outward like an electrical current splitting, running into my arm. I had the sense of time passing – minutes, then longer, maybe hours.

Am I dying? I thought. *Am I dying this time? Finally?*

I sank away and let the past come back again. I was in an airplane, an experimental model I'd helped design at Hughes Aircraft. The test pilot and I were chatting idly, discussing the capabilities of the plane, neither of us having any idea a missile crisis was brewing nearby in Cuba and we were heading into danger . . .

A stab pulled me away from the memory of the flight, dragged me back to the floor of my study. I saw the chair turned sideways, the desk lurking impossibly tall above it, a mountain, the telephone atop.

I could try. I could try for the phone. But there was no motivation, other than a fear of the unknown. Whatever a man's faith, death is still an untraveled country, a place mapped only by others who claim to know what it holds. Annalee would be waiting on the other side of this pain. I had faith in that much, but even more, I had resignation – the surrender of an old man with nothing important left to do. A few regrets, of course, but who hasn't?

The current in my chest blazed again, white-hot in the center, shooting outward into my arm, burning my fingertips.

I shrank away from it, sank into the past again, into another memory – one deeper than all the rest. There was a table, large and freshly polished, the dark wood so sleek I could see my face reflected in it. A boy's face. I smiled at myself, setting out the plates. Seven plates around the table, seven chairs. I could not place the memory, could not tell the story that would surround it, yet it was vivid. I knew the smell of the room – leather and lemon oil, and the faintest scent of gas from the heaters. A woman was singing in the kitchen, her voice full, deep, and melodious.

I knew the voice. I knew the song . . .

'Dad . . . Dad . . . can you hear me?' The words were out of

5

sorts, lacking synchronicity with the time and place in my mind. 'Dad . . . Dad, it's Deborah. Can you hear me?'

There was a lurch of pain, a heartbeat that fluttered strangely, then pain again. Someone was shaking me, causing my head to rattle.

'Dad? Dad, I'm here. Put this under your tongue. The paramedics are on the way.' The voice was Deborah's. I wanted her to leave me be. I wanted to remain in the room with the seven chairs, to decipher their meaning. But Deborah was rousing me, insisting, pulling me toward her. My mind rushed as if I were going through a tunnel on one of the bullet trains in Europe. Images, moments, scraps of past and present flashed past like billboards too closely spaced for adequate viewing.

I opened my eyes, and the world swam – the walls of my study, a blue March sky outside the window, Deborah with her dark hair curling around her face, her brown eyes wide. She wasn't a child, not the thirteen-year-old girl from the days of Apollo, but a woman. A woman with a soft fan of wrinkles beside each eye and a smattering of gray wound into the curls of her ponytail. She looked so much like her mother that for a moment I let myself imagine she was Annalee.

You're here, I wanted to say. *They've been saying that you'd gone. I told them they were wrong. There you are.*

The words wouldn't come, so I only smiled at Annalee. Perhaps I'd died there on the floor, in actuality. Perhaps Annalee was here to show me the way. My life had passed before my eyes, after all. I'd seen it all in fast motion – the pictures flashing by outside the bullet train, a montage beginning with the present and moving into the past, as far back as I could remember, and then the room with the seven chairs.

I could be dead. This could be the end.

Am I? Is this what it's like to die?

But the desk was yet in its place, the chair still tipped sideways. I remembered grabbing it when I fell. The frames remained on the wall – photos and certificates, diplomas and awards for years of service. Items of the sort that do not travel with you when you go. There are no walls for hanging accolades in heaven.

Annalee's fingers touched my lips, left behind a sweet, burning taste. I closed my eyes, pulled in a breath. The air was thick, like breathing gelatin. I tried to speak, to ask her, *Am I dying? Have I died? Are you Annalee, or are you Deborah?*

'Ssshhh,' she whispered. 'It's all right. Just lie still. Give the pills a chance to work.'

The sweetness faded in my mouth, and the burning grew stronger. I heard the heartbeats slowing, felt the pain ebbing, like a wave draining out to sea.

'There, see? You're getting better. What in the world happened? You know you're supposed to carry your pills with you all the time.' The voice was lower now, harder edged, less patient. Not Annalee's. Deborah's. It was Deborah there, kneeling beside me on the floor, calling to check on the ambulance.

I closed my eyes and wished she wouldn't bother. I couldn't tell her that, of course. I couldn't admit that I'd left the pills in the bathroom drawer on purpose and that I'd been doing so for weeks. If . . . when another of these attacks came, I didn't want the temptation of having them close by. But surrendering is not so simple when the time arrives. It's easier to resolve oneself to death in the abstract than to make the choice in the moment of truth.

The pain dulled further, and I let myself sink into exhaustion. There was a throbbing in my head. I'd bumped it on the way down. The corner of the desk, most likely . . .

'Dad? Dad, stay awake. Stay . . .'

Deborah's voice was far from me again, echoing off the walls of the tunnel. It was a selfish thing I was doing, I supposed, trying to leave her this way. It would have been difficult for her if she'd found me too late, crumpled on the floor in a heap, beyond saving. But then, this was difficult, as well, this constant darting away from her work to breeze by my house and look in on me. When Annalee was here, a week or two might go by without Deborah stepping foot in this house. She was busy with her work at the university, engrossed in her biomedical research. I, of all people, should have understood that well enough. She'd learned her intensity from me.

'Dad, stay awake.'

Stay awake, stay awake. For what reason? So she could slip away from her office again to check on me tomorrow, and the next day, and the next? There was nothing here for either one of us – only a big house with no life left in it. Annalee was the heart of this house. I don't suppose I ever told her that, but she had a way of knowing things . . .

I drifted away from the study, slipped back to the memory of the seven chairs. Annalee knew of that memory. She was the only one I'd ever told. We were lying on a college lawn together in our courting days. Her hair spilled over the grass in long, dark ribbons, and her eyes reflected the soft hues of a noonday sky. I wanted to tell her that she was beautiful. I yearned to be the sort to spout flowery epithets, but I was never skilled with such sentiments.

'What's the farthest back you can remember?' she'd asked, looking up from her literature book. 'Your deepest memory.'

'I couldn't say,' I answered, and she poked me in the side, her lips quirking in a playful way.

'Yes, you can.' Rolling onto one elbow, she rested her chin in her hand and gazed at me. 'Tell me. You never tell me anything about yourself, Norman. You never let me in.'

I sighed, and as a young man in love will often do, I tried to give her what she wanted. 'It's an odd memory,' I admitted. 'There's a table – a large table, with seven chairs around it. Four of them have pillows to boost up the seats – for children, I presume – and there's a high chair for a baby, and armchairs at either end. I'm setting out the plates. I must have been five or six years old.'

'Five years old?' she questioned. 'You can't remember anything before you were five?'

'Not a thing,' I admitted. 'Nothing I can put a finger on, anyway.' There were other scraps of memory – the beach house at Galveston, where we spent summer weekends when I was small, a great-grandmother who'd died before I was four, the church in which my baptism was held, the house where we lived in Houston before moving to Dallas. But those memories were static in my mind, flat. They had no movement, no depth. My first vivid memory was of seeing my face reflected in the polished wooden table as I put out the place settings. 'What seems so odd about it is that it's just the table. I can't picture the room around it – only the table and the plates, a red Persian carpet underneath, four children's chairs, and a high chair. I can't imagine where it would have been. I grew up an only child, you know.'

Annalee's nose crinkled as she considered the question. 'Did you ever ask your mother?'

'She told me it was something I dreamed. A scene from a book she read to me when I was young.' I lifted a finger, twirled one of Annalee's curls around it. Her hair was as soft and smooth as satin ribbon, and a bit of poetry came to mind. Yeats. *I am looped in the loops of her hair.* 'But it feels as if it were real.'

Annalee's lips twitched upward at the corners, forming the silly, mischievous smile I'd first noticed over a sales counter in the student union. 'Hmmm ... it's a mystery.' She leaned close, her lips only inches from mine. 'Just one more thing about you I'll have to ferret out ...'

Deborah's voice chased away the memory. I was conscious of paramedics, an ambulance, the emergency room, doctors. I was poked, prodded, assessed, and painfully shocked with the defibrillator to force my heart into a normal rhythm again. I suppose that was a fitting punishment for having left my medication out of reach on purpose. God has

a way of putting a thumb on those who take undue liber-
ties. One experience with a defibrillator would be enough
to convince even a stubborn old man not to leave his pills in
the bathroom drawer again.

Deborah had reached her boiling point by the time they
moved me to a room for observation. She'd lost a whole afternoon at work – missed an online symposium having to do
with cancer cells and a meeting with a foundation that
funded research like hers. She sank into the chair, tapping
away on her cell phone as the nurse settled me into the bed,
then hovered momentarily over my medical chart, seeming
to sense that family drama would erupt the moment she left.

Finally, the nurse instructed me in the use of the call button and the television remote – as if a seventy-six-year-old
man with an irregular heart wouldn't have seen these gadgets already – and then she moved on with her rounds.
Fortunately, Deborah was still busy typing with her thumbs –
catching up on work, or giving her husband, Lloyd, an earful
about my latest bout of bad behavior, no doubt. I closed my
eyes, thinking I'd feign sleep, and Deborah, without the
nerve to wake me after such a traumatic day, would leave
quietly.

On the television, an episode of *Hogan's Heroes* played, the
sound loud enough that it must have been audible even in
the next room. Hogan and LeBeau were preparing to slip
through the secret hatch in the barracks and make an
escape from Stalag 13, so as to accomplish some clandestine
business in town.

Perhaps I could tunnel through the hospital floor and pop from a

11

manhole cover somewhere on the street. A fiendish and clever escape . . .

'Don't even *think* you're going to drift off to sleep before we've talked.' Deborah's voice was an inconvenient interruption – like the entrance of Sergeant Schultz.

I let my head fall to the opposite side, tunneled into the pillow as if I'd already succumbed to sleep and her noise was distressing me. It seems generally wrong for your children speak to you as if *you* are the child. Having been overseas with an engineering position during the declining years of my own parents, I was spared this strangely inverse relationship with them. A housekeeper cared for them, and at the end, my mother went into nursing care. I brought Annalee and the children to visit her when I could. She seemed to understand why it wasn't often. She was peaceful in her final years, with her bridge circles and her television programs. There were no ugly scenes between my mother and me, none like this one.

'I *know* you're not asleep,' Deborah insisted, an edge in her voice. She sighed, and I pictured her leaning over the chair arm, fingertips scrubbing her forehead.

On the television, Sergeant Schultz barked, 'I see nothingk! I know nothingk! I vas not here!'

I'm not here. I'm not. What possible logic could there be in my existence? Surely a man isn't meant to be a prisoner inside his own body, inside his own life. Surely, when his glory is at an end, when his colleagues, his friends, so many of his loved ones are gone, he can will himself to slip through some escape hatch and disappear.

'Look at me!' Deborah insisted, and I heard the flatulent sound of friction against vinyl as she stood up and rounded the bed. I opened my eyes. 'This has *got* to stop. First you ran the car into a ditch, so we took away the car. Then you left the gas on in the house, so we put in an electric stove. You fell down the stairs; Lloyd and I moved all the important stuff downstairs. And now this! What were you doing upstairs in the study, and without your pills? Are you *trying* to hurt yourself?'

I wanted to shake a finger in her face and say, *Don't you take that tone with me, young lady.* But her poking so close to the truth was an embarrassment that wouldn't allow me to produce a haughty answer. 'I was watering the plants, of course.'

Deborah gritted her teeth, pushed air through them. 'You're not supposed to be doing that.'

'Plants must have water. Your mother loved her plants. Am I to let them die?'

'I told you, the new cleaning lady will take care of the upstairs and water the plants every Monday when she comes. You don't need to worry about them. You shouldn't be on the stairs. What if you fall again? What if nobody happens to come by this time?' She wagged a finger at me and then swung it in the general direction of the house. This was Deborah's revenge for all the years I wasn't the father she wanted, for all the times I was on the other side of the world, missing school plays and orchestra performances and birthday parties. This was my penance for not noticing that Annalee was pale and tired the day she died – for not insisting she leave

13

the laundry alone, for letting her lie down on the sofa when she felt poorly after lunch, rather than taking her to the doctor. It was my fault she was gone, and Deborah would never forgive me for that. In truth, Deborah wished it were me, rather than her mother. For two years we'd been prepared for my heart to give out suddenly, but we hadn't been prepared to lose Annalee.

'Mondays aren't enough for the plants,' I said.

Deborah's face reddened, the angry flush traveling down her neck. 'That's all Mother ever watered them – once a week.'

'You can't trust someone who's just been hired, some housekeeper. What will this ... this woman know about your mother's plants?'

Deborah lifted her palms with a jerk, turned, and walked to the window, stood with her hands on her hips, gathering fistfuls of her clothing. 'I'll move every stupid plant in the house downstairs. How about that? Better yet, I'll take the plants home with me.'

'They're Annalee's plants. They're not yours.' My back stiffened, the hairs bristling against the hospital gown. 'I don't want anyone in my house, either. You tell that housekeeper not to come. What's to stop her from stealing something – Annalee's jewelry, or the silver? I can't watch her every moment she's there.'

'You don't need to *watch* her, Dad. She isn't going to steal anything. She's there to clean.'

'How would you know?' It was hard to say why Deborah and I continually butted heads. Even as a child she was difficult for me, determined to have her way, to have the last

14

word. Her brother was much more pliable, with an easy, relaxed nature that made him more like Annalee. Deborah would argue just for the sake of argument. The characteristic was valuable in a researcher, frustrating in a daughter, infuriating in a caretaker. I didn't want to be taken care of, to be told what to do in my own home. 'Look at what happened to Edward and Hanna Beth Parker, just next door to me. That housekeeper of theirs got into their bank accounts and almost robbed them blind. She tried to take their house while Hanna Beth was in the hospital after a stroke. That was just a year ago. You can't trust people.'

Deborah turned around, her chin set in a firm line. Snatching her purse off the night table, she indicated that our conversation was at an end. 'She isn't some *person* I hired off the street. She works for the service that cleans the university offices at night, for heaven's sake.'

Bracing my knuckles against the mattress, I pushed higher in the bed. 'If she already has a job, why does she need to clean my house?'

Deborah's hand flipped through the air. 'What does it matter? Why do you care? Can't you, for once, just be happy with something I've done?'

I turned my face away, staring out the window at the Dallas skyline. 'You can't trust people. You never know what motives they might have.'

Deborah's heels tapped the floor as she crossed the room. There was a loose tile somewhere near the door. It made a hollow sound. 'The housekeeper doesn't have any motives other than to do the job I hired her for. We're all just trying to take care of *you*.' She yanked the door open, and it collided with the wall, sending sound waves through the room. 'Whether you want us to or not.'

Quiet overtook the room as her parting shot faded, and I lay there letting my mind drift slowly through the day, and then farther back. Back, and back, and back, all the way to a place I hadn't visited in years, before today. The house with the seven chairs. Now it was as clear in my mind as it had always been. Was it merely something I'd imagined from a storybook, or was it real, with all its sounds and smells – the woman singing, the clattering of pans in the kitchen, the musty, pine-scented air?

And if it was real, why would my mother have felt the need to convince me that the place never existed?

CHAPTER 2

Epiphany Jones

'Ode to Weeds . . .'

A title like that isn't what a teacher wants after she drags a bunch of high school kids to the Dallas Arboretum and then tells them to write about it. She wants you to get all poetic about roses and daffodils and stuff. Guess I had to learn that the hard way.

You write about weeds and you'll get used as a bad example, while she slings your paper around in the air and says stuff like, 'Y'all think this is some kind of joke? You know what I had to go through to get that field trip approved? Huh? I try to do something extra. Try to help the ones who *might* want something in life, and *this* is what I get? It's supposed to be *free-verse poetry* about a public attraction in Dallas, not some gibberish you scribbled down and ripped out of a spiral notebook. Every one of you go home and do the assignment again!' She gave me a dirty look, and I sank down in my chair, sweat dampening my clothes. The rest of the kids were gonna know I was the one that set her off, and then I'd have more than just getting jumped in the bathroom to worry about. As soon as she let us go, I needed to beat it out of there and get down the street before anybody could catch me.

The teacher went on talking about how she never should've bothered to take losers like us off campus. All we ever did was cause her grief and get in trouble, anyway.

She did have a point, sort of. This school did stink. I'd been here just a few weeks, and I'd already figured out that much. Most of the kids here were on their way to jail or the welfare line, or, if they were lucky and good at sports, maybe college someplace for a little while. But the teacher could've seen *my* point, too. There was a reason I wrote about the weeds in the parking lot instead of the flowers in the gardens. But to her, I was just one more face in a toffee shade of brown, transferred in for the last couple months of the year. She didn't want to know my story. If she would've actually *read* the poem, she would've seen why I thought weeds deserved an ode.

I was one. I always had been.

That teacher'd probably never been a weed in her life.

She didn't know how it was to be someplace you're not wanted. Weeds don't care, is the good thing. They don't need a fancy garden, or somebody petting on them, covering them when it's cold, sprinkling them with drops of Miracle-Gro, or loving all over them. You give a weed a little crack in a sidewalk, and it'll put down roots, and suck up water, and do its thing no matter what else happens. Weeds don't need much from anybody. They can look after themselves.

When you're a weed, you can either die or you can push your way through the concrete and try to survive.

The second bell rang, and I was halfway to the door before that teacher hollered my name. I started to act like I didn't hear her, but someone side-slammed me, and I smashed against the doorframe, and my stuff flew everywhere. A couple girls drop-kicked it on their way out, laughing and cussing and calling me things you're not supposed to say in school, but everybody does. DeRon Lee passed by in the hall with a couple of his homeboys. He laughed and shoulder-butted somebody out of the way so he could grab my backpack. 'Now, how you gon' do new girl that way?' he asked the others, and flashed me a big, toothy grin. 'Don't you know she my lab partner in science? We gon' get us a A-plus-plus.'

I couldn't help it: I laughed. It'd probably be the only A-plus-plus DeRon ever got.

From across the hall, DeRon's sorta girlfriend gave me a look that would've been against the law, if looks could kill. She started in my direction, but the English teacher came out and told DeRon to move on. Then the teacher got ahold of me and pulled me back in the classroom so she could vent on me, saying things like, 'I don't know *what* you learned at whatever podunk school you came from, but in *this* room, *I* run things. You think you're gonna make a joke out of *my* class? Huh? Come in here with your little attitude . . .'

I zoned out and thought about Mrs Lora at my last school – the school in the nice, friendly little town where people didn't cuss me out just because they didn't like the way I looked, or knock my stuff across the hall, or get in the bathroom stall next to mine and tell me I oughta go somewhere and die, or make fun of my English paper in front of the whole class. Mrs

Lora was the kind of teacher who loved every kid the same, even the weeds. She showed me how she felt, one time when we were walking home together. She stopped to look at a little purple flower growing from the road stripe in the middle of the street. 'Well, isn't that something, Epie?' she said. 'Look how it's blooming right there with the cars driving by. Just goes to prove that life doesn't have to be perfect for something beautiful to grow.' Then she hugged me around the shoulders and pulled me close to her big, sweaty body.

I liked Mrs Lora. She rented a room to Mama and me in her tall white house three blocks down from the school. Those two years at Mrs Lora's were the best in my whole life, but like everything with Mama, it had to end.

Mama came across Russ at a flea market. She knew him from way back when she was in high school. Pretty soon, that old flame was burning just like in the country songs Mrs Lora liked. Mama quit her job at the processing plant and moved to Dallas to be with Russ. I stayed back with Mrs Lora for a while, dreaming that maybe I'd get to live with her all the way through high school. She told me I was welcome to. She liked having me help with her house and the apartments she rented. For the first time ever, it felt like somebody really wanted me around. But before I was even through my freshman year, Mrs Lora went from teaching in that little white school to the hospital to a big funeral I never got to see. I was in Dallas with Mama and Russ, trying to find another crack in the sidewalk.

It was harder than I thought it would be. A big-city school is different from the backwater places Mama and me had been before. The neighborhoods off Blue Sky Hill were mostly run-down and rough. The kids ran in packs, and if you got yourself on the wrong side of them, you could end up in a world of hurt. I didn't even have to do anything for that to happen. When you're half Italian and half black, and you talk like you grew up in some hick town, you're just some weird chick nobody wants to know.

By the time that English teacher finished chewing on me, the halls were full of kids and noise, and I pretty much knew what my trip to the front door was gonna be like. Once the teachers went back in their rooms, you were fair game for anyone in the hallway. But it never crossed my mind that it wasn't the kids I needed to worry about; it was the mamas. I ran into one of them right inside the school door, and she about yanked my arm out of the socket.

'You all high-tone, Miss Creamy Caramel,' she said. 'You think you better'n us, 'cuz yo' mama's a wop? You prance 'round here, think you gon' get my daughter's boyfriend? You all smilin' at DeRon and stuff. Yeah, she seen you doin' that ever since you been here. You think you gon' take DeRon from Lesha? Huh?'

I froze up right there in the doorway, which was dumb, because I should've told her to move her big, fat self out of my path. I wasn't the one looking at her daughter's boyfriend, either. DeRon Lee had been into me since the minute I showed up in this school – something new, I guess. The nicer he was to me, the more the other girls got on my case. Now it looked like I'd have their mamas to deal with, too.

'You jus' like yo' old lady.' She pointed a finger right up in my face. 'Yeah, I know yo' mama. She all runnin' around here like she own the place, 'cause she live here back in the day. Well, she a shame befo' God. Go gettin' herself wit' other women's men. That's how she ended up with you. She tell you that? She got a lotta nerve, movin' back to this neighborhood after she took my cousin's man. Yeah, yo' daddy was my cousin's sorry boyfriend. Yo' mama tell you that, either?' She stuck her chin out and got so close I could smell her nasty cigarette-smellin' breath.

'My daddy died before I was born. In the army.' It was rolling around in my head that what she was saying couldn't be true. Mama never wanted to talk about my daddy, but a long time ago I'd heard her tell the registration lady in some school office that he was sent to Somalia before they could get married, which was why she had Salerno for her last name and I had Jones, his name, for mine. This lady *and* her sleazy daughter probably couldn't even spell Somalia, much less figure out where it was or know anything about my daddy. She was just some high-school-dropout, low-rent loser, up here trying to help her daughter nail down DeRon Lee, because he was so good at basketball everybody figured he'd end up in the NBA – if he didn't land in jail first.

She laughed, her long red fingernails fanning the air like the claws on one of the lions at the zoo. 'Girl, you jus' as ign'rant as you look. Yo' daddy ain't in no army. He washed dishes at a restaurant until he got hisself killed in some car wreck. He didn't die before you was born, neither. He jus' didn't want no wop child fo' a daughter. Yo' mama's people didn't want you, neither. They too busy up there on

22

Greenville Avenue, servin' up that fine Italian food at Tuscany Restaurant.'

She must've seen my eyes getting wider and wider, because she threw her head back and laughed. 'Girl, what kinda lies yo' mama been feedin' you? Yo' mama's family jus' a couple miles up the road, but I bet you ain't gettin' no birthday cards, is ya? Them high-class woppas, they don' want no daughter gettin' with some dishwasher boy and makin' some little Oreo moolie. Why you think they kicked yo' mama out when she had you?'

The lady turned around and walked off, and I stood there feeling like a house of glass was cracking all around me. People bumped into me, knocking me back and forth as they squeezed by, and I barely even noticed. After a minute, somebody laughed and yanked my backpack off my shoulder and threw it into the hall. Pencils and papers spilled and scattered around, and the school counselor came out to see what was the matter.

'Epiphany?' She waved and snapped her fingers by my face. 'You all right? Epiphany?'

Epiphany. That long mouthful of a name bounced off and floated into the air, like another trail of smoke. It didn't feel like it belonged to me anymore. Mama'd told me that was the name my soldier daddy picked for me. When he saw the ultrasound pictures from half a world away, he knew I was gonna be something special. Now *Epiphany* didn't mean anything. She didn't exist and neither did the soldier daddy.

There was just Epie, a skinny, long-legged, creamy caramel girl standing there getting in everyone's way. Too skinny, too ugly, too brown, not brown enough, her eyes a strange gray-ish green that came from the Italian restaurant up the street. Just a couple miles away. When Mama would talk about the past at all, she always told me her parents were dead, but now I remembered that we came to Dallas once when I was little. She'd just split up with some guy, and we needed money to keep from ending up at a homeless shelter. We came to this neighborhood, and she went inside a house, and she left me in the car with some crayons and a coloring book. She came back with cash, and we beat it out of town.

She never told me she was visiting family, but now the truth was clear enough. She didn't want whoever was in that house to see me.

I got my backpack together and walked out of the building and turned into Epie. The best thing was that Epie didn't care what that lady thought, or whether some girls would probably try to jump her later for hanging out with DeRon. Instead of heading on home from school, Epie hung around and watched the basketball games, then waited in the alley behind the gym and found DeRon afterward. She rode in his old car, and got her flirt on, and went off to some party with him at the low-rent apartments down the street. It didn't even bother her when everybody was getting wasted, and some ex-convict named Ray came by and smiled and wanted her to go back in the bedroom and smoke. DeRon just laughed and said, 'Go on, Ray. How you be gettin' all up on my girl like that? She with me, and you know me and my boys can't be smokin' that stuff. We got them drug tests alla time. You gon' get me in trouble, my man.' DeRon and Ray bumped fists and laughed.

Right after that, DeRon and his friends got restless and headed out. Epie piled in the car and went right along with them. Next thing she knew, they were down the street in the parking lot of the old white church, and the guys were running around wild, throwing rocks at the building and tipping over benches in the memory garden. Then the police showed up, and the fun went bad in a hurry. The whole thing ended with a ride home in a police car and a parent talk on the front porch. The good news was that the preacher at the old church had told the police officer he wasn't gonna press charges; he just wanted the damages taken care of. The bad news was that Mama was bloodred mad because she'd wasted her whole second-shift lunch hour driving around, thinking there'd been a kidnapping or something. Now she was late getting back to her job as a temp, cleaning classrooms at the university.

Epie didn't feel a thing when the cop left and Mama dragged her into the house, then slammed the door. She figured Mama deserved this. It didn't even seem like there was any point telling what'd happened that afternoon, or bringing up what that lady at school said about the soldier daddy in Somalia. If someone'll lie to you once, they'll lie again.

Fool me once, shame on you. Fool me twice, shame on me, Mrs Lora used to say.

While Mama yelled, and Russ complained about how much gas he'd used up driving around looking for me, Epie sort of faded off. I started thinking that three more years until I got out of high school was too long to stay here. I wanted to move on to someplace where I didn't have to worry about getting jumped at school and there wasn't some lady who knew dirty little secrets about me, and I didn't have relatives down the street who wouldn't let me into their houses. *Maybe I oughta go on down to Greenville Avenue and walk right into that fancy restaurant*, I thought. *See the looks on their faces when their long-lost grandbaby shows up.*

Russ got tired of the argument and headed for the door, dropping his keys on the table. 'You can take my car back to work. I'm goin' on my bike.' A minute later, his Harley rumbled from the carport and he was outta there. Russ knew Mama was ready to come all the way unwound and it was gonna get ugly.

I looked at the clock and wondered if Mama cared about anything else but her wasted lunch hour. Did she even wonder why, after coming right home after school every day for three weeks, and trying to be good, and trying to stay out of the way so her and Russ wouldn't mind having me around, I all of a sudden went and partied till after midnight? Mostly, she just seemed mad that now she'd get her pay docked and have to work late. Like usual, she figured I was trying to make her life harder than it already was. She never thought anything I did was good. I wanted to not care. *She's a liar anyway*, the Epie voice whispered in my head. *She's been lying to you all your life.*

Mama stood in the doorway, her hands shaking as she yanked her dark hair up in a ponytail and grabbed a rubber band from the pile of mail, newspaper ads, and other junk on the end table. Her face was wicked red from her cheeks on down, all the way to where her skin disappeared into the neck of her T-shirt. Her eyelids were droopy and slow. She'd probably calmed herself with a whiskey sour or two when she couldn't find me. But whatever. Anything she wanted to do was her business.

'Stop giving me that dirty look.' She lifted a hand like she was gonna smack me. It wouldn't have been the first time, but if she tried it again, she was in for a shock. I was tired of taking crap off her. All I ever did was try to make Mama like me, and all she ever did was tell me how much trouble I was and how hard it was to keep a roof over our heads and buy everything we needed. Every once in a while, she'd add that things weren't supposed to end up like this. This wasn't the life she'd wanted. 'You're just lucky I've got to get to work, or I swear . . .' She let the threat die in a growl.

I took a step back and tried to make her yelling roll right off. What choice was there, really? I didn't have anywhere else to go. Otherwise, I wouldn't have come home. I would've told that police officer I was a runaway or something. It wasn't like Mama would miss me. I was the worst thing that ever happened to her. If she hadn't gotten herself pregnant with me, her life would've been totally different. Better. She'd be down the road helping to run that fine Italian restaurant.

It hurt to know that – to finally really understand. I didn't want it to hurt. I wanted to be as cold as ice to her, but there was still some part of me that couldn't. There was still some of Epiphany in there with Epie.

'Don't even know if I can get the classrooms finished tonight,' she grumbled, picking up Russ's keys. 'You think this is easy, after cleaning houses all day? I hope you know

how much you screwed up, Epiphany. You selfish little . . .
And for what? Because you want to go run around like
some . . . like some . . . back-alley trash? You get yourself
knocked up, Epiphany, and you're outta here. You're not
staying in my house. You hear me?'

I wanted to say, *You know what? I won't.* But I couldn't say
anything. I just stood there with a big ol' lump gathering in
my throat. I wasn't gonna cry where she could see it, so I
closed my mouth tight over the sound and watched her grab
her cleaning company smock and head out the door. For
half a second, the room felt better without her in it. After
that, it just felt empty. I looked around at the matted-down
sofa, and the end table somebody's dog must've chewed on
before we moved in, and the gold-colored carpet that was
probably three times as old as I was, and I thought there had
to be more to life than this. There had to be something else
out there. I sank down onto the sofa and just thought about
it for a long time.

I hated it here. I hated her. I hated me. I hated who I was.
I hated what I looked like. I hated the color of my skin, and
my stupid, long, kinky hair. All that hate was like a slow
burn, eating me up from the inside. Wasn't there anybody
in this world who wanted me?

What if tomorrow night I got looking superfine, and then
took the bus to Greenville? The street would be lousy with
people partying at the clubs. Guys would give me looks and
stuff, and I'd smile right back. When I made it to that restaurant, I'd walk on in like I belonged there, right past the dudes
in their white shirts and black ties, parking high-class cars out

front. I'd stroll to the counter and find the people who owned the place and make them tell me what'd happened when I was born. I'd make them tell me all the secrets Mama kept.

Her secrets . . .

I knew where she hid her secrets. She'd crammed two boxes in the back of her closet at every place we'd ever lived. The one time I'd messed with the boxes, she'd caught me with her closet torn apart and yanked me up by the arm so quick I felt my shoulder pop. 'Did you open these? Did you?' She pointed at the boxes, her finger shaking.

'I didn't!' I said, and tried to pull away. The way she was holding me hurt a little in my arm, and a lot inside. 'Mama, stop!'

She let go of me finally, shoved the boxes back in the closet, and shut the door hard. 'You leave my things alone,' she hissed, and dragged me out of the room. 'You stay out of here. Stay out of my room!' She headed back to the sofa to watch a movie with some guy from next door.

I was nine then, old enough to finally get it through my stupid head that I was better off keeping my distance – from Mama and her things. It was easier to stay clear of whatever was in the closet, keep my head down when Mama and me were home together, and try not to be a bother to her. It never even crossed my mind that those boxes in the closet might be hiding secrets about me.

My heart started pumping as I headed down the hall, went into her room, opened the closet door, and looked inside. The boxes were still there, a big one with a picture of a tomato can on the side, and a shoe box, stuffed in the corner behind a pile of dirty laundry and junk. I studied all of it, memorized how

29

it looked, then knelt down and started moving things one at a time, making sure I'd know how to piece it all back together. Even though I told myself I didn't care what Mama thought anymore, a part of me remembered what it felt like to be yanked up by the arm and thrown through the doorway.

I set each box on the bedroom floor, leaving tiny trails in the dust. My heart hiccuped into my neck. What if even that was enough for Mama to notice? What if she finally decided she was sick of me and kicked me out on the street? But I had to know. If there was something about me in those boxes, I had a right to it, didn't I?

I slid my fingers around the lid on the shoe box, worked it upward. It popped loose, and I set it to the side, my eyes following it to the floor, then tracking back to the box real slow. I was afraid to look, but I wanted to see.

There was a plain white paper on the top, folded in half. I lifted it out, opened it, read it – the rental agreement for some trailer house we lived in before Mrs Lora's.

I set down the paper and took out an envelope that was underneath it. My birth certificate was inside, and a few other things – vaccination records and stuff. My father's name was on there, Jaylon Jones. It wasn't J. Lon Jones, like I'd always thought. It was Jaylon, all one word. I tried to picture him in my mind, but I couldn't anymore. The hero soldier daddy, who was tall like me and looked a little like Will Smith, had walked right out the door with the nasty lady at school. Jaylon was just some lines on paper. A man I'd had all wrong, just like the name.

A man who didn't want me.

I pushed everything back into the envelope, set it aside, and dug down deeper. There was a Valentine's card – one of the sappy kind you pick out when you're just falling in love with somebody. There was no way to tell whether it was from Mama or to her. The envelope was yellowed, but the flap had never been stuck down and torn open, and in the spot where it should've been signed, it just said, *Me*. Why'd she saved it all these years?

I dug deeper, jumping every time the house settled or creaked, even though I knew that once Russ headed off on his bike, he usually hooked up with some friends and partied for hours.

There were more papers in the box – some medical stuff, the payment book for the car that'd been gone forever, a few of my old report cards and some school papers where teachers wrote notes and said I was smart, a Mother's Day card I'd probably made in day care or Head Start someplace. There was a little gold handprint inside a paper heart on the front of it. It was hard to picture my mama putting that card away in a safe place, like it mattered. Maybe it'd ended up in here by accident. Underneath it was a sheet of school pictures from back in middle school. Only one was cut out. It was probably still on the wall in Mrs Lora's classroom.

Underneath the school pictures were a few from the Christmas pageant at Mrs Lora's church, where I got to wear an angel suit, because I was tall. The pastor, Brother Ben, gave me the pictures when he took them off the bulletin board at the end of the year. I liked Brother Ben's church. People were nice there. I got saved and everything.

I lifted a stack of bills, and under those was a little hand-made book with a blue paper cover. I knew what it was without even pulling it out – the Someday Book from Mrs Lora's seventh-grade class. She gave us ten sheets of blue paper that were blank, except for three words: *Someday I will . . .* We had to fill in the rest and draw pictures. She told us to think hard, to dream big, to put down the things we most wanted to do. To make ten promises to ourselves, and when we were done, she'd bind them into a book. We were supposed to keep the book where we could look at it again and again. *When you look at a promise over and over, it becomes part of who you are*, she said.

Guess I'd lost track of my promises at some point, just like I'd lost track of the book. Now I couldn't even remember what those promises were.

Underneath the blue paper promises was another book, an old one with a yellow satin cover that was stained brown around the edges. A baby book. The cloth felt dry and fragile under my fingers as I wiggled it from under the pile. It slid free, and something blue fell out, dropping into the side of the box. A plastic envelope – the kind that comes from Wal-Mart with photos in it. I picked it up, set it on the floor, then straightened the papers in the box so that they were flat again.

Boots clomped up the porch steps, and I jerked my hands away from the box, listening. The sound of keys rattling sent an air ball into my throat. Russ was back. For some reason, he hadn't stayed out partying, after all.

Panic zipped through me. If Mama found out I'd been in here, I was dead. Shoving the photo envelope, the baby book, and the loose papers back in the shoe box, I hoisted the big box back into the closet, my hands sweating while I tried to wrestle stray shoes out from underneath, so it would sit flat. The locks on the front door were clicking now.

'Come on, c'mon, c'mon,' I whispered, trying to lift the big box and push the junk from underneath. Finally, it plunked into place, and I capped the shoe box, set it on top, then piled the clothes and shoes into the closet. The front door fell open and thumped against the end table, and I slid the closet closed just as Russ was dropping his keys and cell phone on top of the newspapers.

He started up the hall, and I checked the floor by the bed. Air caught in my throat. The Someday Book was still there. I kicked it under the bed, making sure nothing was showing before I moved toward the hall.

'What're you doin' up?' Russ grumbled, swaying a little when he looked down the hallway. 'You got someone here with you?' His eyes narrowed toward my bedroom.

I yawned and stretched like I'd just woken up. 'I heard a mouse.' It wasn't until after I said it that I wished I hadn't. Russ might look under the bed for the mouse. 'I couldn't find it, though.'

On the way down the hall toward me, he slid his Harley jacket off, yawning as I backed away from their bedroom so he could get in the door. 'Go to bed, already. That mouse ain't gonna hurt anything.'

''Kay,' I said, watching the bed skirt shiver in the breeze as he passed by, the corner of a blue paper showing for just a second before the cloth fell into place and hid it again.

CHAPTER 3

J. Norman Alvord

I was no sooner home from my incarceration at the hospital than someone came rapping on the front door and ringing the bell.

'Be there in a minute,' Deborah called, guiding me toward the bedroom as one would an invalid or an inmate in chains.

'Whoever it is, tell them to go away,' I said. 'I don't want anyone here burning incense and saying prayers over me.' Even though it had been four months since Annalee's death, neighbors still insisted on dropping by with invitations to domino nights at the senior center, or with servings of casserole and bowls of soup for one. This was a street of old-money families, and Annalee had made it her business to know everyone on it – a bridge club here, a ladies' tea there, a baby shower three houses down, an Avon party at another place. She also saw to renting out the studio apartment over our garage building near the street, often sharing dinners and baked goods with the tenants. She'd spent so much time alone as I traveled the world for my work that she'd learned to be good with the neighbors – a skill I'd never bothered to cultivate.

'It's the cleaning lady,' Deborah informed me flatly. 'I told you she'd be coming on Monday.'

Indignance swirled within me like the fumes from a chemical reaction, leaking quickly into the room. 'I told you I didn't want anyone.' The topic hadn't come up since Friday afternoon, when I'd landed in the hospital. It had slipped my mind during the plethora of conversations with doctors recommending that we try an internally implanted defibrillator, a pacemaker of sorts, as a way of preventing further heart spells. The doctor could not guarantee that such a surgery would fix my problem, but he thought it was worth a try. I, of course, had no intention of submitting myself to any more surgeries. What would be the point of that, now that Annalee was gone?

'Well, you're having her,' Deborah said, bristling.

'I haven't time to watch her.' I imagined the woman handling Annalee's things, perhaps moving them, even breaking something. Annalee would never have wanted some hired woman carousing through our home. Even when we lived overseas, where domestic help could be had for a pittance, Annalee tended the house herself. She preferred it that way. 'She's probably one of those illegals. If we end up with a fine for hiring her, I won't pay it.'

'Dad, *really*.'

Looping a finger around the bedroom curtain, I peeked outside, looking past our garage building, where an artist, Terrence Clay, was living now. There was no vehicle in the driveway or at the curb. Apparently, the housekeeper had come on foot or by city bus. What sort of a shady house-keeper didn't own a vehicle? A ne'er-do-well. The sort with a dismal credit rating, the sort who spent all her money on alcohol, drugs, or lottery tickets.

The bell rang again.

I pushed my cheek to the glass in an effort to see who was on the front porch. 'Tell her to go away and come back next week. By then I'll have had time to put away the valuables.' The housekeeper stepped off the porch, shading her eyes against the late March sunshine and checking the house number. She hardly looked honest to me – a slight, small woman with dark, curly hair bound haphazardly in a clip. She was dressed in jeans and a T-shirt, from which pro-truded the thin, leather-skinned arms of a lifetime cigarette smoker. She had the appearance of someone who might wait on your table at some out-of-the-way truck stop – not the sort you'd want roaming through your home. Not at all. 'I don't like her. Your mother would never have let a woman like that in this house.'

'How would you know?' Deborah muttered, then turned to leave the room. 'You were never here.' Even now, Debo-rah faulted me for the fact that I had continued to take consulting jobs during my retirement years. Had I stayed home more, been more attentive, Deborah felt that I might have noticed Annalee's dizzy spells and become aware that something was wrong.

'Well, tell her not to come in my room,' I called after her, and then moved to the bedroom door with the intention of

36

closing it. 'I'll be resting.' Deborah didn't reply, and so I added, as she disappeared up the hallway, 'I certainly hope you'll be staying around to supervise her.' Then I pushed the door to, shutting out the remainder of the house and the rest of the world.

I turned on the bedroom television, stripped off the clothing Deborah had brought to the hospital – a sweltering jogging suit that had probably been hanging unused in my closet for twenty years – and climbed into bed, suddenly weary of everything. If I couldn't have sway over my home any longer, at least I could maintain control of my person. I could sleep away the afternoon, and let Deborah deal with this ... this housewoman she'd hired. Surely Deborah wouldn't leave her alone here if she knew I wasn't supervising.

Lying in bed, I turned an ear toward the wall. I could hear the hum of conversation, but not the words. What were they talking about? What was Deborah telling her? I scooted across the bed, strained toward the sound, tried to make it out. Finally, I rose and put an ear to the wall. The words still weren't clear. Deborah and the woman were in the foyer or the front parlor talking; I could tell that much. No work was being done so far. Perhaps they wouldn't be able to settle on a price. Perhaps they hadn't discussed the details previously.

What were they saying? Was Deborah telling her things about me? Untrue things? Making me sound like a dotty old man? I moved toward the door, turned the handle silently, stuck my head into the hallway, then crept out a few steps, pressing close to the wall like a Soviet spy gathering trade secrets in enemy territory. Perhaps Deborah's bringing in the housekeeper was just one more way of building the evidence she would need to oust me from my home and force me into some warehouse for the criminally old.

'. . . isten to him,' Deborah was saying. 'He'll give you trouble, if he can. Just go ahead and do your work. I would say that he's having a difficult time with the death of my mother, but he's always been impossible to deal with.'

'I'm used to it.' The woman's voice was listless, disinterested. 'I clean for a lotta old people. I don't let it bother me.'

'Perfect.' Deborah seemed delighted, disgustingly so. 'I'd be willing to pay extra if you could cook supper for him on Mondays and make sure he eats a good meal. That would give me a night off.' The sentence ended in a dramatic sigh, indicating the breadth and depth of the daily burden I'd become. 'Eventually, we need to work out something more . . . permanent, but for now I'm just trying to get through a day at a time.'

The woman sucked air past her teeth, the hesitant sound one makes in order to up the ante while bargaining in an open-air market on the far side of the world. 'I go into work with the janitorial service at four thirty . . . or I'd do it. I could use the money.'

Of course she could. Of course she could use the money. What had I tried to tell Deborah? A ne'er-do-well, for certain.

'Well, it was an idea.' Deborah's disappointment was obvious. 'I'll just have to –'

'I got a daughter who could do it. She turned sixteen last

month, so she's lookin' for work. Needs something to keep her busy after school. She's a nice girl. Makes good grades – smart at math and stuff. Good cook, too. She helped take care of the lady who rented to us at the last place we lived. A teacher. Got down with diabetes. Epiphany stayed with her and helped when she was sick.'

To her credit, Deborah hesitated. Obviously, some teenager coming and going from my house was out of the question. As soon as I had the chance, I'd let Deborah know in no uncertain terms that I was perfectly capable of feeding myself.

'That sounds perfect.'

My skin flamed at Deborah's answer. The gall!

'I could have her come more than just Mondays, if you want. She's got time, and her school's just up the road a few blocks.'

Certainly not. Not even once per week. I had no need of a babysitter, teenage or otherwise; nor did I intend to tolerate one. The housekeeper was affronting enough. Any more of Deborah's spies coming and going from my house, and I'd have no control over my life at all.

'I'll tell you what. Since you're here on Mondays, you could just leave a supper plate for him to warm or a sandwich. Why don't we start with your daughter coming Tuesdays and Thursdays to cook and maybe take care of the dishes in the kitchen and whatnot? That'll give me a few days a week to catch up on work and such. Since Mother died, it seems like I'm behind in every possible way, and . . .'

At that point, I'd had quite enough of my daughter and some woman making plans for me, as if I were a child.

'Now, just one minute, young lady!' I protested, and was up the hallway in several quite determined strides. A somewhat breezy feeling caught the corner of my mind, but in the heat of anger, I did not let it deter me from my mission. I burst into the living room with a finger pointed. 'I will not tolerate your making arrangements such as these without consulting me. I am not an invalid. I do not need a housekeeper, or someone to cook for me, and . . .'

'Daddy!' Deborah gasped, twisting in the wing chair. The housekeeper was poised on the sofa with her mouth agape. Deborah's eyes widened, taking me in from head to toe, and it was at roughly that juncture that I recognized myself to be standing there in my union suit. A reflection watched me from the glass of the china cabinet across the room – long, thin legs protruding from droopy blue boxer shorts, a midsection in the general shape of an olive, and toothpick-like arms protruding from a tank-style T-shirt. I'd lost a great deal of weight in these months without Annalee. I'd been avoiding mirrors.

Normally, such a display in the living room with the curtains wide-open and two women present would have disturbed me greatly. Today, it was the least of my concerns. In fact, since my goal was to dispose of the housekeeper anyway, this might be a fortuitous opportunity.

The reflection in the glass lifted its chin, straightened its shoulders, and pretended to be oblivious to the lack of attire. 'I'm quite fine here on my own.'

'We can see that.' Deborah blinked, delivering a bug-eyed look my way.

The housekeeper turned her gaze toward the sofa, the corners of her mouth tugging.

I pressed onward. What choice did I have? 'I am not an incompetent. I do know how to make a sandwich or pour a bowl of cereal. I've no need of someone. I don't want the trouble of it. I like my privacy.'

The housekeeper continued investigating the floral print on the sofa and then moved her gaze to the gold sculptured carpet Annalee had wanted to replace for some time now. I should have let her do so when she asked. What had been the point of my stubbornness?

'I don't think someone coming in a few hours a day, twice a week, is going to drain your privacy too much.' Deborah pursed her lips with another glance at her watch. 'Besides, her daughter needs the work. Silvia's right: There isn't much for teenagers to do in this neighborhood. Too many adults and college students are taking the jobs.'

'It isn't my responsibility to employ the neighborhood.' The man in the glass looked less appealing now, less certain of himself. Annalee would have been disappointed in him. She was always the first to purchase Girl Scout cookies or donate books and supplies for after-school programs at the church. Last year, she'd even started volunteering with the free-lunch program in the Summer Kitchen, where they fed the homeless and downtrodden. Had she heard the sad story of this housekeeper's daughter, she would have invited her to dinner *and* given her a job.

But I was never as good a man as Annalee hoped. I didn't want the girl.

41

'Let's give it a try for a few weeks,' Deborah negotiated. 'If you don't like it in, say . . . a month, then we'll think about something else. Meals on Wheels, maybe.'

'I do not need charity. I can afford to buy my meals anywhere I want.' A poor choice of words in front of the housekeeper. Now she'd certainly be looking for valuables.

Deborah's lips curved in a sly fashion, as if she'd known that would be my response. 'True . . . and so it won't be any burden to give a teenager a few hours' work a week, will it? Mom would have liked the idea.'

'Don't bring your mother into this.'

'Well, she would have.'

'I am not your mother.' Therein lay the heart of the problem.

The color drained from Deborah's face, and she swallowed hard, then checked her watch again. 'No, you're not.' Moisture gathered in the corners of her eyes, and I knew I'd finally landed a blow through the armor. The victory felt hollow.

'I'm still against it,' I said, and I could feel the man in the glass dissolving like a sand castle overtaken by a determined tide. 'But I suppose I have no choice.'

By mutual consent we let the argument die there. After a quick tour of the house and an explanation of cleaning duties, for which I put on pants, Deborah left and the housekeeper stayed. Exhaustion had seeped through my body by then – I am convinced that hospital stays do more harm than good, in general – so I stationed myself on the sofa in the front parlor. Long rays of light angled from the leaded glass over the tall west windows and pressed through the transom above the door, chasing rainbows around the room. I watched the housekeeper pass through the beams of light as she came and went, the rainbows sliding over her clothing and skin. She had a Mediterranean look about her, I decided – Greek or Italian, perhaps, with a slight curvature to her nose and eyes a greenish hazel color that seemed eerily bright against her skin. She smelled like cigarette smoke. I didn't like her, and the feeling seemed to be mutual. She went about her work, crossing the room without looking my way.

'Be certain you leave things as you found them,' I instructed when she passed by with Pledge and a dust rag, stopping to spray and wipe a set of shelves where Annalee kept a collection of tiny glass birds gathered in our travels.

'I will.' The answer was neither accommodating nor particularly harsh, but conveyed a resignation to our situation.

'I'll be checking through the house after you leave.'

She muttered something. *I'm sure you will*, I thought she said.

'I have an excellent memory. I'll know if something isn't where it should be.'

Mumbling another reply, she picked up a bird and began rubbing it with the dust rag.

'That's *furniture* cleaner,' I pointed out. 'It contains wax. It will leave a residue on the glass.'

With a huff, she set down the bird and dropped the dust rag on the table, then turned on her heel and exited the room, her arms stiff at her sides.

I decided that she was singularly unpleasant, which was undoubtedly part of Deborah's plan. My daughter intended to irritate me with this woman's invasion, and now her daughter's, three days each week until I finally acquiesced to being sent away with the old and useless.

Her plan wouldn't work. Deborah should have known that I am nothing if not a man of resolve. I could outlast this hard-faced woman. And the teenage daughter would be easy to dissuade. Youth and enthusiasm are no match for old age and treachery. I'd have my house to myself again in no time.

In an odd way, it was refreshing to have a mission in life, a challenge once again.

Leaning back on the sofa, I watched the filtered light paint splotches of color on the ceiling, and I contemplated plans, designed them as I would have an engineering schematic, considering first the end goal, and then slowly calculated what sorts of components might be needed. I was, after all, a member of the Hughes Aircraft team that built *Surveyor 1*, the first American spacecraft to soft-land on the moon. This was a small matter compared to navigating thousands of miles into space.

At some point during my mental calculations, and after telling the woman that several areas of the house were off-limits, including my study and the unused bedroom at the end of the upstairs hall, weariness overtook me, and I nodded off. When I awoke, the prisms of light were gone from the room. The housekeeper was leaning over the sofa and shaking me.

'Mr Al-ford? Mr Al-ford? I need to leave now. Mr Al-ford, are you all right?' She mispronounced and generally eviscerated my name, while apparently attempting to confirm that I was alive at the time of her departure.

I held my eyes closed longer than was necessary, just to

see what she would do. She leaned so close that I felt her breath rustling the wispy hairs that were all that remained of what, in my days at Cape Canaveral, had been a thick head of hair, cut in the requisite flattop style. I smelled fresh cigarette smoke.

'Mr Al-ford?'

I sat up so quickly that she jumped back and slapped a hand to her throat, then stood watching me, wide eyed. 'The pronunciation is Al-*vord*. Alvord, from the original Saxon. There is no "F" in it. That shouldn't be too difficult to remember.'

Her chin pulled upward and back, and she blinked, seeming to have been rendered speechless by my sudden awakening.

'See that your daughter knows how to pronounce it, too,' I instructed, then scooted forward on the sofa in order to push to my feet, so that I could lock the door when she left. 'And there's no smoking in this house. See that your daughter knows that, as well.'

Backing away a few steps, she angled herself toward the door. 'My daughter doesn't smoke.'

'I find that, these days, parents have no idea what their children do.'

She snorted and began fishing through her purse, looking for her keys, I supposed. Apparently I'd made her uncomfortable, and she was in a hurry to be gone, which was as it should be. 'I went outside for the cigarette,' she muttered into the purse.

'Fine lot of good that does. It lingers in clothing.' It occurred to me that, since she hadn't driven here, she couldn't be

45

looking for her keys. Perhaps she was waiting for me to offer some monetary compensation for the day's endeavors. 'I won't be paying you, if that's why you're hovering in my front room. Along with the rest of my life, my daughter has taken over my checkbook.' Deborah felt the need to begin monitoring the accounts after I'd purchased from some wandering Girl Scouts their entire load of cookies as well as the wagon, on the promise that they would tell other neighborhood children I'd stolen their goods, and that this was no longer a safe place to conduct door-to-door sales.

'I was looking for my bus pass.' She stiffened, showing obvious irritation. My strategy was working.

'Perhaps you'll have better luck finding it on the way to the bus stop. It's time for me to lock up my house for the evening. Pull the front shades before you go.'

Cocking an eyebrow, she took in the slanting afternoon sun outside the window. In the entry hall, the clock was just chiming four. 'Kind of early, isn't it?'

On the street, a school bus roared by, and I heard children chattering. 'I don't like to be bothered. I have work to do.'

Shrugging, she took the long pole with the hook on the end, circled the room, and hurriedly lowered the shades. 'I'll get the rest on my way out. You need anything else?' She uttered the last words with a note of exasperation, as if I were intruding on her time.

'Take the mail from the box and put it inside the front door. On the table to the left, not the one to the right. And don't consider slipping anything from the stack. I'll be watching through the window, of course.'

'Table to the left,' she ground out, then started toward the entry hall again, shaking her head and grumbling to herself. She paused before turning the corner and disappearing from view. 'I left a sandwich plate for you on the counter. Your daughter wants to make sure you eat.' The words had the sound of having been forced out between clenched teeth.

'I don't like sandwiches,' I said, which quite conveniently was the straw that broke the camel's determination. She forwent pulling the rest of the shades and didn't bother to bid me a fond farewell on her way out. Nor did she pick up the mail.

I sat back in my chair, self-satisfied, calculating that there was a fair chance of her not showing up at all next week. Surely she could find work in more welcoming places. Not a bad bit of progress, particularly considering my weakened condition. Tomorrow, after a good night's sleep in my own bed, I'd make short work of the teenager, if she bothered to come at all.

Smiling to myself, I rested my head against the sofa cushions. Outside, I could hear the children chattering, and the low, dragging cadence of the neighbor's mentally handicapped son, Teddy – a perpetual child in an adult body. Annalee had developed a particular bond with him. He brought starts of flowers and tiny seedlings to her, and she baked cookies and tea cakes and sent them to Teddy and his parents. From time to time, he still left potted plants on my porch. I brought them inside and put them upstairs with the rest of Annalee's growing things.

Thinking of the plants reminded me that I should go through the house and check to be sure that the housekeeper had properly taken care of everything and hadn't absconded with any valuables in the process. If anything were missing, or the plants had been left too wet or too dry, it would be a strike against her. A deficiency I would most definitely be compelled to mention to Deborah . . .

Something flitted through my mind, fast and featherlight, like the prismatic rainbows slipping over the housekeeper's skin. I'd been dreaming before she'd awakened me. I'd been in a large room with dark, richly paneled walls on all sides. The delighted squeals of children rang in the air, rising like bright butterflies, fluttering upward through the cavernous space. The sounds danced about the heavily polished wood railing on the second-story gallery and echoed along the arch-shaped ceiling, where a fresco sky and clouds had been painted among ornate gold-leafed cornices.

The room was filled with prismatic light – tiny rainbows that were bright in my memory now. I chased them as they moved, tried to capture them. Two little girls ran ahead of me – girls in starched white dresses, flyaway red hair bouncing over their shoulders. Reaching the bottom of a wide staircase, they rounded the corner, their white patent-leather shoes *click-clack*ing against the hardwood floors as they scrambled up the stairs. Hands slapping flat against the oak steps, the girls attempted to capture the beams of light beneath their palms, only to find that the rainbows squirted away each time, disappearing over their wrists and fingers.

Squealing with delight, they turned back to look for me, their faces nearly identical – the same small, pursed lips, round cheeks, wide eyes the fathomless blue of the ocean. 'C'mon,

Willyyyy!' Their voices echoed in my mind. 'Willyyyy! C'mon!' The girl closest to me took a tumble then, and came careening down the stairs in a tangle of fabric and hair and skin. The moment stretched in my mind – her body falling, rolling, the other girl screaming, a baby crying, glass hitting the floor, then shattering, someone running across the room.

'Cecile!' A woman's shrill call split the air above us. A door slammed against the wall. I stepped back from the staircase as the little redhead tumbled to a stop.

I turned to run.

The dream had ended there, when Deborah's house-keeper shook me awake. In my mind, the pictures remained clear even now, as if I should have known them all along. Yet I'd never seen that room before this day, never before experienced that dream. Where was the cavernous house with the dark wooden walls and the blue-sky ceiling?

Was there more to the dream? Would it have come if the housekeeper hadn't awakened me? What did it mean? Why was I seeing it now?

I wanted to tell someone about it, to see what the response would be. Perhaps the most recent incident with my heart had caused a lack of oxygen to the brain. Or perhaps my temporary journey toward death, the scenes outside the bullet train flashing by at indeterminable speed, had unlocked a door in my mind. Was this another dream, merely a fanciful extension of my watching the play of light through the glass earlier?

Or could it be another tiny slice of the past?

CHAPTER 4

Epiphany Jones

The man lived on one of those streets where kids like me don't go. You show up just strollin' down the sidewalks on Blue Sky Hill, people in their big houses figure either you're the hired help or you're casing the place. Kids that live on the Hill don't walk, for one thing. They drive real nice cars, and wear clothes that say, *Yeah, I got money. I belong here and you don't.* Right after I started at this new school, the history teacher brought in an old lady to talk to us about segregation. The lady said there used to be places in Dallas where she just plain couldn't go. She remembered how they used to have 'colored day' at the state fair, and how in most of the stores, she couldn't try on clothes unless she bought them first, and then if it didn't fit she was stuck with it.

She laughed and said, 'But the Lord provides for those that'll try, because that's how I started my own business.' Her cheeks crinkled up and her eyes twinkled like two tiny black dots of fresh paint on an old piece of brown paper. I scooted up in my seat, getting into the story a little. I never thought of myself too much as black, or African-American, whatever you want to call it. On Martin Luther King Day and all that stuff, I was just me. Some weird mix that was just different from everybody else I knew. Mostly in the little towns we lived in, some of the Mexican kids had skin about my shade, but you could tell I wasn't Mexican just by looking.

When I listened to the lady telling her story, I could relate to not being welcome someplace. I liked the idea that God might take that very thing that stunk the worst about your life and change it around into something good.

'I worked in the back at a dry cleaner's.' Her voice was crackly and old. 'When I was done at the end of the day, the man would let me use the sewin' machine, and I'd alter up dresses for all the black women who couldn't return them to the stores – for lots of white women, too, who couldn't fit the sizes, and such. But the black women, they wanted those dresses to fit so they could look good at the jazz clubs down in Deep Ellum. I saved that sewin' money, and it wasn't too many years before I started my own little store.'

She looked around the room then, and her eyes got misty, and she said we kids oughta remember there was a time when some folks had it a lot harder than others. I couldn't see how things were so different now. The upscale neighborhoods in Blue Sky Hill weren't all lily white anymore, but you could be sure their kids didn't wear our kind of clothes, or get free lunches at the Summer Kitchen, or pick up used books and magazines down at the Book Basket store, or go to the public school. These days, it wasn't about what color you were, but how much money you had. The

51

same, only different. It was still people not wanting to be with people who weren't their kind.

I wasn't the *kind* to be heading up the sidewalks of Blue Sky Hill, but Mama'd told me that if I didn't make some money to pay for the damages at the church, I could just get out of her house. After that, she warned me about the man, Mr J. Norman Al-vord. She wanted me to practice saying his name right. I wasn't about to practice some stupid rich guy's stupid name, but I didn't want to end up out on the street either. DeRon had asked me to come with him after basketball practice, and part of me, the Epie part, thought about chucking the Blue Sky Hill job and hanging out with DeRon. I'd started to think that, if I was DeRon's girlfriend, the rest of the kids in that school might leave me alone.

But there I was, lugging my backpack while the private school kids in their nice cars drove by and stared at me like I was an alien from another planet. Guess I wasn't as much Epie as I thought, because I was afraid not to show up for the job.

Just because you're showin' up don't mean you gotta do the job, Epie whispered in my ear. *You let this old man know you ain't the help. Let him find some other sucker to cook for him and clean up his nasty mess. Who's he think he is, anyway? You ain't his aunt Jemima . . .*

What I really wanted to do was go on home. I could have the whole place to myself. After hanging around all weekend, Russ was supposed to pack up his piece-of-junk trailer and head out to a knife and gun show tonight. That was Russ's job, if you could call it that – selling weapons and

52

T-shirts and Harley stuff at gun shows and flea markets. Usually, jobs were supposed to actually make money, but Russ spent about as much as he brought in. Right now, Mama was on Russ's case about money, which was good, because it'd get him out of the house. I'd had to crawl into Mama's bedroom while he was sleeping to take the Some-day Book from under the bed. Tonight, after he left and Mama was gone to the temp job, I was headed for the closet to see what else was in there.

I found Mr J. Norman Alvord's house, and, sure enough, it was high-dollar. The place was old, like most of the houses on Blue Sky Hill. They'd all been put there by folks who got rich off oil back in the roaring twenties or something – the history teacher told us about it – and not far away, there'd be streets crammed full of little houses where the maids and the cooks and the gardeners had lived. You can guess which of those streets was ours.

Who in the world needed three built-in garages and another one out by the street, anyway? The house was like a redbrick castle, three stories high, with about a million long windows that had fancy colored glass around the edges. Other than being a TV star or playing for the Dallas Cowboys, what did a person do to get a house like that? Even the garage out by the street looked like good digs, with a place for cars underneath and an apartment up top. It was, like, twice the size of our place.

One of these days, I'm gonna live in a house like that, I thought. Epie laughed in my head and said, *Girl, you trippin'. You better just turn your little bubble butt around and head on back to your own neighborhood. It ain't even healthy, looking at a house like that.*

I shut Epie down, because by then I wanted to see the inside of that house, job or no job. I'd never been in a place so big.

I headed up the driveway, and a window blind slapped shut, then another, and another, and another. A shiver ran across my shoulders. Maybe I was at the wrong address. What if they called the police, and I got hauled off for trespassing?

The closer I came, the more I felt like I wasn't supposed to be there. The house had a weird vibe to it, and I got the creepy idea that someone in there was watching me. I stopped and looked at the address number again. Yup. This was it. There was a little name-plate above the house number that read, MR. AND MRS. J. NORMAN ALVORD.

I crossed the porch and knocked on the door. Nobody answered, so I leaned close to one of the long, skinny side windows. There was a filmy curtain over it, like the veil a bride wears, so I couldn't see much inside, except a dark hallway and the bottom of a staircase. 'Hey,' I called out, and pushed the doorbell again. 'Hey, I know somebody's in there. I'm supposed to come work this afternoon.' Mama'd warned me that the old man was a real jerk, and whatever he said, I should ignore it, because his daughter was the one writing the checks. She'd even given Mama a little extra. She called it hazard pay.

I wondered if she'd hand me money for sitting on the porch, since I couldn't get in the door.

I pushed the doorbell a half dozen times in a row. Finally the locks clicked and the door swung open. The dude on the other side was pretty much what I expected – an old white guy. He was skinny and kinda stooped over, so that he just about looked me level in the eye, but I could tell he must've been tall before he got, like, way old. He was wearing a tank top thing, with chest hairs and droopy skin hanging out everywhere, and striped pajama pants pulled almost to his armpits. His hair, what there was of it, looked like the fuzz on a baby's head after you pull a T-shirt on in the wintertime and the air crackles with static.

His lips made a big ol' frown, and he tipped his chin up, looking at me through glasses so thick, they were like the magnifier we used in science lab. He seemed like he was waiting for me to say something, and I was waiting for him, I guessed.

'*What?*' he asked finally. 'I told you Girl Scouts not to come here anymore.'

That made me laugh, but he probably didn't mean for it to. I figured he was trying to make trouble so I'd give up. But I was supposed to get twenty dollars for fixing him supper and cleaning up his kitchen – eight dollars each for two hours' work, and another four just for walking over here from school, then riding the city bus home. That wasn't bad money for a little cooking, and I liked to cook, because I used to do it with Mrs Lora.

That look he gave me made Epie pop right to the surface. She worked up some major attitude, just like the mean girls at school would've. Sounded like them, too. 'Mister, I ain't no Girl Scout. I'm here to cook your dinner. My mama cleaned your house yesta'day.'

'Yes-*ter*-day.' He spit out the middle of that word like he was making sure I knew how to say it right. Then he looked me over again, and I could tell what he had on his mind. I'd been getting that look my whole life. You'd think it wouldn't be too hard for people to figure how a white woman gets a brown baby, but people, especially old people, always looked at me like it was some kind of surprise.

'Mmm-hmm, yes-*ter*-day af-*ter*-noon.' I put on the voice we'd learned in after-school enrichment last year, when we got to spend a week pretending we were news broadcasters. 'Your daugh-*ter* said to come at four thirty.' I'm not so dumb, when I don't want to be, but you go talking all proper around the kids in school and somebody'll jump you, thinking you're trying to act like you're too good. This old dude wouldn't know one thing about that.

He kept an arm stretched across from his shoulder to the doorframe, like a bar to shut me out. 'I'm not hungry.'

Mama was right about Mr Alvord. 'Well, your daughter says you are.' I bent down, ducked under his arm, and ended up on the other side of him, in the hallway. All of a sudden, even if I didn't want this job, I was gonna show him he couldn't go trashin' on me. I got a stubborn streak that doesn't give in easy, especially not to some old rich dude with his nose in the air, telling me not to come in his big house.

He turned around, his mouth popping open and shut like one of the little tadpoles the country boys used to catch in

56

the creek behind my old school. They'd hold those things out of the water just to watch them squirm and try to get a breath. I never did know why they did that, but with Mr J. Norman Alvord, it was kind of funny. He looked like he didn't have a clue what to do now.

He coughed, and then pulled out a hankie and coughed some more, then folded whatever he'd hocked up *inside* the hankie and tucked it in the waistband of his pajamas. That was about the nastiest thing I'd ever seen. And these old dudes were the ones complaining about boys wearing their pants sagging? Least people my age didn't hock one up and keep it for later.

'Come back another day,' he barked. 'I have work to do. I'm in the middle of a project.'

I turned my shoulder to him and went a couple more steps into the house. The hallway was big, with paintings hanging in fancy gold frames, like you'd see in a museum. Off to the right side, there was a room with flowered couches and little chairs. That room had doorways to other rooms, and then to the left, a hallway stretched way too far to be in any one person's house. Ahead was a huge staircase with a big stained-glass window halfway up, and what looked like another big room sat off to the right. This guy was seriously loaded, but the place felt like Dracula's castle, with all the shades pulled, shadows everywhere, and the air stale and quiet.

'Tell you what,' I said to Mr J. Norman Alvord. 'You go do your work, and I'm gonna do my work, and we won't bother each other, huh? House like this, you prob'ly won't even know I'm here.'

'Most pro-*ba*-bly I will,' he grumbled, pronouncing the word like I hadn't said it good enough. Then he smacked the front door shut and headed for the stairs without saying another thing.

'Hey, you gonna show me where the kitchen is?' I called after him, but he didn't answer. 'Guess not.'

I stood there for a few minutes, waiting to see if he'd come back. When he didn't, I slid my backpack down and set it on the tile. The zipper hung open where it was broke, and I could see the Someday Book inside. I'd been carrying it with me since I got it out from under the bed. It was mine, after all, and even though the ideas in it seemed stupid now – *someday I'm gonna fly an airplane; someday I'm gonna have a horse; someday I'm gonna have a big bedroom with a roof thing over the bed* – it was still kind of interesting, looking back at what you dreamed about in the seventh grade. Besides, if Mama found it around our place, I'd be dead for sure, because she'd know I'd been in her box.

I wandered through the downstairs, checking out the hallway to the left. A couple bedrooms and bathrooms, and a little room with lots of bookshelves and windows, some sofas at one end, and an old pool table at the other. There were photos in the hall, the old kind with the colors faded – a little girl running in the waves on a beach, a boy playing in the sand under a palm tree, a family standing on the deck of a sailboat, smiling for the camera. Mom, dad, two kids. The perfect postcard. The sailboat was high-dollar, and the man looked enough like J. Norman that I figured out who it was. He had red hair when he was young. He wasn't a bad-looking dude – nothing like the prune-faced guy who'd just opened the door. But the man in the picture didn't look happy, either. The woman and the little girl and the boy were all focused on the camera, but the man was looking off a bit, like he'd pasted on a smile for the picture, but his mind wasn't in it. I stared at it and thought, *If somebody put me on a boat like that, my mind wouldn't be anyplace else.* That looked like the good life, right there.

I wandered on past some more baby pictures and high school graduation pictures, and pictures of J. Norman and his wife. They'd gone on trips all over the world – the Great Wall of China, some pyramids like in Egypt, a big ship out in the ocean, a castle someplace. His wife had on pretty dresses in some of the old pictures, and hats to match, and little white gloves. She was as classy as an old-time movie star, with a big white smile, and red lipstick, and dark hair piled high on her head. From where I was standing, the life in those pictures was a fairy tale.

I left the photos and went back up the hall and across the entryway, past the stairs. I could hear J. Norman up there making noise in one of the rooms. He had a TV on loud, and drawers and cabinets were slamming. Mama'd told me I was supposed to keep an eye on him, and that his daughter didn't want him upstairs, but what was I supposed to do about it – go up there and carry the man down like a big ol' baby? He was a grown-up, after all, and if he felt good enough to be smacking drawers around, he couldn't be in too bad shape.

Then I thought, *Yeah, what if he fell down or something, and that's what all the racket up there is about?* I remembered when Mrs Lora came home from the hospital the first time. The night she got back, she fell in the bathroom and was stuck beside the toilet. I had to break the door lock to get in there and help her out.

Maybe I should check on Mr J. Norman Grouchface Smartmouth Alvord . . .

Then again, if he saw me, he'd probably bite my head off for bothering him. The kitchen was a safer place, since that's where I told him I'd be . . .

I tiptoed up a couple steps and listened, anyway. He was talking to someone up there . . . or talking to himself. Anyway, he wasn't yelling for help, and so I decided he wasn't dying or anything. I left him be and went through the rest of the downstairs. There were so many rooms there, you could get lost. I liked the front room with flowered sofas and lace curtains and a cabinet full of teacups from all over the world. Each one had a little label on the bottom telling where it came from. I could've stayed in that room all day, but I figured I'd better go do the job I was supposed to do.

The kitchen was huge, with green tile countertops, a refrigerator big enough to stuff dead bodies into, and a giant brick archway with pans hanging overhead. Inside it, the shiny new stainless-steel stove looked weird, since everything else in the kitchen was old. Off to the left, a little table sat tucked back by some windows. There were bird feeders hanging all over the backyard – like, fifty of them. Birds darted in and out, checking the feeders, but they were empty and it looked like they'd been that way for a while. I

60

wondered if the pretty lady in the pictures used to fill them. One time when we lived in Odessa, Mama and me rented a trailer house from a lady who fed the birds out back of her house. She said a free bird is good for the soul.

There was an envelope on the counter with my name on it. I opened it and found money and a note inside. J. Norman's daughter wrote the note, I guess. It was full of instructions, step by step, for what I was supposed to cook, and where everything was, and how to turn on the stove, and to be sure to turn it off, and where to set J. Norman's plate, and that I was supposed to hang around and clean up after he ate. Geez. Really, as long as she must've spent writing all that, she could've just fixed him dinner herself. At the bottom, the note said, *I assume your mother told you that my father is not to be climbing the stairs unassisted, under any circumstances. All necessary items have been moved downstairs for him. If he argues with you about this, please call, and I'll talk to him.* After that, there was a phone number and her name, *Deborah*. At the top of the page, the stationery had a fancy emblem from the college, and her full name, Deborah Lewis, PhD. She had perfect handwriting, and the strokes were deep into the paper, like she was pushing hard when she wrote.

Since I'd already messed up in my first thirty minutes on the job, there was no way I was gonna call her. Anyone who'd write a note like that wasn't about to pat me on the head and tell me it was all right.

I was supposed to make some kind of pasta for J. Norman. His daughter'd left all the ingredients in the refrigerator, chopped up in separate little baggies – onions, mushrooms, green peppers, and low-fat imitation hamburger crumbles. There was pasta and a bottle of sauce on the counter, and whole-wheat bread. The note did everything but tell me which side to butter it on. Guess *Deborah* didn't know I'd been cooking since I was old enough to pull a chair up to the stove, because Mama was always too tired, and most of her boyfriends liked food on the table when they came in. I didn't mind it so much. Once I got old enough to come home and stay by myself after school, cooking gave me something to do, and besides, I like to eat.

J. Norman didn't have to worry about me eating *his* food, though. That low-fat fake hamburger smelled nasty, even once I put the vegetables in. I looked around in the refrigerator to see if there was anything else I could add to it, and came up with a little low-fat ham. I chopped it thin and put it in, and fried it all and added the sauce. In about twenty minutes, dinner was done, and it was only four fifty-five. Now what was I gonna do with myself until six, when I was supposed to leave? Four till six Tuesdays and Thursdays. Man, this was gonna stink.

I put the food on the table, made toast and a glass of orange juice (just like the note said), and set a single place at the table. Then I went looking for J. Norman. He was upstairs in a room with the door shut. I knocked on it, and he hollered at me, 'What do you want?'

'Your food's ready,' I told him.

'I'm occupied.'

'Well, it's ready, and it'll get cold.' What was I supposed to do now? Kick in the door, drag the man downstairs, and sit him in front of his plate? This job was such a stupid idea. Why was I even still here?

'What's in it?' Something in the room, a drawer shutting maybe, smacked like the crack of a gun going off, and I jerked back.

'What's in what?'

'The food? What's in the food?' His voice was closer to the door now. Just on the other side, but we were still yelling through the wood.

'The stuff that was in the refrigerator.' *Duh.*

'I don't like those things.' A chair squealed. I guessed he was sitting down in it. Looked like J. Norman wasn't coming to dinner.

I gathered up my *nice* and tried one more time. While I was cooking, I'd started coming up with a use for the money for this job, and I was getting kind of attached to the idea. 'I made it like your daughter said. Like Deborah said. In the note. I know how to cook.'

'She doesn't care what I like.'

'Except I added a little ham.'

'What for?'

'To make it taste better. Like pasta carbonara.' I had pasta carbonara in a restaurant with Mrs Lora once, and I liked it, so me and her found a recipe. Now I couldn't help wondering if that was the Italian in me coming out.

'Never heard of it.' The chair creaked and a drawer slid open. 'I don't like ham.'

'Then why's it in your refrigerator?' He didn't have an answer for that, I guess. He snorted loud, and then the phone rang. I wasn't sure whether I was supposed to answer it or not. I thought about the fact that it might be Deborah, and if nobody answered, she'd think something was wrong. Then she'd come over and find J. Norman upstairs and his dinner all cold on the table. I'd be out of this job in a hurry. Mama would go off on me like crazy.

The phone on the hall table kept ringing and ringing. I could hear one in the office, too. Guess J. Norman wasn't gonna answer no matter what. Maybe I needed to. Maybe I'd get in trouble if I did. Maybe I'd get in trouble if I didn't.

Finally, I grabbed the phone. It was Deborah, and she was mad. 'He's ignoring the phone, isn't he?' she asked, and I heard a click like someone was picking up another receiver. Deborah heard the click, too. 'Is that him? Did he just pick up? Dad, are you on here?'

'I don't think so,' I told her, and I wasn't sure why I said it. The office door opened, and J. Norman poked his head around the corner, the phone cord wrapped across his chin and pulling his left ear down flat. The sunlight reflected off his glasses, so that I couldn't see his eyes, but his mouth was hanging open a little.

'Has he eaten?' Deborah wanted to know. 'Did he give you any trouble about it, because I told him not to . . .'.

'He's eating right now.' Whether I was trying to save J. Norman's rear or my own, I didn't have a clue, but Deborah sounded like she could chew somebody up one side and down the other. 'That's why he didn't pick up the phone.'

J. Norman tilted his head back, squinted at me underneath

64

the black plastic rims of his glasses. He frowned, like I had him all confused.

'You want to talk to him?' I asked. 'Because I can go in the kitchen and get him.'

J. Norman put up a one-handed stop sign and shook his head. He made a sidestep toward the stairs, like he was afraid Deborah could see him right through the phone. The cord stretched tighter and his ear got flatter.

'It's just that he's, like, in the middle of dinner.' I looked him in the eye. He stopped with his hand on the doorframe. 'He likes it a lot, I think.'

His eyes went wide.

'He's eating a *ton?*' I said.

He cocked his head to one side and squinted at me again.

Deborah let out a long, slow sigh, like the mad was flowing out of her. 'No, don't bother him. I'm glad to hear he's eating a good meal, for once. I just wanted to check in.'

'Everything's great. He can't get *enough* of that pasta. He even said he *liked* it.' I stared J. Norman dead in the face, and his mouth dropped open again.

'He did?' Deborah was in full-on shock.

'Yes, ma'am. He even told me "thank you."'

J. Norman coughed like he had a bone in his throat, and he shook a fist in the air.

His daughter said good-bye; then I pushed the button to hang up the phone, pointing the antenna at him. 'You owe me big-time now.'

I had a feeling I wasn't gonna have near as much trouble

with Mr J. Norman anymore, and I was right. By the time I left for the day, we were getting along, if that's what you call it when two people act like they don't notice each other, but they don't argue, either. I cleaned up the rest of the kitchen and left him at the table, eating pasta carbonara. I couldn't tell if he liked it or not, but I didn't really care, so everything was fine.

Russ was gone when I got home, and Mama was already down at the university, trying to get those classrooms shiny clean so she could get promoted from being on a temporary status to full-time with benefits. That meant I was free to finally get in Mama's closet again and pull out the secret boxes.

I opened the big box first this time. It was full of old clothes that smelled kind of musty, but they weren't the kind of clothes Mama would wear anymore. They were nice dresses, like she might've put on for a dance or a party at someplace fancy, but all of them would be too small for her now. Smashed on one side against the cardboard were some things that must've been hers when she was a kid – a china doll in a pretty dress but with her hair moth-eaten; a lacy white little girl's dress, like a wedding dress, only smaller; a pink ballet costume and a pair of crushed ballet shoes. I never even knew my mama was a dancer.

I laid everything back in the box and put it in the closet, feeling like I was digging around in her life. None of it had anything to do with me.

I opened the shoe box next, set aside all the stuff I'd already looked at, and got out the baby book and the pictures in a Wal-Mart envelope. The baby book was mostly blank inside, the notes about first teeth and first steps stopping after I was about a year old. On the page that said, *First Birthday*, there was nothing but an imprint of the Wal-Mart envelope. I guessed Mama had planned to paste the pictures on there, but never got around to it.

I set down the book and picked up the envelope of photos, flipped it open. There wasn't much inside. I counted seven pictures as I spread them out on the carpet. Seven little bits of my life I never knew existed. Three pictures were taken outside some church, and four looked like they were from a picnic in the park. In the church pictures, my mama was standing with five other women – my daddy's family, I guessed. I stared into the faces of those black women – tall, dignified, decked out for church in wide-brimmed hats and matching dresses and heels. They looked like something out of a magazine, like they were about to walk the runway at a fashion show. My mama was dressed like them, but her smile was careful, pasted on, like she felt kind of silly being there. She was so young when that picture was taken. Just eighteen, I guessed, because I was a year old. The birthday girl. The big dress-up celebration in the park was for my birthday. I could tell it was the same day, because none of the dresses changed.

I couldn't remember ever having a birthday party in my life. Some years Mama rushed around at the last minute and brought home a cake. Some years she forgot. Some years a birthday present came along a week or two later, when she ran across something at the grocery store or the dollar store.

I studied my mother's face in the pictures – no hard lines, no cold look in her eye, no dried-up cigarette skin. I could see myself in her – same wide hazel eyes, except hers were darker than mine, same chin, same nose. But those black women were in me, too. Their high cheeks, their long, narrow fingers, and their tall, thin bodies were like mine. Now I knew where the flat chest and the stick legs came from, too. I didn't get my mama's; that was for sure. My mama was short and curvy, even back then.

I sat for a long time looking from one picture to the next, trying to hear the sounds that would go with it, trying to pull the voices from my mind. In one of the pictures, I was sitting on the lap of a woman who looked a hundred years old. I stared into her eyes and tried to decide, *Do I remember her?*

CHAPTER 5

J. Norman Alvord

The girl and I have reached an understanding, of sorts. She stays on the main floor and I stay abovestairs, where I can continue to devote myself to my current project. She does not bother me, and I do not bother her. We do not speak, unless she tells me to eat, or asks where something is located. I have instructed her in the use of the intercom, so that she can warn me if Deborah should make a surprise appearance. When the girl is here, I can search the boxes from my father's estate and lay out my work in my office without fear of being disturbed or discovered. The going is slow, as the collection of items packed by my mother upon my father's death has been haphazardly stored in the crawl space behind my office closet for years. I unearthed some family items, but nothing pertaining to the house with the grand stairway and the seven chairs. I continue on my mission, but to date have learned more from dreams than from research. I have decided that I must widen my search to the remainder of the upstairs closets, and eventually the third-floor attic. Today I will embark upon a plan to make that more feasible. I remain hopeful and committed to the mission.

—JNA
Project Log, April 4

I closed my logbook to the sound of Deborah talking on her cell phone as she crossed the porch. The book was a relic I'd discovered while searching the office closet – a leather-bound project notebook with a fading Hughes Aircraft insignia on the front. No doubt I'd saved it at some point, after a project was complete, a mission accomplished or perhaps aborted after an information leak let valuable secrets go to the Russians, rendering the project no longer viable. There were a few of those. There was a time when our notes were kept closely guarded.

I tucked the book beneath the sofa cushions, then sat drumming my fingers impatiently, wondering how long Deborah would stay before she was satisfied that I wouldn't have the gall to die before morning. A plastic bag crinkled as she came in. She'd brought me something from a restaurant.

That would be as good an excuse as any to execute the next phase of my plan.

I waited until she'd passed by the doorway to the front parlor before I spoke. When I did, she started and nearly dropped the food.

'Oh, I didn't see you there,' she gasped, slapping her car keys against her chest and spinning around in the entry. Sliding her purse off her shoulder, she entered the parlor and sat on the other end of Annalee's flowered settee. Deborah looked somewhat more relaxed today, the lines having softened around her eyes, and the prominent vein in her left temple having retreated into the skin. The evenings of not needing to worry about me were doing her some good. The girl had come four times now to cook for me. Two weeks, Tuesday and Thursday. Now it was Friday again. The disagreeable, sour-faced housekeeper would be here on Monday. She was a horrible woman. No spunk. No determination. The stale smell of cigarettes and occasionally alcohol. She maintained a blank, disinterested stare and had a habit of lurking around the house as if she were looking for something – perhaps trying to catch me doing something forbidden, so that she could report it to my daughter. Deborah would pay her extra for the information, no doubt. I knew they talked occasionally at the university, when the woman picked up her checks. No telling what sort of information they exchanged.

Deborah delivered a perplexed look my way. 'What are you doing here in Mom's parlor?' Throughout our years in this house, Annalee had kept the front room strictly for formal occasions. The furniture was stiff and unpleasant, straight backed, velvet, hot and uncomfortable. But I was close to Annalee here, with her collections of birds and teacups.

'I've just been sunning.' I felt the weight of the project log tucked beneath the center cushion, mere inches from Deborah's hand. 'You look well today,' I offered.

She cocked her head to one side, mistrusting the pleasantry. 'I feel well, I guess. Everything okay here?'

'Yes,' I said. 'Fine.' And I reminded myself not to look

71

toward the stairs. I'd left a box tucked under the desk in the office, which was a risk, but if I didn't tire too quickly this evening, I wanted to look through it. I was like Hogan entertaining Colonel Klink while not having quite covered the secret hatch. The box was heavy, and moving it back to the crawl space would be difficult. Old age was filled with such frustrating limitations – often the penance for the folly of youth. I wished I could go back and tell the young men who kept ashtrays at their desks and filled the block-houses and control rooms with a haze of smoke that they'd one day pay the piper. You do not fully appreciate oxygen until you haven't enough.

I hoped Deborah wouldn't notice that I was still flushed. I'd stayed upstairs too long before finally checking the time and realizing that she could be coming any minute, as it was Friday, and there was no housekeeper and no girl today. Fortunately, Deborah was a bit later than usual, and I'd had time to catch my breath while making notations in my project log.

Still, I undoubtedly didn't look good.

Eyeing me with suspicion, Deborah slipped her fingers through the handles of the restaurant sack. 'I brought a roasted chicken dinner for you.'

'I'm tired of restaurant food,' I replied, and she rolled her head as if she were trying to work out a cramp. This was all part of my plan. I'd thought it out ahead.

'Well, Dad, I could buy something and cook, but you're not happy with anything I make.' If she'd seemed disappointed at that juncture, I might have felt an inconvenient temptation to offer reassurance, but she merely appeared irritated, which was much easier to combat. It fit nicely, as a matter of fact.

'I like the way the girl cooks. You can arrange for her to come four days a week in the afternoons, rather than two, and on Mondays her mother will leave a sandwich. That way, you can spend your weekday evenings at home with Lloyd, rather than dropping by here to look after me. I can get by at lunch on my own, as well. I shouldn't be pulling you away from your work or your husband. The girl can make a little extra for leftovers, and I'll have it the next day. I do know how to operate the microwave.'

Deborah was speechless. Perhaps my sudden reversal was a bit too abrupt to play believably. I'd been complaining about both the girl and the housekeeper for two full weeks, but now it had come to me that I was better off having someone here who didn't poke into my business. The only hurdle was convincing Deborah.

'I'm not leaving you alone all day, every day.' If only Deborah were more like her mother and less like me. Annalee was never a suspicious type.

'I've been behaving myself. It's been two weeks, and I haven't so much as skipped a pill,' I pointed out blandly, trying to affect the sound of an old man resigned to his fate. 'You can call from your office to check on me – speak with the jailer, even.'

Deborah smacked her lips irritably. 'You're not bullying Epiphany, are you? She's only a teenager.'

'I've been a model citizen.' I waved a hand toward the

73

door, as if the girl would be coming in any moment. In reality, this being an off night, Deborah would linger around my house for hours, punching away on her laptop and her cell phone, keeping me from my work. When the girl was here, I had no such problem. She saw to the cooking, or watched TV, or occupied herself with school projects. Her only annoying habit was turning on rock-and-roll music on the old stereo sound system I'd built from surplus Hughes parts in 1965. Occasionally, when I passed by the kitchen and saw her at the breakfast table, tapping to the beat and working her way through algebra problems with impressive speed, my mind went back in time, and I thought it was Deborah there doing her homework, her spindly legs folded into the chair in impossibly uncomfortable positions. *Where's Roy this evening? The* question would cross my mind, and then I'd find myself hearing the answers from days gone by, like an echo clinging in the house. *Must be off down the street with his skateboard or a football, starting up a game. His homework isn't done.* Roy was so much like his mother. Joy was a chosen pursuit in their lives, toil an afterthought. Deborah, on the other hand, would slave away, chained to the kitchen table until her work was finished. By then, the neighborhood mothers would have called the children in for supper, and the time for play would be over. Her social skills suffered for it, but her grades were top-notch.

My mind always came back to the present if the girl looked up at me. There was a spark in her eyes that Deborah had never possessed, and, of course, she was mixed-race of some sort – black and Spanish or Italian, my guess. She looked much like the Creoles I knew while designing levee pump systems in Louisiana. There was a time when people frowned on mixing the races, but it was a different world now. My mother, who was British by descent, abhorred prejudice of all kinds. She was wont to remind me that in her home country, a ginger-head like me would have been teased – the red hair being considered a sign of Irish bloodline. *But you're not Irish, are you? You're my sweet little Normie boy*, she'd say, and ruffle my hair. *So, you see, Norman, it's best not to judge a book by its cover.*

It occurred to me now, as I was talking to Deborah and thinking about the girl, that I couldn't recall ever having met anyone in my family who had red hair.

There must have been someone . . .

'Dad, are you listening to me?' Deborah demanded, and I realized I wasn't.

'Yes, of course. I think four days a week for the girl and one for the housekeeper will be perfect.'

Deborah's nose crinkled in a way that told me I'd gone off topic. She watched me, absently twisting her wedding ring, studying me as if I were an equation, a proof she was struggling to solve. 'All right,' she said finally. 'We'll try it your way. I still think the Villas would be a better solution. They have people on call around the clock, game days, activities, an exercise room, a shuttle that takes residents on day trips. They even offer golf memberships for the apartment residents.' Clearly she'd been going on about the retirement home again, while I was tuned out. No wonder my mind had drifted off.

'I hate golf. I have always hated golf.'

'You hate everything,' she muttered, then lifted the food sack off the coffee table with a quick jerk and stood up. 'Let's go eat.'

'You'll arrange it with the girl?' I pushed myself to my feet as unobtrusively as possible. My legs hurt from all the lifting and moving, and trips up and down the stairs.

Deborah's shoulders heaved with a sigh. 'I'll try. But I'll still be coming by here at lunch.'

I gave up the battle then, and we ate in relative peace. Deborah left quickly afterward, off to some project, I supposed. Over the weekend, she harassed me about the pacemaker issue, which put us at odds. In the end she was quite happy to increase the schedule of afternoon help, so that the two of us would not have to deal with each other as frequently.

On Monday, the housekeeper left a sandwich for me, and on Tuesday, the girl was to come. Deborah had dropped in at lunchtime to check on me and leave food for the girl to cook. Just as I was bidding Deborah good-bye and preparing to embark on my search of the upstairs closets, the tenant in our garage apartment stopped by to discuss repairing a water leak. The pitter-patter of company left me worn, and, after making some notations in my project log, I postponed my plans to dig around upstairs. I was catching a nap on the parlor settee when the girl banged on my door.

I let her in, and she bounced past me and dropped her backpack on the tile, then set some sort of folded display board beside it. More schoolwork, no doubt. Good, since it would keep her busy. 'Hey, J. Norm,' she chirped, like a little bird fluttering through the entry. Somehow, she'd taken to shortening my name. She was an impudent little thing, because she knew she could be. She was aware of my secrets, after all. This overly familiar behavior was blackmail of a sort, but a small price to pay for having Deborah out of the way so that I could work unhindered at least four days per week. Making progress in the upstairs closets and the third-floor attic would require solid blocks of time. The attic, in particular, had always been a black hole, crowded with our castoffs as well as items that had belonged to my parents when they lived in the house. What I was seeking could be hidden in any of the boxes. Or in none.

'Norman,' I corrected. '*Mr Alvord*, to someone as young as you.' We went through this process each time she came. It did not improve things, and I knew it would not. This was merely a dance we did upon meeting – a tango filled with anger and an occasional glimpse of mutual understanding. She'd be insufferable, now that she'd been asked to come four days each week. She would assume I was pleased with her job performance, or worse yet, that I found her presence tolerable in some way.

'Yeah, I know. So what's on the menu tonight?' She asked this question each day upon arrival, as well.

'Deborah left an envelope.'

'How come I'm not surprised?' She shook her head. The envelopes filled with Deborah's detailed instructions as to food and medications had become almost a private joke between the girl and myself. 'She say whether you're supposed to eat with a fork or a spoon today?'

I felt myself struggling to fight off a display of mirth. It was a good quip. 'I think I'm allowed to have my choice tonight.'

'Woo-hoo. Is it your birthday?' She grinned impishly. The girl had a lovely smile, actually – beautiful, straight white teeth, and wide, full lips. It occurred to me that she didn't smile very often. For someone so young, she seemed, in large part, bleak, tired, and resigned. A bit like myself. Such emotions were out of place in a fresh face like hers. I wondered at the cause of this, but considering that harpy of a mother of hers, the girl was doing quite well.

I wasn't developing a fondness for her, of course, and I didn't want her to think I was. 'I have work to do,' I said, and started for the stairs.

'Go for it.' She directed herself toward the kitchen.

'You'll answer the phone if Deborah calls,' I told her. There was a phone in my office, but it was an old hardwired model and had a little hum to it. I feared that if I were to answer, Deborah would discern the slight difference in the sound quality and know where I was. 'And you'll stay belowstairs and buzz me over the intercom if anyone pulls into the driveway.'

'Yup.' The girl headed off to the kitchen. I was pleased that she knew our arrangement was not to change just because she was working four days rather than two.

But as the week progressed, she grew slightly more familiar each day. It was troublesome. By Friday, she was kicking her shoes off in my entry hall. 'Whoa, those were killing me,' she remarked of the sandals.

I frowned at them. 'We do have a shoe closet.' I pointed toward the door next to her. 'Conveniently within reach.'

Shrugging, she opened the door and kicked her shoes in, then slipped her backpack off her shoulder and pulled something from it. She held it up as if she felt I would have an interest. 'Hey, J. Norm, look what I got today.' She lifted it near my face.

I squinted at the box. Unsalted butter, by the look of it. A full pound. Unopened. My mouth watered. I couldn't recall my last taste of real butter – sometime before Annalee put me on a low-fat and low-cholesterol diet two years ago, following my close call with a heart attack and subsequent surgery.

'Butter?' I surmised.

The girl's face lifted into a grin. 'Yeah, I jacked it from the consumer science room at school. Mrs Lora always said nothin' cooked without real cow butter tastes right, and Mrs Lora could cook.'

'*Stolen* butter,' I corrected.

She snorted and rolled her eyes, I suppose to indicate that I was ruining her surprise.

'Yum,' I said blandly, and she smirked at me, then started for the kitchen.

'Don't fall down the dumb stairs and get me in trouble.'

'I will endeavor not to.'

She stopped then, and flashed a glance over her shoulder, her lips pursed. 'What're you doin' up there, anyhow?' Her gaze drifted toward the stairs, curiosity brewing in her odd gray-green eyes. This was the first time she'd shown an interest in my comings and goings, other than to warn me not to cause her to be fired, because she had a use for the money.

'Work,' I answered, and I noted that she had on even more makeup than usual. 'So much makeup is unbecoming on a young lady. My wife never allowed Deborah to wear more than a bit of lipstick when she was in school.'

Momentarily, I thought I'd succeeded in offending the girl, or perhaps in making a point, but she only bobbed her head side to side with a slight shrug of her shoulders. 'Well, you ain't my mama, and besides, you ain't so shiny, neither.'

'Aren't . . . either,' I corrected, and she gave a slow, deliberate blink.

'If the fashion police come by here, they're gonna haul you off first.' She motioned to my attire, and I was reminded that I still had on this morning's pajama pants and slippers. Halfway through dressing, I'd had a thought about the young woman who had lived above the garage and served as a mother's helper in the house when I was quite young. She was a cousin of some sort, as I recalled. She had an older sister who had lived with us briefly, too. I'd adored Frances, and now I remembered that she'd left my mother's employ abruptly. I couldn't recall why. Frances . . . Frances . . . something. It occurred to me that if I could unearth my mother's photo albums, Frances's full name might be written there. No telling whether she would still be alive today – Frances must have been eight or ten years older than myself. I'd had no luck finding Mother's photo albums in the closets. I had finally concluded that they must have been packed and moved to the attic when my mother passed. The albums would not be easy to find. There was no rhyme or reason to the tangle of items stored in the attic – ours, my parents', perhaps even things that had been in the house when my parents had purchased it.

Deborah had come and gone this noon and not even noticed my combination of a worsted button-down shirt and blue pajama bottoms. Perhaps she thought I'd done it to goad her, and so she'd ignored it intentionally.

'I fear they'll arrest both of us. The fashion police,' I remarked, and started up the stairs. I had the urge to turn and look at the girl again. When I did, she was shaking her head and smiling. It seemed a long time since I'd made someone smile.

'Mind the fort,' I told her. 'Keep the front door locked and chained. If Deborah drops by, delay removing the chain until I can make it down the stairs.'

The girl's gaze met mine again, and she winked. 'I got your back, J. Norm.'

I did not correct her, as she seemed determined to persist in the ridiculous nickname. I supposed I was becoming accustomed to it.

After the long climb up the stairs, then through the door at the end of the second-story hall and up the attic stairs, I proceeded with my search for Mother's photo albums. There was an old steamer trunk in which she kept family mementos when I was a child. With any luck, I could spot it among the offal of stored items. The idea that I could perhaps find information about Frances, and that she might still be alive, had fired my imagination. A direct link to the past could answer so many questions. Frances was present in my most remote memories, the ones close to the time of the seven chairs, perhaps slightly after.

The upper deck was unusually warm when I reached it, April sunlight flooding through dormer windows high in the eaves, illuminating stacks of boxes, crates, a rocking horse, a dress dummy, a wooden room divider purchased in Saudi, a clay water pot from Kathmandu, a drugstore Santa Claus that Annalee had dragged home after the season, half price. He stood in the corner now, his red paint gone from the white plastic, giving him the look of a snowman about to be whisked into oblivion by a ray of sunshine.

He just needs a little touch-up, Annalee said cheerfully in my mind. She never tossed out anything. To her, the items here were precious receptacles in which the days of our lives remained stored, frozen in time. It was because of Annalee that the boxes from my parents hadn't been sent to the trash during our many years here. *Someday you'll want these things, Norman*, she'd said.

I'd insisted that I wasn't a sentimental person.

As it turned out, both of us were correct.

It seemed strange that, if my mother's photo albums were here, Annalee had never rescued them from the attic. In later years, she'd developed an interest in genealogy and scrapbooking. She'd spent many an hour poring through old files and photos. My mother was also a preservationist, given to keeping scrapbooks, never one to leave family heirlooms and photos without a notation on the back. Yet I'd never seen Annalee with any of my mother's private things. That seemed odd, now that I considered it.

A sweat broke over me as I worked, and the air in the attic turned stifling. I relocated closer to the stairway, sifting through things piled atop what remained of an old bedroom suite with trundle beds. I remembered moving them up the attic stairs. Roy and I had done it together. At seventeen, he was six-foot-three, having inherited the tall, slim stature of Annalee's father. He'd outgrown the boyish furniture and the child-size bed. Annalee's parents were moving into a nursing home, and she wanted to redo Roy's room with their furniture. The room was never finished. Roy never slept in it. Everything that belonged to him lay carefully boxed, where it had been since the spring of his senior year. Rather than a high school graduation party that April, we arranged a funeral.

I stood in the corner for a moment, looked at the bed, and thought of Roy. There was a stack of boxes under the eaves – model rockets and cars. Annalee had placed them beneath the Christmas tree year after year. She'd thought that Roy and I would build them together, but the models remained in their containers by mutual agreement. Roy wasn't one to stay in the house and I wasn't one to be home. Occasionally, when I was around, I found Deborah working with the models. She was more inclined toward quiet, solitary pastimes. She had a scientific mind, even when she was young.

It occurred to me now to wonder whether my mother's trunk could be in this part of the attic, behind Roy's furniture. That would explain Annalee's never having encountered it while doing her family research in later years. I sidled along the edge of the stairway opening and began laboriously moving bed railings, a headboard, a foot-board. The blue paint was faded and crackled now. It seemed foolish that we'd saved the furniture. I suppose Annalee had been thinking that the little trundle suite might one day be a perfect heirloom, that Roy might pass it along to a son, or paint it pink for a daughter.

Those ideas were too difficult to consider, even now. Too painful. The heart is never prepared for a child who remains frozen in time, for hopes unrealized.

I caught a glimpse of tarnished brass behind the three-drawer chest that held Roy's little-boy clothes. We'd rescued that dresser from a trash heap when we were living on Switch Grass Island. Annalee had painted it to use in our bedroom at the time. I was a young man, working for Hughes Aircraft at Cape Canaveral, in the race of a lifetime. A race beyond all that was known, to the surface of the moon. The hours were long, but the work was important, competing with the Russians an imperative. Annalee was busy with the house and with Deborah. My work was stimulating and challenging. We made the most of my rare days off by enjoying time on the lake in our little boat. Life, it had seemed, couldn't be any more golden.

I stretched across Roy's dresser now, and there was the black steamer trunk, the one my mother kept in her sewing room with a lace quilt draped over it. I was more likely to find something of value in there than in all the boxes I'd sorted through to date.

I went to work moving the rest of the furniture, stopping on occasion to mop my forehead and catch my breath. Good fortune that I hadn't started this project in the summer, or the attic heat would have been unbearable. All the same, I took heart in my ability to clear the furniture out of the way. Only a couple weeks ago, such work would have been beyond my capacity, but all this climbing up and down the stairs and moving the boxes had increased my stamina.

The trunk was wedged a bit, having been shoved under the rafters when we hastily piled Roy's furniture and boxes near the stairway. I bent over, grunting as I threw my weight against the handle. It budged finally, then began grinding across the layer of dust on the floor, the brass corners digging into the wood and producing a loud screech. I paused in a clumsy squat, like a cat burglar listening for awakening home owners. The girl wouldn't come up here, surely. She probably hadn't even noticed the noise.

I attempted to lift the lid of the trunk so as to check the contents, but the lid was either locked or rusted shut. I would need tools, and in reality, I would probably be better off moving the trunk downstairs, so that I could take my time with it, down where the air was cooler. I scooted it a bit farther, pausing at the stairway to consider the potential weight of the trunk, added to the component of gravity and the slope of the stairs. At times, knowledge of physics can be useful. I mentally calculated that the load should be manageable, provided that I stayed in front of it and eased it down a step at a time. The later problem, then, would be what to do with the trunk when I was finished with it. Even empty, it was probably more than I was capable of moving up the stairs.

But first things first. I slipped in front of the trunk, then braced myself with my back against it to slow the descent. Drawing one last fortifying breath, I reached behind myself, tipped the beast off balance, and started the downward trek one step at a time, each very carefully. One, *bump*. Two, *bump*. Three, *bump*.

The process was going well at stair six, moving according to plan, and then suddenly the contents shifted and the trunk began to list onto its side.

I heard a sharp gasp, which I assumed was my own, and next I knew, I was bumping down the steps like a youngster sliding on his backside, the trunk, now askew, pushing me along, moving faster and faster. It toppled off near the bottom, rolled to the side, and burst open, and the contents and I landed in a pile in the hallway.

In the addled moment that followed, I heard the girl rushing up from the first floor, calling my name: 'J. Norm? J. Norm?'

I had, quite literally, exposed the mission, or more properly, the mission had exposed itself.

CHAPTER 6

Epiphany Jones

When I skidded around the corner into the upstairs hall, there was J. Norm, crumpled in the opening to another set of stairs with books and papers all around him. He wasn't dead, at least, which was good. He was trying to get up, but he'd gotten all twisted around with his feet up over his head. Some kind of big black box was wedged between his legs and the wall.

'What'n the world are you doin'?' I hurried down the hall and stepped across a few papers to get a look at the stairway behind him. A lightbulb swung back and forth up top, and I could see an attic with paint cans and boxes. Everything smelled dusty and old, like the closet where the water heater was in Mama and Russ's house. 'Where've you been?'

J. Norm tried to pull his legs around so he could get up, but he was seriously stuck. His face was red and he started raking up papers and old magazines that'd spilled, and shoving them back in the black box, which was a big, old-timey trunk. 'I told you not to come up here,' he hollered at me, panting.

'You don't want me up here, you shouldn't make noise like that. I thought the house was caving in.' I took another step and my foot slid on a magazine until I was halfway to the splits. 'You been climbin' up those stairs?' Man, if his daughter found this out, she'd shoot us both. If she didn't want him on the big, pretty stairs with the carpet and the nice handrail, she sure didn't want him going up these rough ones with nothing to hold on to.

'Those stairs are none of your business.' He tried to get a handhold to turn himself around, but he couldn't do it. His arm quivered and caved in, and he slid on the magazines again, then just stayed there, breathing hard. I felt sorry for him, until he opened his mouth again. 'They're *my* stairs. I can climb them if I wish.'

He brought out the Epie in me, and she brought the attitude. 'Well, that ain't what your daughter says.'

'I'll thank you not to use such grammar in my house. Poor grammar is a hallmark of poor education. I suspect you're a more intelligent girl than you portray. I've seen you doing your homework.'

I wasn't sure whether I should get insulted or feel like he'd paid me a compliment.

'Well, listen at you, Mr High and Mighty,' I said. 'I'm not the one on the floor, now, am I?'

He snorted, grabbing his own leg and trying to pull it around. 'As you've already invaded my privacy here, you could help me to my feet.'

'I don't know if I want to.' Shoot, it might be good for him to stay there on the floor awhile. 'I help you up, you'll go climb the stairs again. Maybe I ought to just go ahead and call your daughter. She can figure out how to keep you off the stairs.' I looked the mess over, and I could pretty much figure out what'd happened. 'Were you trying to move that big old trunk down here?'

'It slipped,' he said, like it was an excuse. 'Otherwise, I was getting along just fine.'

'Yup. You look fine.' I cleared out some papers and stuff so I could get in behind him and hook my elbows under his armpits, the way I'd learned to do with Mrs Lora after she got so sick. The worst part about helping somebody out of a spot like that wasn't the lifting; it was that it was embarrassing. While I was dragging J. Norm off the stairs, I thought the same thing I used to when I helped Mrs Lora off the bathroom floor: *Man, if I ever get like this, I'm gonna find a gun and shoot myself.* I wondered sometimes if God would hold it against a person if they got in such bad shape that they couldn't take it anymore, and so they did something. I knew the answer, of course. One thing me and Mrs Lora did together was go to church. Every time the doors were open. Mrs Lora was a Southern Baptist, and so the doors were open a lot. Even after she got weak and wobbly, and her skin turned yellow and thin, I'd help her to the car on church nights, and we'd putter the six blocks across town. I drove, even though I barely had my learner's permit. It wasn't far, and we never went over thirty.

I dragged J. Norm off the last couple steps. He groaned, because I was yanking his arms off, but I didn't have any choice. By the time we got out of the opening, both of us

89

were huffing and puffing. J. Norm rolled over and sat up against the wall with his legs folded to one side and his head leaned back, and I slid down against the doorway.

'You all right?' If we had to call an ambulance, we'd be in so much trouble. What would I do tomorrow if I didn't come here? If I got caught anyplace but at school, Mama's house, or work, I could kiss my happy home good-bye. At least being here was better than being at home.

'You think I better call the doctor?' I asked.

'Most certainly . . . not.' J. Norm cracked one eye open – just a little slice of blue with bloodred around it, but it looked like he meant business.

'You at least gonna take the pills your daughter said you should eat if you got a heart spell?' His shirt pocket was hanging open a little, something round inside. I figured it was the pill bottle. He patted a hand over it, like he was making sure.

'Just need to . . . catch my breath.' He wheezed and coughed, the sound weak, thin, and hacky.

I didn't know if I should believe him or not. A couple times, Mama'd laughed and called this job *the suicide watch*. She figured someone as nasty as J. Norman Alvord didn't deserve all the fuss. 'But you'll take the medicine if you need it, right?'

His eye closed, and he pulled his lips together over his teeth, then swallowed hard, his chin jerking up and down like it hurt to do. 'I . . . believe so.'

'You promise?'

The one eye opened again. 'Beware. You . . . could be

mistaken ... for someone ... who actually cares.' He spit the words out in little breaths.

Heat went into my cheeks and drained down to my shoulders. Was he teasing with me? Maybe his plan was to keep me talking until it was too late for me to force a couple of the pills into his mouth. Maybe that's why his teeth were clamped so tight. 'I just don't want you to go and have a big, stupid heart attack while I'm here, all right? At least not till after I get paid for this week. I got plans for that money.' Every week, my money was in an envelope on the counter with Deborah's supper note. Cash, the cold, hard kind. I'd been socking it away, not giving it to the church to pay for damages like Mama thought. DeRon had told me that some anonymous athletic booster was gonna pay off all the broken stuff, so the basketball boys wouldn't end up in trouble. If Mama knew that, my money would be gone to pay the light bill, or buy beer, but she didn't know, so it was all good.

J. Norm kind of laughed, or maybe he was just coughing. Finally, he settled down again and some color came back into his skin. 'I'll endeavor ... not to expire ... before next payday.' He opened both eyes and watched me like he was trying to figure me out. It made me feel weird. Mostly, people don't look at you real close when you're sixteen. They don't try to see inside. They just take a pass at what clothes you've got on and your makeup and whatever, and put you in some box or other. Good kid, bad kid, sexy kid, regular kid, poor kid, rich kid, got potential, got none. That's okay, sorta. It keeps you from having to work too hard to show them anything.

'Well, because where else am I gonna get me a job around here?' I pointed out.

'Get *myself* a job.'

'Yeah, exactly.'

He smiled a little. It looked like his pasty old face might crack, but he did it. 'I suspect that you could do anything you set your mind to.'

I stared at him for a sec, trying to figure out what he meant by that, because at first it sounded like J. Norm had actually said something nice. 'You sure you're all right? I'm not gonna need to, like, do CPR on you or anything, am I? They taught us that in health class at my old school.'

'A frightening thought. Health class ... CPR.' J. Norm closed his eyes and shook his head, static fuzzing his little hairs against the paneling. 'I don't think any lifesaving measures ... will be necessary.' He sat there a minute longer, then turned toward the wall and started to fold his feet under him, his hands pushing for support.

I got up and stood behind him with my arms out like I might catch him. I guessed I would've if he'd needed it, but he didn't. He wobbled a little on his feet, looking at the mess that'd come out of the trunk. 'Magazines,' he grumbled. '*Life* magazines.'

'These are seriously old-school.' I leaned down and grabbed one. It had a sailor kissing a girl on the front. 'Where'd you get all these?'

Taking a hankie out of his pocket, J. Norm wiped his forehead. 'They were my mother's, I'm sure. She was a woman given to reading and to saving things.'

'Looks like it.'

He reached for one of the magazines, but stumbled instead.

I caught his arm. 'Tell you what, J. Norm. How about you go sit down in that room you lock yourself in all the time, and I'll pick up the stuff here? You want me to take it back up the steps, or what?' I looked at the stairs, trying to figure if I could get the box up there or not. But if we left it like this, Deborah would see it when she came, and there'd be trouble. One way or another, I had to get J. Norm's mess cleaned up.

He shook his head, looking at the trunk. 'Nothing but magazines. Trash.'

The magazines were cool, actually. I picked up a couple more. 'What was supposed to be in there?'

He sighed, his shoulders sinking. 'A dream,' he whispered as he walked away. 'A midsummer night's dream.'

I cleaned up the mess and hauled it all back upstairs. The attic was, like, three times the size of our house. From the center part around the stairway, the peaks of the roof ran out in four long tunnels, each one with a window, so there was plenty of light. The place was dusty and smelled old, and cobwebs hung in the eaves like Halloween decorations, but it was quiet and kind of interesting up there. When I finished putting everything back, I stood on the top stair a minute, looking at old doll furniture and a three-story doll-house I would've killed for when I was little. There were boxes of toys that'd never been opened – rockets you could put together and shoot off, and model cars, and a coffee can filled with brushes and paints that were all dried up. The space near the stairway was like a toy store, frozen in time. It was hard to imagine having all that stuff – so much you crammed it in the attic and left it there.

I picked out a few of the magazines to ask J. Norm if I could keep them and look at them. We had a paper to do in my stupid English class, for one thing. Maybe I could get stuff out of the articles. If Mrs Brown didn't like stuff about weeds, maybe she'd like stuff about the John F. Kennedy assassination.

Finally, I went back and found J. Norm in his office at the top of the stairs. He was sitting in the chair with his elbow braced on the desk and his head resting on his hand, his face turned the other way.

'I cleaned everything up,' I said, standing in the doorway. 'Can I borrow a couple of these to read? I like history all right.'

'Take any you like. Keep them. I don't want them.'

'The trunk and the magazines and all. It's back up in the attic.'

'You should have called me to help.' He turned slowly toward me. 'That trunk is too heavy for you.' But he didn't look ready to get out of that chair. He looked worn-out.

'Oh, no,' I told him. 'First of all, no *way* you're falling down the stairs again. If you want something from up there, you've gotta tell me, okay? I'll go up and get it. And second of all, I hauled the trunk up and *then* put the magazines in it. I'm not stupid.'

'No, you're not.' It was weird having J. Norm actually

be nice to me. It worried me a little. Sitting there at the desk, he looked shrunk up and sad, just staring at the wall again.

'What were you really looking for in that trunk?' I took a step into the room, then another. The wall in front of his desk was crowded with certificates in frames, pictures, and plaques with his name on them. J. Norm went to school at Clemson University once upon a time. His folks must've had money, just like he did. The only place I'd ever seen that much official stuff was in the doctor's office.

'Clues.' The word came out in a long, slow sigh.

'What kind of clues?' I held the little stack of magazines against my chest and moved a little farther in. Beside the college degrees, there was a black-and-white picture of a young guy in a graduation robe standing with his mama and daddy. The face looked a little like J. Norm's, but sometimes it's hard to see who somebody was in who they are now. 'This you and your folks?'

'Yes.' The word was flat, like he wasn't really interested in talking about it. 'Graduation from Clemson. I went for a master's degree after that.'

'Man.' There was a big brick building in the back of the picture, an important-looking place like a queen would live in. 'You must've been some kind of smart.'

'Failure wasn't an option in my family. Success was expected.'

'You still had to be smart, though.' Next to the diplomas there was a picture of J. Norm and some other guys in front of a rocket like they used to shoot off to the moon. They all had on white shirts and thin neckties and dark pants, and a whole chain of name badges hanging off their shirts.

'I worked hard.' His voice perked up a little. 'It was an exciting time. An important time.'

I looked into the eyes of those young guys in the picture and wondered what they were thinking, standing there by that giant rocket. Maybe they wanted to hop in and ride it to Mars. 'You shoot rockets into outer space, or is that, like, a missile or something?' Maybe J. Norm invented the A-bomb or the computer. He was probably old enough.

In the corner of my eye, I saw him lean around to see what picture I was looking at. 'That's an Atlas/Centaur rocket.'

'You bomb somebody with it?'

'Just launchpad thirty-six-A. That particular rocket caused the worst explosion in the history of Cape Canaveral.' He rolled the chair up closer, so that he was just behind me and off to one side.

'Whoa, really?'

He rocked back in his chair, and when I glanced over at him, his eyes seemed far away. Lacing fingertips together, he cupped them behind his head. 'A tiny, ten-dollar part failed. It's a bit of a long story.' His hands turned loose, then went down to his lap and hung there.

'You got someplace important to be?' I leaned up against the wall to listen. One of the plaques tipped off square a little, and he watched it like he was afraid it was gonna fall. ' 'Cause I don't. I'm here till six.' I caught the plaque with two fingers and pushed it back onto the nail, reading the words underneath the picture:

Let it be recorded that:

When future generations look back on man's conquest of space, the soft landing of an instrumented spacecraft on the lunar surface will mark a most significant milestone ... advancing man's technological capabilities and providing the world its first close-up look at a celestial body, and that

J. Norman Alvord

as a member of the Surveyor team shared in this exciting venture and contributed to the successful achievement of the program goals ... paving the way for man's journey to the planets.

'Whoa,' I said. 'That's you.' But J. Norm didn't answer. When I turned around, he had his grouchy look back.

'We'd better go downstairs now. Deborah may come by,' he said, and scooted to the edge of the chair, pushing himself to his feet, his arms wobbling like licorice ropes. 'Straighten that frame properly, will you?'

I fixed the plaque and checked my watch. I didn't really want to go downstairs. It was more interesting up here. I hadn't looked over this territory yet. 'She's not usually here till it's time for me to go.' Lots of nights she didn't stop by at all when I was there. For a sec, I thought about asking what in the world was the problem with him and his daughter. It seemed like if you lived in a house like this and had all the stuff they had, you could get along. Mostly, Mama and me fought because I cost her money.

I walked out of the office with J. Norm, then followed him

to the stairs, carrying my magazines. He caught a toe and stumbled a little, so I slipped around and got in front. 'Here, hold on to my shoulder. You already did the backstroke down the stairs once today, remember?'

He put a hand on my shirt and leaned harder than I thought he would, and we moved on. 'More of a swan dive, actually,' he said.

I laughed a little. 'Well, Mr J. Norm, I think you just made a joke.' Who would've thought it, but J. Norm had a sense of humor – kind of like an appendix, I guess, since he didn't use it for much. 'That was pretty good.'

We got to the halfway point where the stairs turned, and he stopped to rub his leg. 'I won't make a habit of it.'

'I didn't figure you would.' After that, there didn't seem to be much to say. I took him to the room off the kitchen, where he could watch TV. He held the chair arms and lowered himself in like a crippled man.

'I could bring your dinner in here if you want,' I said, feeling sorry for him.

He shook his head and grabbed the TV remote. 'I'll get to it later. I do know how to use the microwave.' He slumped back in his chair, like he didn't want to talk to me, and he turned on a show, then picked up one of those big, thick newspapers he kept piled by his chair. The *New York Times*.

'Whatever.' I knew I'd better go in another room before things got ugly, but for some reason, I stopped halfway to the kitchen door. 'Did you really do all the things on the wall up there? Shoot off rockets and stuff?'

He opened the newspaper and disappeared behind it, trying to get rid of me, probably. 'Yes.'

'So did you ever, like, bomb anybody?'

Lowering the paper, he frowned like he was really into the *New York Times* and I was bothering him. 'It was a different sort of battle. A battle to see who could get there first. To the moon. The fate of the free world depended on it – at least, that was how we felt about it at the time.'

'No joke?' I wondered if he was pulling my leg.

He pointed at my magazines. I'd forgotten I was still carrying them. 'There might be a bit about it in some of those. I don't know if those were my mother's or Annalee's. My wife saved everything, too. "It's our history, Norman," she always said.'

I looked down at the magazines and thought maybe I shouldn't take them, after all. Then I guessed it didn't matter. If he wanted that stuff, it wouldn't be packed away in the attic. I wondered how long his wife had been dead, but I knew better than to ask. People didn't like to talk about that kind of thing, and talking with J. Norm felt like walking on ice over a pond. The ice could break any minute, and you'd be up to your nose in cold water. 'That why there's so much junk up there?'

'You collect things over the years.'

'Guess so.' I thought about our little house. There wasn't anyplace to collect stuff. Everything my mama'd kept – our history – was in a couple boxes stuffed in the corner of a closet. There wasn't much worth saving, I guessed.

I still wanted to know why J. Norm was up in that attic.

'So tomorrow I can help you look in the attic some more.' Maybe it was because I'd been digging in my own family secrets, or maybe it was because J. Norm had some cool stuff up there, but I didn't want him to find things without me.

'Tomorrow is Saturday.' He chewed the side of his lip, looking toward the stairs. He was thinking about taking himself up there again; I could tell.

'I can come anyway,' I said, and he gave me a suspicious look, like he thought maybe I was trying to pull something over on him. I toned down the enthusiasm. 'Well, like, the more days I work, the sooner I can get the money I need and get out of here. It's not exactly party central. I've got a social life, you know.'

He rubbed his chin, turning the idea over in his mind. Finally he leaned back, deflating like a birthday balloon, and the newspaper came up again. 'Deborah will be here.'

'Tell her you don't need her to come,' I said. 'Tell her I'm gonna be here, so she can do whatever she likes to do on Saturday.'

The paper lowered. He squinted over it. 'She'll wonder what's going on.'

I looked down at my magazines, and an idea hit me. 'Tell her I've got to write a research report this weekend about . . . rockets, and you're helping me. We do have some stupid semester project. We're supposed to write about some . . . history . . . something. I forget what the English teacher said. It's not due Monday, but nobody has to know that except you and me, right? Deborah will think I asked you to help me out.'

J. Norm chewed his lip some more, and then he started to nod real slow. 'You're a clever girl.'

I liked the way he said that – like he was impressed. Mrs Lora used to tell me I was smart, but in this new school, it didn't seem like anyone even knew I was there. When you're toffee brown, and you don't have all the fine clothes, and you live in a run-down house off the Hill, people don't think you're smart. 'I just know that the minute I'm not here, you're gonna go back up those stairs,' I said.

Norman just smiled at me and lifted the *New York Times* so he could hide behind it. He knew I'd figured him out.

CHAPTER 7

J. Norman Alvord

I see the grand stairway again. This time I am walking up it. The stairs are smooth, polished wood, and my shoes are slick. The stiff leather soles click and slide upon each landing. The stairs are tall, and I'm taking them one at a time, looking down at my feet in the brown leather shoes, a boy's dress shoes with mud on them. There's a spate of fear, quick like a charley horse twisting my ribs. The mud shouldn't be on the shoes. I am afraid I may be punished for it. I'm afraid of being hurt – spanked, perhaps? I stop and look down the stairs and consider not going up at all. But there's someone at the top I want to see. I have flowers in my hand, the sort a child might pluck from a garden without asking. I look at them, then gaze upward to the hallway. The doors are open, morning light tumbling from them, but it is the closed door that holds my interest. The one with only a dingy gray glow underneath, evidence that the curtains are still pulled in the room. I move up another step, and then two, on tiptoe. I am trying to make the shoes land silently. I don't want anyone to know I'm here.

Finally, I reach the upper hall, take a few steps toward the door. There's a crash, and I stop short. My fingers tighten around the flowers, crushing and bending the stems, drawing water into my hand. A rose makes a pinprick on my thumb. I wonder if it's bleeding, but I cannot look. I'm frozen in place.

Another crash, and then a man's voice shouts, 'Get up out of that bed! You put on this dress. Do you hear me? You harlot! You cheap, stinking scrap of trash. You get out of that bed and make yourself decent today, or I'll give you what you really deserve. What you ask for every day!' Something strikes the door then, and it vibrates in and out. I catch a breath, move back a step, then two, feeling my way. There's something warm on my leg. It oozes slowly downward, soaking the fabric of my short pants and draining into the tall socks that lead into my shoes. I look down and see the muddy tracks on the floor. Terror races through me. I can only think to run. I drop the flowers, spin around, prepare to take flight. An arm catches me, robbing my breath so that I cannot cry out.

'Ssshhh!' A hand goes over my mouth. The hand smells of lard and flour, and I am suddenly comforted. Her lips brush close to my ear. 'Git on down in the kitchen now, honeylove.' The arm releases me, and I grab the banister to sprint away. From the corner of my eye, I see the gray fabric of a woman's skirts, her white apron folding as she kneels on the floor and reaches for the flowers. I hear the handle turn in the door down the hall . . .

The dream vanished like smoke, and I was aware of Deborah shaking me awake. I caught my breath in a gush of air and sat up so quickly that we nearly butted heads. It wouldn't have been the first time, of course.

'Deborah!' I gasped, and discerned that I was in my recliner. Judging by the light outside, it was early morning. Friday . . . no, Saturday. It was Saturday. I must have fallen asleep in the living room and stayed there through the night, after the girl left.

Last night's plate of food was sitting beside me, dehydrated now. The girl had insisted on putting it there before she went out the door. 'Don't you forget to eat that,' she'd said, and wagged a finger at me in that haughty way of hers. 'I don't wanna find that here tomorrow.'

Now Deborah was frowning at the plate. 'Is that last night's supper?'

'Leftovers,' I answered, thinking quickly. 'A second helping. I thought I might eat it, but then I decided against. How are you this morning?'

Deborah drew herself upward, taken aback by what might have passed for a pleasantry had it not been coming from me and offered in her general direction. 'Fine . . .' She surveyed the room, trying to piece together the reason for my being in my chair so early and wearing yesterday's clothing. The clock in the hall chimed, and I counted. Seven.

'Did you sleep here all night?' Deborah queried.

Shaking my head, I folded the footrest and sat up, making an effort to appear alert and fully within my faculties. 'Of course not. I was up early and couldn't go back to sleep, so I decided to warm some leftovers. I suppose I wasn't as wide-awake as I thought.'

Deborah seemed to debate the explanation, but then she abandoned her investigation and held up a bag of take-out food. 'Well, I brought a breakfast sandwich for you. I'm going into work for a little while this morning. It's so much easier to get things done on Saturday, when the building is quiet.' She sat down and opened the bag, then began placing the contents on the coffee table. Two bottles of orange juice, and a variety of paper-wrapped food.

'I imagine you're backlogged. I don't want to keep you from your projects,' I offered, to encourage her along. I had plans in the attic again today. The girl was coming to help at nine o'clock. 'I always found weekends to be a productive time at work.'

She flashed a glance my way – a wounded look, I thought. 'Yes, you did,' she bit out, and I knew I'd chosen the wrong comment. Most of her life and Roy's, Saturdays had been spent without me. It became the usual way of things – so much so that even Annalee seemed to accept it.

'You need not have stopped by. I've asked the girl to come today. She can watch me eat.' That brought another glance from Deborah and an irritated narrowing of her eyes.

Deborah raised a brow suspiciously. 'She has a name, Dad. Epiphany.'

'Epiphany?' I repeated. 'She refers to herself as Epie, I think.'

'That's a nickname, I guess. Her mother calls her Epiphany. Either way, she does have a name, other than "the girl."' Deborah opened my orange juice and set it on the end table, then unwrapped a breakfast sandwich and laid it in proximity of my hand. 'So you are at least being decent to her?'

'Certainly. Why wouldn't I?'

'Just to be stubborn. Because you don't think you need anyone here.'

I paused to swallow a lump of pride along with the first bite of my biscuit, and worked up some encouraging words. When a mission is under way, sacrifices must be made. 'I don't mind her so much. It was a good idea you had. Aside from that, I can be a help to her in her schooling. I'm of the impression that she isn't afforded much assistance at home. That mother of hers is a crass, disagreeable woman. Smokes, too. Brings that smell into my house. It's her I don't need. I'll be working with the girl on some of her schoolwork today – a research project of a sort.' That much was not entirely untrue, and I prided myself on being quite convincing.

Deborah's expression remained incredulous. 'Well, that sounds lovely. I just find it a little hard to believe. All of a sudden you're helping her with her homework?'

'It's good to be useful . . . to someone.' I took another bite of my biscuit, but it came with a bitter taste.

Deborah leaned against the sofa as if she intended to stay a while. 'Please tell me you're not using her so you can . . . do something again.'

'Do something?' Of course, I knew very well what Deborah meant.

'To yourself. Please tell me you're not just trying to keep me out of the house because you're planning something.'

That had always been the trouble with Deborah. If you

tried to pull the wool over her eyes, she'd quickly break down the DNA of it. 'I've been a model citizen.'

'Stop saying that!' She yanked the straw up and down in her cup, and the plastic emitted a loud whine. 'You're not in prison. I'm trying to take care of you. I'm trying to do what I promised Mom I would.'

I turned my face away. Therein lay the heart of our discontent. Deborah was caring for me only out of a sense of duty to her mother. Annalee was wrong to have put that burden on her, but since Annalee had placed it there, I had no power to remove it. My reassurances that I was perfectly capable of caring for myself would mean nothing to Deborah. Anything I said to her now would be twisted into a knife.

We fell into silence, and I finished my sandwich. That, at least, would make her happy. I drank the orange juice, too. Afterward, I read the label. 'Frozen reconstituted. What a waste of perfectly good oranges.'

'I'm sure it's not the kind you like,' Deborah said wearily.

'The only way to drink it is fresh out of the grove, like we did when we lived on Switch Grass Island. There were stands selling it fresh all along the highway there.' My mind went back, and I smelled the orange groves, the scent of blossoms hanging so sweet and thick that the air itself was a pleasant drink. I heard the earthy call of the lake, took in its warm, moist scents – pine, and Spanish moss, and oleander.

Deborah didn't want to hear about life at the cape, of

course. The ones closest to you grow weary of your glory days. To her, the glory days were the enemy – the very demon that had initiated the wrestling match between work and family.

It crossed my mind that when my work had afforded opportunities to travel in the early days, Annalee had sometimes gone with me before Roy was born. Deborah had stayed with my mother. By that time, my mother and father were spending summers at a beach house near Mother's family in Galveston. Deborah was young, but she might remember something. 'Deborah? Do you recall before Roy was born, those times you stayed with Grandmother and Grandfather Alvord and Aunt Fleeta?' A younger cousin of my father's often visited with them when Deborah was there, and Deborah adored her, as I recalled.

My mention of those long-ago times drew a confused frown from Deborah. 'A little. That was a lot of years ago, Dad. By the time I was in the second grade, Roy came along, and Mom stayed home with us.'

'I know. I just thought you might remember something of those last summers on the coast.'

Deborah's face softened a bit, and I sensed that we'd finally found a mutually agreeable topic of conversation. 'What kinds of things?'

I thought about my dreams, mentally thumbed through the notations in my project notebook. 'Do you recall any of the relatives' houses, other than Aunt Fleeta's? Places you might have visited in Houston? Perhaps one with a tall, open room and a grand staircase at one end. The walls were dark wood paneling. They had a maid working there. A black woman.' I'd begun wondering if the house plaguing my dreams might have been a relative's. Perhaps the patchwork of memories I'd experienced hailed from some time when my mother had left me in the care of a cousin or friend in a house that was strange to me. My parents did travel, on occasion, just as Annalee and I had.

Deborah's lips twisted to one side, a smirk she'd inherited from Annalee. 'That description fits most of the relatives and everyone in Grandmother's bridge club. They all had those big, two-story houses down in the old-money neighborhoods. They all had black maids, too. Everybody did. Except Grandmother had the college girls. You know, she loved to flout the unwritten rules of the bridge club set there in Houston and Galveston. I remember her and Aunt Fleeta having a knockdown, drag-out fight one time because Grandmother wanted to go pay her respects at a black funeral, and Aunt Fleeta thought that was about the worst idea in the world. I thought Grandmother was going to run over Aunt Fleeta in the driveway. I hadn't ever seen adults get in a wrangle like that. I mean, you and Mom hardly ever fought, or not where we kids could see it. I don't remember whose funeral Grandmother was headed to, though.'

I wondered at the picture of my mother planning to cross to the other side of town to attend a funeral. It must have been for someone who mattered to her a great deal. 'But you don't recall a house with a tall room like that, with a balcony on the second floor? There were stained-glass windows in transoms above the doors. I recall the shape of a script letter in them, the letter V. The maid there was named Cecile.' Imagining the windows brought back a scrap of memory. It floated by, tumbling as a bit of birthday wrap might on a windy day. I chased it, but couldn't catch it quickly enough. I recalled something to do with smoke, and papers burning . . .

'Nope.' Deborah set down her sandwich and fished a napkin from the bag. Her hands hung in midair with the napkin between them. 'Why? What's this about?'

I pretended to be busy cleaning crumbs off my pants. How much should I tell her? If I revealed too much, she might think my mind was going, along with my circulatory system. 'I've been having some dreams. Things in the past, I think. I've been trying to sort them out – making a study of them, so to speak, while there's still time. It seems as though it's something important. Do you suppose it's possible to forget entire blocks of your life?' I stopped short of telling her that I'd been wondering whether the memories could have been awakened by my recent flirtation with death.

She took in a breath that shuddered in her throat. Her fist tightened around the napkin, squeezed it as if she were trying to contain some emotion within it. 'You've been dealing with a serious loss these last few months. Right now, I think you need to focus on your health and the future. Have you thought any more about that grief recovery group at the Villas?'

'I can't see what good that would do.' Deborah and her agendas – anything to lure me down to the old-age home. It

110

was no surprise that rather than considering the question I'd asked, she would use it to turn the conversation in the direction she wanted. 'And aside from that, how would I get there? Certainly not in my car, since you've taken the keys away.'

Deborah bristled. 'Do we have to do this today? I just came by to bring you some breakfast and make sure you're all right.' Her defenses went up, as impenetrable as the heat shields that protected our Apollo capsules upon reentry.

'Well, clearly I am all right.' It would always be this way between us, I supposed. Deborah and I on opposite sides of the divide.

'Clearly,' she muttered, then rose to her feet, scooped up the trash from breakfast, and stuffed it into the bag. She didn't say another word, just breezed through the living room, gathered her things, and headed for the door. The *click-click* of her footsteps paused in the entryway. I waited, trying to peer around the corner. I could feel Annalee beside me, nudging my shoulder and saying, *Go tell her you're sorry.*

But an apology, a softening, would soon lead to the discussion of grief recovery groups, medical treatments, and the merits of the conveniently located old-persons' village, which Deborah had already visited, priced, and decided upon in her own mind. She'd move me there and conduct an estate sale here – *a cleaning out*, as she'd called it after Annalee passed. Answers to the family secrets, if they were hidden in this house, would be lost forever. The pieces of my life would be sold to the highest bidder. My daughter would manage me as if I were some nincompoop, some incompetent incapable of making my own decisions.

For this reason, I let her go out the door without another word between us. With Deborah, there was no aimless conversation. With Deborah, there was little pretense. She merely wanted to dispense with matters as quickly and easily as possible. There was no room for the idea that I might have something left to do in life.

I waited for the girl to arrive. I waited until nine, and then half past, and then ten thirty-five, forty, fifty-two. Having no phone number or other means by which to contact her, I had little choice but to pace the floors. Perhaps she wasn't coming. Perhaps, after the stairway incident, she'd decided to divest herself of me altogether.

The idea was disappointing to a degree for which I was not prepared. I stood in the entryway, considering the situation. I could, of course, climb the stairs and proceed to the attic, moving along with my project myself. Until yesterday's incident, I'd been doing fine. I was sore from the fall down the stairs, but not incapable of making my way up there.

Instead, I found myself hovering near the front door, listening as each car passed, even though I knew that the girl normally walked here from school. How was she planning to travel here today? By city bus, I supposed, since that mother of hers didn't seem to have a vehicle. Where did they live? How far away? I hadn't asked. I hadn't so much as inquired about a phone number.

Frustration finally took me outside to look up and down the street. The yard was a disaster that would have mortified Annalee. The grass had been mowed by the lawn service, but Annalee's flower beds, which she'd always groomed herself, lay in ruin, her roses never pruned in the winter, and now unprepared for spring. Only the plants around the detached garage had been properly trimmed and cared for – no doubt by Terrence. Today he stood at the curb speaking with my next-door neighbor, Hanna Beth, and her mentally handicapped adult son, Teddy. All three of them turned my way at once, and then proceeded in my direction, Teddy helping his mother navigate the sidewalk with a walker and Terrence trailing behind them.

'Hallooo!' Teddy called, waving his arm in that enthusiastic, clumsy way of his. 'Hallooo, Mis-ser Al-bird.'

Teddy's mother waved as well. Terrence pushed his hands into his pockets, as if he were as uncomfortable with this invasion of my space as I was. A man should be able to stand in his own yard without being accosted by the neighbors.

I steeled myself for the inevitable social niceties – *how are you, we haven't seen you, is there anything we can do for you, how are you feeling* . . . These things were, in part, the reason I kept myself indoors.

I met them at the sidewalk, so as to discourage the idea of an invitation into the house or yard. Terrence shook my hand, Teddy waved shyly again, Hanna Beth greeted me with a sympathetic touch to my shoulder, and we cycled through a likewise uncomfortable conversational greeting. Terrence let me know that, so as not to bother me, he had given the recent repair bills for the apartment to Deborah. I nodded to confirm that I appreciated his efforts to stay out of my way. For the most part, he came and went from the property like a ghost. If not for his car lights and the occasional sound of a door closing on the garage building, I would never have known he was there.

'I'm just waiting for the girl who helps me around the house,' I said, to imply that this wasn't a visit to the curb to catch up with the neighbors. 'She's late today.'

'Oh, Teddy and I met her a few days ago while Teddy was out pruning the roses,' Hanna Beth said, smiling. 'Hard to believe it's April already. The birds have come in. Teddy was out filling the feeders this morning. He'd be happy to come by and prune your roses, by the way. Terrence hired him to do the ones around the apartment.' She indicated the detached garage, and it occurred to me that Teddy must have spent a fair bit of time on those flower beds. Life was going on in the world, and I wasn't a part of it. My mind was trapped in the winter, frozen in mid-November, when Annalee lay down to rest, feeling unwell, and never rose again.

'Send me the bill for the gardening,' I told Terrence. 'It isn't your responsibility.'

Terrence circled a hand, palm out, as if he were washing a window. 'No, dude, it's all right. It was my deal. Sesay, my helper, and my girlfriend, MJ, are plant freaks. MJ has been on me about the rosebushes, you know?' He gave me the somewhat helpless look of a man under the spell of a woman. My mind wound back in time, and I recalled that feeling. Annalee and I had married only six months after we met, and I was so smitten that I'd made a flower bed for her outside our college apartment. It was her first summer not to go home to her parents' farm in Maine, and she was homesick. I wanted her to be happy, as happy as I was. I had

everything – a beautiful wife, my studies, job offers waiting, the promise of an exciting career ahead. Annalee and I
basked in the glow of young love, and it was all I could see.
But slowly, I'd let that dim. I'd buried it beneath the mortar
and stone of building a life, let it go to seed like this yard,
while my back was turned.

A stab of regret found some tender place inside me and
drew blood. I didn't want to be near anyone. I wanted to be
alone in my house. 'I should go back inside now. Send me
the bill for the gardening.'

'No, no, it's a gift,' Terrence countered.

Teddy added, 'I gone come fill yer bird feeds, too, 'kay?
Got lotta hungry bird. Got mornin' dove, 'n' meadow-ark,
'n' rob-bin, 'n' pretty red bird.'

'I don't want any gifts.' My emotions threatened to tumble out of control, and just as quickly, I was angry. I was
angry with life. I was angry with the neighbors. I was angry
with Annalee for leaving. Even in the midst of it, my lack of
ability to control the outburst was humiliating. 'I don't
need sympathy, or plates of cookies, or neighbors knocking
at my door. I am perfectly fine on my own.' I turned and
started toward the house, so as not to make a greater spec-
tacle of myself.

Clearly, the girl wasn't coming today. I shouldn't have
been surprised. She was a teenager, after all. Bound to be
unreliable. Perhaps she'd found a new means by which to
earn the money she was so interested in, and she would
never come back here at all.

CHAPTER 8

Epiphany Jones

Sometimes it's not till after you do something stupid that you see how dumb it was. I never should've gotten in DeRon's car instead of waiting to catch the city bus over to J. Norm's house. It was Saturday morning, though, and the buses would be slow and crowded. When DeRon pulled up and said he'd give me a ride, I figured that would be faster. I couldn't have been more wrong.

So far, we'd cruised up and down Vista Street three times, been to that low-rent apartment complex where I'd left behind a night I really wanted to forget, gone by the furniture store to try to hustle some money from DeRon's cousin who worked there, and picked up three of DeRon's friends. Now we were sitting in front of some dumpy little house waiting on another friend, who I guessed was gonna be in somebody's lap. There were a bunch of dudes on the porch, looking our way and leaning over, trying to see who was in the car. I pushed my hands between my knees and slid down in the seat, because I didn't want them to see me. At least one of those dudes, the big white guy with the tattoos up and down his arm, Big Ray, was fresh out of jail for dealing crack, and the night of the party, he was bragging about it right before he asked me to go to the bedroom with him and smoke. He was the reason we'd headed off down the street with DeRon's friends. After that, we passed by the church and got in trouble anyway.

Now Big Ray was looking at me through the car window and licking his nasty lips, like he hoped I was gonna come in there. No stinkin' way.

The friend DeRon was waiting for stepped out on the porch and waved for us to come on. Big Ray grabbed him around the neck and wrestled him some, just messing with him, but really Ray looked like he oughta be on *The Ultimate Fighter*. He could probably break somebody's neck. The three losers in DeRon's backseat jumped out and ran on up to the house to get in on the action. I felt better without them in the car. Things had been getting a little weird, and I didn't like how it felt.

They all started wrestling and goofing around on the porch, and DeRon reached for his door handle.

'Where are you going?' I asked.

He nudged me in the shoulder. 'Let's go chill a minute.'

'No *way*.' A sick feeling gurgled in my stomach, and all of a sudden, I wanted to be anyplace else. 'C'mon, DeRon. I've gotta get to work. I'm late already.' I looked at the clock on the dash. After ten. I should've been at J. Norm's at least an hour ago. So far, this morning had started bad and gotten worse. Russ and Mama were headed to camp out at one of their gun shows this weekend. Russ needed to make some money, because he'd spent the rent buying new inventory from some dude at the last gun show, and Mama was mad as a wet cat.

Russ was supposed to have gotten his trailer all packed last night, but a bunch of his biker buddies came by while Mama was at work, and they'd hung out watching some game on TV. When they got done, the living room was trashed.

This morning, Russ's trailer wasn't ready, and Mama went off on him. Russ didn't care at first, because he was still passed out, mostly. By the time Mama stomped out the door to work on the trailer, they'd had a big fight, like usual. Russ told me to clean up the mess in the house. I knew better than to argue with Russ when he was like that. It was easier to do what he said. So I cleaned up their stupid mess and then helped finish stocking the trailer. After that, I listened while Mama told me I was dead meat if I didn't come straight home after work and lock myself in the house while her and Russ were gone. She acted like she was gonna check with the neighbors to see how I did, which was such a crock. Mama and Russ weren't about to waste their weekend worrying about me, and it wasn't like they could call the house, since we didn't have a phone, except Russ's *business* phone, which went wherever Russ went.

By the time they finally left, I was late heading for the bus stop. I'd missed the bus and was waiting for the next one when DeRon drove by. I figured nobody'd know about me getting in DeRon's car. Besides, I needed the ride.

I didn't think I was gonna end up stuck outside some crack house with Big Ray licking his lips at me. 'You said you were gonna give me a ride to *work*, DeRon.'

He jerked away like he was trying to get a better look at me. 'What you wanna be workin' in that old white dude big house fo'? You know they jus' gonna jump yo' case at school fo' that. They thinkin' you a little Aunt Jemima.' He blinked at me and grinned, like it was all a joke. DeRon had a smile that could melt butter, I swear. 'Come on, Epie. It Sat-aday. You too fine to be workin' on Sat-aday.' He slid a hand over my shoulder and into my hair and tipped my chin up and kissed me, and I leaned into it. It felt so good to have somebody touch me like that. His thumb rubbed a soft circle over the hollow of my throat. Little tingles went through my skin, and for a minute, I couldn't think.

DeRon kissed me again, harder this time.

On the porch, Big Ray thumbed toward the house and said he had a room in there, and we could use it. DeRon's friends hollered something you wouldn't say in front of your mama, and DeRon shot them the finger out the window; then he pulled me close and rested his forehead against mine. 'Let's ditch 'em and go someplace. Jus' you and me.'

'Yeah, all right,' I heard myself say. Anywhere was better than here, with a half dozen guys acting crazy. Right then, I wanted to be alone with DeRon, anyway. I could tell myself twenty dozen times that DeRon was a bad idea, but when he was right there, with that big smile and those eyes, all I could think was that nobody'd ever looked at me like that before. I could see myself in the bleachers at the basketball games, cheering him on. If I worked at it a little, I could probably get away some and go do stuff with DeRon – maybe tell Mama I was staying late at J. Norm's. If I kept putting DeRon off, that other girl he'd been crushin' on was gonna have him wrapped around her finger, and everybody at school would be taking free shots at me again. Right now, they left me alone because DeRon said to.

DeRon started the car and stuck a hand out the window, waved, and hollered, 'Catch y'all later.'

They hooted, and one of them stood on the edge of the porch and did something nasty. I pretended I didn't see it, but a big ol' lump came up in my throat. DeRon slid his hand over and put it on my thigh and started to rub. The muscles underneath went stiff, and then relaxed, but my mind was spinning ninety miles an hour, like the simulator car in driver's ed class when it hits a water puddle. I couldn't think that fast.

I wanted DeRon. I wanted to be his girlfriend, but I hadn't ever *been* with anybody. In Mrs Lora's school, I was like a fly in a puddle of milk. Those lily-white farm boys didn't want to be with me, and their mamas and daddies weren't gonna let them, anyway. This thing with DeRon was a whole new deal. It's not every day the guy all the girls want decides he wants you. I could picture how life could be a whole lot more fun with DeRon around.

'I hadn't ever met anybody like you, Epie,' he said, and smiled on one side, and his hand slid up a little bit. The muscles went tight, then loose again. His fingers stopped for a minute while he was scoping the traffic to turn onto Vista Street. 'How come you let them other girls push you around? They hadn't got nothin' on you, girl. You fine like you oughta be on a magazine cover or somethin', and you smart.' He grinned and winked at me, and I felt like I could be on a magazine cover, right then. Nobody'd ever talked to me like that before.

'Those girls are stupid.' I leaned back in my seat, let my head turn toward DeRon, tried to look like I knew what I was doing. 'I got no use for them.' I pulled my bottom lip into my mouth and chewed on it, because all of a sudden I was nervous again.

DeRon sucked in a breath and blew it out. 'Man, Epie, you drivin' me crazy.'

It felt good to drive somebody crazy – but at the same time, there was a knot in my throat so big, I could hardly get air past it. I knew where me and DeRon were headed – well, not where, exactly, but that look in his eyes told me what he had in mind. *Lust of the flesh*, Mrs Lora would've called it. She was against it, and the preacher at her church was, too. There was stuff about it all through the Bible. They did a whole purity class for us girls when we were in the seventh grade. It was all about the reasons you shouldn't have sex, and you should wait until you're married and stuff. I didn't listen much. I was skinny as the Feed the Children commercial back then and flat as a board. I just kept thinking, *Who're they talkin' to? Nobody's ever gonna want me.*

Guess I should've paid more attention. If Mrs Lora could see me right now, she'd drag me out to that old swing in her backyard, and we'd have us a talk.

If I got myself pregnant, Mama would kick me out of the house for sure. She'd been telling me that since back in the eighth grade, when I started to develop. *You get yourself pregnant, Epiphany, you're on your own. Then you can just see how hard it is. See what I go through* . . . Other than that, it didn't seem like it'd be such a big deal. There were pregnant girls all over the school. Nobody cared. They even had a special club for get-togethers and stuff. Mama probably didn't really care, either. She just didn't want a baby to take care of. She didn't really even want me.

DeRon kept rubbing my leg. I wanted him to want me. I wanted somebody to. I got a little picture in my mind ... me, DeRon, a baby. I could get out of Mama's house for good. We'd have our own place. I could help DeRon with school, like I did in science class now, and he could make it big in basketball. In a few years, we wouldn't be living off the Hill. We'd be living on it – in a big house with a swimming pool.

Yeah, right, who're you kidding? another part of me said. *You'll end up in some welfare line ...*

It was like there were two people inside me, with two different minds. Mrs Lora called it the angel and the demon. She said usually the flesh is on the demon's side. My body was on DeRon's side right now, if that meant anything.

I caught a breath and tried to think straight, but there was too much going on in me. The preacher said that when temptation comes, you've got to pray. I closed my eyes, but I didn't think I wanted to bring Jesus into this whole situation right now. I figured I knew what He'd say, anyhow. I shouldn't be with some boy in the backseat of a car, no matter how fine he was. That all sounds good in church, but when you're out in the real world, it's hard.

When I opened my eyes, we were pulling into the parking lot of a closed-down grocery store across from the school. We were just a few blocks from J. Norm's house, where I was actually supposed to be right now.

'Hey, listen, take me down the street, okay?' I said, and DeRon gave me the *you're-crazy* look.

'Say wha'?'

'I just . . . I gotta go by work and check on him and make sure he's all right. He falls down sometimes and stuff.' I needed more time. I needed to think about things for a minute – away from DeRon.

DeRon's smile fell straight, and his mouth hung open like somebody'd whacked him upside the head. 'You kiddin', right?' He started to smile again, slow, first on one side, then the other. The car drifted along behind the store and turned into an old loading dock, so that we were parked down in the carved-out truck ramp, and nobody could see us from the street. There was just enough room in there for the car, and the concrete walls were higher than my door, so I couldn't get out, either.

A pulse went wild in my neck, and my skin turned cold, but I was sweating. The radio cranked out a rap song, and I felt the drumbeats inside me.

DeRon leaned over and slid a hand into my hair, but it didn't feel good this time. 'C'mere, baby,' he purred, and leaned in to kiss me on the neck. 'This ain't your first time, right? Man, you're so hot, Epie. I been wantin' you bad.'

He got up on his knees and crawled over the console half-way onto me. I felt his finger hook under the strap on my tank top and slide it down.

My heart punched like a fist beating my ribs. My eyes darted toward the backseat. I tried to see if the doors were high enough above the cement walls to open.

DeRon laughed against my skin. 'You wanna go back there?' He shifted a little, like he was gonna crawl into the backseat. I moved and got an arm between us. He hung on to my tank top, and I felt it stretch and slide down. I grabbed it with one hand and tried to push him off with the other.

'You bes' quit teasin' me.' His voice wasn't so soft anymore. 'C'mon, Epie, you was all ready to give it out the other night at Big Ray's apartment, and jus' a little while ago, you tellin' me to leave my homeboys so we can be alone. Jus' lay back and let DeRon show you how it's good, girl.'

My head spun, and I felt him pulling the tank top farther, trying to take it, and me, with him into the backseat. Something tore. I pushed my knee between us, and it caught a soft spot in his stomach, and he coughed out air. The strap on my tank top broke, letting him tumble into the backseat.

He got tangled in the floorboard a minute, and I grabbed what was left of my shirt, felt my heart bumping against the broken strap.

DeRon roared and cussed a blue streak.

I looked around the car, panic crackling through me, making my thoughts rush and spin. Even if I rolled down the window in front, I wasn't sure I could shinny between the car and the walls of the loading ramp. I thought of some guy Mama had lived with right before we moved to Mrs Lora's. He beat her black and blue, and then dragged her off to the bedroom. I saw it happen. 'I've gotta go to work,' I said. 'I'll lose my job.'

DeRon snorted. 'C'mon, girl, stop messin' wit' me and take that thang off.' He pointed at my shirt. He'd lost a shoe somewhere, and he had his long ol' legs all crunched up in front of him. It would've been funny if I wasn't so scared.

Think, I told myself. *Think of something.* And then I heard J. Norm in my head, saying, *You're a clever girl* . . .

There was more space between the car and the wall on the driver's side.

'You first,' I said, and DeRon went for his pants. While he was busy, I scooted over into the driver's seat and hit the window switch. The radio was so loud, and DeRon was so busy, he didn't even notice until I was squatting in the seat and grabbing the keys. He looked up when the radio went off, but by then, I already had my feet on the window frame and I was shinnying between the side of the dock and the car.

'Hey, what're you doin'?' he yelled, and made a lunge for my foot. I ducked out of the way and took a chunk of skin off my arm, rolling onto the dock.

'I'm leaving, you jerk! Your keys are out here.' I threw his keys where it'd take him a while to get to them, and then I turned and ran. I didn't look back to see how DeRon got out of the car, or whether he tried to follow me. I just kept running – through the streets of small houses around the school, past the new condos that were changing the neighborhood, all the way to J. Norm's street.

By then, I couldn't run anymore. My lungs were burning, and my legs felt like rubber. I stopped by someone's yard fence, wiped my face, looked at my arm where it was bleeding, and tried to decide if there was some way I could tie my tank top back together.

I heard DeRon's car roaring up the street behind me, so I just started walking, holding up my tank top with one hand. Only eight more houses before J. Norm's, and I figured I was as safe on the sidewalk as anyplace. This was the kind of neighborhood where, if you screamed, someone'd probably do something about it.

DeRon pulled up beside me, the front tire bumping over the curb. Rolling down the passenger window, he leaned across the console. 'Man, Epie, what're you doin'?'

'I'm going to *work*.' I didn't look at him, just kept walking. If I'd had a baseball bat in my hand, I probably would've knocked out his window with it. All of a sudden, I remembered that my stuff was still in his car, too. 'Give me my backpack.'

'Come 'n' get it.' DeRon smiled, then swerved around a parked car. When he pulled back to the curb, he was holding my backpack just inside the window. 'You want your stuff?' His eyes curved upward, like he thought it was funny. My books from school were in there. If I lost the books, somebody would have to pay for them, and all the money I'd been saving up would be gone.

I stopped walking and moved toward the car, then reached for the backpack. DeRon laughed and pulled it away.

'Give me my stuff!' I yelled. My hands were shaking, so I squeezed them into fists.

DeRon jerked his chin back like he couldn't believe I wasn't playing along. He caught sight of my arm. 'Girl, you bleedin'.'

'Yeah, nice, huh?' I tried to look like it didn't bother me, what'd happened in his car, or that I was stuck on the sidewalk now, holding my shirt together.

He popped the door open. 'Girl, get in this car.'

'No.' I started walking again, a creepy feeling sliding over my shoulders now that the car door was open. J. Norm's place was only three doors down. I'd just have to worry about the backpack later.

DeRon followed me, revving the engine, then hitting the brakes again and again, so that the car bounced up and down. Now that I thought about it, I wondered how he got a car like that, anyway. His mama didn't have any money, and you didn't get paid for playing high school basketball, no matter how good you were. Maybe Big Ray was so friendly with him for a reason.

A shiver went through me, and I wanted to kick myself. I was so stupid. Of course DeRon and Big Ray were so tight for a reason. Just because DeRon didn't use that stuff didn't mean he didn't deal in it. Shoot, kids at school would probably buy from DeRon just to get in good with him.

I looked ahead, hoping J. Norm's next-door neighbor, Teddy, or the guy in the garage apartment, Terrence, would be out trimming the bushes or something, but there was nobody. J. Norm wouldn't be outside. He never was.

DeRon bumped up onto the curb far enough that I jumped sideways into somebody's lawn. 'C'mon, Epie. Knock it off. I'll give you a ride home.'

I kept walking, and DeRon drove a half-moon on the sidewalk, then bounced back onto the street. Something scraped under the car, and he cussed a blue streak and yelled out a half dozen names for me. He sounded like Russ during a fight. Russ could call Mama stuff that would make your ears burn.

DeRon squealed ahead to J. Norm's house, pulled the car

up and parked it, and got out. 'Yeah, I know which house it is.' He stood on the sidewalk, looking like he wasn't even worried that in this neighborhood somebody might call the police on you just for driving a car like DeRon's and wearing a do-rag. 'I seen you walkin' down here after school, like you his little ol' housemaid. Now ain't that sweet?'

I turned off to cut across the yard, but he got in front of me. He grabbed my arm and twisted it until he could see the place where the skin was scraped. Tears popped into my eyes because it hurt, and I remembered what it felt like to have somebody yank you around. That guy Mama dated before we moved to Mrs Lora's wasn't near as mellow as Russ.

DeRon's eyes were hard as glass when he looked at the blood on my arm. 'Don't you go tellin' people I did that to you. I didn't do nothin'.'

I tried to pull my arm away, but he was strong. He lifted a hand and wrapped it around my throat, then smiled and dragged his fingers across my chest. 'Come on, baby. We got a good thing. You know you want it.'

Let go! I opened my mouth to say it, but the words wouldn't come out. I pulled against his grip, but he twisted harder. My eyes filled up, and I felt like that little girl hiding behind the sofa while Mama got into it with some guy. DeRon disappeared behind a blur.

'I got it.' He leaned close, and I felt his lips against my ear, his breath hot on my skin. 'You gonna make me work for it, huh?' He kissed my neck, moved his hand up my arm until he was holding on to the raw place. 'C'mon, Epie. Stop jerkin' me around.'

He squeezed harder, and I squirmed. I heard a door open somewhere nearby. 'Something wrong down there?' The voice came from overhead, and I figured it was Terrence in the garage apartment.

'Ain't nothin' wrong,' DeRon answered, letting go of my arm and backing off a step. He looked toward the apartment. I could hear Terrence coming out. There were other people with him, more than one coming down the steps.

I wiped my eyes and tried to get hold of myself. The last thing I needed was someone making a federal case out of this and thinking they should tell Mama.

'We just talkin',' DeRon said.

'That true, Epie?' Terrence was just a few feet behind me now. Someone else had stopped on the steps. I could hear the bottom one creaking. I looked over my shoulder and saw Terrence's girlfriend, MJ. She ran the Book Basket store across from the church and knew every kid in the neighborhood. She was probably the one who called the police the night we got in trouble in the memory garden.

'That true, DeRon?' she asked, and tossed a long, dark ponytail of braids over her shoulder, like she was ready to whoop up on somebody if she needed to.

'Yez, ma'am,' DeRon said, backing off another step, smiling at her. 'I just brung Epie in for work.'

'Epie?' Terrence's voice was low and serious. I wanted to turn around and let him see the ripped shirt and the bloody arm.

I swallowed hard. 'Yeah, it's fine. I gotta get up to the house. I'm late, and J. Norm's probably wondering where I am.' I circled around toward DeRon, so Terrence and MJ wouldn't see the broken strap, and I headed across the yard. My legs went soft and my feet felt like they were sinking in quicksand. Every step seemed like a mile.

'I'll hang on to yo' stuff for you, Epie,' DeRon called after me, and I knew this wasn't over. After I was done with work, I'd have to head home tonight, for one thing.

I didn't turn around and look back at him. I just ran up onto the porch and pounded on the door until finally the lock clicked. The door opened, and I felt my body melting. I pushed a hand over my mouth, but it didn't help. My lips shook, and a sob came out, and when I saw J. Norm on the other side, I started to cry.

'What in heaven's name?' His raspy voice was a whisper against the rush of blood in my ears. His hand slid under my elbow, and he pulled me through the door. 'Good heavens, what's happened to you?'

Another sob busted out. I tried to swallow it. It came again. I heard J. Norm close the door and lock it. His hand touched my shoulder, like he wasn't sure he should put it there, and he moved me to the sofa in the front room. The cushions squished and leaned when he sat down next to me. I felt something soft in my hand and saw his hankie.

'All right, now. All right.' He patted my shoulder with stiff fingers and cleared his throat, like he didn't know what else to do or say. 'What's happened? Did you fall down? Get hit by a car? You've scratched yourself up a bit.' He touched the raw skin, and I jerked away. I let my head drop forward, so that my hair went over my shoulders, covering the scratches and the ripped shirt.

'Now, then, no real harm done.' J. Norm's voice got softer. 'It doesn't look too bad. Just a skin contusion. We'll put a little peroxide on it. Are you injured anywhere else?'

I shook my head, wiped my eyes with the hankie, hoped it wasn't one that'd already been used. I tried to think of what to do next. DeRon had all my stuff. Mama and Russ were gone tonight. As soon as I headed home, I was dead.

Another sob came out. I pushed the hankie over my eyes.

'There, now.' J. Norm patted my head like a puppy's. 'It'll be all right. Tell me what's happened. You're safe now.' His voice was soft and kind. I would've never thought he had a voice like that in him. It broke me wide-open, and without even meaning to, I started babbling out the whole thing – Mama and Russ fighting, the bus stop, DeRon, his friends, the car, the loading dock in back of the old grocery store, DeRon taking off with my backpack in his car.

The words came out like a river, rushing and crashing against each other, breaking over the tops of all the walls inside me. I didn't want to tell J. Norm that stuff. I didn't want him to see me like this, but I couldn't help it. I needed somebody to promise me it was gonna be all right. I needed somebody to help me.

'There, now,' J. Norm said again, when I'd calmed down a little. He went and got a kitchen towel, and when he came back, he took the soaked hankie and put the towel in my hands. 'Enough of that, now. Dry those tears. We'll clean up the scratches, and then we'll figure out what to do.'

CHAPTER 9

J. Norman Alvord

We went to Annalee's closet to find a shirt. It seemed strange to be in there among her things – neither Deborah nor I had yet attempted the handling of Annalee's personal belongings – but what else was I to do? I could hardly let the girl run around in disarray, and short of my attempting to operate a needle and thread, which had always been Annalee's domain as well, a loan of clothing seemed the wisest choice. Annalee would have done the same. She was a few inches shorter than this girl's lanky frame, but I surmised them to be roughly the same size.

The girl stood in the doorway of the walk-in closet, watching while I held up various shirts I thought might serve. My judgment of women's clothing being rudimentary, she laughed at some of my choices, still sniffling and choking on leftover tears.

Her gaze took in the long row of Annalee's suits and dresses, then the wide rack of shoes at the back of the closet, and finally the stack of hatboxes overhead. In my corporate days, there were always banquets and Christmas parties, awards ceremonies and speeches to attend. Those events were never to my liking, but Annalee was a butterfly, brightly colored and fully alive in all social situations. She rescued me from my own awkwardness, and when the need to maintain polite conversation became too oppressive, she whisked me off to the dance floor, where no conversation was required.

The girl selected a red plaid shirt that Annalee had used for gardening; then she stood gazing at the section of dancing dresses. 'Whoa. Your wife was, like, totally a fashionista.'

I felt Annalee there beside me, smiling at the comment. She was fashionable. Always. Many of the gowns she'd either sewn or altered herself, merely because she enjoyed clothing. She'd even sewn the bridal gown for Deborah's late-in-life wedding, two years ago. After waiting all these years for our daughter to fall in love, Annalee wasn't about to miss the opportunity. It had been a beautiful wedding on Jupiter Beach in Florida – a place Deborah remembered from her childhood. The trip was a stroll down Memory Lane for Annalee and me, a reminder of the glory days of our young family. I'd let melancholy overtake me more than I should have on that trip. Those years at the cape were the glory days, and they were over. Had I known that the trip to Deborah's wedding would be my last vacation with Annalee, I would have lived more fully in the moment, realized how easily a perfect day can slip by unnoticed. Any day is the glory day, if you choose to see the glory in it.

'We had many occasions to go out socially over the years,' I said. 'There were parties related to my work, technology

133

conferences, and charities in which Annalee involved her-self.' The past came back as unexpectedly as the gush of a breeze when a door is opened. It smelled fresh and pleasant. 'In my days at Cape Canaveral, the social events were a way to appease the wives, to make penance for the fact that our work occupied so much of our time. We were desperate to get ahead of the Russians, of course. Kennedy wanted to be the first to put a man on the moon. We devoted our lives to it, and when our wives grew frustrated and cross, we took them out for fine food and dancing. Annalee loved to dance.'

The girl's face brightened, and I was glad to see that the tears had been forgotten. 'Whoa, J. Norm, you're a dancer?' She looked me over, as if it were hard to see Fred Astaire inside the rumpled blue dress shirt and navy pants that hung two sizes too large on what was left of my body.

The memories surrounded me, sweet and fragrant like the gardenias at the cape. Bright, beautiful, pungent to my mind. 'I've been known to take a turn.'

She responded with a wide, precocious grin that left dimples in her milky brown cheeks. 'Like, a *dancer* dancer? Like ballroom stuff, like they do on that TV show? Fox-trots and the Vietnamese waltz, and that stuff?'

'Viennese waltz,' I corrected. 'I knew them all. My mother saw to that with several years of charm school.'

'Charm school!' She sniffled and then choked on laughter. 'J. Norm, you been to charm school?' Oddly enough, Annalee had offered much the same reaction when, at her college sorority's spring cotillion, I proved to be reasonably compe-tent in the finer arts. *Norman*, she'd said, after I gallantly dipped her at the end of a dance, *I didn't know you had that in you!* I was quite pleased with myself at that moment and thankful for my mother. A boy from the lacrosse team had been eyeing my date that evening – a young man known for being good with the ladies. I was afraid to leave Annalee alone even long enough for a trip to the punch bowl.

'I feel certain there's a graduation certificate somewhere in the attic,' I told the girl. 'Mrs Hardin's School of the Social Arts.'

'You *graduated* from charm school?' Epiphany coughed in exaggerated disbelief, smirking at me. 'I think you oughta go ask for a refund.'

'I'll have you know, young lady, that I was a model pupil.' I pretended to be offended by the insinuation that I was less than charming to be around. She wasn't fooled. She laughed at my answer, and I felt a tremble in my stomach, an urge to laugh along with her.

Slipping on the shirt, she moved a few steps into the closet, touching one of the dresses. 'Man,' she whispered, trailing her finger along smooth sky-blue satin. 'These are, like, red-carpet stuff. What's up there in the boxes?'

'Hats,' I told her, and she regarded me with such curiosity that I felt compelled to take down a container for her. Inside were two pillbox hats and some gloves, things Annalee might have worn to church on a Sunday, back when such was the fashion. 'And gloves, it would seem.'

She peered over the side of the box, moved her fingers toward the hat, then stopped. 'Can I touch it?'

'I don't see that it would hurt.'

Taking out a pale green hat with a feathered clip and gloves that had undoubtedly been perfectly matched at one time, she clicked her tongue against her teeth, then whispered, 'Whoa. These are cool.' She stepped back into the room and stood in front of the mirror to put them on. Her face lit as she braced her hands on her hips, admiring herself from side to side, the bruised shoulder and torn shirt seemingly forgotten. 'Whew-eee! Look at me. I look like Jackie O. Kennedy. I read about her and Camelot and stuff in those magazines you gave me.'

My mind fell into a memory – one of Deborah as a child, dressed in one of her mother's gowns, her tiny feet hidden in the toes of Annalee's heeled shoes. I'd passed by the doorway as she was gazing at herself in the mirror. *Look at me, Daddy! Look at me! Am I a pretty girl?*

It matters more for a girl to be smart, I'd said. *Beauty is subject to the beholder, but intelligence is undeniable. Shouldn't you be attending to your studies? It's after seven thirty . . .* I'd continued on about my business without looking back. The moment had seemed insignificant then. Now I wished I could stand in the doorway again and watch my daughter pretend in her mother's shoes. I wished I had told her how beautiful she was.

The girl frowned into the mirror, her bottom lip pouching on one side. 'You think I look like Jackie Kennedy, J. Norm? You think I'm ever gonna be pretty, like she was?' Her face narrowed, as if she were trying to imagine the answer for herself.

I think it's more important for a girl to be smart. The words were on the tip of my tongue, but it's a foolish man who willingly tastes the dish of regret once he knows how bitter it is.

'I mean,' she went on, her gaze sliding over and catching mine, her odd silver-green eyes bright in this light, 'I was just wonderin'. Not in some kind of weird way, 'cause I'm young and you're old and stuff, but if you were young, would you think I was, like, pretty?'

For reasons I could not grasp, the words that had never come to my lips for Deborah came now for this child. 'I think you are beautiful. A beautiful young lady. Like Jackie Kennedy.'

She smiled, bashful for the first time since I'd known her. Looking down at her hands, she slipped off a glove. 'No prince from Camelot's gonna be sweeping me off to Kitty-bunkport, though, probably.'

I felt obliged to make a point. 'Well, certainly that boy, that Dron, is no prince, now, is he? Not the sort a princess should be going around with.'

Her gaze slid toward me again. 'De-Ron,' she corrected.

'Precisely. That sort of boy isn't worth the trouble.'

She drew back, offended. 'You don't *know* DeRon. He scored more points in basketball than any high school player in Dallas last year. He's set to get a college scholarship. Every girl in school wants to be DeRon's girlfriend.'

I suddenly wondered how I'd allowed myself to be drawn into such a ludicrous conversation. I knew nothing of high school romance. 'In my day, there were standards. A young man was expected to behave in a proper way. A young woman who thought anything of herself insisted on it.'

'Whatever.' She reached for the hat, wincing when her lacerated skin touched the fabric of the overshirt. 'Well, that's not how it is anymore. You go acting like you're some kind of princess, you can sit home by yourself on Saturday night.'

'Would that be the worst thing?'

Her thumb caressed the feathers on the hatband, as if she felt the need to admire it a moment longer. 'It would be in my house. I hate it there.' The words ended in a sigh. 'DeRon's just ... I just want someone to ... want me around, you know?' Her chin trembled and she swallowed hard, then fluttered a glance my way, as if she were waiting for an answer. What was I to say? I could guide a rocket to the moon or design systems to track missile launches halfway across the world, but I knew nothing of advising a teenage girl, of offering comfort or pertinent information. Yet, there she was, her eyes soft and round, the color of spring leaves, expectant.

I remembered something an elder colleague once told me when I was considering a position overseas. The job included a long-term contract requiring me to be absent for extended periods in the lives of our young children. I repeated the advice now, because it seemed to apply. 'We all make trade-offs to get what we want. But no matter what you stand to gain, when the thing you're asked to trade is yourself, the price is too high.' *What shall it profit a man if he shall gain the whole world and lose his own soul?* My father, with whom I'd engaged in perhaps only one or two lengthy conversations in my life, was a successful oilman who often quoted the wisdom of Proverbs.

Placing Annalee's hat and gloves into the box, the girl gave the contents a narrow look. 'You don't live where I live.'

'Admittedly, Epiphany, I don't. But some principles are universal to the human condition. "What shall it profit a man if he shall gain the whole world and lose his own soul?"' I shifted the cover onto the box, thinking about the hat and gloves. Annalee had so many pieces of clothing, so many accessories. She probably wouldn't even have remembered where these were purchased.

'That's from the Bible. Who told you my name is Epiphany, anyway? It's Epie. That's what people call me now.'

'Why?' I turned to put the box back on the shelf, then stood holding it instead.

'Because I like it. Because Epiphany's a stupid name.'

'It's a charming name.'

'Yeah, like somebody in charm school.' She pushed her hands onto her hips and smirked at me. 'It doesn't fit, you know?'

'I think it fits nicely. It's the sort of name that sets expectation.'

She blew out a puff of air, her eyes casting toward the ceiling in the way of an exasperated teenager.

'Do you even know where it hails from?' I asked. 'The origin of your name . . . Epiphany?'

A shadow crossed her face. Apparently I'd hit upon a dark subject. 'My mama picked it out of a hat, I guess. It don't . . . doesn't mean anything.'

I continued, despite her look of disinterest. I'd worked in

Greece and Italy both, at different times. The name wasn't so uncommon there. 'It's from the Greek *epiphaneia*, meaning "appearance" or "manifestation." It hails back to the feast of the Epiphany in January, which celebrates the revelation of God in human form. It was an important holy day in early Christian traditions. A special day. It's a name to be proud of.'

Tilting her head to one side, Epiphany considered her reflection in the mirror, as if she were seeing something new. 'Huh,' she murmured. 'It means all that? My mama probably hasn't got a clue.'

I stood behind her, watching her watch herself. 'The point is that now you know.'

'Guess I do.' She considered her reflection a moment longer, then turned away, clapping her hands together in front of herself. 'Suppose we oughta go on upstairs and get to work, huh?'

'I suppose we should.' I held the box out to her. 'You take these home with you. You keep them.'

She blinked, her expression filling with such pleasure that I was tempted to allow her to keep anything she wanted from the closet. I should have, but I couldn't bring myself to disturb the way Annalee had left things.

'You mean the whole box?'

'Yes. You think about Jackie Kennedy the next time DeRon comes around. You're as worthy of Camelot as anyone, Epiphany.'

The conversation ended there. Epiphany set the box outside the bedroom door, and we proceeded upstairs to work. The attic was hot today, and before long, a gloss of perspiration coated

Epiphany's skin as she lugged storage containers up and down the stairs.

'Man,' she panted during one of her trips to the office. 'It gets any hotter up there and I'm gonna need one of the pills you got in your pocket.' Swiping a wrist across her forehead, she craned toward my desk, where I was sorting through yet another tub. This one appeared to be filled with old quilts. So far, I'd found nothing of use in a potpourri of containers – just aging holiday decorations, packages upon packages of plastic eggs from some long-forgotten egg hunt, old toys and stuffed animals, yellowed baby clothes.

My hand settled on a Matchbox car, a green metal station wagon with a pull-behind Airstream trailer. A memory whisked across my consciousness, the stroke of a broom stirring up dust that had settled long ago. I was driving along a quiet, winding road near Yellowstone, the tall shadows of the pines falling lazily over the car, sunlight passing in patches. I looked in the rearview mirror. Roy lay curled in the large window ledge above the backseat, his legs knobby and brown, feet small and bare, crusts of dirt between his toes. He drove the miniature car and camper along the top of the seat, annoying his sister. Deborah was busy with a coloring book.

Annalee had purchased the toys for them at a tourist stop to placate their road weariness. Roy met my gaze in the mirror, his eyes sky blue beneath a tussle of red hair. He smiled, a smile so complete in its trust, in its contentment, that the memory, the moment of perfect peace, all of us together in that small space, stayed with me. The moment was fleeting.

Roy soon dangled a foot in Deborah's hair, and she squealed. *Oh, gross, Moh-om! Tell him to stop touching me!*

Examining the tiny car and trailer now, I remembered my son's smile, the instant when everything was perfect, the sense of being fully in the present, fully there. So rare are those moments in a father's life. In my life.

'You findin' anything good in that stuff?' Epiphany's question pulled me from the memory.

'Not what I was looking for.' I set the car on the desk, dug deeper. Baby clothes, more toys, a fairy princess costume to which I could attach no memory. Perhaps it meant something to Annalee. Perhaps it marked a Halloween or a school play during which I was away on business or working overseas.

I finished digging and closed the lid, then slid the container toward Epiphany. This method of searching the attic was slow and unproductive. Were I up there, I could have peeked into these tubs and identified them as being too recent to contain clues to the mystery of the seven chairs. Epiphany, of course, had no idea; nor had I told her exactly what we were searching for.

Frowning at the most recent container, she employed her long lime green fingernails as grooming equipment of sorts, combing and tugging her hair into a springy ponytail. 'You got a rubber band in there anyplace?'

I opened the desk drawer and considered what sort of rubber band might best serve as a hair retention device. Nestled in the tray was an old ink pen – the sort of souvenir a tourist might have bought near the cape. Inside the upper section, a tiny rocket floated between the Earth and the moon. By tipping it, one could cause the rocket to travel through space, then sink back to Earth. I handed it to Epiphany, said, 'Here, you might like this.' Then I felt foolish about it. What would a sixteen-year-old girl want with such a trinket?

Epiphany looked at it, tipping the pen back and forth, watching it as I held a rubber band out to her. She hooked the rubber band between two fingers without handing back the pen. 'Cool.' Lips pursing, she studied the tiny rocket. 'J. Norm, do you think I could, like, borrow some of your rocket stuff? A couple of them . . . those pictures, or maybe one of the rockets in a box that's up in the attic?'

My chair squealed as I leaned back in it, taking a wider view of her. 'What could you possibly want with those things?'

Moving the pen back and forth, she watched the miniature spacecraft. 'That paper for English class – the research report. Well, we've gotta do a talk in history class, too, for a test grade, and I thought I could use the same stuff – you know, kill two birds. The talk has to be about something we think made history different, like an event that changed things. Something important. I read some about the rockets in the magazines you gave me. The rockets were important, right?'

'Yes, they were,' I agreed.

Epiphany nodded. 'I mean, they went to the moon, right? Nobody ever did that before.'

'There were many who didn't even think it was possible.' My thoughts took a fresh breath then, filling with information, facts, dates, and numbers. Old stories bubbled to the surface and I found myself reliving them in the way a worn-out, overweight laborer rehashes his days in high school football. 'But when Howard Hughes put together Hughes Space and Communications, he believed we could. Kennedy wanted a moon landing, and Hughes secured the contract, and we designed and built *Surveyor 1* out in California; then when it was ready, we took it to Cape Canaveral to put it in the nose of an Atlas/Centaur rocket.'

Epiphany's focus turned to me. I had suddenly become more interesting than the pen. 'Whoa, J. Norm, you knew Howard Hughes? I saw a movie about him.'

'Not directly, but his presence, his enthusiasm for the challenge was always felt on our team. We accomplished incredible things at Hughes.' Epiphany's gaze met mine, and I saw myself all those years ago, a youngster not so far out of college, stepping into a man's job, into an important moment in history, feeling as if I might not measure up, as if I were an impostor and might be found out. 'Don't let anyone discourage you because you're young, Epiphany. There was a time when the moon seemed an impossible distance away. People, well-known scientists, believed that if we were able to get *Surveyor 1* to the moon, it would sink beneath the surface and disappear under several feet of dust upon landing. They believed our solar arrays would be covered, and the batteries wouldn't operate at the impossibly cold temperatures of the lunar surface. But you see, there on the wall is the first picture *Surveyor* sent back to Earth, and she is still up there today, asleep on the lunar surface in the Ocean of Storms. So many things are impossible only because we limit ourselves to what others tell us we are capable of.'

Epiphany shifted from one foot to the other and looked at the pen again, breaking the connection between us. 'Geez, you sound like my history teacher. She's young. She hasn't been at this school long enough to know what it's like here.'

'Don't tell her,' I said. 'Let her keep believing. It's a kinder thing.'

Epiphany quirked a one-sided grin and twisted the rubber band around her hair, securing her ponytail. 'You're not gonna go all soft on me, are you, J. Norm? Because you won't be near as much fun that way.'

I chuckled. 'I will endeavor to remain as unpleasant as ever. We should get back to work, then, shouldn't we?'

She walked to the doorway and regarded the attic stairs with a weary expression. I was reminded again of the inefficiency of our process. In the attic alone, I could accomplish so much more. 'Why don't you go down and fix a drink and a sandwich for us?' I suggested, but somehow I must have subconsciously hinted at my intentions, because Epiphany stood her ground in the doorway, shaking her head.

'Because you'll go right up the stairs the minute I turn my back.' She wagged her head side to side in a manner most confrontational. 'It's *hot* up there, too. Way too hot.'

I slapped a hand on the desk, suddenly frustrated, tired, losing hope. 'What we're doing is not efficient. We have to find a better way.'

'Well, you're not going up there, or I'm gonna tell Deborah. You and me made a deal, remember? And what's the major rush, anyhow? That attic's not going anywhere.'

But I could be, I thought, even though I didn't say it. There was never any telling when a turn in my health could render me incapable of living in this house, or whether Deborah would finally manage to force me out. If the clue to the seven chairs was here, I had to find it before it was too late. Sometime last night, I'd dreamed about a house on fire. I'd smelled the smoke, seen the flames. It was the house with the seven chairs. Something had happened there. Something real, something horrible. An event that was part of who I was. A hidden part. I couldn't leave this world without finding it.

Epiphany's posture softened, her silver-flecked eyes blinking slowly, the long lashes hovering a moment on her cheeks before she looked at me again. 'J. Norm, what in the world are you really lookin' for up there?'

'Myself,' I said, and then I told her the story of the house on fire.

CHAPTER 10

Epiphany Jones

After J. Norm told me about the house with the seven chairs, I wanted to dig through every box in the attic. It was a mystery, and I like mysteries, so I kept working even after J. Norm got sleepy and went downstairs for a nap. I was afraid he'd say I needed to go on home now, but he didn't, and I was glad. Home was the last place I wanted to be.

The closer it came toward evening, the more nervous I got. Sooner or later, I'd have to leave, and with Mama and Russ gone, there was DeRon to think about. What if he came by tonight? Part of me was still saying I was stupid for not doing whatever it took to be DeRon's girlfriend. Guys like DeRon expected a real woman. Of course he figured that if we were going out, we were gonna go out *all* the way. DeRon knew his way around a girl . . .

I felt sick, standing there thinking about it. *You're as worthy of Camelot as anyone, Epiphany.* J. Norm's voice was in my head. It wasn't Camelot to have some guy grope all over you in a car and tear your shirt. What if I was alone with DeRon again, and I panicked again, and this time he went ahead and got what he wanted?

Maybe it'd be easier to just give in, I thought, and my brain went through the whole thing again. *Yes. No. Why not? What if? Who else is ever gonna like me?* If I didn't make up with DeRon, school would be torture. Everybody would be on me, and DeRon would be right in there with them.

Finally, I went downstairs. It was time to catch the bus home before it got too dark. My insides were bubbling like water in a hot pot when I found J. Norm in the living room.

'Any luck in the attic?' he asked, giving the stairs a tired look. He was probably too wiped out to go up there and get in any trouble tonight. His skin was chalky and kind of bluish.

'Not so far, but I'll find it. There's lots of cool things in the attic, though. I got a little distracted looking at the toy rockets and stuff. Sorry.'

'Take any of those models you'd like for your project.' He backhanded toward the stairs like he didn't care what I got from up there. 'Most of them are in pieces inside the boxes, though. I could help you with the assembly when you come on Tuesday, if you like.'

Tuesday . . . Tuesday seemed like a long way off – a whole night and a day at home by myself and then two days at school. 'Sure, that'd be cool.' I took a step toward the door and it felt like somebody was pulling a piano wire tight inside me, wrapping it around and around my lungs. I stopped in the entryway door, blurted out, 'Hey, I got an idea. We could do it now.' By the time we put some rocket together, it'd be dark and way too late for me to catch the bus. I could bunk on J. Norm's couch. Nobody'd know the difference but him and me.

J. Norm's bottom lip pushed up into his top one, making halfmoon wrinkles in his chin. 'You'll miss your bus.'

I swallowed a lump the size of a baseball and words came out. 'I could just stay here. I was thinking I could come back in the morning anyhow, since tomorrow's Sunday. If I just stayed, I could keep looking through boxes till way late, maybe all night, because I don't sleep a lot. But if I get tired, I can just, like, crash on the sofa. I'll call my mom and tell her. It'll be all right with her, so long as I'm working. She doesn't care.' That last part was both true and a lie, of course. Mama didn't care, but I wasn't about to call her.

Rocking back in the recliner, J. Norm scrunched his nose like he smelled stink. 'It's a bit difficult to feature, a parent not caring whether her daughter stays overnight in a house with a single man.'

'Geez, J. Norm. Yuck!' If I wasn't sick before, I was after he said that. 'I'm not staying *with* you; I'm crashing on your sofa, and besides that, you're *old*. You could, like, be my *grandpa*. It's not the same thing at all.'

He drummed his fingers on the arm of the chair. 'But I'm not your grandfather.'

He said it like he was glad, and for a second I felt a little stab – the kind that always comes when you know somebody just wants to get rid of you. Big, stupid tears needled my eyes and I felt like an idiot. 'Yeah, well, lucky for you, right?' Of course J. Norm didn't want me hanging around all night.

I looked past him out the window. In the backyard, all the birds were gone and the shadows of the trees hung long and deep. I needed to leave now, walk out the door and head for the bus. I had a little money in my pocket. I could ride the bus around all night, then go back home and change clothes in the morning.

J. Norm was blabbering on. 'It wasn't my intention to offend . . . I mean to say that . . . I was . . . I was merely considering the practicalities of –'

I cut him off. 'You know what, just never mind, all right? I was stupid to bring it up.'

I heard the footrest click shut on his chair. 'But you aren't stupid, Epiphany, so you must have a reason. One other than putting together rockets or spending the evening sifting through old boxes. Suppose you try being honest with me, then?'

'Whatever,' I said. 'I gotta go catch the bus. I shouldn't have bothered you.' I looked around for my stuff and then realized I didn't have it – just my keys in my pocket. It was time to quit being such a baby about the thing with DeRon. I was sixteen, after all. I was probably, like, the only girl in the school who hadn't been with somebody. Afterward, I'd probably be glad I just . . . got it all over with. At least everybody would think I was normal.

'Are there problems at home, Epiphany?' I heard J. Norm suck air through his teeth when he stood up. He stumbled a little when the chair bounced back. 'We don't mince words, you and I, now, do we?'

'There's nothing wrong at home.' It figured he would

150

make a federal case about this. Adults were always that way. 'I gotta go.' I heard him shuffling across the room as I headed for the door. He turned and started down the hall toward his bedroom, and even that hurt me a little bit. I guess I wanted him to chase me down or something.

I messed around turning the locks, then opened the door and smelled night coming. Chills went over me. J. Norm was coming up the hall, puffing air like he'd just run a mile. He rounded the corner with the hatbox in his hands, but he took one look at my face and set the box on a side table.

'What in heaven's name . . .' he muttered.

'Look, there's just nobody at home, and I don't want to go there tonight, okay?' I said. 'Mama and Russ are gone selling at a gun show for the weekend, and it's just . . . well . . . DeRon, okay. He's probably still ticked at me.'

J. Norm blinked real slow, like I wasn't making sense. 'I believe it's you who should be . . . *ticked*, Epiphany.'

'Whatever.' The last thing I wanted right then was a lecture. 'So can I stay here or not?'

J. Norm stuck his hands in his pockets and jingled some coins in there, like he was going to decide the answer by how they sounded. Then finally he said, 'All right. Provided your mother approves.'

I thought about pretending to call Mama, but then if J. Norm said something to her about it when she came to clean his house, there'd be a problem. 'Listen, since we're not keeping secrets and all, I'll just tell you. There's nobody to call. They're at some campground someplace, and they probably can't get cell service. They're not gonna call home to check on me. They never do, and we don't even have a home phone anymore. They don't want to be bothered. That's just how they are, okay?'

J. Norm took a long time to answer again. For a minute I thought he'd tell me no, but then he shrugged like it was all the same to him. He backed up a few steps so I could shut the door behind me. 'I don't approve of this business with that boy, that DeRon, though. If he's threatening you, something should be done about it. An assault like that should be reported – to your mother and to the authorities.'

Panic zipped through me like an electric shock, but I tried to keep my face calm, so it wouldn't show. 'Listen, DeRon and me were just goofing around. It was my fault, too, and if Mama finds out, there's no telling what she'll do to me for being in DeRon's car. The whole thing is no big deal. Guys like DeRon just . . . expect stuff, okay?' I wished I hadn't brought up DeRon again. I didn't want to talk about him or think about it anymore. 'You don't know how things are nowdays, J. Norm, that's all.'

'I don't believe I want to.' He headed for the living room, shaking his head. 'Let's have some dinner, and then we'll get back to work. We'll leave the rocket building until morning, when the light is better and my eyes are good.'

'Yeah.' I let out a sigh, but under my breath where he couldn't hear it.

We ate a quick sandwich in the kitchen, and then went back to work. The attic was cooler after the sun went down, but it was dark up there, too, with just a couple lights overhead. The house creaked and groaned, and tree branches

152

scratched on the walls, so that it felt like I wasn't alone in there. I thought about how many people must've lived and died in a house this old. I don't really believe in ghosts, but still, it was creepy.

I figured out some things about J. Norm while I was up getting boxes for him. There was a reason he had a stack of boys' furniture and toys in the attic and an empty room on the second floor of the house. J. Norm had a son, Roy. He died in a car wreck when he was a senior in high school. In one of the plastic tubs, I found a bunch of his old books and drawings – cards he'd made on Mother's Day, school projects, some trophies he won in sports, and school pictures of him. Somebody had packed his stuff away real carefully, and on top of it all was the paper from his funeral. There was also a diary his mom wrote – just letters to him, telling how much she missed him. I thought about asking J. Norm about Roy, but I decided I shouldn't.

While J. Norm was looking through boxes, he told me more about the dreams he'd been having and how he wanted to know if it was something that'd really happened. 'The odd thing is that each time it occurs, I see something new – just scattered bits, puzzle pieces tossed at random.'

'I only dream about stuff that's not true – like flying and things like that,' I told him. He was closing the boxes, and I could see myself about to take another trip up the stairs. 'But I guess somebody could have true dreams. Maybe even see things they didn't know they remembered.' I thought about my father. Did he ever see me or hold me when I was little, before he died? He must've, because that had to be his family in the shoe box pictures at home. If I tried really hard, maybe I could dream about him and see what he was like.

I took the latest load of rejects and headed back up the attic stairs, and for a while, it was up, down, up, down, up, down. Finally, J. Norm was ready to turn in for the night. He showed me where I could sleep. 'This was Deborah's room,' he said, opening the door to a room that had lacy curtains, a bed with four tall white posts, and a ruffled canopy like the one I dreamed about in my Someday Book. The shelves on the other side of the room looked like they could've been a boy's, though. They were loaded down with model cars and rockets and gadgets made out of old Tinkertoys, nails, screws, bottle caps, and other stuff.

'Cool,' I said, swinging a pendulum on one of them and wondering what it was meant to do. 'Who made all these?'

On his way out the door, J. Norm gave the shelves a glance. 'Those are Deborah's creations. You can see that she had more interest in those than in dolls. She steadfastly resisted her mother's attempts to turn her into a girl. Stubborn to the last.' His lips squeezed up like he'd just swallowed a spoonful of vinegar. He always looked like that when he talked about Deborah – like he had a bad taste in his mouth.

For a sec, I felt sorry for her. I knew what it was like to have somebody who should love you not like you very much. 'That's cool,' I said. 'You think she'd care if I used a couple of these rockets for my project?'

'I don't think she cares about any of it.' He went out the door, and I thought about what it'd be like to grow up in a place like this. It seemed like a girl who got this kind of a room would have to be happy, but whenever Deborah and J. Norm had anything to do with each other, they seemed about as unhappy as people could get. It must've been hard for J. Norm's wife, loving two people who hated each other, and also having a dead son. *Maybe she's glad not to be here, having to deal with it anymore*, I thought. After going to a bunch of funerals with Mrs Lora, I'd decided that, once you get to heaven, you don't have family fights anymore. Everybody just gets along and loves everybody else. That's what makes it heaven.

I went back up to the attic to work some more on the pile of plastic boxes where J. Norm's wife had stored their family memories. It was after midnight when I finished. By then, the moon had come up outside one of the windows where the roof jutted out in a long tunnel. The peak was barely high enough for me to stand in, and old boxes and trunks sat piled against both walls, so there was just a narrow path to the window. On the other side of the glass, the moon was big and bright, so close it seemed like I could stretch out an arm and touch its face.

I took a few steps toward the glass, the attic floor creaking under my feet. Around me, the air was musty and still, so thick with dust it hung gritty in my throat. Outside, the moon glowed with patches of dark and light, the shadows of hills and valleys and craters. Somewhere up there, J. Norm's machine, *Surveyor I*, was sitting in the shallow dust, as silent as the toy rockets on Deborah's shelf, a relic nobody thought about anymore. But it meant something once. Once, it was the most important thing in the world.

It was still there, even if no one could see it. Maybe it would sit all alone for a hundred more years, or a thousand. What would it feel like to look at the moon and know that what you built was up there? One of these days, I was gonna do something like that – something so big it would change the world, and people would talk about it forever. I didn't want to be like Mama, or DeRon, or the rest of those losers at school. I was gonna be different . . .

My mind flew a million miles away, left the attic behind for a minute. I thought about the future, and what it might be like . . . and then I heard scratching and chewing in the wall right next to me. *Yeah, this part of the attic can wait until daylight*, I decided, and backed away. My foot caught the edge of some picture frames, and they fell, sending up a clatter that made my heart jump.

A sliver of moonlight caught the place where the frames had been. It pressed through the wall of boxes and reflected against something metal. I leaned in, got closer. Something *was* back there, tucked way under the eaves – a trunk with brass corners. It looked like the one that'd chased J. Norm down the stairs, only smaller.

Scooting the boxes a couple inches, I checked it out a little more. Maybe if I could push it along under the eaves, I could get it loose without unstacking all the stuff in front of it.

Whatever was chewing inside the wall stopped when I scooted into the narrow triangle between the boxes and the roof. Cobwebs slid over my arm, and I caught a breath, the sound dying in the dark space by the wall. All of a sudden, I felt like things were crawling all over my skin – creepy little things with six or eight legs. I pictured red-eyed rats, and black bats, and other creatures you'd see on Halloween. J. Norm was so gonna owe me extra for this. But if I didn't haul the trunk out of here now, I probably never would. Once I got out of this spot, no way I was crawling back in here again.

I sat down and wedged my feet against the trunk, bracing my hands behind me and pushing it through the tunnel. The metal corners let out a long, high whine as they scraped along. I felt them grinding deeper and deeper into the wood floor before the trunk hit a rafter and wedged solid. Hopefully, it was far enough that I could grab it from the other end and wiggle it on out.

A few minutes later and a few pulls from the other side, and the trunk came loose all at once, toppling over. Something shattered inside, and right then I felt a breeze on my shoulders, like someone was behind me breathing on the back of my neck, waiting for me to tip the box upright. I heard whispering, and a quick, high-pitched sound, like a little girl laughing. I thought about J. Norm's story – the little red-haired girls playing on the stairs and then his dream about a fire. Maybe he'd had friends or relatives that'd died when a house burned down, and they were, like, haunting this trunk, and whoever opened it would be in trouble.

'All right,' I told myself. 'You been in the attic w-a-a-ay too long. There's probably fumes up here.'

Pieces of glass filtered down like sand in an hourglass as I turned the trunk over. One thing was for sure: This baby wasn't full of magazines.

Something dark, like a shadow, moved in the corner of my eye. I thought about that TV show where they go to old houses and hunt for ghosts.

Then again, maybe this thing was hidden for a reason . . .

Leaning close, I studied the latches, tried the sliders different ways, but they wouldn't budge. There was an old-timey keyhole in the center, which probably meant the trunk was locked. No telling where a key might be, or if there even was a key. After all that work, I was out of luck.

Crossing my arms on the trunk, I sagged over it and let my forehead rest against the cool metal.

So much for my big discovery.

CHAPTER 11

J. Norman Alvord

The little girls came to me in a dream again. They were running on a lawn this time. I stood at the edge of a brick patio, my feet in small, brown polished-leather shoes, with socks that stretched to the height of knobby knees, meeting gray short pants. A toddler boy ran with the girls, his red hair in curls like theirs. They'd discovered a patch of dandelions near an ornate wrought-iron fence. The girls picked a few and the toddler stood very still while they held the flowers under his chin. 'See if you like butter,' they cried. 'See if you like butter, Johnny!'

The boy's name was Johnny. I realized now that I knew it. I had always known it.

'He does! He does like butter! His chin's all yella!' The girls squealed, and the little boy fingered his neck, trying to feel the change in color. 'Johnny likes butter!' The girls darted off across the yard, their dandelion bouquets leading the way. 'Cecile, let's see if you like butter.'

'I don' like no buttah.' The maid, Cecile, was sitting on a concrete bench with lion's paws capping the legs. She held a baby, a chubby-cheeked, red-haired cherub, loosely in front of herself, dangling the baby's tiny feet, letting the grass tickle them. Smiling, Cecile lifted her chin to accommodate the dandelion bouquets. 'I don' like no buttah, no how. No, ma'am.'

The girls squatted in the grass, craning to gain a view of her neck. The skin there was as smooth and dark as a coffee bean, glistening with a sheen of perspiration. The day was warm, the girls dressed in simple white smocks, their thin, freckled arms dangling from oval-shaped openings that left their shoulders bare.

'Yes, you do!' squealed the bolder of the two, Erin. I knew her name now. I knew it as if I had always known. Erin, the bold one, and Emma, fully an inch shorter, more timid than Erin. The twins. 'You like butter!' they squealed in perfect unison, as if it were planned. They lowered the flowers to the baby's chin. 'Poobie likes butter, too!'

'I bet big bubbie like buttah.' Cecile nodded toward me, tipping her chin up, her lips pressing to one side so as to form a dimple in her cheek. 'Bet he like it a lot, much as he like to eat him a biscuit.' Her gaze met mine, and she winked. 'You like that dandelion buttah, Willie-boy?'

'No,' I said. I was in a foul mood, determined not to enjoy the dandelion game or any other. When the twins ran to me with their flowers, I rose onto my toes, slapped their hands away. Stretching her bouquet upward, Emma grabbed my arm. Even her slight weight caused pain, and I pushed her away hard enough that she stumbled off the patio and fell backward into the grass.

'Stop it, Willie!' Stiff armed, Erin threw her weight against me, her palms colliding with my chest. I let her bounce off and pretended to laugh at her. Stomping a foot, she plucked Emma off the ground, and they darted away, their dandelion bouquets scattered in the damp grass. With the bottom of my shoe, I ground the flowers into the soil until only dirty yellow shreds remained, and then I grabbed my arm where Emma had touched it, rubbed it because it hurt. I was aching in more places than just that one. The pain was Erin's doing.

She'd made the racket that caused it to happen.

Yet today she could run and laugh and play the butter game. It wasn't fair. Everything was different today. Wrong. There was a heaviness inside me, a newly cast shadow that kept me from playing with the girls every bit as much as the pain did. I was angry, afraid, ashamed, hiding a painful secret now, moving quietly through the world so as to go unnoticed. Worse yet, I knew this was only the beginning of something terrible. Something that would continue to worsen.

Together, the girls moved to the corner of the yard to pluck tiny puffs filled with dandelion parachutes.

I watched them show Johnny how to blow across them, sending the little soldiers skyward with their miniature canopies of silk.

I wanted to rip every last seed head from the yard, grind all of them into dust so that no one could play with them, so that no one could laugh, and run, and make noise.

I felt Cecile's gaze upon me, and I turned my attention

her way. Her dark eyes narrowed and her wide lips pursed. The angle of her head was thoughtful, pensive, wary. Her gaze moved to the house, sweeping upward, reflecting brick and stone and sky. On the second story, she paused and honed in, then quickly looked away.

I turned to check over my shoulder. A woman was in the window, a filmy white nightgown outlining her breasts, draping off one thin shoulder. A slip of red hair fell over her cheek, and she pushed it aside with the back of her wrist.

She looked down at me. I turned away. I let my arm fall to my side. I stopped rubbing it. I didn't want anyone to see.

It would only cause more pain. More fighting . . .

I woke from the dream with a familiar ache. *There are some old fractures here*, a doctor had told me while reading my X-rays after a minor car accident in college. He'd been surprised to find evidence of an injury from long ago. *There's some damage that never healed properly. Any idea why?*

None, I'd said. My mother had always been meticulous about shots and doctor visits, protective to the point of not allowing me beyond the yard fence when I was a boy. She'd never mentioned my having broken an arm when I was very small. I didn't recall having broken an arm.

The doctor tilted his face toward the X-ray again. *Hard to believe that. This must have been quite painful.* Shaking his head, he turned off the light.

Maybe I blocked it out, I said flippantly, and laughed it off. At the time, I had no memory of holding my arm that day in the yard while the girls played with dandelions. Strange that I remembered it so clearly now.

How is it possible to find a part of the past that was never there before?

The question haunted me as I went to the kitchen for coffee. It was warm and ready, thanks to the timer on the pot – one of those many modern conveniences for which I should have been grateful. Still, I missed the days when the sun rose to the sound of Annalee's slippers in the kitchen and the percolator belching, draining, belching again. The mornings had a rhythm then, the sense of a life building toward something, brewing like the coffee in the percolator, giving off a tantalizing aroma.

Now the coffee brewed quickly, and the morning's aroma was stale.

I'd never realized the difference until now, hadn't given a conscious thought to Annalee's morning sounds, but the memory was there nonetheless. An unexamined fragment, until this moment. It is possible, I concluded, to lose a bit of life – a moment, a sensation, a memory – for it to lie trapped like a bit of paper along the curb of a walking path. A stiff wind passes and it suddenly tumbles free, drifts past your eyes, so that you see it now.

Gazing through the window into the yard, I noticed for the first time that dandelions had sprouted near Annalee's bird feeders. Like my memories, they seemed to have appeared overnight, but in reality, they'd been growing for a while. Beneath the surface, the roots were deep.

I heard the water running upstairs and my mind hiccuped. Someone was singing, a girl's voice. For an instant I was lost in time, and Deborah was upstairs, dressing for church. Any moment now, Annalee would come around the corner on her way to force Roy from his bed and into the Sunday clothes he didn't want to wear.

I turned and checked the coffeemaker. Modern, sleek, with a digital clock on the front. Deborah and Roy weren't upstairs.

A melancholy fell over me, but then I recalled Epiphany and our mission, and life spiraled back to order. She came loping down the stairs a few minutes later, bounded through the living room and slid around the corner into the kitchen, dark hair bouncing in a ponytail of long spirals, her eyes wide and full of excitement. 'You're gonna be so glad you said I could stay last night.'

'And why would that be?' I did my best to affect the look of a curmudgeon. I couldn't, after all, be giving off the impression that last night's arrangements implied a repeat invitation.

'Just guess,' she chirped.

'I couldn't begin to.'

'Oh, come on, J. Norm, be a little fun for once.' Without hesitation, she helped herself to a mug from the cabinet and poured a cup of coffee, then added sugar and milk.

'Fun?' Her enthusiasm traveled on the coffee fumes, slipping up my nose like an infectious disease. I snorted, tried to rub it away. 'Fun isn't the goal. This is a working arrangement, after all. What is *fun* about digging around in an old man's attic?'

Opening the refrigerator again, she leaned down and looked inside, splaying her lanky legs like a colt trying to

164

reach fresh grass. 'It's fun when you find something.' She opened and closed a drawer. 'You got *anything* here for breakfast?'

'I don't like breakfast.'

She blew out a laugh. 'Why doesn't that surprise me?' Shrugging, she pulled out a loaf of bread and set it on the counter. 'Fine, then, I'll just sit here and I won't even tell you what I found last night. Just about broke my neck getting it out, but that's okay. If you don't wanna know, then I'll make me a piece of toast and go watch some cartoons. Same difference to me.'

'It's an oxymoron – same difference. Things are either the same or they're different.'

Sighing, she pushed the bread aside. 'How come you do that?' Her attention turned my way. 'Argue about everything? Act hateful.'

It was a fair question, one for which I did not have a good answer. 'It entertains me.'

My reply elicited a one-sided smirk. 'Yeah, well, then you need to get a life.'

'I'll take that under advisement.' I waited for her to tell me what she'd found upstairs, but she returned to making toast, ignoring me completely. Finally she smacked the butter knife down so hard that it rang against the plate. 'Geez, J. Norm, are you gonna ask what I found upstairs or not?'

'I supposed you'd tell me soon enough,' I answered, disproportionately triumphant.

Snorting, she leaned over her folded arms. 'I found a trunk. Another one, just like the one with all the magazines

165

in it, only smaller.' Her hands flipped through the air, the palms turning upward. 'What can I say? I am goo-oo-ood.'

'I couldn't agree more,' I answered, and was out of my chair in a whistle.

In short order, we were in the second-story hall with the trunk and a toolbox. We'd lowered the trunk down the attic stairs using a rope and pulley – rather ingenious, if I do say so myself. The lock was a more complicated matter, however.

While I went to work with a screwdriver and an ice pick, Epiphany chewed a fingernail. 'If it's more magazines and junk, I'm gonna snatch somebody's hair out.'

Anticipation filled me, seeming almost overwhelming. 'Well, not mine, please. I haven't much left.'

She jittered impatiently, leaning closer as I managed to trip the lock and prepared to throw open the lid. 'Ten . . . nine . . . eight . . . seven . . . six . . . five . . .'

But as the trunk began to creak open and the odor of must and yellowed paper wafted into the hall, Epiphany grabbed my arm. 'Ssshhh! J. Norm, hold still.' She cocked an ear toward the stairway, as if she'd heard something. A moment later, I caught it, too. The sound of the front door locks turning, then the door colliding with the security chain. 'Deborah!' I whispered, and Epiphany nodded. I stood up and started down the stairs. 'Drag that into Roy's room and stay there with it.' I pointed down the hall. It was too early to explain Epiphany's presence here on a Sunday, and most certainly I couldn't let Deborah know that Epiphany had been here overnight. Deborah would be suspicious, concerned that I was getting in over my head, letting myself be taken advantage of. She'd feel the need to involve herself, perhaps discuss the issue with Epiphany's mother. My best hope was to be as agreeable as possible and send Deborah on her way quickly.

I descended to the entry, surprised to find that the door had been pulled to, and Deborah was no longer trying to breach the security chain. Perhaps she'd decided to come in through the garage. Moving to the parlor window, I pulled the sheers aside. A car was rolling up to the curb out front – the older-model sort that didn't belong in this neighborhood, and Deborah had started across the lawn. From her body language, it was clear that the driver had called her over.

A young man with some sort of scarf tied around his head leaned out the car window and flipped a hand haughtily toward the house, as if he were demanding information. Deborah, being Deborah, undoubtedly answered him curtly, then pointed toward the street in a way that indicated he should move along now. She glanced toward her vehicle in front of the garage, where my math professor son-in-law, a laid-back fellow not given to unnecessary socializing, appeared to be unbuckling his seat belt. My daughter was a confident woman, accustomed to ruling over college-age research assistants and graduate students, but even Lloyd recognized that neither this young man nor his behavior belonged here.

Lloyd opened his car door as Deborah pointed toward the street, telling the young man in the car once again that he should move on. Finally, he withdrew through the window, then slung something out. It skittered across the driveway, and he bade it farewell with an obscene hand gesture before leaving the premises with a squeal of tires. On her way back to the house, Deborah scooped up his discard, and I recognized it as Epiphany's backpack. Clearly the boy in the car was the infamous DeRon, and he hadn't come to apologize.

I unlocked the front door and let Deborah enter on her own. Lloyd, who had probably intended to wait in the vehicle, followed her into the house. He hovered in the living room doorway, seeming wary of potential family drama as Deborah dropped the backpack on the sofa. 'How late did your little helper stay last night?'

'Why do you ask?' I replied, and then exchanged morning pleasantries with my son-in-law.

Deborah's brow furrowed. 'Well, apparently Epiphany didn't come home last night. There was someone . . . either a brother or a boyfriend outside just now, looking for her. He wasn't very nice about it, and he didn't want to take no for an answer. Sounds to me like she's in some sort of trouble.'

'I'm sure she's fine.' I rushed the words out, and then realized they sounded callously unconcerned. 'Undoubtedly, she stayed over with a friend and forgot to leave word. You know how teenagers can be.'

Deborah rubbed her arms, and I could see the wheels turning. She was thinking that this arrangement with Epiphany might not be a good idea any longer. 'You didn't see the way that boy was acting out there. If she has . . . issues, I don't want her here.'

I shifted quickly to damage control. 'Nonsense. She's been very reliable. She already called this morning to confirm that she was coming again today to work on her school project. She's writing about the rocket launches. She'll be here later this morning.'

Deborah smacked her lips irritably. 'You're going to church with us today, remember? They're having a special luncheon after the service. They're dedicating the paving stones in the memory garden, including Mom's.' Since Annalee's death, Deborah had become a regular in church again, and active in the project of paving the sidewalks in the memory garden with stones dedicated to members who had passed on. Deborah felt she owed this to her mother, I supposed, as Annalee had always been the driving force behind our involvement with the church. Annalee would patiently endure my long work hours and the months I was away in foreign countries, but she would not stand for taking the Lord's name in vain or missing service on Sundays. These days, I could not bear to set foot in that place without her, and in truth, God and I didn't have much to say to each other. We'd ceased to be on speaking terms. Aside from that, Deborah's foremost mission on any trip out of the house was to drag me by the Villas.

'You and Lloyd go ahead without me. I'm not up to it today.' I turned away to avoid seeing her disappointment. She was proud of the memory walk project, of course.

'I knew I shouldn't have bothered.' Deborah's words were sharp edged and bitter. In the doorway, Lloyd winced and looked at his feet.

'I've had a difficult night,' I added, attempting to soften my posture a little. 'It isn't a good time.'

'It never is.' She proceeded toward the door, her dress shoes clicking across the entryway in a rapid tattoo. Lloyd gave me an apologetic look.

'Tell her I'm sorry. I simply don't feel well,' I said, a damper falling on the morning. Why was it that Deborah and I could never avoid treating each other badly, nipping from opposite sides of the fence?

'I will.' Lloyd said good-bye and followed Deborah out the door.

After they were gone, I proceeded upstairs and tried to leave the trouble with Deborah behind me.

Epiphany was sitting in my office, doodling on a notepad. She angled a frown my way. 'She left kinda quick. What'd she want?'

'To drag me off to church,' I answered, the sour mood clinging to me, flavoring everything.

'You could've gone. I would've waited.'

'I have no desire to go,' I said, surprised that Epiphany's mind wasn't squarely on the trunk. 'Next thing, those people would begin coming around with casseroles and inviting me to domino games again. I don't want the bother of it.'

Epiphany responded with a sardonic look. 'Geez, J. Norm. People are just trying to be nice. You might try being nice back once in a while.'

'I think I'm beyond needing the counsel of a sixteen-year-old.' The comment was harsh, and I regretted it, but couldn't bring myself to say so.

'You know . . . whatever.' Setting down the pen, she stood up behind the desk. 'But I'm not the one going around with some big ol' frown on my face, hating everybody. Maybe you'd be happier if you'd eat a few casseroles and go to some domino games. Just sayin'.'

'I'll renew my attendance in a house of worship the day they wheel me through in a coffin.' The words were meant to shock the conversation to a standstill. Deborah would have found them horrifying, but Epiphany only scoffed under her breath, as if she knew I hadn't the courage to face my own death when the moment came.

'Seems like that's a bad time to start back to church,' she said blandly.

Any appropriate retort escaped me. 'I'll thank you to stay out of my personal life.'

'Pppff!' She rolled her eyes. 'What personal life?'

'There is a history between Deborah and me that you know nothing about,' I countered. Deborah had been heaping her resentments upon me for as long as I could recall. She blamed me for ruining her life, for being indirectly responsible for Roy's death and Annalee's, for moving the family to Dallas when Deborah was fifteen and forcing her to leave behind her friends, for her difficulty forming lasting relationships with men, for the fact that she'd devoted herself to work rather than having a family, for her struggle with a midlife marriage. Every problem in her life hailed back to my inadequacy as a father. It was all my fault.

Never once had she been the least bit grateful for the sacrifices I'd made, for the work I did to provide a comfortable future for her – good neighborhoods, private lessons, expensive schools, clothes, and cars, and country club memberships. A man sacrifices his life for those things, and then everyone criticizes him for it.

'Sure, whatever.' Epiphany looked away, her smile dimming. I'd wounded her this time.

Silence fell over us, and the office seemed claustrophobic. I felt compelled to say something. 'Did you hear Deborah when she came in? That boy, DeRon, was outside. She saw him.'

Epiphany's eyes widened, her mouth falling open. Her hand slid upward unconsciously, touched the place where the strap was missing on the shirt underneath the one that was Annalee's. 'DeRon was here? What did he want?'

'You,' I replied. 'It would appear that he went by your home last night looking for you.'

Slapping a hand to her stomach, she clenched her fingers over the shirt and turned her attention to the street outside the window. 'He knows I didn't go home . . .'

'It's a good thing you didn't,' I pointed out. 'I don't like the look of him – the way he acts, the way he behaved toward Deborah. In front of my home, no less. He has a nerve coming here, making demands. I think we should have the police go by and give him a talking-to.'

'No!' she snapped almost before I could finish the sentence. 'Leave it alone, all right? You'll make it worse.'

'I don't see how putting the boy on notice can be a bad idea. He should understand that such behavior won't be tolerated – that other people know about it, and aside from that, a bully doesn't operate well in the light of day.'

She faced me, her lips tight with fury. 'I said *no*, all right? Just leave it alone. I got a personal life, too, all right? I can take care of myself.' She picked up the piece of paper and pitched it in the trash. 'Let's just go open the stupid trunk.'

'All right,' I agreed, but the problem of DeRon remained in the corner of my mind like a spider on a web as we proceeded to Roy's room. Epiphany moved to the trunk, placing her hands on her hips with an impatient expression. I remembered Deborah, a little girl with a big mind, stomping her feet and assuming the same stance, her hair bouncing from side to side as she directed her brother in games of playing house, or Simon Says, or freeze tag. It was no wonder she was successful in her career. She'd determined herself ruler of the world from the very start. In the wake of the thought came a sensation of profound emptiness. Why were those memories usually so far away from me? Why was it so much easier to see the bitterness between us, the same resentments, stale and musty like the air rising from the old trunk as I lifted the lid?

Epiphany leaned over my shoulder, fanning her nose as the contents came into view. A tattered quilt lay on top – a baby quilt made of blocks embroidered with terrier puppies in faded blue and red. I slid a hand over the fabric, felt its crusty threads beneath my fingers.

In my mind, the fabric became new, soft, comforting. I smelled washing soap, the fresh air of the clothesline, saw the way light passed through the weave. I was hiding underneath the quilt. A man thundered past in the hallway, his voice rising, a wire rug beater striking his pants leg and scraping the wall, the sound echoing through the house.

'J. Norm? Are you okay? What's wrong?' Epiphany's fingers touched my arm, and I jerked away.

'No . . . no . . . I only . . . I remember this blanket.' Never, under any circumstances, would my father, a dignified, self-controlled person who put most of his efforts into his business, have behaved in such a manner. Never would my mother have left me in a house in which I was not safe – even under the care of a neighbor, a friend, or a relative. A mother who wouldn't even allow her child down to the corner for a sidewalk game of marbles would never do that.

She wouldn't have left me in the house with the seven chairs. Nor would she have abided the ranting and threatening, the drunken slurs of a man. My mother was a formidable woman, tall, rawboned, stately, direct, not to be trifled with.

She loved me to distraction.

Would she have kept some part of my history secreted away all my life?

Would she have crafted falsehoods, convinced me to believe things about myself that weren't true? Would she have lied about who I was? Could there have been a time when I wasn't with her? Could there have been a life before?

But what could account for the baby pictures hanging in the hallway of our home when I was young? There were black-and-white photographs of her holding a chubby-cheeked cherub in a long white christening gown. I knew all the details of our life in Houston, before my father had moved his offices to Dallas. Mother spoke often of our home there, of the magnolia trees and how I loved to play under them, of our little summerhouse by the seashore where I ran about in the waves. I remembered those places. I knew exactly how they looked. I remembered the towering palms in front of the original beach house, the one that had been swept away by a hurricane when I was young.

'What is it, J. Norm?' Epiphany squeezed my arm, her voice laced with intrigue. 'What do you remember?'

'I . . . don't know.' Lifting the quilt, I fingered the fabric. The memory of the quilt was different from those bits of early family history my mother so often told me about. The quilt was unlike the beach house or our home in Houston. The memory of the quilt was full, and real, tactile. I knew not only the sight of it, but also the feel, the touch, the scent, the sound. The memory surrounded me, wound through me, transported me, so that I was once again in the body of a young boy, wrapped beneath that quilt. I was cuddling it under my chin this time, ready for bed in the house with the seven chairs. The night was peaceful, but still I was afraid.

A hand stroked my hair; a smooth, dark arm grazed my forehead. Soft lips kissed the skin there. 'Don' worry, Willie-boy,' she whispered, her voice melodious and low, as if she caressed the words in her throat before releasing them. 'Cecile gon' watch over. I gon' be right here.' She moved then to a fainting couch in the corner of the room and hummed a hymn. 'Children Go Where I Send Thee.' I let my eyes fall closed, fingered the edge of the blanket, touched something I knew would be there.

Children, go where I send thee,
How shall I send thee?
I'm gonna send thee one-by-one,
One for the little baby boy . . .

Now I unfolded the blanket on Roy's floor, searched the corner, found the threads my fingers had stroked in the memory – an embroidered heart, red at one time, outlined in blue, now faded to gray and lavender.

Inside the heart lay the name of the maker who had so painstakingly created the patchwork of plaid terrier pups. *Cecile.* The letters were a clumsy block, part capital, part small, but the name inside the heart was unmistakable. Cecile was real, and she'd sewn this quilt and put me to bed in it, and watched over me as I slept.

'My mother didn't have a black maid when I was a boy,' I said, and Epiphany leaned away from me.

'What?'

'She couldn't abide the rules of it. There were rules in those days – ordinances, segregation laws, social conventions. My mother was from Boston, and she couldn't abide the rules for having help in the South. There was a Polish woman who cooked for us, and Mother took in young single women – girls who came to attend secretarial school or college. They lived with us and helped with the domestic work, and Mother mentored them. Mother believed that a young woman should be capable of making her own way.'

Epiphany craned to see the embroidered letters inside

the heart. 'Okay . . . so what's that got to do with this blanket? Who's Cecile?'

'The woman who took care of me. A black woman. I remember her from when I was young. She was in the house with the seven chairs, but I don't remember her anywhere else. I don't remember her in our home in Houston, or my parents' vacation cottage at the beach. If Cecile looked after my care, why wouldn't I remember her in those places, too?'

Epiphany scratched her head, smoothing dark curls away from her face. 'People don't remember *everything* from when they were young, J. Norm. Sometimes there's stuff you don't want to remember.' Her gaze sought mine, and I wondered what things she was trying to forget.

'This is different,' I said. 'It's as if there are two sets of memories, and one doesn't match the other. Both can't be valid. It is impossible for a person to be in two places at once.'

'Well . . .' Epiphany knelt beside the trunk as if she intended to be there awhile. 'Guess there's only one way we're gonna find that out. Let's see what else is in this trunk.'

CHAPTER 12

Epiphany Jones

It wasn't long before J. Norm and me figured out that finding clues wouldn't be easy. The trunk was full of all kinds of stuff from J. Norm's mother. There were photo albums with crispy sheets of black paper crammed full of pictures from school plays and high school dances, Christmases and birthday parties. There were scrapbooks from trips to Europe, Egypt, Asia, a tiny pair of white leather toddler shoes, coloring books he'd colored in, a chart of stars and a book on astronomy some teacher gave him, a stack of his mother's ledgers about household accounts, a tattered book of Bible stories, some baby clothes his mama had saved, a long, white christening gown. We separated everything into stacks, and then looked at photo books until our eyes were crossed. Finally, we took a break for lunch. J. Norm fell asleep in his chair, and I left him there and went back upstairs.

I started in on some old scrapbooks and ledgers that had been his mama's. That woman must've written down everything she ever spent money on and every place she went. It was weird to think about that being somebody's life – paying housekeepers and gardeners, and spending your time going to things like Ladies' Tea, and the Christian Aid Society. J. Norm's people were rich, like you saw in the movies.

He came back up after his nap, and we found what we figured must've been the mother's helper he remembered from when they came to Dallas. She was in a couple pictures with him at his birthday party, all of them smiling on the front lawn. She got paid every week out of the household account, but only the first name was in there – Frances, like her last name didn't matter. She was there working for a couple years, according to the checks.

After Frances, there was another young girl, Lydia, and all the while there was a Polish lady, Irenka, getting paid for cooking and housekeeping. The weird thing was that J. Norm's mama was also writing housekeeping checks to a third person the whole time she had Irenka and one of the younger girls there. The third housekeeper's name wasn't even in the book – just her initials, T.C., and the word *housekeeping* in the notations column. J. Norm didn't remember a third person ever being there, but T.C. got paid for years and years, until J. Norm was grown and married. The money went out twice a month, right on schedule.

I laid the picture book with Frances in it open by my knee, looked down into her face, and wondered what she was thinking the minute someone snapped that photo. She was young, maybe even younger than me, already off in the world. 'So why did they have to come work here instead of living with their own families?' I asked. 'Frances and Lydia, and the other mother's helpers, I mean?'

J. Norm kept flipping through the ledgers, reading his mama's handwriting. 'It was a different time. Young women didn't have so many options open to them. Families often had more children than they could afford, or sometimes the parents died and the children had to go to work. Frances was a distant cousin of some sort. A poor relation sent to my mother for an education. She had an older sister who stayed with us for a short while, too. Possibly they'd lost their parents or some such. My mother helped a number of young women through the years. I don't know if Frances was with our family before my parents moved to Dallas. I don't remember much of life in Houston.'

'Do you think Frances liked it here?' She was smiling in the pictures, but she had a worried look in her eyes. What was behind that look?

There was a line across her cheek, a shadow, I thought at first, but when I picked up the book and looked again, I could see that the line had bled through from behind. Sliding a finger over the picture, I lifted the corner as far as it would go before the glue clung to the black paper. Then I held the book up so that I could see the back of the photo.

'J. Norm, there's writing on the backs of these,' I said, and he looked down at me from the chair we'd wheeled into the room.

'Writing?'

'Yeah.' I lifted a little more, heard just the tiniest bit of ripping, then yanked my fingernail away.

He leaned forward in his seat, flipping a hand at me. 'Well, go on. Tear it off. Let's see if it's anything useful.'

I stuck a fingernail under the corner, and the same creepy feeling I'd had in the attic crawled over my skin again – like someone was standing right over my shoulder, breathing on my neck. My shoulders did a shimmy, and I handed the book up to J. Norm. 'You do it. It'll mess up the book. I don't want anyone mad at me.' If J. Norm's mama was a ghost in this house, I sure didn't want her coming after me.

A bushy eyebrow went low over one of his eyes. 'I assure you that I have absolutely no plans for these old things, and Deborah isn't the type for sentimental study of family history. The minute I'm gone, she'll have a moving company in here to empty out that attic. She was after Annalee to do it for years.'

I held my hands up, away from the photo book. 'I'm not doing it.' I wondered what Deborah would really say if she could see all the books. If I had a whole trunk full of stuff about my family, it'd mean something to me. All I had was a shoe box, and almost everything in there seemed important. When you've only got a little of the puzzle, every piece matters.

J. Norm tore the pictures off the page in one quick sweep, and about a half second later, we knew the name of the girl in the picture. Frances Gibbs. After that, we hunted up all the pictures of other hired help and tore them off the pages, too. We also found the photos of some of J. Norm's mama's neighbors and friends, and a few photos of neighbors' kids he'd played with. We made a list of names of people who were there when he was little, people who might've known something or heard something.

I told him we could try looking up the names on the Internet, if we had some way to get to the Internet. 'You can find people's addresses, and stuff like newspaper articles they've been in, or sometimes their obituaries, or if somebody put them on a family tree when they were looking up their ancestors, or if they're on Facebook. We used to do it in classes at my old school – look up famous people in history and stuff.' Now, with all those names on J. Norm's list, I thought about my daddy. His name was on my birth certificate. I wondered if I could find out anything about him or his family on the Internet. 'I could probably do it at school, if I could get one of the teachers to let me on a computer. They're picky about it here, because the kids at this school will wreck it or look up porn.'

J. Norm blinked, surprised. Guess he didn't have a clue what kids did with computers these days. 'No doubt those computers are for schoolwork. I had a computer here for e-mail and whatnot, but it was old and slow. Deborah took it home so that Lloyd could rehab it, and he pronounced it a lost cause. They're busy salvaging Annalee's photos off of it now, I think. I don't want you getting into trouble trying to use the one at school on my account.'

'I won't,' I said, and started gathering the pictures. 'I don't know if I'll find anything, anyway. Most of these people are probably dead by now. They'd be, like, even older than –' I bit off the last word of that sentence just in time.

'Me,' J. Norm finished.

'I was gonna say *dirt*,' I told him, and he smiled – a real smile, not the kind that looked like it was painful to make.

We slipped the photos into an envelope, then headed downstairs to do a little work on my research report before I had to go catch the bus home.

'That hoodlum DeRon did return your backpack, at least,' he said to me when we got downstairs. He grabbed it and handed it to me in the entryway. 'Or rather, he threw it at Deborah.'

I let out a breath when I felt the weight of the backpack. DeRon couldn't be too mad at me. The backpack was still heavy, so everything must be in there – some math homework, a couple books, J. Norm's old magazines. The night I took the magazines home, I'd started reading the articles about the Apollo launches, and there was plenty of stuff in there to make a report and do the talk in history class. It wouldn't matter much what I said, anyway. Nobody would be listening.

The zipper on the backpack was gummy when I tried to open it. It stuck in one place, and I sat down on the stairs to wiggle it free. 'Hang . . . on . . . a . . . sec. It's hung up or something.'

'We could try a screwdriver or a pair of pliers.' J. Norm actually seemed kind of excited about helping me with the report.

'No . . . I can get . . . There it goes.' The zipper started moving again, but it was still sticky and slow. 'I worked on the project a little bit from the articles, and . . .' The zipper turned the second corner, and the flap flopped open, and I felt sick. I yanked my fingers back and they were wet and bloodred. My breath caught, I dropped the backpack, and it rolled down the stairs.

A sharp smell wound up my nose, and I knew what it was on my hand. Not blood. Paint. DeRon and his friends had spray-painted the inside of my backpack. Everything was ruined. 'I'm sor ... sorry,' I whispered. Annalee's magazines, and the rocket pen ...

J. Norm opened the backpack, pinched one of the magazines between two fingers, and took it out. I felt my cheeks going hot, the tears spilling over. I didn't want to be at J. Norm's house all of a sudden. I didn't want to be anywhere. I wanted to find DeRon and kill him, or else run away and never come back. I hated DeRon. I hated it here in Dallas. I hated everything about being here.

I didn't even say anything else to J. Norm. I just got up, ran across the entry hall, opened the door, then took off before he could stop me. I ran across the yard with him yelling after me. I kept running, and running, and running, until finally I caught the bus back to my part of the neighborhood.

Walking home from the bus stop, I wondered if DeRon was still trolling around. I pictured him driving up in his car, and after that, the picture went one of two ways. In one picture, I knocked him out with a right cross to the jaw. In the other picture, he had the rest of his loser friends with him, and they were looking for a party girl, and they didn't want to take no for an answer.

Russ was out front unhooking his flea market trailer when I got home. For once, I was glad to see him.

'Where you been?' he asked, and gave my borrowed shirt

a once-over. I pulled it tighter over the ripped tank top. If Russ or Mama found out what'd happened in DeRon's car, they'd say it was my fault for being stupid. It probably was.

'At work,' I said. 'I don't feel so good. I'm gonna shower and go to bed.'

Russ just shrugged and told me to clean up the kitchen first. 'Your mama's ticked.'

What's new? I thought. Nothing ever changed here. Somebody was always mad.

Today Mama was on the sofa with a headache, trying to sleep off the weekend fun. I started picking up dishes, but she cracked open an eye and yelled at me to quit making noise, so I gave up and hurried to take a shower while Russ was outside. The lock on the bathroom door didn't work, and if Russ needed to use the toilet, he'd just walk on in whether someone was in the shower or not. He never did anything but come and do his business, but it was creepy knowing he was right on the other side of the curtain, so I tried to get my showering done when he was asleep or when he and Mama were holed up in the bedroom together.

After the shower, I scooted past Mama to the kitchen, grabbed a sandwich and a soda, and headed to my room. Outside, a couple Harleys rumbled up, and I heard Russ shooting the breeze with some friends. The old refrigerator in the carport opened and shut, and Russ and his buddies popped the tops on some brews. They'd be there awhile.

Tiptoeing barefoot out of the room again, I looked down the hall and checked Mama on the sofa. She was out for the count, her mouth hanging open and her hair curling wild

185

on pillows, splayed out like a lion's mane. She'd probably taken one of the sleeping pills Russ's VA doctor prescribed, and she'd be there all night.

I decided it was safe enough to go into Mama's room and get the shoe box. The laundry in the closet was piled so high now, she wouldn't notice it was gone, even if she did wake up. All this business with J. Norm hunting for his people had me thinking that I wanted to check the backs of my pictures for clues, too.

I shut myself in my room, wedged a chair under the doorknob, and laid out all the pictures on my bed. The voices outside, the rumble of another bike pulling up, and the noise from a siren somewhere in the distance faded off. I studied the photos, felt myself sinking in, looking at the women standing there with my mother as she balanced me on her hip the day of my first birthday party.

I wondered what those women thought about me when we all stood there together. Did they think I was pretty? Or did they just feel, like Mama did, that I was a problem to have around?

Did they love my daddy? Was he right outside the picture frame, saying, 'Okay, everybody smile!' Or was he miles away already, about to land himself in the wrong place at the wrong time and end up dead?

Pictures couldn't answer questions like that, so I got busy looking for questions that could be answered. Where were the pictures taken? What were the names of the people in them? There were kids at the birthday party. Where were they now? Who were they? Friends? Cousins?

Maybe brothers and sisters?

Did my father have other kids before me?

There was a church in the background of one of the photos. I wrote down what I could read of the name on the sign and then moved on. In one of the pictures, an old woman was holding me, her hands dark and wrinkled against my white dress, her smile missing a few teeth. She looked really old, but her eyes were bright and happy.

It almost felt like I could remember her, like I knew how it felt, sitting on her lap that day.

There was a baseball field in the background. *Greg Nash Park*, the scoreboard read. I wrote down the name, turned the picture over, and looked at the back. The words written in pencil had almost faded, but I held the photo to the light and I could see the indentation they'd made. *From Neesie. Mama Leela, 99 years old.*

If the woman in the picture lived to be one hundred, there might've been something about it in the paper. They ran stories sometimes about people who were turning a hundred.

But the newspapers where?

I wrote down, *Neesie, Mama Leela, hundred years old?*

There weren't any other clues in the pictures, but I looked at them until my eyes got tired; then I copied my father's full name off my birth certificate and put everything back in the box. I slid the box into the top drawer of my dresser until morning, because Russ was back inside. He was trying to wake Mama up and get romantic in the living room, but she was out cold. He wasn't happy about it.

I decided the best place for me was in bed, so I turned off the light and climbed in. I left the chair in front of the door and went to sleep.

In the morning, Mama headed off early. She was doubling up some of her housecleaning jobs into the first days of the week, because Russ and her wanted to drive to Oklahoma to sell at some flea market this weekend. Since it was her day to clean at J. Norm's and fix him supper, I wasn't supposed to go there. I got dressed for school, and then stood looking at myself in the mirror, and I couldn't deal with it. I didn't have my books, because they were at J. Norm's with paint all over them. Now that DeRon was mad at me, walking down the halls at school would be like stepping into a war zone. Just thinking about it made me feel like I was gonna throw up, so I put my sweats back on and went out to the living room to get Russ to call me in sick at school. Russ wouldn't mind, I figured. He was in a good mood. He was busy digging through some boxes of cheap flip knives and bandannas he'd traded for over the weekend. I told him I'd help get the stuff sorted and priced if he'd call me in sick, and we had a deal. Mama never knew a thing about it, which Russ thought was kind of funny, like we had a special little secret between us.

Tuesday morning, he asked if I wanted him to call me in again. He was heading over to DeSoto to make a trade with a guy from Craigslist, and then he was going to some warehouse auction out in Greenville, and if that went well, he and Mama would have some good stuff for the flea market in Oklahoma next weekend. He asked if I wanted to go with him and help out.

For about half a second, I thought about saying yes, but I knew it was a stupid idea. If you got in the truck with Russ, you were likely to end up at some biker bar, and besides, Mama didn't like it if I got too friendly with her men.

'I better go catch the school bus,' I said, and my stomach knotted up like one of those shoestrings you'll never get untied.

'Yeah, well, you're about as much fun as the ol' lady. If you see her this afternoon, tell her I'll be late getting back tonight.' Russ belched and set his first brew of the day on the coffee table.

'She's got houses to clean this afternoon, and then she goes straight to work cleaning classrooms. I won't see her.' With Russ and Mama gone, there wouldn't be any reason for me to hurry home from J. Norm's tonight.

'You need some beer money?' Russ grabbed the chain on his wallet and started to pull it out. That was his way of saying I'd helped him out yesterday, and asking if I needed money for lunch. Russ could be all right, sometimes.

'Yeah, sure.'

Russ handed over a five and winked at me. 'There ya go. Buy a round for your friends.'

''Kay.' I slipped the money into my pocket, and since we were buddies and everything, I asked him if, sometime soon, he could help me get my driver's license.

'What's in it for me?' He looked between some pillows for the TV remote, then smiled a little under his bushy mustache. 'Yeah, sure, kid. Soon as I get a chance, and speakin' of cars, you tell that little punk in the Chevy Caprice if he don't quit drivin' by here, he's gonna get a load of scatter-shot right through the front window, understand? You got something goin' on with that boy?' Russ looked hard at me for a minute, and I didn't like the way it felt. I backed a couple steps toward the door and shook my head. 'You tell him you're jailbait.' Russ pointed a finger at me. 'He gives you any trouble, you let me know.'

'Oh . . . okay.' I headed out the door feeing itchy and strange under my clothes, partly because DeRon had been driving by the house, and partly because Russ'd never, ever asked me anything like that before. He only cared about stuff that had something to do with him.

When I got to school, the basketball boys were gone to some kind of college tour day, and I was glad, because that meant I wouldn't run into DeRon. Everything seemed normal enough. I kept my head down and tried to get by without anybody noticing I was there.

In study hall, I talked the teacher into letting me use the computer so I could work on my research report. She let me do it, since she liked me. She never had to peel me off the ceiling, or chase me down the hall, or bust me out of a fight, which put me at the head of the class.

I sat at the computer desk and looked up the names on J. Norm's list, and even shot some stuff to the printer while the teacher was busy with some jerk who'd passed out in the back of the room. I knew pretty quick, though, that finding anything useful about J. Norm's people was gonna take a while. Mostly I just clicked from one dead end to another. I'd never have enough time to do it at school.

The teacher figured out I wasn't working on a research report, and she kicked me off the computer just when I was about to look up the names and places on my own list. After that, I knew I wouldn't have any more chances at a computer. I finished up the afternoon mostly trying to keep my head down and catch up on my work. By the time I made it to the last class of the day, all I could think about was getting out of the building as soon as the bell rang. Just because DeRon was gone earlier today didn't mean he might not be back now.

Five minutes before class was supposed to get out, the teacher got a note, and the next thing I knew, she was handing the note to me and telling me to get my stuff and go to the office.

A million things went through my mind on the way down the hall, but if I'd of had ten years to come up with ideas, I wouldn't have guessed what I saw through the glass when I turned the corner by the secretary's desk. Standing right there in the principal's office were DeRon and one of the basketball coaches. The principal was rubbing his eyes like he was tired, and the coach looked like he was set to blow.

A half second later, I figured out what was going on. Someone was sitting in the chair across from the principal. He didn't have to turn around for me to know who it was.

J. Norm. And my backpack was on the desk with red-painted stuff strung all over the place.

DeRon saw me coming. His eyes went narrow, and his lips got tight and straight, and I knew if he'd had a gun in his hand, I'd be dead already.

CHAPTER 13

J. Norman Alvord

Epiphany refused to offer the least bit of testimony against the boy. She meekly agreed with his version of events – that the spray-painted books were an accident, the result of a prank gone wrong. The can of spray paint had ended up in her backpack accidentally and it had exploded.

The coach, standing with his hand possessively on the boy's shoulder, nodded along with that explanation and was anxious to hustle his player back to an ongoing practice.

I was the villain now – a fussy old man sticking his nose in where it didn't belong, offended, perhaps, that a boy from 'off Hill' had disturbed my quiet, upscale street with a noisy, older-model car. Given Epiphany's reaction to my school visit, perhaps it would have been better if I'd minded my own business, but it had seemed the right thing to do, taking the backpack to the school and seeing to it that the boy was held responsible for vandalizing the textbooks. I would have come first thing on Monday, but the principal had put me off until this afternoon. While waiting, I'd had time to work up a full head of steam. What sort of school would let such heinous activity go unpunished?

'This is a good boy,' the coach remarked. 'He's on his way to a D-one college scholarship.'

'Then perhaps he should mind his extracurricular activities accordingly,' I replied, and the boy delivered a silent, openmouthed reply. Behind the mask, his eyes held a wickedness, a simmering anger that caused me to press the point. 'Perhaps we should ask Epiphany for her side of the story – *without* an audience present.'

Epiphany, however, had other ideas. Crossing her arms over her stomach, she sagged in her chair, looking at the floor. 'It's no big deal. There's nothing to tell. It was an accident.'

The coach and the principal were pleased to accept that answer and give us the bum's rush. Epiphany followed me to my car, stiff armed, and didn't offer a word until we'd traveled the few blocks to my house.

'You shouldn't have done it!' Her protest exploded as the garage door rolled closed. I parked the car exactly where I'd found it. With any luck, Deborah would never notice that I'd used the hide-a-key and gone out for a drive. In reality, extricating the car had been a lengthy procedure involving trickle-charging the battery overnight with an ancient battery charger I hadn't even realized I owned, then carefully backing the car out of the garage and creeping slowly down the street. Since my recent spate of heart trouble, my reactions had gone downhill, I had discovered. Driving was more of a challenge than I'd thought it would be, but I was determined. I was not, however, receiving any cheers for my efforts now.

'You shouldn't have lied for the boy, particularly after what he did to you. Why would you lie for him?' I demanded. 'It isn't right that you should be responsible for the books, and since that neophyte of a principal won't force the boy to pay for them, then I will. I've already told the principal to give you new ones tomorrow, and –'

'I'm not your little charity case, all right?' Epiphany exploded from the car, slamming the door behind her. 'I don't need you taking care of me.'

'A girl who is afraid to go home at night does need someone's help.' I climbed from the car, my legs weak after the afternoon's excitement. 'A ...' *Friend* came to mind, but I didn't use the word. 'An advocate, at the very least.'

She didn't answer at first, just stood there with her fingernails sinking into her hair. 'I've *got* a mama, okay? I don't need another one. And don't say anything to her about this, either. She doesn't want to know.' Without waiting for my reply, she went into the house, the *slap-slap* of her flip-flops echoing against the walls. She was in the kitchen next, slamming the pots and pans. I let her be and stepped outside, because Terrence was in the driveway, and I wanted to speak with him about something. I had an idea.

After I came in from conducting my business with Terrence, Epiphany seemed to have cooled down a bit. She was preparing some sort of boneless, skinless, nearly chickenless chicken breast. Another of Deborah's healthy meals, no doubt.

'I think we should go to a restaurant and pick up something,' I said, hoping to make amends for having embarrassed her at school. I wasn't wrong in what I'd done, but it had offended her. Having dealt with Deborah and Roy as teenagers, I might have known. 'We could both stand to get out of the house.'

'Don't think I don't know you're not supposed to be driving that car.' She flung open a drawer and began rummaging for utensils. 'If Deborah finds out, she'll have a fit for sure.'

'Considering the rest of our crimes these past few days, I think the car is the least of our worries,' I pointed out. 'And Deborah won't be by this evening. She has a symposium overnight in Fort Worth. I've promised not to do anything that can be construed as an attempted suicide while she's gone.'

Epiphany stiffened, bracing her arms on the counter. 'That's not even funny, okay?'

It occurred to me that I hadn't, in quite some time, considered potential means of hastening my own death. Epiphany and the mystery of the seven chairs had changed the roads my mind traveled. 'Let's go out for something to eat before Terrence comes by.'

'Terrence?'

'He's agreed to loan us his laptop computer this evening. He had to run to an appointment just now, but he'll be back in forty-five minutes to show us how to attach it to the Internet. It uses cellular communications.'

Epiphany's face brightened with enthusiasm, and if she was still angry with me, it didn't show. 'Cool. All right. But if we're going somewhere, I'm driving. You ran up on the curb three times on the way home, and slow as you go, one of those construction trucks might come along and wipe us out.'

Switching off the burner, she set the pan aside, wiped her hands on a kitchen towel, and moved to the doorway, her hand held out in buoyant anticipation. 'Where's the car key?'

'Have you a license?'

'I've got a learner's permit,' she replied haughtily, and patted a bulge in her pocket – a wallet, I guessed. 'I passed driver's ed.'

'That gives me the utmost confidence,' I said, and we proceeded with our newest mission.

After thirty harrowing minutes, we'd accomplished the trip to Stump's Barbecue and back. When the doorbell rang, we were sharing supper, and I was telling Epiphany about Fat Boy's Barbecue near Cape Canaveral, which still glittered in my memory. 'Many were the times we held a late-night meeting at Fat Boy's. I think that's why we beat the Soviets. We had Fat Boy's, and they didn't. If the KGB had known, they could have dressed their spies as waitresses and stolen all our secrets.'

Epiphany grinned as she stood up to answer the door. 'Maybe I can put that in my report. We've got to work on that after a while, okay?'

'Most certainly,' I agreed, admiring the fact that, despite a lack of supervision from her mother or encouragement from the school, she was a conscientious student. 'We can use Terrence's computer for that, as well.'

After a short lesson from Terrence, Epiphany and I busied ourselves with our work. As with most puzzles, it was challenging. The neighbors and relatives named in my mother's photographs were mentioned in death indexes and electronic copies of old obituaries, but the information led us no farther. Frances Gibbs was too common a name and was contained in so many entries that discerning our target was like searching for a needle in not just one haystack, but many. We created notes and charts to continue narrowing our search.

Finally, I insisted that we proceed to Epiphany's school project. After having caused a stir in the principal's office, I did not want to be responsible for keeping her from her homework.

'Can I look up a couple more things first?' she asked, and flipped the sheet of paper. On the back, she'd made some notes that I didn't recognize.

'What are these?' I turned the paper and squinted through my glasses.

'Just something for another project.' She moved it farther away from me. 'I have to find out where these places are.'

'For a school project?'

'Sorta.' Her answer was oddly evasive.

'Well, I can tell you who Greg Nash was.' Reaching across the table, I tapped the paper, where she'd written, *Greg Nash Park*. 'He was a baseball player with the Tampa Tarpons, minor leagues. Played in the company of greats like of Johnny Bench and Catfish Hunter. Could knock the skin right off the ball, but every time he'd move up to the big leagues, he'd drink himself right back down to the minors. I think the team owners finally figured out that he just couldn't handle too much money in his pocket at once. You know, the sad thing about him was that he was having his best-ever season in the majors when he died in a hotel fire.'

She cast a glance my way. 'How do you know all that?'

'Annalee and I lived in Florida for almost seven years before we moved away for another job,' I reminded her. 'Deborah was small then, and Roy was born there. We lived in a little cabin on Switch Grass Island. Beautiful place right on Lake Poinsett – sat up on piers over the water. You could fish off the back porch.'

Memories flooded my mind, raindrops falling faster, faster, faster, bigger and heavier. A deluge. I quickly forgot my reason for bringing up those days on Switch Grass. My mind flew away from Blue Sky Hill. 'The fishermen woke us each morning about four a.m. as they trolled through the channel with their fishing boats. Nearly drove us batty the first few months we were there, but finally we grew accustomed to the racket of the boats coming and going, and we learned to love the place.' The mention of the boats caught a tether in my mind, brought it back to the original question. 'Living on the water, we had a small boat, and many of our friends owned boats, so when we had a little time off, we packed our coolers and trailered the boats to this or that park for a picnic or an overnight campout. If we were near a town where a minor league team was playing, we'd pile into one of the cars and drive to the game – have a hot dog and enjoy the entertainment.'

'So you think Greg Nash Park is in Florida?' Epiphany's interest grew intense. 'I mean, you sure?'

'Hard to say,' I answered. 'I suppose a park could have been named for him in whatever town he hailed from, but he played in Tampa. There was a park not too far from the ball fields at one time. I don't recall much about it, except that the facilities were fairly rudimentary – picnic sites, a great deal of sand, a bit of playground equipment. We once mired Annalee's Volkswagen Beetle up to the axles trying to back up to a picnic table. It was just the four of us that day. Roy was howling in Annalee's arms, and Deborah was crying in the backseat. Annalee didn't have another bottle for the baby, and there wasn't another soul in the park. Then the sky broke open, and the rain poured down, and we thought we were goners, for sure.'

I laughed to myself, my mind in the past again. How drastic that situation had seemed in the moment. 'That day was Roy's introduction to 7UP. It was always his beverage of choice, and Deborah's as well, after that.' In my mind, the memory was clear and beautiful, like an aged Polaroid suddenly regaining the brightness of its original color. I saw Annalee curled in the passenger seat of the little Bug, her hair falling over her shoulder, Roy in her arms, water draining down the glass in tiny rivers all around them. Nowhere to go, because we couldn't.

I'd taught Deborah how to play Rock-Paper-Scissors, to quiet her. Before long, we were laughing despite the rain.

I smiled now at the memory, a glorious moment that had slipped by unnoticed, like a pearl in the sand along the edge of a path.

Epiphany folded the paper in half and set it aside. 'You oughta tell Deborah about the 7UP. She might not even know why she likes it.'

'I'm sure her mother told her that story many times.'

The conversation ran dry, and finally Epiphany turned back to the computer. 'I guess we better do the research for the project about the rockets. I can look up my other junk later.'

I studied her for a moment longer, wondering what was going on behind that inquisitive face of hers. There was more to her interest in Greg Nash Park than just a school project. As we started to work on her report, I found myself mulling the possible reasons, but I didn't question her further. We talked, instead, about things that pertained to her report – my days as a young man, my position at Hughes. 'We started our work on the *Surveyor* out in Culver City, California,' I said. 'It was an adventure, but I was secretly afraid. I was going off into the world on my own, taking on a huge challenge, and with a wife and child to support. But Howard Hughes had put together a crackerjack team. That was one thing he believed in – hiring the best people and letting them do their jobs. He was nothing like the history books say, by the way. You get a sense of a man when you work for him. He encouraged, gave us the room to perform to our potential, to attempt the impossible. We were doing things that had never been done. We needed someone to do the believing for us, at first, and Hughes did. Because of that, we landed on the moon. Those were amazing times, Epiphany. That was my Camelot. I was young; exciting things were happening. I was in love, just starting out in raising a family. It was as if the world were exploding all around me, everything lit up with bright colors.'

Epiphany stopped writing and looked at me. 'How'd you meet your wife?'

'I doubt that information will fit into your project.'

She doodled wistfully on the corner of the paper. 'I was just wondering.' She shrugged, as if to indicate that it didn't matter.

The past tugged a smile from me. 'I was never much of a ladies' man,' I began, and Epiphany rolled an unsurprised glance my way.

'Nah, really?'

'Do you want to hear my story or not?'

'I asked, didn't I?'

I took a sip of my root beer, swilling it around in my mouth and thinking of where to begin. The rush of fat and calories from our barbecue supper was catching up with me. I'd begun to feel foggy and tired. 'It was back when I was in college. I went out one day to buy a pennant or sweater or souvenir of some sort to send home to my mother for her birthday. I walked into a little store and quite literally reached across the counter and ended up in a tug-of-war over a burnt-orange scarf. When I looked up, the most beautiful girl was hand in hand with me. I suppose, at first, she assumed I might be picking out a gift for a girlfriend, but being a resourceful fellow, I quickly let her know I was shopping for my mother's birthday, and I enlisted her help. Everything she suggested, I vetoed for some reason or other, so as to keep her there shopping with me. She did confess later that she'd never seen a boy so worried about finding the right gift for his mother, but my ploy worked. I kept her attention until I'd finally worked up the courage to ask whether I might take her for ice cream, as a thank-you for her help. When she agreed, I couldn't believe my good fortune. This girl, this beautiful young woman, wanted to spend time with me. We talked for hours, sitting at a corner table in the ice cream parlor. Once I had the seat next to her, I was afraid to leave even long enough for a trip to the men's room.'

Epiphany giggled. 'Well, that must've got rough after a while.'

'Ah, Epiphany, the things a young man will do when he's smitten by a pretty girl. Nothing else seems to matter in a moment like that.' The jubilant feeling of sitting at that table with Annalee and the sounds of the campus were suddenly as real as if they'd happened yesterday. I could see her eyes, the carefully painted bow of her lips, her beautiful smile. Her laugh jingled in my ear. 'You'll know that sort of feeling one day.'

Resting her chin on her hand, she returned her attention to her doodle – a pencil sketch of a rose. 'Yeah, right.'

'And not with some hoodlum like that DeRon character, either.' I recalled the boy sauntering into the principal's office with his coach in tow, then hooking one leg over the principal's credenza, regarding me through half-mast eyes, attempting to silently cast a threat across the room.

Epiphany bent over her paper, embarrassed. She quickly changed the subject. 'So what happened when the thing . . . the lander didn't sink into the moon? Did everybody cheer or what?'

Without thinking, I reached across the space between us, slipped a curled, crooked hand, the hand of an old man, under her chin, turned her face my way. 'You wait, Epiphany. Don't be in such a hurry for a boy. Wait for that young man who knows what a treasure you are, who shows you respect.' The moment seemed to slow and stretch then. I thought of Annalee. She was the most beautiful thing in the world to me when we met. Over the years, I hadn't told her that nearly enough.

I pulled my hand away, folded it over the other. 'She was studying to be a teacher, my Annalee. She was from a small town in south Texas, and her dream was to return there and teach in a public school, but we met and . . .' A connection blazed in my mind, like a circuit suddenly going live, illuminating an area that had been dark.

Eyeing me quizzically, Epiphany sat back in her chair. 'J. Norm?' When I didn't answer, she leaned close and waved a hand in front of my face. 'You eat too much barbecue? You need one of your pills or something?'

'The sister worked in a school,' I muttered, long-lost details rushing back to me. 'The cousin who lived with us, Frances, her older sister was a teacher. The sister came to visit and brought some books to me – grade-school readers, an alphabet book, an arithmetic book, and a social studies text with maps and pictures. They were things that the school was discarding, and she thought I might like to have them. My mother had decided to keep me home for another year, rather than starting me in grade school, and I remember that Frances's sister – her name started with an F, as well . . . Flora . . . no . . . Faye – talked to Mother about the school where she'd just accepted a teaching job. Faye wanted my mother to send me there, but my mother was reluctant to let me go. In the end, I continued with tutoring at home and didn't start in a formal school until I was nine years old. I always thought it was because I was a late-in-life child, but maybe there was something more. I think the truth could be that I was adopted, and she didn't want me to know it. But even that doesn't explain her fear of letting me out of the house. I suspect there was some secret involved – some scandal.' The past swirled and dipped in the corner of my mind, tantalizing, alluring, a dancer slowly shedding veils. I closed my eyes, saw my hands, small and pale, turning the pages in the first-grade reader as I sat on the floor. 'My mother argued with Faye during that visit. Faye said she would watch over me if Mother would send me to her school.'

I heard Faye's voice, quiet, calm, attempting to placate my mother. Frances had left the room to go after tea. I was watching the door for her to return. Even though Faye had brought the books to me, I was nervous about her being there. She smiled, as if to reassure me. I looked away. 'I'll have a close eye on him, Aunt Phoebe. You can't keep him hidden away here forever. He's a bright boy. He needs to be out in the world, around people, around other children.'

'Not enough time has passed.' My mother's voice was frayed, and she was uncharacteristically close to tears. 'It's too big a risk. His red hair, for one thing.'

'Many children have red hair, Aunt Phoebe. You're putting up excuses.'

'He's afraid,' my mother protested. 'Even when neighbors

come here, or when we entertain, he's terribly shy of strangers.'

'And he will be forever,' Faye replied. 'He'll never improve if he isn't allowed to move into the world, to begin to see that he can trust people. St Clare's is a very small and nurturing school. There are only fourteen children in my class. I'll be there with him.'

My mother stiffened, sat forward on the parlor sofa, her spine ramrod straight, her hands folded in her lap one over the other, her neck stretching upward, giving her the posture of the regal springer spaniels in the portrait over the fireplace. I understood the meaning of that posture. I wouldn't be going off to school, to Faye's classroom or any other. Not this year.

I was relieved. Sitting very still with the books, I endeavored to go unnoticed, hoping the discussion was over. I didn't like being the topic. I was afraid of it.

'No. Absolutely not. Not now. It isn't time yet.' Mother shifted forward on the sofa, the decision made. 'In another year or two, when he's grown and matured somewhat.'

Faye stood abruptly, placing her teacup into the saucer and setting it loudly on the table. 'It's been almost two years. Two years of your keeping him closeted. You're only teaching him greater fear; don't you see that? He's worse, not better. Look at him over there, in his own world. He hasn't heard a word we're saying.'

My mother remained seated. 'You have no way of knowing what he hears. You don't see the progress he's made. You are not here on a daily basis.'

'What you're doing is wrong, Aunt Phoebe,' Faye protested. 'I don't want my sister to be around it any longer. I won't have Frances learning any more about it than she already knows. I've taken a house near the school, and I'll be moving her there to live with me. She can pursue her education at St Clare's. Perhaps even attain a teaching certificate of her own, when she's older.'

Frances entered the room with a tea tray, and the conversation ended abruptly. I slid closer to my mother, leaving the books behind, and wedged myself into the comfortable space between her leg and the front of the divan. Laying my head on her knee, I took in her scent, a safe scent. Her hand slid tenderly over my hair, the red hair that was a bad thing, I concluded. A reason the other children would not like me at school. A reason not to go.

Frances left our home shortly after that. Because of my red hair. Because it prevented me from going to school with Faye . . .

I turned to Epiphany, my mind whirling with new details. 'Frances's sister was a teacher. I think Frances may have become one, as well. Faye taught at a private school. St Clare's. It couldn't have been too terribly far away. My mother would never have considered sending me a long distance.'

Epiphany's face brightened with interest. 'You just remembered all that?'

'I think so,' I replied. 'Faye argued with my mother over sending me to school. Their conversation didn't end well. Faye would surely have passed away by now, but Frances was younger, not so many years older than me.'

Epiphany slid the computer closer, touched the keyboard. The screen blinked on. 'Maybe that'll help narrow down our people.' She typed Frances's name into the computer again, then added, *St Clare School*.

Within moments, her search had produced something. A Web site filled with history, the history of St Clare's School. Among the pages was a faded photograph of smiling children and their teacher, a brighteyed, round-faced young woman with her blonde hair pulled back in a bow. I knew her. 'That's her. That's Frances.' I pointed. 'Is there anything more?'

'Hang on.' Epiphany scrolled down the page, her slim finger touching the screen now and again, pointing out images of Frances working with children, cleaning a blackboard, sitting at a writing desk. 'There's a link under this one. Something about a hundredth anniversary of the school.' Epiphany brought up a new page, and the screen was suddenly filled by a newspaper article, a copy like a microfiche in very small print.

I squinted, trying to read the blurry text.

Fortunately, Epiphany's eyes were young. 'She wrote this for the hundredth anniversary of the school.' She pointed to the byline underneath the title. 'She was married by then. Look at the name. Frances Lynne Wilson.'

Epiphany's fingers flew over the keyboard, the screen changed again, then again, and my cohort sat back in her chair, her mouth hanging open. 'Whoa, she's got an address just north of Dallas in McKinney. There's even a phone number. Geez, J. Norm, we could call her right now.'

CHAPTER 14

Epiphany Jones

The phone call to Frances Wilson connected us to a guy who'd had that number only a couple months. Since then, he'd had about a million calls for Mrs Wilson. From what he could tell, she'd moved to the nursing home there in McKinney. We called the nursing home, but the front desk wouldn't give out any resident information.

By then, I had to leave to catch the bus home. J. Norm wouldn't admit it, but while I was packing up the computer, he was thinking about going to that nursing home tomorrow. When he thought I was upstairs, he pulled a map out of the stereo cabinet in the living room. I watched him trace the roads with his finger. He didn't know it, but the car key was still in my pocket. I kept it when I headed out the door, just in case he got some wild idea. If he was going to McKinney to look for Frances Wilson, I was going, too. No way I was letting him drive across town by himself, for one thing, and besides, I was deep into the mystery, and I didn't want him solving it without me. We were a team now, J. Norm and me.

On the way back to Mama's house, I made plans for

ducking school tomorrow. Turned out it wasn't even hard, really. I went home and told Russ and Mama I was sick, and the next morning I got Russ to call the school. Like usual, he was fine with it. He was headed out to do a motorcycle escort thing at a soldier's funeral. He asked if I wanted to go along.

'Thanks, but I don't feel good enough, okay?' I put a hand over my stomach and looked pukey. 'You gonna be home for dinner?'

Russ's tongue snaked out and caught the corner of his mustache. He chewed it a minute. 'You got some plan to have that black boy over here?'

A weird vibe went between Russ and me. 'Geez, Russ. No. It's *that* time of the month, okay? I've got cramps. That's why I don't feel good.'

That shut Russ up, but the suspicious look got deeper, sort of hard and cold. 'I ever come home and find you in my house with that boy, somebody'll wind up with lead poisoning.'

The way Russ looked at me made my skin itch, and I crossed my arms, rubbing the itch away. 'Look, I just need to take a couple Midol and go back to bed awhile, and then I'm gonna go to work. I told J. Norm I'd be there.'

Russ rubbed his beer gut, his head tipping back and to one side. 'That old man payin' you good? Because you could come work for me. Springtime business is looking pretty good. I got a bunch of shows lined up.'

I tried to look like I really believed that Russ would have money to actually pay me – money that didn't get turned right around into beer, flea market finds, his Harley, and poker games with his buddies. 'He pays great,' I said. 'And it's, like, the easiest job in the world. I just sit and do my homework. Once the mess at the church is paid for, I'm gonna save for a car, for whenever *somebody* takes me to get my driver's license.'

That wasn't true about the church, of course, but I *was* saving my money – for however long I could get away with it. I stashed it under my bed and added to it every time Deborah left my pay in the envelope on J. Norm's counter. Once I had enough, I'd pick one of those weekends when Russ and Mama went away to a biker rally or a gun show, and I'd head out to find those women in the shoe box pictures – in Florida, or wherever they were. Sooner or later, I'd turn up the right clue to find them, and when I did, I'd be ready.

Russ grinned and slapped me on the shoulder, then grabbed his keys. 'Keep outta trouble. You see that boy, you tell him again to quit drivin' by this house. He rolled by here at least a half dozen times yesterday. You tell him he thinks he's so bad, he can stop on in. We'll see who's bad.'

My throat went tight, and I just nodded.

Russ headed for the door. 'I won't be home till late again. Pass that on to the old lady, if you see her. Looks like that trip to Oklahoma's gonna work out, too. Gotta leave Friday morning, so she better get her houses cleaned ahead.'

'Okay, I'll tell her.' I hung around the living room, waiting for him to get his trailer hooked up and pull out of the driveway. By the time he left and I caught the bus over to J. Norm's house, I was worried. I hoped there weren't any more hidden keys to J. Norm's car, or he'd be gone by now.

J. Norm didn't answer when I rang the doorbell, so I got

the key out of the hiding spot and let myself in. The house was dark, but the TV was blaring. In the living room, J. Norm's chair was empty, and for a minute I was afraid he'd taken off, but then I heard him thumping around in the kitchen. When I turned the corner, I slipped on the wrapper off a stick of butter. There was trash everywhere.

'What're you *doing*?' I asked, and J. Norm nearly jumped out of his skin.

He stumbled back from the pantry, trash still in his hands. He was sweating, and his face was red. 'You are supposed to be in school.'

I kicked some of the mess out of the way. 'If you're going to McKinney, I'm going to McKinney. You need someone who can drive, for one thing. Somebody who can go over twenty-five and not hit a curb.'

He whipped a suspicious look my way. 'What have you done with my car key?' Grabbing a kitchen towel, he wiped the sweat off his face. He looked seriously mad. 'Did you hide it?'

Right then, I had the sinking feeling I'd really screwed up. 'No, but ... ummm ... it ended up in my pocket ... uhhh ... last night.'

'And what about the paper with the nursing home address on it? Where is that?' His mouth squeezed together into a hard line with no lips.

'It's in the end table with the stereo controls. I hid it so Deborah wouldn't see it, if she came around.' Actually, I hid the paper for the same reason I took the key.

'Ffff! Deborah!' he snapped. 'She'd be thrilled to find me

211

looking up addresses for nursing homes. She's newly determined to boot me out of my house. She wrote a deposit
check for the Villas. From my account! Without so much as
a word to me. Once the money was spent, she thought I'd
give in. She's got another think coming. All she wants is my
money and to be rid of the trouble I am. And do you know
what excuse she used? Do you know what she said?'

I shook my head. My mind was whirling. If Deborah
moved J. Norm away, everything would change. I'd lose my
job. J. Norm would have to leave all his stuff – the rockets
upstairs, Roy's room, the things in the attic that reminded
him of Annalee. I'd never get enough money together to
leave Dallas and go find my daddy's family. Deborah could
ruin everything.

'She can't do that,' I whispered. No matter how much
Deborah didn't get along with her dad, you couldn't tell a
grown-up where to live – not like you could with kids.

He made a soft sound – something between a laugh and
a snort. 'She thinks she can do it without my permission. Do
you know what she said to me? "I hoped you wouldn't make
me seek a guardianship"; that's what she said. She'd like to
have me declared mentally unfit so that she can take over my
life. She's consulted a lawyer, of all things! I told her not to
come back here. She isn't welcome in my house any longer.'

I backed off a step, not knowing what to say. 'Well . . . but . . .
she can't *make* you leave, can she? I mean, you didn't do anything wrong. It's not like you're mental or something.'

He mopped his forehead with the towel again. 'According
to her, I'm a danger to myself. She's been plotting this all

along. Even before she brought you here to work, she was plotting this. You were only a stopgap measure, something to distract me. Did you know what she was up to? Did she tell you?' Throwing the towel down on the counter, he braced a hand on the sink and gave me a mean look. 'Have you been spying on me?'

I shook my head, my mouth falling open. 'Of course not.' The palms of my hands turned clammy and hot, and I wiped them on my jeans. 'She never told me anything like that. If she goes to court, I'd come testify for you. I'd do it in a heartbeat.' Mama'd been through enough divorces, three altogether, for me to know what court was like.

J. Norm stared at me like he was trying to cut a hole all the way inside, so he could see what was there.

'I'm *not* lying.' Tears popped into my eyes. I didn't know until right then how much coming here mattered to me. It mattered that I was the only one J. Norm liked, the only one he trusted, the one he counted on. The only other person that'd ever been that way with me was Mrs Lora. I couldn't lose J. Norm the way I'd lost her. 'You and me . . . we're like a team, J. Norm. Like that show you watch so much, *Hogan's Heroes*. I'll tell Deborah that. I'll tell a judge that. I'll tell Deborah she's crazy for wanting to get rid of this house. I mean, Roy's room is here, and all your wife's hats, and the stuff in the attic, and your rockets. You can't just . . . throw that away. Shoot, I'll go tell Deborah right now, if you want me to.'

His eyes went moist, the water fanning out into the little creases around the edges. He didn't answer for a minute, and then finally he lifted a hand, his arm shaking. 'Get our things ready. We're going to McKinney.' He crossed the room in slow steps, shuffling from side to side, finally reaching for a kitchen chair and lowering himself into it.

I watched him for a minute. He didn't look good. His face was chalky pale and covered with beads of sweat. 'We could wait and go tomorrow, if you're tired now. I could call into school again. Russ won't care. Or you could just call in for me and say you're Russ.'

'No, Epiphany.' His voice was so soft I could barely hear it, just words with hardly any breath to float them into the air. 'We'll go today. I have a feeling our time is running out.'

Something inside me sank. I wanted to tell him not to talk that way, but I didn't. He'd feel better once we cleaned up this mess and got on the road.

An hour later, J. Norm and me were headed to McKinney. I had a white-knuckle grip on the steering wheel, and J. Norm was about to rip the armrest off the door, hanging on. Every time we came within twenty feet of another car, he'd stomp an invisible brake pedal through the floor, his hand shooting out like he was bracing for impact. If I heard 'Watch out!' or 'Be careful to . . .' one more time, I was gonna bail out of the car going sixty down the interstate and take my chances. *Be careful to leave plenty of space, be careful not to tailgate, check the other lane, check the rearview, turn on the blinker, watch the speed . . .*

'Cut it out!' I hollered finally. 'You're making me so nervous, I can't drive.' Crossing Dallas was a lot different from tooling around Mrs Lora's quiet little town or taking J. Norm down to the barbecue joint.

By the time we got to McKinney and found the nursing

home, which was hooked to the back side of a big hospital, I was so wiped out, I just pulled into a parking space, turned off the engine, and fell back against the seat. I felt like I hadn't breathed since we'd backed out of J. Norm's garage.

'We made it,' I whispered.

'Praise all ye heavenly hosts.' J. Norm let go of the armrest.

'Thanks a lot.' We looked at each other, and the next thing I knew a laugh bubbled up my throat. 'Guess I know how to drive on the highway now.'

J. Norm blinked at me. 'Meaning you didn't before? I thought you had your learner's permit.'

'All they do is make you take the written test to get your learner's permit. Your parents have to help you practice. Russ says he'll take me to get my license, but he won't.'

J. Norm nodded slowly, his lips pouching out like he was tasting a thought. 'Well, we'll just have to work on all that, won't we?' He reached for the door handle and opened the door. '*Before* today's drive would have been a better time to reveal this information, but now that we've arrived in one piece, let's go inside and see what we can find out.'

'Cool.' I couldn't help smiling as I got out. Guess I'd found myself a driving teacher.

Inside the nursing home, it took us a while to get Frances Wilson's room number and find our way to the right hall. By then J. Norm was walking slower and slower. My heart was up in my neck, the way it used to be when I'd step into Mrs Lora's house, and she'd call out, *Epiphany, I have a surprise for you . . .* Something great was always waiting in the kitchen when she said that – some clothes or a book she thought I'd like, or maybe cookies she'd baked, or something that'd grown in the garden we worked on together. One time, there was a little baby kitten she'd found under the porch. We named him Tigger – not too original, but it fit. I didn't even know where Tigger was now. I couldn't take him when I left Mrs Lora's.

Walking down that hallway in the nursing home felt like getting ready to run through that kitchen door and see what was on the other side. The nursing home didn't smell sweet and good like Mrs Lora's house, though. When we moved past the doorways, I could see furniture painted bright colors, like it was meant to cheer up the people curled in metal beds, their bodies so thin and sunk down into the mattresses that it was like the beds and the people were fused together. I was glad Mrs Lora hadn't ended up in a place like this. How could Deborah even think about putting J. Norm in one? The only thing he'd do here would be curl up and die.

Behind me, he stopped and grabbed hold of the handrail along the wall, leaning on it and catching his breath.

'You know, you need get out and exercise more,' I said, frustrated. We were at room B-32, and Frances Wilson's was B-43. Right down the hall. 'When we get home, we're gonna start exercising, taking walks, get outside and stuff.' I'd have him in such good shape, there wouldn't be any way Deborah could talk some judge into sending him to a nursing home.

He swatted at me the way you'd shoo a fly. 'Go on and find her room. I'll be right there.'

I spun around and ran-walked the rest of the way to B-43. The door was hanging open just enough that I could see the corner of a bright blue dresser and the foot of the bed. 'Hello?' I whispered, leaning close to the opening. 'Mrs Wilson? Frances Wilson?'

'She's not in there.' A voice from behind made me jump just about out of my skin. A nurse was in a doorway across the hall, looking at me. 'Are you a family member?'

'Just . . . ummm . . . a friend . . . and . . . Where is she?'

The nurse gave me a sad look. 'She's been transferred to the hospital. Her room is scheduled to be cleaned out. I'm sorry.'

J. Norm caught up and turned to the nurse. 'Is she able to see visitors?' He leaned on the rail, looking worried. We both knew what it meant when they transferred you to the hospital and cleaned out your room.

'Hard to say,' she answered. 'I was by to check on her yesterday, and she wasn't doing well. It's not expected to be long. I'm sorry. She's a sweet lady. She was always one of my favorites.'

J. Norm got the room number and some directions about how to find our way, and we headed toward the hospital to see if we could learn Frances Wilson's secrets before she took them with her.

'What're you gonna say if we get to see her?' I asked while we were working our way over there. J. Norm was so slow, I wanted to hijack a wheelchair and push him in it.

'*Going to.* That's two words – *going to.*' Leave it to him to rag on me about grammar when the answer to the biggest mystery of his life might be right around the corner. 'I'm not certain I know what I'm *going to* say.'

'You scared?'

'Anxious,' he admitted.

'I bet we find out something great.' I wanted that to be true.

J. Norm patted my hand, then held on to my elbow while we walked the rest of the way.

When we got to the room, the door was cracked open. No one answered when we knocked, so I peeked inside. The lady in the bed was asleep as far as I could tell. She looked about a hundred years old.

'Is that her?' I whispered to J. Norm, as I pushed the door open farther.

He shuffled into the room, staring down at the woman like he was trying to find anything he recognized. 'I believe it could be.'

The two of us leaned over the bed from either side. The woman didn't move. I was afraid to touch her. She looked breakable, her skin as thin as paper, dotted with brown spots and veins and purple pools of blood just under the surface.

A sneaker squeaked in the doorway, and both J. Norm and me jerked upright. A girl who wasn't much older than me walked in. She wasn't wearing a uniform – just jeans and a T-shirt, but she didn't look like a relative, either. She was Asian or something. 'Can I help you?' she asked.

J. Norm vapor-locked, so I answered. 'We . . . ummm . . . The nursing home told us she was here. My . . .' I didn't have a clue what to call J. Norm. 'He wanted to visit. Mrs Wilson's his cousin, but they haven't seen each other in a long time. Right, J. Norman?'

The girl gave J. Norm a surprised look, almost like she knew him. 'Are you Norman? My grandmother has been asking and asking about you.' She moved closer to the bed then. 'Let me see if I can wake her. She's in and out, but I know she'll want to see you if she can.' Leaning over the bed, she rubbed her hands up and down the old woman's arms. 'Grammie? Gram? It's Kelly. Can you hear me? Norman's here. He came to see you. Do you think you can wake up and talk to him? Gram? Norman's here.'

The woman's eyelids fluttered, creeping upward like old roller shades with the springs worn out. Her granddaughter kept talking and rubbing, shaking her awake. Finally, some life came into her eyes. 'Sweet . . . heart,' she whispered, her voice raspy and faint.

Taking a water cup from the bedside table, Kelly tried to give her a drink, but the old woman turned her head to one side.

'Just fine,' she whispered, and smiled a little. 'Don't . . . worry.'

Kelly leaned close and kissed her forehead, then smoothed the gray hairs that were tangled against the pillow. She motioned for Norman to come closer. 'Grammie, Norman's here. You remember Norman? You were asking about him today.'

'Oh . . . Nor-mee . . .'

J. Norm leaned over the bed, and Mrs Wilson slowly rolled her head to the other side, squinting like she was trying to see him. She lifted a hand. 'What . . . happened to your . . . red hair?'

J. Norm laughed softly, taking her hand. 'I've gotten old and exchanged it for silver, but I couldn't afford more than a dusting of it.'

Mrs Wilson laughed, then coughed like she was choking on air. Her granddaughter took a tissue and wiped her chin. 'Gram, did you want to tell Norman something?'

'Not old.' Smiling again, Mrs Wilson let her eyes fall closed. 'Just a spring . . . chick . . . chicken.'

Holding her hand between both of his, J. Norm pressed her fingers against his chest. 'I need to ask a question of you. About my mother. About what happened.'

'Of course . . .' Mrs Wilson let out a long, slow sigh, her body seeming to dissolve into the sheets.

From across the bed, Kelly gave a sad look and shook her head. I knew her grandma was fading again.

Norman leaned closer to the bed, his chin almost on the railing. 'What was my mother hiding from me?'

'I give you . . . some . . . thing?' Mrs Wilson whispered, the words growing softer and softer, fading along with her. '. . . from the bl . . . blue . . .' She took another breath, her fingers slack in Norman's hand. One more word came when she breathed out the air. '. . . dresser?'

She closed her eyes and Kelly gave us a sad frown, then mouthed, *I'm sorry.* She said we could wait if we wanted, but she doubted that her grandma would wake up again that afternoon, and maybe not at all. J. Norm brought Frances's hand to his lips and kissed it, then lowered it gently to the bed. He stood looking at her a minute longer before we left, remembering the past, I guessed.

We didn't talk until we were back in the car, and J. Norm was looking at the map, trying to figure out how to get us out of McKinney and back on the highway.

'Turn left,' he said when we got to the street. Easy for him to say. Left was across three lanes of traffic. I'd never turned across three lanes of traffic in my life.

I held my breath and hit the gas and hoped I didn't take anybody's bumper off. The car lurched out of the parking lot, and J. Norm's head snapped. 'Slowly!' he barked.

'I can't go slow! There's cars everywhere!' All of a sudden there was traffic all around, everybody whizzing along faster than we were, turning off in all directions.

J. Norm pointed his finger toward the window and swung it sideways. 'Right at the next corner. Right. Right!'

I looked over my shoulder at all those cars coming a million miles an hour, and sweat started dripping down my back. 'I'm *not* turning right. It's too hard.'

He pointed again, his hand wagging like one of those dashboard dogs on a spring. 'That way to the highway entrance. That way!'

'I don't want to go that way.' *Breathe, breathe, just keep breathing. The left lane has to go someplace.*

'You're taking us into town!'

Every muscle in my body went stiff, and my stomach wriggled and twisted. A gap opened up to the right of us, and I whipped across two lanes, into the parking lot of a used-furniture store. I hit the brakes so fast that both of us swung forward, then back. 'Do *you* want to drive, because I . . .'

J. Norm wasn't looking at me. He was staring at some

junky scratched-up furniture in the store window. Someone'd painted it bright red and electric blue and glued Power Ranger pictures all over it. J. Norm's head tipped to one side, and he rolled down his window to get a closer look.

'What're you doing?' I leaned across the console to see if there was anything interesting in that window.

He pointed toward the furniture. 'What color was the furniture in the nursing home? In Frances's room. Did you see the dresser?'

My mind zipped through a half dozen tunnels, like a mouse slipping through the walls of Mama's house. 'Blue.' J. Norm turned to look at me, and both at the same time, we said, 'The blue dresser.'

Sliding back into my seat, I gripped the steering wheel. 'How do we get back to that nursing home?'

His mouth worked into a grin. 'Turn left.'

'Yeah, see, I was right all along,' I said. 'I knew you'd figure it out about the blue dresser here in a minute. I was just trying to make you feel good about yourself.'

He shook his head, but he was trying not to smile, I could tell.

I pulled out, and we headed back to the nursing home. On the way around the block, we came up with a plan. I'd go into Mrs Wilson's old room and push the door shut where people wouldn't see me snooping around, and J. Norm would hang around down the hall. If any of the workers came by, he'd stop them and ask them questions to keep them distracted, and if he had to, he'd even slip and fall down or something.

It was a good plan, and when we got to the nursing home, it went just like we'd pictured. There was a lady making her way down the hall with a laundry cart, but she was three rooms away from Mrs Wilson's, and I figured I'd have enough time to case the joint before she got there. She went into another room, and I ducked into Mrs Wilson's. There were actually two beds in there, and a lady was asleep in the other one, but she didn't look like she knew a thing. I checked out the blue dresser on Mrs Wilson's side, but the drawers were empty. Somebody'd already started cleaning the place out.

The old lady in the next bed moaned and stuck her hand up when I moved to the closet. 'Ssshhh,' I whispered. 'It's okay. Mrs Wilson wants her stuff from the blue dresser.'

The lady moaned louder, and I stopped where I was. Should I try to get her to quiet down, or check the closet real quick and scoot on out the door? Finally I went for the closet, and sure enough, there were boxes in the bottom, and they had Frances Wilson's name on them.

The lady in the bed kept moaning and moaning.

I popped opened a box. Clothes. I checked the other one. Clothes. I opened the third, and it was mostly empty – a few old pictures in picture frames, some printed pages from the Web site about St Clare's school. Some greeting cards, a couple of pretty bows that must've come on flower arrangements, a lace thing like you'd put on the top of a dresser, some loose stationery for writing letters, another box of greeting cards.

I heard J. Norm in the hall, talking to someone. Hooking a finger under the lid of the greeting card box, I pulled it up, looked inside, and there it was – an envelope with *Norman* written on it.

There were voices right outside the door now. J. Norm was talking loud, asking the laundry lady how often the sheets were changed here and whether the food was good, like he was either thinking of moving in or doing an inspection of the place.

I heard the squeal of another set of shoes coming up the hall. 'You'd better check on her,' the person talking with J. Norm said, and I figured that in about two and a half seconds, the moaning lady and I were gonna have company. Grabbing the envelope and one of the greeting cards, I pushed the closet door shut right as a nurse walked into the room. She didn't notice me at first. I took a step toward the door, and she saw me, and I glanced at J. Norm, who was wide-eyed outside with the laundry lady.

I held up the greeting card I'd lifted from Mrs Wilson's box. 'I don't know what's the matter. I just came in here to bring a card, but I think that lady needs something.' Before the nurse could ask me who I was, I set the card on the blue dresser and scooted out the door with J. Norm's envelope in my hand. I didn't even look at him. I just kept going until I was out the front of the building and in the car.

J. Norm must've found the switch for old-guy hyperdrive, because he wasn't far behind me. I was still trying to get my breath when he slid into his seat. 'What did you find?'

I held up the envelope. 'Home run.'

Taking it from my hand, he touched the place where his name was written and said, 'Drive.'

CHAPTER 15

J. Norman Alvord

I left the envelope unopened until we reached home. I wasn't certain why, other than the knowledge that the mere act of traveling across town with Epiphany at the wheel was excitement enough. I had the sense that the envelope contained something of significance – a life-altering bit of history that shouldn't be discovered while clinging to the seat by my fingernails as the car threaded through rush-hour traffic. Epiphany didn't argue the matter greatly. She was busy trying to deliver us home in one piece.

At slightly after five thirty we reached my house, having both perhaps sacrificed a year or more of life span. I was never so relieved to be pulling into my own driveway.

Safely back in the house, I sank into my chair, sliding my fingers along the crease of the plain brown envelope. The paper was crisp, somewhat aged in feel. The envelope had a pliability to the edges and a stiffness farther in, indicating that whatever was inside hadn't been intended for this particular package.

'Open it!' Dropping to her knees, Epiphany squirmed into

the narrow space beside my chair. 'I risked my life for that thing. It better not be last year's Christmas card.'

I examined the crease again, partially just to torment her, but there was also a sense of foreboding in me. If my mother had chosen to hide whatever knowledge this envelope contained, perhaps there was a good reason. 'Now, that would make both of us look foolish, wouldn't it? All this running around for a Christmas card.'

'Well, hey, at least I know how to drive in rush-hour traffic now, right?' Epiphany's hands flipped through the air, mobile exclamation points.

'I presume you're using that term loosely.'

She blew a raspberry at me. 'I got us back here. Open the stupid envelope.'

I slid a finger under the flap, and the glue popped free quickly. Inside was a single sheet of floral stationery folded around a newspaper clipping.

'What is it?' Epiphany leaned close, her chin touching my arm. 'What's it say?'

My hands shook as I unfolded the paper. At the top, my name had been written in shaky cursive, and beneath that, the single paragraph of writing ran downhill, the scrawl labored, crooked, almost illegible. I lifted it closer to my face, trying to make out the words. In my mind, I heard the voice from my childhood, Frances's voice.

Norman, I fear I cannot take this secret to my grave. Please know that I believe your mother had your best interests at heart. I suspect that to her dying breath she would have told you that you were always hers, but you came to her at five years old, following a trauma of some sort. You dreamed often of a house fire. I believe you had or may yet have siblings. A woman who helped with parties in your mother's Houston circle, Aldamae, may have known something of this. She was a black woman from Groveland. She came to the back door late one night and spoke privately with your mother. Shortly afterward, you were brought into the family. Aldamae knew your history, I am certain. I overheard things later on. There were secrets which your mother never confided to me, but . . .

The words became indiscernible then, except for the final few . . .

from Groveland, I think . . .

The letter ended abruptly, unsigned.

'Whoa,' Epiphany breathed, leaning away to look at me, her eyes wide circles of tarnished silver. 'That's like something out of a movie.'

'Except that it isn't a movie.' Everything I had suspected was true. The christening pictures that my mother had placed in my baby book, the grainy photographs of her building sand castles with a toddler at the beach house, were bits of someone else's history. My hair had not darkened from sandy blond to red, as she had always asserted when she'd shown those pictures of a towheaded child. In reality, I was not the child in those photographs.

I was another child. Someone *else's* child.

Epiphany squeezed out of the corner and stood up. 'You think we can get Terrence's computer again today?'

I glanced toward the door. 'He's out of town. When I spoke with him this morning, he said he was leaving for an art show in Oklahoma, and then he'd be spending a couple days with his daughter, Dell. She's expecting his first grand-child.' Epiphany's look of consternation took me aback slightly. 'Why did you want the computer again?'

She paced to the entry doorway and back, her fingertips drumming together. 'The library's closed by now. We need to get to a computer . . .'

'For what purpose, exactly?' Clearly I'd been left in the dust of a speedy, youthful mind.

Her face was alive with possibilities I hadn't yet seen. 'To look it up, J. Norm – just like that stuff we found about Frances and the school. I mean, a big house burns down and there's kids in the house, and some people must've died, or you wouldn't have been up for adoption. A fire like that would've been a big deal, right? Even though it was a long time ago, it would've been a big story. We think it might've happened in Groveland. Maybe it made the papers, or got on some history site – like the one we looked at about St Clare's school. We know *what* happened, and we sort of know *when* it happened – I mean, you know about how old you were when you were in the house with the seven chairs, so we can figure out what year the house might've burned down, right? You said you remembered four other kids and you, all redheaded. It's not every day five redheaded kids are in a house that burns down. You'd be surprised what's on the

Internet – all kinds of memories people have written about, old newspaper articles, lots of history. It's worth a shot.'

'Smart thinking,' I said, and my mind picked up its walking cane and chased after hers. 'We need a computer.'

'That's what I said.' She lifted her hands, then let them slap to her thighs.

But she hadn't gotten my point. 'No, I mean to say, we *need* a computer. Wal-Mart is only a few blocks. They sell those at Wal-Mart, correct? And the cellular apparatus for the Internet connection. Do they sell those?'

'Well, yeah, I guess. They got a whole cell phone store right there in Wal-Mart. You can buy anything. Shoot, when we go shopping, we can pick me up a cell phone while we're there.' She delivered the last sentence in a sarcastic tone, but with a hopeful gleam in her eye. 'You know a computer's expensive, right? And the cell phone Internet thing probably is, too.'

'Cost is not an issue. We have work to do.' Tucking the letter carefully back into the envelope, I scooted to the front of my chair, the joints in my legs popping and protesting. 'You can use it for your schoolwork, as well. When you have a need.'

'Cool!' Backing away from my chair, Epiphany cast a quizzical look in my direction and then toward the clock. 'You mean we're going right now? To Wal-Mart to buy a computer?'

A check of my wristwatch told me it was almost time for Epiphany to go to the city bus stop. 'Perhaps you should let your mother know you'll be working late. I can take you home in the car after we're finished.'

She looked askance heavenward in the way of a mother exasperated by a child's repetitive questions. 'Nobody's there, J. Norm. Mama's gone to her night shift by now, and Russ said he'd be away until late. He doesn't want me calling him while he's out doing his thing, believe me.' The answer held a nonchalance that made me wonder if anyone was looking after this child. She seemed to operate in her mother's house as if she were a miniature adult, living with roommates she didn't particularly like. I found the concept difficult to imagine. When I was her age, my mother could barely summon the courage to allow me to pick up a date and drive to the spring cotillion. When the time came for me to actually fly the nest, Mother wept for weeks, trailed me with letters, phone calls, care packages, and too-frequent visits.

And, in truth, I wasn't even hers by blood. Yet she was my mother in every meaningful sense of the word.

Oddly, I found myself both missing my mother and admiring Epiphany as we proceeded to the car and drove to Wal-Mart. Based on Frances's letter and my dreams, I suspected that my mother had saved me from a situation like Epiphany's, or worse. Given a set of circumstances like Epiphany's, would I have been as resilient, as determined to make a life for myself as she was?

'You're sure you want to do this?' Epiphany asked when we pulled into a handicapped space in the parking lot. Being old does have its advantages, occasionally – handicapped tags, for one.

'Quite. We'll purchase a computer and anything else that will be helpful in our search.'

Less than forty minutes later, Wal-Mart being the multi-purpose mecca that it is, we were walking out the door with food from the deli, a new backpack for Epiphany, and a computer, complete with all the necessary accessories, some of which the charming pimple-faced boy at the counter had given us for free with our purchase. The total cost, including the Internet cell phone connection, and a pair of barbecue dinners from the deli, was less than nine hundred dollars. A pittance, really, considering that I well remembered the day when computers occupied entire warehouses and carried price tags in the millions. Comparatively, our new laptop device was a bargain. Nonetheless, Epiphany was stunned on the way home.

'Must be nice to have all that money,' she muttered as we pulled into the garage again.

I considered the quest that had consumed a great deal of my life – not so much a lust for money as for success, for accomplishment. Money had been a natural result of it, however. 'Money follows hard work,' I said, perhaps by way of defending myself.

Getting out of the car, Epiphany scoffed. 'It helps if you got money to start with, J. Norm.'

Her answer frustrated me, because of the implicit helplessness of it. 'It helps if you're tall, and athletic, and dashingly handsome, too, but I was not. I suppose I would have preferred it if I'd been placed in the body of one of those charmed young men for whom the world seems to roll out like a red carpet, but what good would it have done me to complain about it? I came to this earth with an acute mind and an unwavering curiosity, and I made use of those assets. One of the secrets to life, Epiphany, is to find your gifts and focus on those. Leave your liabilities in the dust of the road not taken. The world is an imperfect place. Everyone struggles. Successful people see trials as growth experiences, rather than stumbling blocks. You have everything you need for success. You're a beautiful young woman, and you're strong, and you have a clever mind. If you let anyone convince you otherwise, you steal from yourself.'

'Now you sound like my history teacher,' she complained as we took the computer upstairs and set up a card table in Roy's room, a clandestine location where our equipment wouldn't be found, should Deborah ever decide to come back.

While we ate our deli meals and configured the computer, I told Epiphany about the early Block I Apollo Guidance Computers and the giant Sperry UNIVAC 1100 and IBM mainframes, which took up the space of whole rooms, operated via punch cards, and used reel-to-reel tape to store information. 'Hard to believe how things have changed,' I admitted, pointing to the computer. 'Those are kilobytes and gigabytes of information, flashing through the air all around us, encrypted and encoded. We could have used that technology, back in the day. The Russian trawlers wouldn't have given us so much trouble with our rockets.'

'The Russian what?' She paused with a fork halfway to her mouth.

'The trawlers – fishing boats off the coast,' I explained, thinking back to those cloak-and-dagger days when the Russians attempted to thwart us at every turn. 'In preparation for sending the real *Surveyor* into space, we moved our operations from California to Cape Canaveral to test a dynamic model, placed in an Atlas/Centaur rocket. But time after time, we experienced communications failure. Before we figured out that the Russians were using fishing boats off the coast to jam our radio signals, we'd changed out two complete radio transmitter systems, thinking they weren't working correctly. It took a couple of days each time, which was expensive – not to mention the costs of the hardware. After we discerned that the Russians were waiting for our launches each time, we began announcing fake launch times, then performing the real launch tests in secret. Our tests stopped failing after that.'

'Whoa, that's seriously James Bond,' Epiphany commented, and then turned her attention back to the computer. The software had finished installing, and she restarted the computer to allow it to take effect. It was only when the screen came on again that I noticed the time. I shouldn't have been so surprised, as it was dark outside.

'We should be getting you home,' I told her. 'It's after eight thirty.'

Her response was the usual incredulous, 'J. Norm, nobody cares. Besides, it's not like *you* know how to do a search on the browser. Anyway, you aren't driving me home.'

'I most certainly am. It's not as though you can be walking to and from the bus stop in the dark. I won't allow it.'

With an indignant cough, she opened the browser window. 'I can handle myself.'

'Well, then, humor me,' I replied. Epiphany would have a

career in the Senate someday. Winning an argument with her was almost impossible. 'Allow me to feel useful.'

She ignored me and typed something into the computer. 'What year were you born?'

'Nineteen thirty-five. I am driving you home.'

'So if you were five or six when the fire happened, that was 1940 or 1941, right?' Epiphany typed the information into the computer, adding bits and pieces of my life story. Clues. 'Not without taking out a few street signs and a fire hydrant or two, I bet. You barely got us home from the school, remember? There were five kids in your dream, right?'

'Five, including myself. I was the eldest.'

She added the words *five children,* and then pushed the ENTER key, sending the kilobytes of my history floating off into the ether. As the computer whirred, she swung my way like the pendulum striking on a clock. 'Look, Deborah told my mom that a couple months ago, you ran your other car into a tree and almost killed yourself. You're not driving me home.'

'Deborah exaggerates.' I could hardly admit that, at the time of the accident, I'd been driving Annalee's car. I'd brought it out with the intention only of circling the block a few times to run the engine. As the sunlight streamed into the interior, warming the seats, the scent of Annalee's perfume became so clear, so convincing, that I'd been certain she must be there in the car. Her voice echoed in my ear, and I'd turned toward the passenger seat, seen her or imagined her there, her head tipping back in laughter, her hair curling over her shoulders. I'd reached for her, and then the next thing . . . impact.

Epiphany touched my hand now, but instead I felt Annalee. They were Annalee's eyes that I saw, large, beseeching, brimming along the bottom. 'I don't want anything to happen to you, okay?' she whispered.

A tenderness swelled inside me – vulnerability of the sort I hadn't felt since . . . since Roy was alive? Was that when I threw myself so completely into my work, walling myself off from Deborah and Annalee, allowing them to process their grief together, without me? 'We're at an impasse, then, aren't we?' I observed. 'Either way, someone is at risk.' *Risk.* I'd been unwilling to take the risk of showing my pain to Deborah and Annalee, of letting them see the depth of my grief and guilt, of even experiencing it myself. I'd helped Roy choose that car, the Mustang, never stopping to consider what sort of trouble a fast car could lead a boy into.

I shook off the past, shedding it like water from an impermeable barrier. What was the point in revisiting old wounds? 'I'll call next door and speak with Hanna Beth. She has two nurses who live in her upstairs apartment. One of them leaves for the night shift a bit before ten. I can pay her a little something to drive you home.'

'I can take the . . .'

I whipped a hand upward to stop the argument. 'It's settled. I can't let you go walking off in the dark, and by the by, no gentleman would. You'll do well to remember that, in terms of dating in the future. Any boy who expects to pick you up and drop you off at the curb is not worth your time.

A young lady must respect herself if she's to demand respect from a boy.'

Epiphany didn't answer. She'd turned her attention back to the screen, her rounded shoulders indicating that she was weary of my lectures. I only hoped they were penetrating her armor. 'J. Norm, look,' she whispered, pointing to the screen. 'It came up with something. There's a listing about books.'

I leaned close to make out the text. *An East Texas Timber Town History, by M. L. White, Pinewood Publishing Company*, it read in blue type, and below in black, a listing for a book with two hundred and fifty pages, published in 1991, and following that, a quote: . . . *tramps along the railroad. I remember in January of 1940 a big house along the track burned down, with five children, their mother, and a black maid inside. My daddy was the sheriff at the time, and there was a suspicion that hobos off the train had caused the fire, but* . . .

'My word,' I breathed.

Epiphany nodded, then moved the arrow to the listing and pushed the button. She seemed to be holding her breath, as was I.

The hourglass spun and spun.

We waited.

Epiphany tapped her fingernail impatiently against the button.

'What's wrong?' I asked.

She shook her head. 'I don't know. It's not coming up, or . . .' The screen changed finally, turning white at first, and then a notification appearing: *Address not found.*

Muttering, Epiphany tried again, and then searched for the author, M. L. White, with the same results. I went to the phone and called next door to arrange a ride for Epiphany, while she searched for further information about the book or the publishing company. She came up with an address in Groveland, Texas, and a phone number. After completing my call next door, I dialed the publishing company's number, thinking to receive an automated message regarding business hours, but the number now belonged to a dollar store in Groveland, Texas. The teenager who answered the phone had never heard of the book or the publisher. A call to directory assistance confirmed that there was no current listing for the Pinewood Publishing Company.

'Tomorrow I'll try the library in Groveland,' I told Epiphany, as we went to Deborah's room and selected a few model rockets for Epiphany's history project. 'With any luck, the Groveland library will have the book in their collection, or they can direct me to a place that might – a museum or historical society. I'm sure that with enough digging, we can track down something.'

'I hope so,' Epiphany said, and then we proceeded downstairs to wait for Hanna Beth's nurse to swing by. Epiphany was still thinking about the Internet listing. 'Where's Groveland, Texas?'

'East and south, down in the Piney Woods,' I told her. 'Not so far from here. Perhaps three hours' drive, I'd say.'

She chewed her lip, and to my surprise I realized that I'd come to know her well enough to understand the meaning of that expression. She was cooking something up. 'We could go there. This weekend. We could take your car. I could drive.'

I was momentarily blindsided. 'I hardly think your mother . . .'

Her mouth hung open, as if I were a numbskull. 'Russ and her are heading to Oklahoma this weekend, on Friday. They'll never even know. If we went to Groveland in person, we could find out everything.' Her eyes widened, and her mouth lifted into a slow, crafty smile that beamed with the light of the rising idea. 'Just think about it, J. Norm. You and me on a road trip.'

I'm ashamed to say that I actually found myself considering it, the taste of an adventure tantalizing the dusty, understimulated corners of my mind. 'And then there's Deborah.'

'Maybe she'll stay mad. She didn't come by today. Maybe she won't all weekend.'

'There's no telling, with Deborah.'

'If she doesn't come by tomorrow or Friday, can we go?'

Lights shone in the driveway, and I unlocked the door for Epiphany to leave, but she wouldn't. 'Come on, J. Norm. It'll be an adventure – like launching for the moon. Who knows what we'll find in Groveland?'

I wrung my hands, the temptation overwhelming. An adventure into the unknown, when I'd thought all the great adventures of my life were past. Camelot, one more time. 'We'll see how the remainder of the week develops,' I answered finally.

Not yes. But not no, either.

The possibility remained.

CHAPTER 16

Epiphany Jones

I got Russ to call me in sick again on Thursday, but by Friday morning, I didn't have any choice except to go to school. Russ was busy getting ready for the flea market in Oklahoma, and Mama was crashed out in bed after working like crazy to get ahead on cleaning her houses so she could go on the big weekend trip. She'd had a cancel today, so she was done for the week, and she'd already called in sick to work for tonight so they could leave. When I passed by in the hall, she rolled over with her eyes closed and babbled out, '. . . uuungo to shhh-school.' Which was more than I usually got. She sure didn't want me hanging around bugging her today.

When I passed by Russ in the kitchen, he asked if I wanted to go to Oklahoma, like maybe he felt bad about leaving me here for three days again. I told him I had to finish my English essay and do my report in history class today, so I couldn't skip school, and then J. Norm needed me at work. I didn't want anybody getting ideas about making me get in the truck and go to some swap meet all weekend. I couldn't think of much that would be worse than being smushed in the front seat with Russ and Mama while they either cuddled or fought all the way to Oklahoma.

For once, I wasn't really lying, anyway. J. Norm and me did have plans, and I really did need to get the stupid speech over with in history. The teacher had already warned us that ditching school wouldn't get us out of it, and besides, if I stayed home any longer, I was gonna be so far behind, I'd never catch up. Hopefully, now that a couple days had gone by since J. Norm's big visit to the principal's office, DeRon would be cooled down. I'd basically saved his rear on the backpack deal, anyway, and J. Norm was paying for the damaged books, so DeRon came out of it all right. I couldn't keep hiding out from him forever. There were still six weeks to go before summer. Six weeks and one day, if I lived that long, and we'd be done for the year. By the time summer was over and it was time to go back again, I wasn't gonna be here. With the money I was stashing away, and now having J. Norm's computer for research, I could blow this joint by the middle of the summer, go look for my daddy's family, and find out the truth about all those ladies in the big hats and the beautiful dresses who bothered to pose for pictures with me at my first and only birthday party.

Turning that plan over in the back of my mind made it easier to gather up the stuff for my history report and walk down the street to the school bus stop, looking over my shoulder for DeRon all the way. My stomach bubbled and curled like plastic in a fire when I thought about getting on the bus, with people giving me looks and saying things like, 'Hey, cream pie, yo' mama get that shirt outta the trash somewhere?' or, 'You want some chewin' gum, Jemima?' And then they'd throw some used gum across the bus, or come by and try to smash it into my hair. When I moved out of the way, they'd be like, 'What, you too good for my gum?'

This morning wasn't any different, of course. Now that DeRon wasn't on my side anymore, we were back to the same stupid stuff, except they'd all heard what had happened in DeRon's car, and how I ran to J. Norm's house after that, and they were all making jokes about it, like, 'Yeah, you jus' like 7-Eleven, got a open-door policy. Take 'em young and old. You got you a old-dude boyfriend, cream pie? Maybe somebody betta tell him watch his back. You gonna give it to him like you done with DeRon, then go call the principal 'cuz he don' wanna be your boyfriend after? Who gonna be a boyfriend wit' some nasty thang like you, anyway?'

'What you got in that bag, there, cream pie? Awww, you got a little toy rocket? You gonna blast off back to the moon?'

By the time I got to school, I was tired. Tired of ducking and dodging, tired of listening and not saying anything, tired of trying to keep the gurgling pool of rotten breakfast inside me from coming up. Tired of everything.

I was sorry I'd brought stuff from J. Norm's for the history report. It just gave them another reason to rag on me. I shouldn't have bothered. If you did your work at this school, it just made the other kids pick on you.

I put everything in my locker as quick as I could, so there was one less thing to worry about. Walking down the halls, I kept watching for DeRon. It didn't take me long to figure out that he'd gotten a couple days of in-school suspension, because after the principal'd talked to us, he'd grilled a couple of the kids who ran around with DeRon, and somebody leaked it that he spray-painted my backpack on purpose. Now the other kids hated me worse than usual. Of course, the story going around was that I'd gone all the way with DeRon in his car, and then I was mad when he wouldn't be my boyfriend.

By ten o'clock, I'd decided that if I made it to the end of school in one piece, it was gonna be a miracle.

During lunch, I went in the bathroom and pulled my feet up above the stall and just hid out there, because I knew what would happen in the cafeteria. Even on a good day, there weren't enough teachers to keep people from throwing food and walking by and poking you with forks, and today wasn't a good day.

By the time history class came along, my stomach was so empty I was sick, and my head was pounding. I botched the report about rockets, not that anybody cared. Mostly, they slept through it. DeRon's old girlfriend, Lesha, stared me down and let me know I was dead if she and her bunch got ahold of me.

As soon as the bell rang, I scooted out of there, dumped stuff in my locker, and moved down the hall to my next class. Once I was there, I let out a big ol' sigh and laid my head on my desk, thinking, *I just want to get out of here.* In

English class, we watched a movie, but I couldn't pay attention to it. A hammer was banging in my head and I felt like
I was ready to throw up. Before class was over, I told the
teacher I was sick, and I took off for the bathroom. That
turned out to be the biggest mistake of the day. The hallway
was empty, and all of sudden there was DeRon. He caught
me by the arm, and before I knew what was happening,
he'd pulled me into the boys' bathroom and pinned me
against the wall, his body solid and heavy, pressing me into
the cement blocks. The smell of hair wax and sweat and bad
breath filled my nose, and my stomach rolled over, then
clenched. I couldn't remember what I ever liked about
him – why I thought I wanted to be his girlfriend.

'Hey, babe.' His lips pulled back into a sick kind of smile –
not the smile he used to charm the ladies, but the kind that
said he was thinking of something bad and already imagining how it was gonna feel. 'You been tryin' to hide out?' He
opened his fingers where they held my wrist pinned against
the wall, slid his palm slowly over my skin. My arm stayed
frozen there, like it'd been tied to the cinder blocks. For a
second, I couldn't move. All I could think about was that
day in the car. If I hadn't climbed out the window, what
would've happened? Would he have pulled me into the
backseat and pinned my body like this?

'Cut it out.' My voice was weak and thready. 'Leave me a –'
His lips came down, covered mine, pressed hard, and took
away the rest of the words. His hand moved lower, his thumb
and fingers circling my neck. Then he lifted his head again,
leaned back to look down at me, his thumb stroking back

and forth over my windpipe, just hard enough that it hurt a little. 'Yeah, you still want me,' he murmured, and grinned again. 'You got a little game on, gettin' me in-school suspension. Tellin' everyone I messed up them books.'

'You know I didn't tell them anything,' I bit out, the words going higher and lower when he pressed on my throat. What was he doing in the hall, anyway? Kids in the in-school suspension room weren't allowed to go anywhere on their own. Did he sneak out, or did the teacher let him go? How much longer until somebody came looking for him, or the bell rang? How many minutes? There was a security camera right outside the bathroom door, a class right across the hall. DeRon couldn't do much to me here. Could he? If I screamed, someone would hear. Right?

But I knew better, really. Just a month before I came, some girl got a concussion in the restroom. People still talked about it in the lunch line. Next week, they could be talking about me. My heart lurched and fluttered so hard I was sure DeRon could feel it through my skin.

'Your old-man boyfriend told 'em I messed with them books, though, didn't he?' DeRon's eyes narrowed, two black beads as cold as glass. They didn't fit with his thick, dark lashes. 'You been givin' that old man some, Epiphany? He pay you good for it?'

'You're sick.' I turned my face away, and he pulled it back, pushed on my throat hard enough that I coughed. I was afraid to turn away again.

'You wanna sell it, girl, we can make us a little money. I know guys that'll pay.' He blinked real slow, like he was enjoying watching my eyes go wide and my mouth drop open. 'You don't mind old guys, I can get us some real money.'

I moved my hand off the wall, slammed both palms against his shoulders, tried to push him off, but he didn't move. I wasn't getting out of here until the bell rang or he let me go. My mind raced ahead, looking for a way I could get free. There was no car window to crawl through this time. 'Get away from me, DeRon. You do anything to me, you get in any more trouble, you'll be off the basketball team, and then what'll happen to all those big scholarships you're always talking about, huh? You'll just be another loser like all the rest of the losers walking the streets around here.'

His lashes flared; then narrowed again. 'Well, you just too good for all us now, are ya? Miss A-plus-plus? I wanna see what somethin' that good tastes like.' He kissed me again, his fingers massaging my neck, squeezing, then letting go, pushing little puffs of air between our lips, his body pressing against mine before he whispered, 'Come on, baby, don't be so cold. I know you been givin' it to that old man. I seen you stayin' at his house all night long when yo' mama ain't home. You think I didn't come lookin' fo' you that night after you ran outta my car?'

He lost his balance a little, his body arching away from mine. Twisting in the empty space, I shoved him off me. He stumbled to one side, his foot tangling between mine.

The bell rang, and all I could think was, *Thank you, God.* Any second now, the hallway would be full of kids heading for the lockers and teachers and security guards trying to make sure nobody got in a fight.

DeRon knew he had to give it up before he got caught in here with me. Standing between me and the door, he rubbed a hand over his hair. 'You bes' stop gamin' on me, Epie.'

I pulled my T-shirt straight, tried to keep my hands from shaking. 'I'm not gamin', DeRon. I'm not *with* you, and I'm not gonna be. Ever. You got girls lined up out the door, anyway. Go find one of them.'

He grinned again, the flirty kind of grin this time, like we were just playing. 'I been with all a' them, Epiphany. I want me somethin' new.'

'Leave me alone, DeRon.' I took a step toward the door, grabbed the handle to see if he'd move. He stuck his foot in front of the door, blocking it just an inch open; then he leaned over me from behind. 'Guess I better go do me a public service, then.' His voice was low, deep in his throat, the growl of a dog that's already decided to bite. 'Guess I better go tell the counselor and the principal that old man been gettin' it on with you, keepin' you at his big ol' house overnight. Lettin' you drive around in his car, buyin' you stuff. Yeah, I seen you at Wal-Mart the other day. You all smilin' at him, and him shuckin' off that credit card like it ain't nothin'.'

My mind went off a cliff. DeRon saw us buying the computer? 'He's just a friend.' What would happen if DeRon told the counselor or the principal those things?

'That's not what you said to me.' DeRon's breath was hot against my skin. 'You said that if you give him some, he gonna buy you anything you want up to the Wal-Mart. Guess you made him pay good.'

'That's not true. I never said that.' I yanked the door again, and it bounced off DeRon's toe.

'Sho' it is.' He laughed. 'And what you think that old redneck yo' mama lives with gonna do when the school gives yo' mama a call about it? And, man, then the police gonna have to investigate, and you know, anytime word get out about somethin' like that, everybody believe it. They can't *wait* to believe it. Why else some old man got some sweet young thang stayin' at his house overnight?'

'He needs my help. I take care of him.' I yanked on the door, and DeRon moved his foot so quick the door came back and hit me in the forehead hard enough that I saw stars.

'I bet you do.' Shoving the door open wider, he pushed past me and headed down the hall, weaving through the crowd. Laughing, he chest-bumped with one of his friends, like he didn't have a worry in the world. I stood there feeling dizzy for a minute, and then I staggered off to my locker. My hands were shaking as I pulled out books and crammed them into my backpack. Some girl passed by and shoved me from behind and laughed when I fell against my locker. I barely even noticed. I was thinking about DeRon. He wouldn't actually do it – walk into the office and tell the principal I had something going on with J. Norm. Would he?

If he did, that'd sure make DeRon look good, like he was concerned about me or something. Just doing his civic duty.

A cold feeling went down my spine, an ice cube sliding along my skin, leaving chills behind. Someone called my name across the crush of people in the hall – a teacher, the

247

counselor, someone – and I knew there was only one reason they'd be calling me like that. They wanted me in the office.

I wondered if I could make them see that J. Norm was . . . well, not a friend exactly, but kind of like a friend. More like a grandpa. I'd never had a grandpa before, but if I did, it seemed like he'd be like J. Norm – a little grouchy, a little bossy, too full of advice, but also somebody who had time to do things, like tell you stories about the old days, or put together rockets, or turn off the TV when you came in, like he'd been waiting for you all day. A grandpa would shake his stupid finger at you, and call you things like *young lady*, but also laugh when you popped off at him, and he'd tell you you're a beautiful young woman, even though you're not. I hadn't ever really thought about it before, but a grandpa, if I had one, would be a whole lot like J. Norm.

But no matter what I said to the principal, it'd be my word against DeRon's, and DeRon was on the basketball team, after all. He was gonna get a scholarship and make the school look good. I was just . . . well . . . some kid who moved in from out of town. Not white, not black. Not an athlete. Not anything special. Once they'd talked to both DeRon and me, then the next thing they'd do would be try to figure out if I really did spend the night at J. Norm's house and if we really were at Wal-Mart buying expensive stuff together. The facts were on DeRon's side. After that, trouble would break loose – wild, and crazy, and tearing through everything.

I pretended I didn't hear the voice calling my name over the crowd. Grabbing my stuff, I started to take off down the hall the other way. The back doors were right around the corner. If I could just make it there . . .

A hand caught my arm, and I jerked back, sucking in a breath.

'Mrs Lavon is calling you.' It was the science teacher who had me. I looked up, and he was pointing down the hall. Mrs Lavon, the assistant principal, waved at me over the crowd, a concerned look on her face.

'Oh.' I felt myself sinking, everything spinning around me. 'But I've got . . . to go to work.' If I could just get to the door, just get out . . .

The science teacher chuckled. 'Better hold on a minute and see what she wants. I'm sure it won't take long.'

The hall started clearing as he turned loose of me, and I headed toward the assistant principal, moving one step at a time, thoughts tumbling through my head. Mrs Lavon slid an arm over my shoulders, and she turned me toward the office, and I could feel a freight train rushing toward me.

'I've got to head for work. I'll be late,' I said, like that would get me out of anything.

'It's all right.' Her fingers patted my shoulder the way you would if you were trying to comfort a baby, which was weird, considering that Mrs Lavon and me had never said a word to each other the whole time I'd been at this school. 'Let's step into my office for a minute.' By then, we were already walking past the secretary's desk, so there wasn't much choice. I glanced over and saw DeRon sitting in the counselor's office, his back turned toward me. Everything went in slow motion after that. Mrs Lavon took me into her

249

office, asked me if I wanted to sit down. I said I didn't. I told her again that I needed to go. She put her hands on my shoulders, looked me in the eye, and I thought, *Here it comes – something like, 'Now, Epiphany, I don't want you to be afraid. You're not in trouble, but I want you to tell me the truth about this man Norman . . .'*

Instead, she said, 'Epiphany, there's been an accident.'

The first thing I thought about was J. Norm. He'd taken the car for a drive without me, and something terrible had happened, and it'd be my fault because I got him started by finding the stuff about his family and driving him to the nursing home yesterday. 'A . . . a what?'

'An accident. Your . . .' It seemed like she was searching for a word, and then she finally settled for, '. . . stepfather's truck.'

My . . . who? I thought, and then I realized she meant Russ. Russ had an accident? Mama and Russ were in Oklahoma together.

'Everyone's going to be all right.' She answered my question before I could ask it. 'But it was a rollover and the truck caught on fire, and both your mother and your stepfather are in an Oklahoma City hospital overnight for observation.' Leaning across her desk, she grabbed a sticky note and handed it to me. 'They called here and asked that we let you know what had happened.'

'Oh . . .' I stammered, looking at the sticky note. My mother's name, Russ's, a hospital, and a phone number were all written in Mrs Lavon's careful, loopy handwriting. 'Okay.' I didn't know what else to say. I was busy trying to figure out what this meant, or what I should do about it. Meantime, in the office next door, DeRon was probably blabbing his brains out. Any minute now, the counselor would come and haul me in there. 'But they're all right . . . Mama and Russ?'

'Yes. The injuries weren't serious.'

'Well . . . when will they be back?' A plan was forming in my mind, taking shape the way clay sculptures do in art class, ideas pinching here and there like fingers.

'I'm not sure. It sounds like it might be early next week before they can get the insurance taken care of and arrange for transportation home.' Mrs Lavon's phone buzzed, and she looked sideways at it. 'Your mother said you had relatives next door to your house who could look after you.'

Relatives. That was Mama code for, *Don't tell these people anything.* Like I would be stupid enough to tell Mrs Lavon that I was home by myself all the time, and a few more days wouldn't make any difference. The truth was that Mama wouldn't have been getting in touch with me at school if she'd had any other way to tell me what was going on. Guess she didn't think to call J. Norm's, or maybe she didn't have the number with her. 'Oh, sure. We've got all kinds of relatives. No problem. Can I go now, Mrs Lavon?' The phone on her desk buzzed again, and I thought, *What if that's the counselor calling over here? Did she see me go by a minute ago? Does she know I'm in Mrs Lavon's office?* I needed to get out now. Mrs Lavon had her mind on the phone, so it wasn't too hard. I told her good-bye, stuck her note in my pocket, and walked out.

Through the glass, I saw DeRon, now in the principal's

office with the counselor. I passed on by in a hurry, and as far as I could tell, they didn't see me. Three minutes later I was out the back door, heading across the parking lot as fast as I could. Slipping around behind the gym, I went through the alley where all the lunch trash stayed tangled in the fence. A man was out there cutting weeds, and farther down the fence, a homeless guy was checking out a Dumpster, but they hardly seemed to notice me. A siren sounded somewhere off in the distance, and I wanted to run, but I made myself walk. The police car wasn't after me. Shoot, the school probably didn't even know I took off so quick. If DeRon had them looking for me, they'd probably check around the campus first.

I ran the rest of the distance to J. Norm's. The way I figured it, depending on what story DeRon was feeding the principal and the counselor, and whether they believed it, the police or somebody could show up at J. Norm's house sooner or later. The plan in my mind was solid now, clear as if somebody'd written it on paper. All I had to do was convince J. Norm.

There wasn't any time to waste.

I was panting on the doorstep, out of breath when he opened the door. For the first second, he looked at me like he didn't know who in the world I was, and then he checked his watch. 'You're early today,' he said, like I couldn't come in unless it was time. Then he stepped back so I could get into the house.

I heard the sirens off in the distance again as I slid past J. Norm. 'Let me in, okay.' The words came out in a breath, and I dropped my backpack in the entryway, then leaned against the wall. For a sec, I just closed my eyes, the day running through my head like YouTube videos gone wild. The school bus, hiding in the bathroom at lunch, DeRon grabbing me, the counselor's office, Mama's accident, Mrs Lavon giving me her concerned look. It was perfect, like she'd practiced it. She'd really be concerned once she heard DeRon's story. I'd be lucky if I didn't end up with social services on my doorstep before Mama even made it home, and when she did, I'd be in trouble for giving her grief. She and Russ might decide to go ahead and kick me out after all.

But if I wasn't *there* when social services knocked on the door, they'd all just figure the relatives had taken me to Oklahoma to be with my mama in the hospital. By the time I got back, this whole thing about J. Norm would've died down, DeRon would be off suspension, and the people in the school office would be on to the next problem. Maybe I could even get Mama to help out and tell them J. Norm was as harmless as a growly old dog with no teeth.

If I came back at all. I was still working that part out in my mind. Maybe it was time for me to go ahead and leave for good, head for Florida and keep doing research about my daddy's family on the way. Could be that'd be the best plan. I hadn't ever seen the ocean, for one thing, and if there was somebody somewhere in Florida who'd cared enough to dress me up and take pictures once upon a time, I wanted to know it. While J. Norm and me were on our trip, I could do some more searching for names and addresses and stuff. Once I had that, all I needed was money. Like the nine hundred dollars J. Norm had plunked down for the computer. I could tell him I needed money to get up to Oklahoma to see Mama in the hospital. Maybe he'd give it to me . . .

The idea was hard to picture, like the mystery packets Mrs Lora used to put in my school lunches, the food wrapped in aluminum foil so that you could see the shape but only guess what was inside. What would it be like to lie to the only person who ever looked forward to seeing you? How would I feel if I took his money and then ran off?

I wasn't sure I could lie to J. Norm that way. Right now I didn't have to, though. 'We've gotta go,' I said. 'J. Norm, we've gotta go now.'

He frowned, his chin pulling back into his neck so that he looked like a bullfrog about to croak. 'Go where?'

'To Groveland.'

Shaking his head, he hooked his thumbs in his belt and pulled his pants higher on his old-man belly. 'This isn't a good day for jokes, Epiphany. Deborah's been after me with her lawyer again.'

A new worry tunneled under my skin, burrowing in like a tick. If J. Norm's daughter heard about this stuff from the school, if she found out I'd stayed here overnight, and we'd been to Wal-Mart in the car, she'd use it against him. The trouble at school would seem like small potatoes then. 'J. Norm,' I said, looking him flat in the eye, 'I'm not joking. We have to go. Now.'

CHAPTER 17

J. Norman Alvord

Perhaps Deborah was correct, after all, in her assessment of my diminished mental capacity, or perhaps it was merely a momentary inability to resist Epiphany's pleading, but in short order, we were hitting the open road. In the back, we had a bag of random snack food, the computer, and my hastily packed overnight bag, as well as Epiphany's backpack and two grocery-store sacks bearing whatever belongings she'd gathered during a rushed stop at her mother's house. While Epiphany had threaded her way through scattered motorcycle parts on the porch and disappeared into the run-down structure, I'd sat outside, keeping watch. A few moments later, she'd skidded out the door, turned the lock, rushed back to the driver's seat, and we were off. No turning back now.

The mad scramble and our escape were exhilarating, like a somewhat silly dream from which I was bound to awaken any moment. A man my age didn't do things like this in real life, surely. But as we left Blue Sky Hill behind and accelerated onto the highway ramp, I felt a burst of freedom, a rush of adrenaline like nothing I'd experienced since *Surveyor* rocketed into the stratosphere on Memorial Day 1966, headed for the moon.

Whether it was the compulsion to discover the secrets of my past, or the misbegotten sense of finally taking back control of my own life, I felt at first like rolling down the windows and bursting into song. 'My Way,' or something of the like, seemed appropriate.

Oddly enough, it was the closing in of rush-hour traffic that derailed my euphoria, scrambling the impulses in my mind like one of the Russian trawlers hacking our radio signals, attempting to send a perfectly good launch and all the hopes attached to it plunging into the sea. I felt the chill of the water, cold, unavoidable, abrupt. I couldn't abscond with someone's child, a minor, without permission. A teenage girl, no less. If this boy, this DeRon, were to continue with these ridiculous accusations of his, this trip would only add fuel to the fire, proof that I was up to something inappropriate with a young girl. Leaving at this time of day, we'd have no choice but to stay overnight. Overnight in a strange town, the two of us.

The idea was appalling. Appallingly improper.

'It's time to go back,' I said, after considering the words for a moment. Even so, they tasted bitter, a disappointment. 'We cannot just leave on a trip without permission, especially with your mother and ... what's-his-name in the hospital.' While I'd packed my bag, Epiphany had called the hospital and spoken with her mother's boyfriend or husband, Ross or Russ, something like that. Epiphany's mother was sleeping off a dose of pain medication, her companion being in somewhat better shape. Epiphany had told him nothing of our trip, of course, but she had managed to ascertain that it would be early next week before arrangements could be made for the wrecked vehicle and trailer. They hoped to return home on Tuesday. Nonetheless, this trip was a foolish idea, and the only responsible thing would be to end it before it went any further.

'I knew you'd say that.' Epiphany's voice was infused with frustration and disappointment. 'I knew you'd try to chicken out.'

I was insulted at first, but then I pointed out to myself that she was only a child. It was easy to forget that fact, as she was intelligent and resourceful. She was, however, a sixteen-year-old girl. I should have reminded myself of that fact at the outset. To her, this was a grand adventure. She could not possibly anticipate all the potential repercussions. 'I am not chickening out. I'm being practical.' Practicality was my strong suit, after all. Had I not spent my life considering projects analytically, developing contingency plans, calculating everything that could go wrong? Careful forethought was the difference between success and failure, in terms of engineering. A lack of forethought could produce disaster.

'Turn the car around.' I scouted for an off-ramp as we limped along in traffic. 'Take this next exit and make a U-turn under the highway.'

Epiphany's neck stiffened, her head angling away from me. That posture I knew well by now. The next words from her mouth would not be, *Yes, sir.* 'Huh-uh.'

'Epiphany, now, you listen here.' This would be war, of course. The girl was nothing if not stubborn.

'No. We're going. We're already gone.' In truth, we weren't. We were stuck in traffic less than twenty miles from home. The highway was moving well in the opposite direction. We could be back at my house in less than half an hour.

The thought was heavy, confining, a rubber raincoat on a sunny day. 'Turn around, I said.'

'No.'

'This is *my* car.' I smacked a palm against the dash, but she only gripped the steering wheel more tightly, her reaction minimal.

'Well, then, you're getting kidnapped.' Her chin bobbed back and forth, lending punctuation to the words, defying my challenge. 'If we get caught later, that's what I'll tell everybody. It was my idea. I made you do it.'

'Nobody would believe it.' I considered reaching for the steering wheel, but in the middle of rush-hour traffic, with an inexperienced driver, it seemed a bad idea. A fine sheen of sweat had broken over her skin as semitrucks squeezed close on either side of us, walling us in. Her gaze held fast to the window, her eyes twitching from one lane to another, as if at any moment she expected us to be obliterated. She was frightened half out of her mind, yet she wouldn't give in.

In truth, I shouldn't have been stirring her up. I might stir the two of us right into an accident, and then our problems would go from bad to worse. I imagined the police coming to the scene, discovering me with a young girl to whom I was not related, with computer equipment and suitcases in the back. They'd think I was some sort of deviant, a child pornographer like the ones reported about on television. 'Epiphany,' I said more gently, 'this is madness. It's insanity.'

She lifted a hand from the steering wheel long enough to swipe the back of a wrist across her brow and tuck spirals of thick, dark hair behind her ear. For a moment, I thought she wouldn't answer at all. Perhaps this was to be a silent kidnapping now. Then she gripped the steering wheel again, the set of her jaw hard, resolute. 'They said the *Surveyor* would sink under the moon dust, but it didn't, did it?'

Her point dawned in my mind like the earth rising slowly, large and blue, over the lunar surface. Only impossible journeys achieve the impossible.

I felt myself acquiescing, giving in, against all good sense. 'True enough.' Caution began to fall away as we worked a path through the traffic, creeping toward the unknown like a rocket moving toward the launchpad on crawlers, the progress so slow it could barely be seen with the naked eye. But beneath what could be seen, there was an anticipation of fire, speed, discovery. One last journey into the unknown. One last mission impossible in my life.

Beside me, my copilot allowed a self-satisfied smirk. She'd won, of course, and she was delighted. 'Don't worry, J. Norm. I'll take care of you.'

'That's what I'm afraid of.' I rested my head against the seat back. 'Kidnapping is illegal, you know.' My eyes fell closed just as her smirk became a genuine smile.

My mind drifted away to visions of Camelot, but slowly

Camelot became another place, a space deeper within me, the memories in light and shadow, like a forest floor with sunbeams filtering through here and there, burning off the murk. I was on a wide front porch with tall white pillars. Cecile sat on the porch swing, balancing the baby on her knee as she helped Emma, the quiet one, to weave a chain of dandelions and daisies. Nearby, Erin created a rhythmic *tap, tap, tap* with her skipping rope at the top of the steps, while Johnny rode a squatty metal baby scooter to the gate and back along the front walk. Seeds with feathery white sails tumbled from Emma's gathering of flowers and slid across the porch, swirling in the whip of air from Erin's rope, then sailing away. I watched the lacy parachutes travel, rising slowly at first, then launching toward faraway places, at the mercy of wind and water. I yearned to follow those seeds, to fly away from that house and the terrible things that were happening there. Watching the girls run and play, I felt envy, then sadness. *They'll be next*, I thought. *Their time will come.* My body ached in so many places, but the bruises on my soul yielded a deeper pain.

There were burns of some sort on my wrists, red and angry and new. Even though it was summer, I wore long sleeves to cover them. Rubbing the fabric that hid the wounds, I glared through the screen door, hated the woman upstairs in her gauzy white nightgown. I hated her because she didn't stop it from happening.

I hated her, and yet I wanted her love . . .

When I woke, a breeze was sliding softly over my skin, cooling the perspiration on the back of my neck. The car clicked steadily over joints in the concrete, so that I knew before coming fully to consciousness that we had left the traffic behind. Outside the car, there were no sounds of the city – just the occasional hum and swish of a car passing in the other direction, and the gentle rocking of an old two-lane highway.

A thought troubled my mind, a leftover corollary to the dream, I supposed. Given the bit of text we'd seen on the Internet, it was likely this trip would prove that the twin girls in my dream, the toddler boy, the baby, and Cecile, were all dead. The victims of a tragedy of such a monumental proportion that it lived for years hidden inside me, and found light only in the memoirs of some person who'd published a book about the history of a little timber town in the Piney Woods.

How much time had passed after that day on the porch, when I'd stood stiff and sore, hiding my bruises as the girls blithely skipped rope and gathered flowers? How much time before the fire? It couldn't have been long. The legs I'd seen when I looked down at my feet were the wiry, sun-tanned legs of a boy, narrow cords of muscle winding into knobby knees. I must have been at least five, perhaps even six. I was seven or eight when my mother argued with Frances about sending me to the first grade at St Clare's school, and by then I'd been with her long enough that she'd taught me my letters and numbers at home. We'd moved from Houston to Dallas, and I knew my way around the house. It was my home. I felt settled there.

Was the memory of the dandelion chain, of that quiet

day on the porch, my last memory in the house with the seven chairs?

Was I prepared to discover that it was the last day or week or month that those children, with their wide blue eyes and deep red hair, or Cecile, with her large, kind hands and her patient smile, lived upon this earth? Was a memory like that worth regaining? Would I be allowing those ghosts into my life only so that they could haunt me?

The mother who'd raised me to adulthood, *my* mother, had loved me, as had my father in his own stoic way. What they'd done to hide the past, they'd undoubtedly done for my benefit. What they'd kept hidden was perhaps better left in the dark.

Yet I felt compelled to find the truth. I felt the questions calling to me.

Yawning and stretching, I straightened in my seat, looking out the open window, watching stands of spring clover and primrose sway in the muted evening light. In a pasture, a lone white horse grazed, unperturbed by our passing. Nearby, tall pines towered above a farmhouse with green asbestos siding. We'd come quite a ways already. We were into the pines.

Behind the wheel, Epiphany appeared relaxed, one hand resting in her lap, as if she'd become fully accustomed to the pilot's chair while I slept in suspended animation. My body was stiff, the bones in my spine popping like the pods on the purple hull peas Mother's Polish cook had shelled on the back porch when I was a boy.

'You done complaining?' Epiphany asked. 'Because if you're not, you can just go on back to sleep.'

'Where are we?' I surveyed the passing territory, looking for road signs or landmarks. Did Epiphany have any idea where we were? Before leaving my house, I'd briefly shown her the map, told her we would take I-20 east, but I'd given her no instructions after that. We weren't on I-20 anymore.

She didn't appear the least bit worried that we might be lost. 'We been out of Dallas a couple hours, at least. I think it's about fifty miles more to Groveland.'

'Fifty miles?' Good gumption, I'd slept almost the entire trip! 'Are you certain? You should have awakened me so that I could help you with the route.'

She cast a sideways glance and held it a bit too long, actually. We drifted onto the shoulder, then veered back to the road. Fortunately, there weren't any lumber trucks coming. 'You were getting kidnapped, remember? Besides, I can read a map.' She patted the atlas lying open on the console between us. 'My mama liked to hit the road a lot. Sometimes she took me with her.'

I studied her for a moment, wondering at the meaning of those words. 'Where did you stay the rest of the time?' I was almost afraid to ask.

'Wherever, kind of.' She didn't offer any further information, and I felt the need to pry.

'And you lived where, before this?'

She shrugged. 'Oh, lots of places, but right before Dallas, I was in a little town out by Abilene. You wouldn't know it. I told you about Mrs Lora, my teacher from seventh grade, didn't I? I stayed on with her after Mama ran across Russ and moved to Dallas. They wanted, like, time alone, and anyway, Mrs Lora needed somebody to help around the house and the garden and stuff.'

'So you just lived with this woman while your mother moved away?' The concept was appalling. What sort of parent would leave a child behind that way?

Epiphany shrugged. 'Yeah, sure. It worked out. I would've stayed there through high school, but Mrs Lora's diabetes got her and she was really sick, and then she died. So I had to come here. I liked the school there a lot. I mean, I was like a little brown bug in a bucket of milk, but at least you didn't have to worry about getting jumped in the bathroom. I hate the school here. I'm not going back. I'll get a GED or something, if I have to.' Swallowing hard, she tipped her face away, as if she hadn't meant to reveal that much information. Clearly, though, it had been on her mind.

'You're far too smart to be settling for your GED,' I pointed out. 'There are your college exams to think about, scholarships and applications. Your future. I've seen you whip through your algebra homework. Few students have that ability. If this school administration won't see to it that you have the opportunities you deserve, then there are other schools.'

She laughed, a soft, rueful sound. 'Yeah, all that stuff takes money,' she said softly.

The conversation ended there. For a time, we drove in silence. I watched towering pines pass, and drank in the scents of grass, and water, and wildflowers growing along the roadsides. As always, my mind was plotting ahead, considering the possible ramifications and the odd practicalities of this trip – overnight accommodations being one. The library and any type of downtown stores or historical museums would be closed by this time of the evening. We'd need a hotel of some sort. I could hardly share a room with a young girl to whom I wasn't related . . .

'J. Norm, the gas thingy's on empty.' Epiphany broke into my thoughts. 'You want me to stop up there?' She pointed ahead to a small gas station at a crossroads.

'That will be fine.' I scooted upward in my seat as we came closer to the store. A small picnic area beckoned from the shade of some magnolia trees off to one side. 'Let's get gas, then buy ice cream bars. We can sit outside and take a little time to enjoy the evening breeze. I need to stretch my legs a bit.'

''Kay.' Navigating into the parking lot, Epiphany smiled. 'Like a picnic, huh?'

'Like a picnic,' I agreed, thinking back. When the children were small, Annalee found any opportunity to stop off at picnic grounds while we were traveling. Against my admonitions that a restaurant would be faster and easier, she packed coolers and sandwiches, and searched for roadside parks or other points of interest. Those trips off the map tended to frustrate me, as I'd already precalculated the mileage to our destination, our expected arrival time, and roughly the delay afforded by stops for gas and, with two small children, restroom breaks. Long lunches with cement dinosaurs, Viking rune stones, Joshua trees, and the world's largest ball of twine weren't anywhere on my agenda. *It's a vacation*, Annalee would say. *It's about discovering what there is to see. No sense rushing from here to there.*

But the world's largest ball of twine? I'd counter.

Annalee would only laugh and flap a hand at me, her bracelets jingling. *I want to see it all . . .*

I would have missed so many things, so many of the best things, had it not been for Annalee. I would have worried and calculated and scheduled my way past the grandeur of ordinary life.

I exited the car, determined not to fret my way through this trip, this adventure with Epiphany.

As it turned out, the stopover created a worry of its own, however. After pumping the gas, we went inside to pay, and I asked the woman at the counter if she knew of a place to stay in Groveland. She gave me an odd look, her eyes sliding from me to Epiphany and back. Her brows, penciled on in high arches, lowered over buggy eyes that were lined with thin red veins, as if she spent too much time looking into things that were none of her affair. 'You and *her*?' she asked incredulously, the words cool and unwelcoming, accusatory in a way that sent a bead of discomfort down my spine.

'Yes, a room for each of us,' I stipulated as Epiphany wandered to the candy counter to look at chocolate bars.

Grabbing a notepad from behind the cash register, the woman wrote, *Pine View Motel*, and handed it to me. 'You on the road to someplace?' The butt of the pen tapped the counter, and her gaze slid toward Epiphany again.

I willed myself not to seem uncomfortable, but I was. I hadn't anticipated a reaction like this one. What if something was afoot and we were yet unaware of it? What if some sort of missing persons alert had been broadcast regarding the two of us? Was the woman behind the cash register trying to decide where she'd seen us before? Slowly connecting the dots?

'Yes. I'm on my way to see family.' I thought it best, then, that the woman not know that our destination was less than thirty miles down the road. 'In . . . Florida. Lake Poinsett.'

'Long trip.' The clerk continued eyeballing Epiphany as I handed over the money for our purchases, then received change. I would have sworn that she sneaked a glance inside my wallet, too, as if everything about us were of above-normal interest.

I took our ice cream bars and drinks, and we hurried out the door. We didn't stay for a picnic. Back in the car, Epiphany gave the store a narrow-eyed glare as we circled the parking lot. 'Yeah, she was wondering if I was gonna steal a candy bar.'

'*Going to.* It's two words.' I resisted the urge to look over my shoulder, though I half expected the woman to be standing in the doorway, taking down our license plate number. 'I fear she thought I was some sort of dirty old man or the like.'

'Ffff!' Epiphany scoffed. 'J. Norm, you're too old for somebody to think you're a dirty old man.'

As was often the case with Epiphany, I was stumped as to how to reply to the comment. 'Well, certainly all that scrutiny wasn't only over candy bars. And aside from that, she was looking at us before you moved to the candy counter.'

Epiphany pulled onto the road. 'Norman, you been living in the big city all your life? She was lookin' at you and wondering, were you my grandpa or did you just pick me up on the side of the road someplace? You go showing up in small towns with a little brown girl, inquiring minds wanna know – get what I mean? Mama and me lived in lots of places like this, and everywhere you go, somebody's looking and wondering, *That her child?* Mama hates that. She says it's embarrassing.'

A heaviness settled in my chest, and I didn't reply, but only watched Epiphany navigate the highway as I replayed her words in my mind, searching for any hint of emotion. How would it feel to know that your own mother was embarrassed to be seen with you? What would a lifetime of that do to a child?

Epiphany continued on, 'So, ummm . . . I been thinking, though. Since that lady acted that way and all, maybe when we go in someplace I oughta just call you . . . well, like, Uncle Norm, or maybe Grandpa or something . . .' Flicking a tentative glance my way, she let the sentence hang unfinished, then added, 'I mean, it might make things easier, you know? So people don't ask questions, but if you don't want to, it's okay.' Her mouth pursed as if she'd had a taste of something troublesome, and she swallowed hard. 'No big deal, all right?'

'I think "Grandpa" would do nicely.' I remembered that the ice cream bars were melting in the bag, and I pulled them out. When I looked up, she was smiling slightly, watching me as if she expected me to say something more. 'But don't be surprised if I don't think to answer right away. I've never been "Grandpa" before.'

'Well, I've never had one before, either.'

Emotion thickened in my throat, and I swallowed it, unwilling to explore the underlying causes. 'Pull over in that gravel patch up there, and we'll eat our ice cream.'

'I can eat it and drive.' She reached for the ice cream bar, and I held it away.

'Grandpa says no.'

Snorting, she guided the car onto the wide spot beside the road. 'Just 'cuz I call you that name, it doesn't mean you get to boss me around.' She took the snack from my hand, unwrapped it, and noisily slurped drips before enjoying a first bite. There were times when I suspected that Epiphany had been raised in a barn.

'On the contrary, it intimates that I am older and wiser.' I reveled in the first taste of my ice cream sandwich – sugar, chocolate, cholesterol, saturated fat. Heaven. All the joys that had been stolen from me in a quest to force me into a longer life. 'Which, indeed, is the case.'

Epiphany snorted again, choking on a bite. For a moment, I thought I'd have to drag her out of the car and do the Heimlich. When she recovered, she shook her head. 'Man, you're gonna be hard to live with now, huh?'

'Perhaps. *Going to*.'

We ate our sandwiches in peace, and then continued on our trek. It was after eight o'clock when we reached Groveland. The town was sleepy and quiet, stately old Victorian homes languishing in the shade of towering pines and lofty magnolias as the sun slowly surrendered the day. Yards bloomed with daffodils and iris, and early spring roses painted trellises with impossible bursts of color. The scents in the air, the sound of the tires clicking along in the edges of the gutter, the rocking of the car seemed familiar. *Have I a memory of this place?* I wondered.

Passing through downtown, I gazed upward at the buildings, their high brick and stone façades rising against the darkening sky, the years of their establishment, many in the eighteen hundreds, etched in capstones. The buildings had been around much longer than I. The bank building, a tall redbrick structure with ornate parapets at all four corners, caught my gaze. I couldn't help thinking that I knew the place. An odd feeling of déjà vu crept over me, and then a sense of foreboding.

A few blocks farther down, we passed the Pine View Motel, a squat motor court of sixties vintage. Judging by the dried-up swimming pool and the aging billboard with forlorn bits of broken neon dangling, the place had seen better days. It had the look of a spot where truckers might come and go at all hours of the night. I could hardly leave a sixteen-year-old girl alone in a room at such a place, and having Epiphany in the room with me was . . . well, improper at best. At worst, it would prove DeRon's case in the future.

Epiphany switched on the blinker. 'Guess that's it.'

'Keep going,' I told her. 'The Pine View isn't up to our standards.'

She craned her head away, surprised by the notion of standards, I guess. 'Okay, but I'm ready to get out of this car.' Rubbing the back of her neck, she rolled her head to one side, then the other.

'Both hands on the wheel,' I told her.

As it turned out, our passing up the Pine View was fortuitous, since just a few blocks farther we found a charming bed-and-breakfast in a two-story historic home with a veranda running around two sides. It looked to me to be perfect for our purposes. After a short negotiation with a friendly young couple who ran the place along with the wife's aunt, my new granddaughter and I were booked into two rooms on the second floor.

Epiphany's eyes were wide as we brought our things into the cavernous entry hall. The proprietress gave our ragtag smattering of suitcases, grocery sacks, and computer equipment a questioning look, and Epiphany sidled a few steps away, then bent over to peek under the chandelier at a semi-circular staircase worthy of Scarlett O'Hara. 'Whoa, J . . . Grandpa. This place is even bigger than your house.'

The proprietress, Sharla, chuckled as she dusted crumbs from her ample bosom and winked at me. She smelled of fresh-baked apple pie and chocolate-chip cookies, which gave me great hope for breakfast the next day. 'If y'all want the tour first, Chris can take your belongings upstairs.' She indicated her husband, who also looked as if he ate regularly and well, which increased my faith that breakfast tomorrow would be worth the price of the rooms.

Chris gathered our things. Epiphany came to stand beside me again, ready for the tour, and Chris lumbered toward the stairs, burdened by our baggage. The computer case swayed on his shoulder, nearly striking the chair rail as he rounded the corner. Epiphany ran after him. 'I can help carry it up,' she said, sliding the bag off his shoulder, and taking charge of her backpack, as well. 'I'll be back down in a minute. Don't start the big tour without me, Grandpa!' she called with no hint of awkwardness. Who knew she had such acting talent?

Sharla and I passed five minutes or so strolling in the front parlor, discussing photos of Ward House in its younger years, when the surrounding land comprised portions of a riverside trading post that had been scratched from the Piney Woods by Hayden Ward, Sharla's great-great-grandfather. We passed another five minutes looking at a coffee-table book with pictures of early-day Groveland, while Sharla pointed out family members and shared stories of the Wards' long history in the town. Her aunt Charlotte, referred to as Char, joined us and contributed yet more bits and pieces of Groveland lore.

It was clear to me, while we were talking, that both Char and Sharla were well-grounded in the history of this place and their family heritage, which could be traced back to Davy Crockett, a Texas legend. Sharla's parents and grandparents had rooted her in the blood and soil of family history, created the ties that bind. It crossed my mind that I'd failed to do that for Deborah. I'd never shared much about my mother's family or my father's. Such things hadn't seemed important. I was a man of the future, not the past. But now I wondered if that tendency in me had come about because the past was never real. My father's history in the oil business, my mother's connection to the Rockefeller family, felt more like a suit I had put on, a garment that didn't quite fit. Perhaps I'd always sensed on some level that those bits of ancestry were no more connected to me than a story told at random.

After fifteen minutes had passed, Sharla cast a worried glance toward the stairs. 'Where are they?' She looked at Aunt Char before seeming to answer her own question. 'Oh, mercy, I bet my husband is up there filling your granddaughter's head full of ghost stories.' Without pausing to excuse herself, she made a dash for the stairs, leaving me alone with Aunt Char, who wasted no time in inquiring about my business in town.

I considered telling her the truth about my visit to Groveland, but some inner caution compelled me to play things close to the vest. My mother had gone to great lengths to dissociate me from my past. She feared it, even after I was grown, even to her deathbed. If her part in whatever happened here could in any way bring shame to her memory or to the family name, I had to prevent it from seeing the light of day. 'Oh, just a little vacation,' I replied. 'And acquainting my granddaughter with a bit of family history. My father made his fortune in the oil fields not far from here, back in the day. He had relatives in Groveland, I think.'

She asked my father's name, and I told her, and of course she didn't know him. My father had never lived in Groveland, and most likely his business would never have brought him here. Yet I had a feeling that my mother had found me here. What were the circumstances? How had that come about? What fears haunted her?

'Well, there's a scad of books about the area, and the oil

273

patch, and the pulpwood mills upstairs in the parlor library,' Aunt Char offered. I had the sense of watching two sevens roll up on the slot machine and waiting for the third. 'I haven't read most of 'em. Don't need to. Mercy, I've heard the stories all my life, sugar. I just buy the books here and there, when there's a book signin' at the library, or somebody speaks at the ladies' club or the church, and I put 'em upstairs for the customers.'

'There's one in particular I'm looking for,' I told her, my hopes inching up and up and up. 'A book about the early-day timber industry. There was a mention of some of my relatives in it, I think. *An East Texas Timber Town History*. The author's name is White, I believe. M. L. White.'

Aunt Char's eyes widened, and she slapped a hand to her chest. I suspected I'd said the wrong thing until she threw her head back and laughed. 'Oh, scat! You won't find a copy of that rag upstairs. Mrs Mercy White wrote that book. Her daddy was the sheriff in Groveland for some years. Don't let the name fool you, either. She was a nasty, spiteful woman. Told all sorts of tales in her book, only about half of them true, but she got her revenge on folks, I guess, before she died. That book was like the *National Enquirer* of the whole county, hon. I think by now the ladies' auxiliary has gathered up every copy and burned them. Mercy White embarrassed most of those women, too.'

'I see.' Suddenly I was back to square one, my roll of the dice having come up empty. It seemed that Epiphany and I had gone on the lam and traveled all the way to east Texas in search of the rarest book in the county.

I heard the clatter of feet on the stairs, and Aunt Char and I left the front room to meet Epiphany and Sharla in the entry hall. Chris lumbered along behind them and quickly excused himself, having the look of a man whose wife had just given him a dressing-down.

Epiphany's eyes were as wide as Easter eggs. 'You're not gonna believe this place!' she breathed, seemingly somewhere between awe and trepidation. 'It's like . . . Oh, man, and there's all kinds of . . . You just don't even know . . . and *Ghost Finders* was here, and they filmed a show. Lyndon B. Johnson slept up there, too, and there was this little girl that fell out the window, and a baby that died of pneumonia. Her picture's in my *room*.' Her gaze rolled upward, her lip curling with it, as if she were considering the proposition of sharing space with a ghost.

Sharla touched her apologetically. 'I knew I shouldn't have let Chris take her up there. Sorry. He loves to tell those silly old stories. But, honestly, I grew up in this house, and I never saw any ghosts here.' She emphasized *never* and *any* in a way that had the air of protesting too much, and perhaps seeing my concern, she added, '*Ghost Finders* didn't find anything, truly. And they had equipment all over the house. Chris just likes to tease. He shouldn't have been scaring your granddaughter.'

In the periphery of my vision, Aunt Char, who had been watching Epiphany with no small curiosity, blinked in obvious surprise. Epiphany saw it, too, I could tell, and she flashed a knowing look my way, proving the point she'd made earlier in the car, I supposed. People considered us an unlikely-looking pair.

'Oh, not to worry.' I addressed the reply to both Sharla and Aunt Char, but also to Epiphany. 'My granddaughter is a smart girl. She's very practical, good with science and math and the like, not the type to get caught up in tall tales and ghost stories. Right, Epiphany?'

Epiphany nodded, then shrugged, then shook her head, a mixed bag of answers. Threading her arms over her stomach, she swiveled a glance up the stairs. I had a feeling she was wishing we'd stayed at the Pine View Motel with the truckers. 'Yeah, I guess not.' Despite her halfhearted display of bravery, she followed close on my heels as we toured the house.

After the tour and a late-night snack in the kitchen, Epiphany and I went upstairs to settle in for the evening and search through the vast library of local-subject-matter books there. We were soon frustrated with the volume of information, though, and descended into a disagreement over whether to leave for home tomorrow if we hadn't yet found what we were seeking. It was becoming clearer to me that this trip could be a proverbial wild-goose chase, and that the longer we stayed, the more likely we were to provide fuel for the flash fires that could be waiting for us at home. At this point, we had no way of knowing whether our absence had been reported, whether anyone was looking for us, or whether that hoodlum, DeRon, had actually made good on his threat of false accusations.

Finally, we left the argument unsettled, and our subsequent good night felt more like a mutual good riddance. Armed with a book about historic towns in the Piney

Woods, I proceeded to my room, slipped into my pajamas, brushed my teeth, and climbed into bed. The old house creaked and groaned, a spring breeze rattling the veranda doors as I thumbed through the book, searching for applicable bits of history or mention of a tragic house fire during the right time frame. So far, though, what I'd found regarding the thirties and early forties largely discussed the boom days of oil and timber, and the trade in alcohol during Prohibition, when rumrunners brought their wares through ports on the Gulf of Mexico. According to the text, they were flamboyant and dangerous men who made their fortunes transporting illegal liquor northward.

A little *tap-tap-tap* came at the door, and I folded the book on my lap. 'Yes?'

The door creaked open a crack. 'J. Norm, you decent?'

'Completely in the buff. Horrible to see,' I answered, and the door opened wider.

Outside in the hall stood Epiphany in a T-shirt with the neck torn out and a pair of baggy sweatpants, hugging a lacy floral-print pillow like a giant teddy bear. 'Did you hear that?' she whispered, as if someone might be listening. Her shoulders shuddered, and she stepped into the room without waiting to be invited. 'There's someone walking in the hall. They stopped right outside my bedroom.'

'I've been up reading.' Which was the story of my life, really. I seldom slept a solid night anymore. 'I didn't hear anything.'

'It *woke* me up.' Her eyes widened further, which I would have thought impossible.

'There was no noise,' I assured her.

She shifted from one foot to the other, her slim fingers kneading the pillow. Finally, she huffed, and said, 'Can I just stay in here with you?' She moved a few steps toward a fainting couch on the other side of the room.

'Epiphany, I hardly –'

'You're not even gonna know I'm here, I promise.' Another few steps. Behind her, the door creaked shut on its own. She squeaked and scampered to the sofa, then jumped onto it like a child playing Sharks in the Water, and pulled an afghan over herself.

I leaned back in my bed and opened my book again. 'I don't see what help I'll be if there are ghosts around. They'd hardly be afraid of a crippled old man with a bad heart.'

Satisfied that she wasn't being sent back to her own room, Epiphany snuggled down, burrowing into the feather pillow. 'You can tell them rocket stories until they get bored and leave.'

I smirked at her over the top of my book.

She yawned, gazing past me toward the veranda doors. 'I'm just joking, you know. I like your stories.'

'I know,' I said.

She inhaled and exhaled, her lashes falling to half-mast as she gazed through the veranda doors to the backyard, where blooming magnolias gleamed in the moonlight. 'Chris said those were slave cabins out back. They made some of the slaves live in the attic, too – the people who worked in the house. They beat people and chained them to the beds up there and stuff, too.'

I laid the book against my knees, looked at her, but her eyes were falling closed. 'I suspect so. History is filled with terrible events that were rationalized by the masses.' I wondered if she really understood that the world in which I'd grown up was vastly different from hers. So much change in a single lifetime. From milk trucks rumbling through the streets to a man on the moon. From a time when her aunts and grandmothers would have taken work in houses like these, oiling the banisters, cooking meals, and providing nursery care for the children, to a time when her opportunities were as big as her ability to dream them and her gumption to make them come true.

'It's weird . . . to think about,' she whispered, then yawned again, breathed out a long, slow breath, and let herself sink away.

'Yes, it is,' I answered quietly.

While browsing the book awhile longer, I watched her sleep. Quiet now, curled into a ball with fistfuls of blanket tucked under her chin, she looked angelic, innocent. I was reminded of Deborah, not much younger than this, curled in her sleeping bag on the floor of our master bedroom. While Annalee was gone to a long-running PTA meeting, Deborah had stumbled across *The Exorcist* on television, after Roy was in bed. I hadn't stopped her from watching it. My mind was on some project I'd brought home with me. I'd been forced to leave the office early due to the sudden cancellation of the babysitter Annalee had arranged.

But the work was forgotten, and somehow I'd ended up on the sofa beside Deborah, watching the movie with horrible fascination, something that I later said (in my own defense, because Annalee was furious with me) should never have been on television where children might find it. When it was finally over, Deborah wouldn't go to bed in her own room. For weeks she dragged her sleeping pallet into our room, until finally her bad memories of the movie faded.

It was the last time I was ever called upon to babysit. I was deemed a complete failure at the task.

But now I remembered that on nights when I worked late or left early, I stood above that pallet and gazed at my daughter, silent and peaceful in her sleep, her dark hair curling around her. She was an angel so perfect that it was hard to believe I could have had a part in creating her. Each time before I left, I knelt down and kissed her, and whispered in her ear, *Sweet dreams, Deborah.*

Did Deborah remember those nights so long ago, so short, so sweet to me in their recollection?

Setting the book aside, I took a pad of Ward House stationery from the bedside table, opened to a fresh page, and began to write. If anything should happen to me in this odd quest to find my family, Deborah should know that inside the man who'd overlooked her in favor of his work and his projects was the father who'd stood over her while she slept and thought her as beautiful as an angel. I wrote:

Dear Deborah,

Words do not come easily for so many men. We are taught to be strong, to provide, to put away our emotions. A father can work his way through his days and never see that his years are going by. If I could go back in time, I would say some things to that young father as he holds, somewhat uncertainly, his daughter for the very first time. These are the things I would say:

When you hear the first whimper in the night, go to the nursery and leave your wife sleeping. Rock in a chair, walk the floor, sing a lullaby so that she will know a man can be gentle.

When Mother is away for the evening, come home from work, do the babysitting. Learn to cook a hotdog or a pot of spaghetti, so that your daughter will know a man can serve another's needs.

When she performs in school plays or dances in recitals, arrive early, sit in the front seat, devote your full attention. Clap the loudest, so that she will know a man can have eyes only for her.

When she asks for a tree house, don't just build it, but build it with her. Sit high among the branches and talk about clouds, and caterpillars, and leaves. Ask her about her dreams and wait for her answers, so that she will know a man can listen.

When you pass by her door as she dresses for a date, tell her she is beautiful. Take her on a date yourself. Open doors, buy flowers, look her in the eye, so that she will know a man can respect her.

When she moves away from home, send a card, write a note, call on the phone. If something reminds you of her, take a minute to tell her, so that she will know a man can think of her even when she is away.

Tell her you love her, so that she will know a man can say the words.

If you hurt her, apologize, so that she will know a man can admit that he's wrong.

These seem like such small things, such a fraction of time in the course of two lives. But a thread does not require much space. It can be too fine for the eye to see, yet, it is the very thing that binds, that takes pieces and laces them into a whole.

Without it, there are tatters.

It is never too late for a man to learn to stitch, to begin mending.

These are the things I would tell that young father, if I could.

A daughter grows up quickly. There isn't time to waste.

I love you,
Dad

CHAPTER 18

Epiphany Jones

J. Norm and me figured out on our first morning in town that the quickest way to make enemies in Groveland, Texas, was to go around looking for a copy of Mrs Mercy White's book. People gave us weird looks anyway, when we walked into places like the library, and the Timber and Railroad Museum, and some antique and junk stores that dealt in books. I guessed it wasn't every day they saw an old white guy in nice clothes hanging around with a teenage girl who for sure wasn't white, but once I called him *Grandpa* a time or two, they got the picture. After that, how they'd react was anybody's guess. Sometimes people were friendly enough, sometimes they gave us hateful sneers, and sometimes they caught J. Norm's eye with a sympathetic look, like they were trying to tell him they knew it wasn't his fault his daughter'd got herself knocked up by some guy who wasn't white. Some redneck dude in a junk shop was just plain unfriendly. When J. Norm asked him about Mercy White's book, he curled his lip and said, 'We don't have *anything* like that in here.' Then he shrugged toward the door, like that's where we oughta be going.

J. Norm blinked at the man once, twice. J. Norm probably hadn't ever been treated that way in his life, but it didn't surprise me. Mama and me had been in enough backwater places for me to know how things were. Mrs Lora always said to just ignore it. *Nasty comes from the inside*, she told me. *It doesn't have anything to do with you.*

Just to get on the junk shop guy's last nerve, I took a few more steps away from the door, toward the aisles and aisles of flea market booths in his big old metal building. 'Hey, look here, Grandpa.' I pointed to a booth that had old hats like the one J. Norm gave me out of his wife's closet. 'Hats.'

The man at the counter flashed a dirty look, and I just smiled, like, *Yeah, what are you gonna do about it? It's a free country.*

J. Norm played right along. 'I believe we'll look around awhile.' He egged me on while I tried on hats and feather boas, and pretended I was going to buy the prettiest dancing dress I'd ever seen. I held it up in front of me and waltzed along the aisle. The dress floated like a patch of blue sky, glittery up top, and the bottom was made of net, like the skirt of a ballerina, only longer. It was in perfect shape, but I could tell it was old. Someone must've kept it in a closet, all wrapped up in plastic, like J. Norm's wife did her clothes.

'Beautiful!' J. Norm said. 'You're a vision, an . . . epiphany, even.' Both of us laughed, and I danced a little more. It was fun having somebody around who wasn't too tired, too busy, or too ticked off to bother with me. If that'd been

Mama standing there, she would've told me to put that stupid thing down and quit messing around before I broke something.

But J. Norm just clapped and laughed, and treated me like Cinderella in glass slippers. It felt good.

After we figured we'd annoyed the shop guy long enough, we left without buying anything. On the way out, J. Norm said it was a good thing we hadn't found our book there, because it would've been against his principles to give that guy any money.

'If he'd of had it, we'd of bought it, though, right?' I asked as we walked along Main Street. J. Norm had spotted a sign on a corner store that said, HAND-DIPPED BLUE BELL, and he was in an ice cream mood again.

'Most likely not.' He was looking up at the buildings, his mind in another place. 'A person must have principles, Epiphany. That's the one thing no one can take from you. The only way you can lose your principles is to give them up. Remember that.' He went on studying the buildings, like that was all he had to say on that subject.

I thought about it while we walked. Principles. I guess I'd always figured those were something for old people and rich people – something you could only afford if you were part of the group who could chunk down nine hundred dollars for a computer and not even bat an eye. The rest of us lived in the real world. Whenever I complained about how things were for us, Mama always said, *Well, who do you think you are, the princess and the pea?* The way Mama figured it, you did what you had to do to get by. Like putting up with some lousy job or living with some loser who treated you bad. She wanted me to know that's how it was for people like us and I shouldn't expect anything different.

But now I wondered if J. Norm was right. Maybe anybody could stand for something, if they wanted to. You could make up your mind that you weren't gonna drop out of high school and shack up with some loser like DeRon, and have some baby you didn't even want, and then end up doing a job you hated and spending your weekends camped out at swap meets or in a bar someplace. You could decide that you were gonna have principles and then not let anybody take them away.

We got to the ice cream shop, and J. Norm opened the door. Like always, he waited for me to go through first. Every once in a while when he did that, he'd say, *Any man who doesn't hold the door open for a lady is no gentleman, Epiphany. You keep that in mind.* But this time he didn't say anything. He didn't follow me in, either. He sort of hung in the opening with the door pushing against his back.

'J. Norm?' I said, stopping in front of a counter that looked like something from an old-time movie. A long bar with bar stools ran along the wall and curved into a cash register area at the end. Behind the bar, there were old mixers and soda fountains, and lots of wooden shelves with glasses on them, and a big mirror, like in the saloons in those old John Wayne movies Russ liked to watch. The place was empty right now, but I could hear noises in the back. 'J. Norm?' I said again, but he was just standing there. Finally, I walked back and waved a hand in front of his face. 'Are you all right?'

286

He blinked, then shook his head. 'I remember this place . . .' His eyes glazed over, and he tripped on the little rim where the wood floor met a square of tiny white octagon-shaped tiles. I jumped to catch him, but he stumbled sideways, grabbing one of the bar stools.

'You mean, like, from when you were little?' I looked around the store, and goose bumps prickled on my arms.

J. Norm put both hands on the barstool, stared down at it, smoothed his fingers across the seat, then twirled it hard enough that it rattled. 'I loved to run along here and spin each one, and Cecile would say, "Little Mis'a Willie, you best cut out that nonsense, or there ain't gonna be no soda float for you." '

'But your name's not Willie.' A cold feeling passed over my skin, like it had when the guy at Ward House told me about the little girl who died when she fell out the window, and about all the slaves they used to keep upstairs in the attic, even little children sometimes. I felt like I was surrounded by dead people.

J. Norm's face went white, and the rims of his eyes, where the skin sagged tired and red, turned moist and teary. 'I think it was. That was my name. Willie . . . William.'

A cloud went across the sun outside, and the room turned shadowy. I touched a bar stool, then pictured a little red-headed boy running along, twirling each one. It was almost like he was really there.

A swinging door smacked open halfway down the counter, and both J. Norm and me jumped. 'Afternoon!' A man came through the door carrying a tray of tall drink glasses.

287

'I help you folks?' He tipped his head back, squinting at us through eyeglasses with black rims around the edges. His thick gray hair was slicked back on the sides, and kind of combed into a puffy swirl on top, like J. Norm in that old picture where he looked like a redheaded Elvis. 'Y'all from out of town?' he asked when neither of us answered.

'Yes, sir,' I told him, and laid on the manners, because I figured it couldn't hurt to make a good impression on the guy who was about to dip up your ice cream. J. Norm was still staring at the walls like there was no one else in the room. 'My grandpa says he remembers this place. He used to live here when he was little.'

The man braced his hands on the counter and leaned up against it, giving J. Norm an interested look. If it bothered him that there wasn't any family resemblance between my grandpa and me, he didn't show it. He just smiled at me and said, 'When abouts was that?'

'We're not real sure.' I looked over my shoulder, and J. Norm was wandering down the aisles of candy and groceries like he was gone in the head. 'A long time ago, maybe 1941, but he remembers this store.'

The man seemed proud of that. 'Oh, well, lots of kids would. This store's been in my family since my dad bought it in the forties, but it was around a long time before that. Lots of kids been through here for penny candy, and Coke floats, and ice cream sun-deys.'

The back of my mouth started to water. I wished J. Norm would snap out of it so we could order. He was just wandering around the store, looking up and down the walls, taking

288

in old metal bread signs and advertisements and a few black-and-white pictures of the town.

The ice cream man stuck his hand over the counter and shook mine. 'Al Nelson.'

I told him my name and stayed on my best behavior. It wasn't until after I said my name that I thought about the fact that I'd used my real name, and maybe that was a bad idea. But then, really, why would Al Nelson in the corner store in Groveland, Texas, care? Nobody from back in Dallas even knew I was gone. Nobody'd be looking for me.

Unless the principal and the counselor had called the police after they talked to DeRon, and the police were looking for us . . .

I put that thought out of my head, and since I had Al's attention, I decided I'd come right out and ask about the house fire. J. Norm acted like he didn't want people to know why we were here, but I figured at this point we needed to make progress any way we could. It didn't look like we'd be finding a copy of Mrs Mercy White's book anytime soon. 'My grandpa remembers something about a big house burning down. Some kids died in the fire. Five kids. We were trying to figure out where that house was, so we could, like, drive by that spot, maybe. Grandpa thinks he probably lived on that same street, but he doesn't know for sure, and my great-grandparents are dead, so there's nobody to ask. We just thought if we came here, like, for a little vacation, he could remember some stuff.' The lies slipped right out, smooth as silk, which made me wonder about that talk earlier about principles. Considering all those times Mrs Lora had brought me to church, she was probably turning over in her grave right now.

But so far, J. Norm and me were getting nowhere fast, and half the day was gone already. We couldn't stay in Groveland forever, although if it took a few more days, that wouldn't bother me any. Mama and Russ wouldn't be home for a while yet.

Mr Al Nelson drummed all ten fingers on the counter, thinking. 'You're talking about when the VanDraan house burned down, I bet,' he said, nodding. 'That was a little before my time, but my sister used to tell that story. Whole family died in that fire, the mama, five little kids, and the black nanny, too. I remember that the old house stood there burned-out for years. Could be that's why your grandpa remembers it.'

'Was it near here?' My mind tingled with the idea, and I noticed that in the back of the store, J. Norm had stopped and turned our way, finally dialing in.

Mr Nelson pointed out the door. 'A mile and a half down Main, right on Dogwood Street, go three blocks, but there's a mini storage there now. For years, the lot was empty – nothing but some rocks from the foundation and a three-story chimney. City finally took over the lot for taxes and knocked the chimney down. The town kids used to play a game – see who was brave enough to run up there and touch the chimney. Many a ghost story was told about that place. Passel of tall tales. Not really anything left of the house now, except you can still see where the stone corner posts were, and there's a bit of the iron fence back there in the weeds. The whole VanDraan family is buried about two miles farther down, in the old Dogwood Cemetery.' Mr Nelson leaned on the counter, like he had all day to visit. J. Norm came back from the other end of the store, now that the conversation had turned interesting. I decided that maybe we wouldn't need Mrs Mercy White's book, after all.

'Well ... how'd the fire start?' I asked, because that seemed like the *logical next question*, as J. Norm would say. 'Didn't anybody get out? I mean, did the whole family die?' If there was nobody left, then how could J. Norm remember the fire? Maybe he didn't live in the VanDraan house after all, but someplace near it. He could've gone over and played with the kids, and that was why he knew them. 'Couldn't the neighbors or the fire department help them get out?'

Mr Nelson seemed surprised that I was so interested, but he was happy enough to go on talking. 'Well, like I said, that was before my day, so I don't know all the facts. The daddy, Mr VanDraan, didn't die until years later. He was playing cards in a poker joint when the big house fire happened. There's been a lot of rumors and speculation about that whole deal over the years, but mostly, people kept the whispers behind their hands. Mr VanDraan was a powerful man in this town. Had money. Owned the mill, the bank, the timber company, and this store before my pap bought it. Most of the folks in Groveland worked for him in one way or another, or owed him for the notes on their farms and houses. But a town doesn't forget about six people in one family lost all at once, you know?'

I nodded, but I was thinking, *Six people?* He'd said *six*. But there were seven. The maid died, too. She didn't count because she wasn't white? 'And the maid.' I couldn't help it. I said it out loud. I didn't know why I cared about something that happened that long ago, but I did.

Mr Nelson clicked his tongue against his teeth, like he was sorry for the maid, too, he guessed. 'Yeah, I imagine she's buried outside the cemetery somewhere. That's usually how it was done back in those days. The black families either had to lay theirs to rest in a patch out back of the fence, or go over to the graveyard on Hakey Creek. Those were different times, I guess you'd say. Folks only mixed in certain ways. Black folks'd come over, keep care of the yards, or tend the houses or the kids; maybe live in a maid's room at one of the big houses, but other than that, they lived over on their side of town, and we lived on ours. Black kids went to one school; we went to another. They went to their movie house; we went to ours. Sundays, we went to our church; they went to theirs. Guess we were all talkin' to the same God, though.'

Mr Nelson shook his head, looking out the window of his shop like he was seeing the town how it was before. 'Back then, I had a little friend, Gordy. His daddy worked the stockroom and ran deliveries around town for my daddy. Many a summer Gordy and I spent fishing the banks of Rye Creek, or hiking off through the woods, or sittin' straddle on an old tree branch and riding it like it was a horse and we were Roy Rogers. Gordy always had to be the Indian, but he didn't mind, I guess. His mama kept house at our place. She packed us the best lunches – fried chicken and corn bread, and homemade biscuits and jelly she'd wrap up in a little bit of butcher paper from my daddy's store. I didn't have a mama, so them lunches felt mighty special to me.

'I remember one time when we were about twelve or thirteen, some of the boys from town saw us walking down under the bridge. They chased ol' Gordy off, and called me *Sambo* for having him as a friend, and slapped me around pretty good. After that, my pap said probably Gordy and I'd better not run together anymore. It was about time for Gordy to go to work, anyhow. A lot of the black kids quit school and went to work young, back then.' He scratched his head and smiled, his eyes a little sad behind his thick glasses. 'Gordy Finn. He died in Vietnam when he was twenty-one years old. Buried in Arlington National Cemetery. Looked up his name on the wall when I visited the memorial once.' He pointed to a pencil rubbing of Gordy's name hanging in a frame behind the cash register. 'Funny thing, he was probably the first one in his family to have his name carved into a granite marker.'

A lump came up in my throat, and I swallowed hard. I didn't know what I should say, really, or how I ought to feel. In my mind, I could see Gordy – barefoot in overalls with the bottoms rolled up, walking down the creek with his friend, a fishing pole and a sack lunch over his shoulder. It was weird to think that his history was my history in some way. I never thought much about my daddy's side of the family. Maybe I had people who were buried out back of some cemetery somewhere. Maybe I had a grandpa or an uncle who died in World War II or Vietnam. Unless I found those women from my mama's photographs, I'd never know.

J. Norm's mind wasn't where mine was, of course. He only glanced at the rubbing of Gordy's name, like it didn't really matter. 'Were there any other family members – of the Van-Draans', I mean? Anyone who might still be in the area?'

Tipping his head to one side, Mr Nelson pushed his glasses higher on his nose, like he was trying to get a better look at J. Norm. 'No, sir. Not that I know of. Mr VanDraan did marry again, built the big white house up on the hill, west of town, but his second wife died before they had any children. Drowned in the river out behind the house. Can't remember all the details, but he married a third time after that, and when that wife passed unexpectedly, there was speculation around town, of course, and her family had some political pull in the county. They vowed to do away with VanDraan, either by legal means or some other. Van-Draan up and sold everything then, and left Groveland. That was when my daddy bought the store, but you can still see VanDraan's name on the header stone of the building, and in the tile there by the door. My mama used to keep a rug over it. She never quite forgave my daddy for doing business with VanDraan. My mama was a good Christian woman and involved in the temperance movement, and everybody knew VanDraan had made a lot of his money running liquor off ships in Galveston harbor.' Laughing, he shook his head. 'My daddy was a good man, but he wasn't above taking a little nip. He appreciated a good smooth Southern whiskey.'

J. Norm and me looked at the tile in the doorway, reading the name VanDraan. I couldn't tell from looking at J. Norm whether he recognized it or not. It seemed like he was trying to figure that out himself. 'I suppose he would be mentioned in books about the area – this VanDraan?' he asked finally.

'Oh, sure.' Mr Nelson started down the counter, motioning for J. Norm to follow. 'We've got a few here for sale. Mostly stuff written by folks from around the Piney Woods.' He moved to a bookshelf on the back wall, and J. Norm met up with him there. I was listening, but I took a minute to check out the ice cream case. That stuff looked good, and come to think of it, the big breakfast at Ward House was wearing off.

I debated ice cream flavors while Mr Nelson showed J. Norm some books from the area. After a minute, J. Norm said, 'I'll take one of each.'

My eyes got wide, and so did Mr Nelson's. There were at least eight different kinds of books on that shelf. A couple of them were big hardbacks with lots of pictures. I knew those weren't cheap. Altogether, J. Norm had probably ordered over two hundred dollars' worth of books. The day my mama ever dropped a hundred dollars on books would be the day pigs grew wings.

'Sounds like my granddaughter and I have some reading to do,' J. Norm told Mr Nelson when they were walking back to the cash register. I liked it that he said *my granddaughter*, even though he didn't have to right then.

'Guess we do, Grandpa.' I don't know why I answered that

way, because Mr Nelson was already convinced, as far as I could tell. I guess it just felt good.

When Mr Nelson was ringing up our books and two ice cream cones, J. Norm asked him if he had the book we'd been hunting all day. The one by Mrs Mercy White. Mr Nelson threw his head back and whistled. 'Hoo-eee! Where'd you hear about that book? If I carried that thing in here, I'd be out of business in a week. That book ruffled more feathers than a stray dog in a chicken yard. The lady who wrote that hadn't lived here in years. Her daddy was the sheriff, but he eventually got crosswise of the wrong people and got himself run out of town. Guess Mercy had been waiting her whole life to grind some axes, but she sure shook up the town when she put that stuff in print. The poor fella who published that book, Leland Lowenstein, eventually had so many lawsuits and threats put against him that he just shut up his little printing company and moved out of the county. Bought the newspaper down in Littlewood. That's been, oh ... fifteen, maybe twenty years ago now. Since then, interested parties have pretty much gathered up every copy and performed proper burials, so to speak.'

After that, we walked out of the store lugging J. Norm's haul of books and eating double-dippers. They were dripping fast, so we sat on the bench across the street for a minute, taking in the warm spring day.

While we were working our way down to the cones, I picked one of the books out of the sack – one of the big hardbacks with lots of pictures and some town history here and there. 'You know,' I told J. Norm in between bites of ice cream, 'they probably have all of these at Ward House.' I recognized some of the titles. 'We could've just looked at them there and saved the money.'

J. Norm was leaning back in the sun, enjoying his mint chocolate chip. 'I felt the need for my own copies. If our trip doesn't pan out today, I can take them home to Dallas with me and keep looking at them. Something might ring a bell.'

It bothered me that he was talking about giving up. I wasn't ready. Even though all I had with me was a couple pairs of jeans, two T-shirts, underwear, a toothbrush, and the envelope of money I'd been stashing under my bed, this trip was like a promise. A promise to figure out the mystery. I didn't want to quit until the promise was kept, and besides that, I wasn't going back to Dallas. I didn't know yet what my plan was, but I wasn't going back.

I read the name carved in stone on the building across the street. VANDRAAN, in big, block letters, kind of oozy and black around the edges where rainwater had drained down. 'That name doesn't ring a bell – VanDraan?' I flipped to the back of the book, to the 'V's in the index.

Norman shook his head. 'It's odd. There are only bits and pieces in my memory. Like random factors of an equation, nothing more. Not enough to solve it.'

The name was in the index. VanDraan, Luther. I popped the rest of my ice cream cone into my mouth – not very ladylike, because my cheeks bulged, but I needed both hands. Swiping off on my jeans, I split the book down the middle and started turning toward page 136.

Page 132 . . . some train.

Page 133 ... a herd of cows and cowboys at the stockyards.

Page 134 ... a picture of an old petition from back in 1911.

Page 135 ... a bunch of soldiers marching through the town in World War I.

Page 136 fell open, and there were pictures. Five of them. The bank building, the store, a big white house with three stories and an iron fence around it. Under that, there was a picture of three black ladies working in the kitchen, dressed in maids' uniforms.

In the last photo on the page, underneath the maids' picture, I found what I was looking for. The VanDraans.

CHAPTER 19

J. Norman Alvord

Gazing at the pictures was a waking dream. Could it be that after all this time, I was coming face-to-face with the ghosts that had haunted me, the past I'd always felt but never recognized until the day my near death had unlocked some long-closed door?

I knew these pictures. I knew the house. I knew the people. The women in the kitchen, I could hear them laughing, and I knew that sometimes they would sing as they worked – hymns, blues songs by W. C. Handy or Mamie Smith. One of the women pictured was Cecile. She was young, even younger than I might have thought her in my dream. In the photo, she was lowering a rack of mason jars into a boiling pot. They were canning. I knew how the kitchen would smell – like steam and vinegar, paraffin and seared vegetables. From the corner, a baby in a high chair looked on, chubby cheeked, with pale skin and downy curls. The fluff of hair was red. Red, like mine. I knew this despite the lack of color in the photo. I knew the children in the next photo also. The girls, twins, their flyaway waves of hair gathered into bows, and the boy, a stout-legged toddler, red hair also, blue eyes, a little button of a nose that made him look as if he'd grow to be a rascal, given half a chance.

My finger traced the photo, trembled upward from the children's faces to the woman standing to their left. A beautiful woman. She was wearing a stylish floral-print dress, a fashionable belt cinched tightly at her waist. Her hair had been pinned up under a wide-brimmed hat, as if she were attired for an occasion. Some holiday, Easter perhaps. She'd turned her face slightly away from the camera, so that the shadow of the hat brim made her no more than a ghost in the picture. A ghost with murky features and eyes that said nothing. In the right of the frame sat a man in a chair, his posture straight and stern, the baby poised on his knee. A hand rested on his shoulder, a boy's hand. My hand. My gaze traveled upward, and I looked into my own eyes.

Epiphany touched the photo, pointed as if to make certain I'd seen. 'J. Norm, that's you.' She breathed the words with obvious surprise, as if she hadn't believed until now that all of this was real.

'Yes, it is.' There was no doubt. I'd seen enough of my own childhood pictures to know myself, and so had Epiphany. The mother who raised me had photographed me within an inch of my life, but there had always been a gap in those photos. There were pictures of me as a baby, even pictures of me in her arms. *He looked more like you when he was young,* acquaintances would say to my mother when they came to visit our home.

Mother would only laugh and reply, *Norman takes resemblance from my father. My father had red hair and a cleft in his chin, God rest him.*

Did those friends on our street in Dallas ever look, really look at those baby pictures, and wonder?

I traced a finger along the names in the caption beneath the photo. *The VanDraan family*, it read. *Front, Luther Van-Draan, wife Fern. Children, left to right, Erin, Emma, Johnny, Paul (infant), and Luther William VanDraan Jr (called Willie), shortly before a fire destroyed VanDraan House, taking the lives of the five children, as well as Fern VanDraan, and an African-American housekeeper, Cecile Bell.*

Cecile Bell. She had a last name now, and I had a name, too: Luther William VanDraan, called Willie. The name became a part of me as I looked into the eyes of the boy. The boy who had not perished in that fire, but somehow, through an unknown set of circumstances, had been transported to another life. This was the secret my mother had been hiding all these years. The reason she was afraid to send me to school or allow me beyond the perimeter of our yard when I was small. She was waiting. Waiting for me to grow, to change, to fully become someone else, all traces of my past gone from my memory and from the rest of the world.

'J. Norm.' Epiphany's tone was grave, contemplative. 'If you didn't die in that fire, maybe the rest of them didn't either.' As usual, her mind was one step ahead of my own. That was the thought I had been reaching for, the next section of track to be laid into the uncharted lands. What was true and what was untrue, and how would I know the difference?

Closing the page, Epiphany stood up, then dropped the book in the sack and scooped it off the bench. 'Let's go, J. Norm. We need to see the graveyard and where the house was.'

I stood up too quickly, and my heart rapped hard against my chest, lurching unevenly in a way that caused the street to narrow and then expand before me. These past two days, with so much activity and excitement, were far outside my normal routine. I gripped the back of the bench, steadying myself.

Epiphany didn't notice. 'C'mon, J. Norm.' She trotted ahead toward the car, her dark hair swinging from side to side over her shoulders, her long legs covering ground in enthusiastic, confident strides. Turning, she walked backward a few steps. 'Hey, just stay there. I'll go get the car.' She began hurrying off without waiting for an answer.

I called after her anyway, 'You're not allowed to drive alone!'

'It's just up the street!' Checking for traffic, she jogged across, then hurried along the other sidewalk to the car. Obstinate as usual, she put the books in the back, climbed in, pulled onto the street, and turned around in the drive-way of a pharmacy before I had any hope of stopping her. She was beaming when she pulled to the curb beside me and rolled down the window. 'Hey, dude, need a ride?'

I shouldn't have laughed. It would only encourage her.

'Learner's *permit*,' I reminded her, as I slid into my seat. I'd put a pill under my tongue while she was gone, and my heart was settling now, the tightness fading. Still, I felt oddly off balance. Perhaps it was the photos, or perhaps I wasn't certain I wanted to see the graves. It's a strange thing to think about viewing one's own resting place.

'I know, I know,' she huffed. 'But you gotta admit, I'm getting better at driving.'

'A bit,' I allowed, and she beamed again.

'Come on, J. Norm. You couldn't have figured all this stuff out without me. We're like Bonnie and Clyde.'

'Bonnie and Clyde robbed banks.'

'Same difference.' Shrugging, she repeated the shopkeeper's directions under her breath, 'Right on Dogwood Street, three blocks . . . right on Dogwood Street . . .'

We continued along the road and turned on Dogwood. The mini storage sat on a corner lot next to a yellow Victorian house that may have been grand once, but now looked as though it were slowly surrendering to the wind and the weather. Across the street, a low-income rental complex had been built, and beyond that, several lots had been cleared for trailer homes. Down the block, a number of old homes had undergone what appeared to be haphazard renovations. On the whole, it was clear that the neighborhood, once upscale and the toast of Groveland, had long since fallen into decline.

There appeared to be no on-site supervision at the mini storage, so Epiphany and I drove in as if we owned the place. 'Circle around to the back,' I said. 'See if the fence is still there.'

''Kay.' She cast worried looks toward the side mirrors while navigating the narrow aisle between two storage buildings. 'Man, this is skinny. How do they expect people to drive through here?'

I leaned toward my window to see around the corner to the back of the lot, where weeds, wild grapevines, and brambles grew in a tangle, like the wall of thorns around Sleeping Beauty's castle. My breath caught in anticipation. Somehow, it seemed that if I could touch a bit of the house, hold it in my hand, the rest of my memories might come flooding back.

As we cleared the building, I saw the corner post among the weeds, a thick, heavy brick structure with an ornamental iron finial atop – the head of a lion entwined with vines, encrusted with a patina of dirt and rust and moss. In my mind, it was freshly painted, the teeth catching the noonday sun, sending a chill of foreboding over me.

Epiphany turned off the car and stepped out, but I was barely conscious of her. My mind cartwheeled back in time as I started toward the corner post. A section of iron fencing lay sideways in the weeds, the vines winding in and out like threads in a needlework canvas. Epiphany leaned over the tangle of grass and brush, reached, then pulled her hand away without touching. 'Oh, shoot, there's poison ivy everywhere.' She pointed, and, indeed, she was right.

Bracing a hand on one knee, I bent toward the grass. Epiphany caught my arm protectively. 'J. Norm, don't. You'll catch pois –'

I plucked a dandelion from the edge of the brush, stood up again. Staring at the flower, yellow and lacy, I saw the hands of my little sisters, heard their laughter. My sisters.

My brother. And the baby. Another boy. My sisters. My brothers. Two of each. All these years, I'd been an only child, but in truth I wasn't.

Reaching across the weeds, I laid a hand against the corner post, willed the memories to come back, but they remained a garden in the mist, alluring, tempting, yet impossible to make out.

'Did you remember something?' Epiphany asked.

I shook my head, looking up at the iron finial. The lion's mouth made me shudder, even now. In my mind, I saw another one like it, a smaller version capping an iron post, perhaps for tying horses. It was near a stable. There had been a stable at the house. The lion's mouth held a ring. A rope was strung through it, tied tightly, wrapped around my wrists.

The backs of my legs were raw, sticky, flies crawling over them, dining on little trickles of blood.

The windows in the stable were going dark, night coming.

Cecile was there, her hands shaking as she untied the rope. 'Oh, Willie-boy,' she whispered. 'Oh, child. Hush, now . . .'

I pulled my hand away from the cool stone, the memory stopping abruptly, catching in my throat, seeming to suck the air from the space around me, leaving a vacuum.

'J. Norm?' Epiphany gripped my arm again. 'You all right?'

'Let's go back to the car,' I said, allowing her to help me navigate the uneven patches of dirt and crabgrass. Safely in my seat again, I noticed the dandelion still in my hand. I tossed it into the grass, afraid of the memories it might conjure. My remembrances were an unpredictable mix. Some

305

were hard, cold, unyielding, like the stone post. Some were soft, beautiful, and resilient, like the dandelion. To find one, I would have to come near the other. Perhaps this was the reason my mind had locked away the memories long ago, and the reason my mother had never told me the truth. Unimaginable things had happened to me in that house, terrible things that should never have been done to any child, to any human being. Cecile had attempted to protect me, but as a young black woman of that day, a maid in the home of a wealthy man, she would have been in danger herself. What had she risked in order to look after me and the other children; what had she endured? Had she survived in the end, or had she perished in that house?

As we drove to the graveyard, I tried to imagine who I might have become, if not for the mother who raised me and the gentle, quiet father who quoted from Proverbs and encouraged me to be an honest, enterprising man. Their love for me had erased everything about this town, all the pain and trauma of those early years. Did they know of that when they took me in, or had they discovered later that they'd been given a damaged, broken little boy? At what moment had they decided to extend the time and patience that would be needed, and keep me anyway?

We found the graveyard easily enough. It lay in a field beside an old clapboard church that was no longer used, other than as a historic site. The headstones were more recent in front, older in back, although it was evident that, like the church, the cemetery wasn't generally in use anymore. Walking past the rows of stones, Epiphany carried

the book with the VanDraan family photo in it. She lin-
gered over some of the tombstones as I moved on, searching
for any markers bearing the VanDraan names.

'Find anything?' she asked, trotting to catch up with me
after a bit. With a shudder, she threaded her arms and
pressed the book to her stomach.

'Not yet.'

She sighed impatiently as we walked. 'I used to live down
the road from a graveyard like this. When I got bored, I'd go
read the stones, or sometimes I'd dig up flowers from the
ditch and plant them on the graves for the little kids. It
seemed like, if you were a kid, and you never got to grow
up, you wouldn't know the difference between weeds and
real flowers, right? Weeds are tougher, and just as pretty,
anyway. Flowers are just weeds somebody decided were
special. Like those dandelions back there at the mini storage. I mean, if people called them flowers and sold the seeds
in little packages, they'd be flowers, right?'

'I believe they would,' I agreed, and it occurred to me that
Epiphany's analysis wasn't entirely random. She'd been considering the question, thinking about her life, or mine, or
both. We'd both been cast adrift as youngsters, Epiphany
and I, and she seemed to be searching for an anchor as des-
perately as I had been when I sat at the feet of the mother
who raised me, and clung to her knee. My mother was
everything to me – comfort, security, safety, love. Epiphany
needed those things as much as I had. Who could say why
God would have selected an old curmudgeon like me for
such a task, but I wanted to be the mentor she needed, the

person who would make a difference. Here at the end of my life, I found myself yearning for the things on which I'd placed so little importance in my adult years – a connection, someone to listen to my stories, a sense that my life would matter after I was gone. A ripple in the pool.

Stopping suddenly, Epiphany pointed ahead, her eyes widening. 'There it is! VanDraan. That big one over there. J. Norm, look!'

I turned my gaze in the direction she indicated, and indeed I saw it, not more than twenty feet away now – a wrought-iron fence, aged and leaning, that marked a private plot for several graves. At the center, an obelisk of granite proclaimed the name VanDraan. The letters were black with mildew, grown over with moss, so that they seemed to spread, twining into the dark threads of the rock as if they had been forged along with it, deep in the earth. I took an unsteady step, moving closer, felt breathless, my heart fluttering, but not painfully, not dangerously. The flutter was anticipation, the sense of being so caught in the moment that I could think of nothing else, even breathing.

Epiphany's hand slid under my elbow. 'It's okay. I'm right here,' she said quietly, and I moved my fingers to clutch hers. Together, we walked closer. The gate creaked, protesting as I opened it. At the base of the stone tower, there was a name. Like the face of the father in the book, it was meaningless to me. LUTHER WILLIAM VANDRAAN SR. Any memory of his name had been erased so cleanly from my memory that it no longer existed. All traces of those words were gone forever.

Staring at the letters, thinking of the family photo, I tried to excavate the memory, exhume it like a body needed to solve a cold case. But there was nothing.

Epiphany gasped, released my arm. 'There are the kids.' Side-stepping, she opened the book, thumbed through the pages until she'd found the VanDraan photo again. She read the names out loud, pointing to each of them in the book, 'Paul, Johnny, Erin, Emma, and Luther William VanDraan Jr – Willie.' She turned to look over her shoulder, her gaze rolling slowly upward to catch mine, her eyes flinty, filled with questions. 'You.'

I couldn't say how long we stood there, numbly studying the graves, looking at the pictures. Five plots, youngest to eldest in sequence, each tombstone slightly larger than the last, an odd physical depiction of the dates on either side of the hyphens, the short spans of young lives. And beside those, next to the grave of Luther VanDraan, who had lived fully twenty years beyond the deaths of his family, was the grave marked, FERN, WIFE AND MOTHER.

My mother. I could remember her, if I tried. Her hair was red, long. Her eyes blue, sad, vacant. She was a pretty woman, but thin and pale, a shadow. Helpless, afraid, confused. Weak. These were the impressions that came to me with the picture, with the name. They rose from her grave like restless spirits, surrounding me.

She played the piano sometimes. Long, haunting melodies that drifted through the halls of the house, filling every corner, choking the air like smoke, drowning out the voices of the women in the kitchen, the laughter of the children. Who was she, this woman in the grave? *Was* she in this grave? Was she there under the soil, a victim of a fire that took some lives, but not all?

How many lives? Had the mother who raised me known? Had she known who was buried here and who wasn't? How had she become involved to begin with, and if the baby on her lap in our family albums wasn't me, what had happened to that child?

So many questions, and I'd arrived so late in my life to search for the answers . . .

Epiphany handed the book to me and slipped away. I watched as she walked across the cemetery, the shade sliding over her skin, painting her the color of rich earth in shadow, a golden hue in the light.

Finally, I closed the book and left the family plot, unsure of my feelings about it. Should I sense a connection or not? I was no longer that boy named on the stone. I was James Norman Alvord. An engineer, a scientist, a man who'd lived a full life, who'd been fortunate enough to exist in a time when the world was changing, when America was making unprecedented strides in innovation and technology. I'd seized opportunity when it came my way, sometimes stumbled upon it, always tried to do good business, to be enterprising. My father had taught me that – and my mother. They'd made me who I was. These people on the gravestones were strangers. What good could come of learning all of this now?

I started toward the car, calling after Epiphany, but she was walking through the weeds, crossing out of the graveyard at the back, where the fence had rusted through, the strands of wire hanging in uneven curls. I called to her again, but she paused only for a moment, then ducked under a hackberry branch and continued on.

'Just a minute.' Her voice drifted back as I came closer to the fence. 'I want to see.'

'To see what?' A sharp, narrow fingernail of irritation scratched along my spine. 'We've found the graves. It's time to go.' Inside me, there was an almost desperate need to get out, to move away, but Epiphany was weaving deeper into the scrappy grove of hackberries, her knees rising high as she tromped over weeds and fallen branches. Finally she disappeared in the brush, and I had the sense of being there alone. It slid over me with the chill of ice water. 'Epiphany,' I called again. It was foolish, being afraid. She was still nearby, of course. I was acting like a child, as silly as Epiphany last night when she carried her pillow into my room and curled up on the fainting couch.

Even so, I moved to the point where the groomed area stopped and the weeds began. 'Epiphany?' I called again.

'They're really out here.' Her voice was quieter now, intimate. The rustle of leaves and grass had stilled. 'The graves, J. Norm. You can see where they were.'

The graves? I didn't understand her meaning at first. We'd already discovered the VanDraan graves. They were easy enough to find, prominent actually. VanDraan may not have been well liked, but certainly he could afford to leave his resting place clearly marked.

I stepped closer to the fence, bending low over what was

left of the wire in an effort to catch sight of Epiphany. I could not, and so I traversed the single strand that lay tangled along the ground. Brambles tugged at my pants, as if to stop me from moving farther. My foot settled on something uneven, solid, and in bending to wrest my pants loose from the brambles, I realized what it was. A marker. A flat piece of simple brown rock, once buried in the soil to stand upright, now listing at a forty-five-degree angle. A gravestone, worn by the wind and the weather. The words, BABY AMOS 1947, 2 MONTHS, were barely visible now, crudely carved in a mixture of small letters and capitals.

Epiphany had found the other part of the cemetery, the hidden place Mr Nelson had mentioned. The place where those not permitted within the fence were laid to rest, their markers hand-hewn by loved ones, many undoubtedly made of wood and long since destroyed. It was odd to realize now that as a young man, I would not have thought anything about this. How many times had I passed by the churchyard in my mother's car and watched funeral lines proceeding beyond the fence to another area? I'd never given the reasons even a measure of consideration. It was just the way things were done. What we knew. What we had been taught. What we had accepted.

If Cecile, that young woman who had mothered me, cared for me, loved me, *saved* me, was buried here, the chances were that her marker, like so many others, was long gone. It seemed wrong that she should be the one to lie unmarked, and not my mother, who had failed to protect me, or my father, who had wounded me in unspeakable ways.

I stepped back through the fence, walked to the car, and waited for Epiphany to come. When she did, we drove back to town without conversing. I wondered what was in her thoughts, but I didn't ask. I could send a rocket to the moon, but emotion had always been a mystery to me.

Of all things, the words that finally came to my lips were, 'Let's stop for barbecue.'

Epiphany seemed almost relieved that I'd rekindled the conversation. 'Can we have something else? We've had a lot of barbecue lately.'

'All right, then, you pick.'

After a meal of drive-through hamburgers and horrible cylinder-shaped fried potato nuggets, which we ate in the car, we proceeded back to Ward House, both of us having resumed our normal rhythm.

'I looked for Cecile's grave out there, but I didn't find it,' Epiphany said as we exited the car at Ward House. 'There were lots that weren't marked, though. Lots of babies' graves, too.'

'It was the way of things,' I admitted, and then realized there was a baby's grave in the family that had raised me, as well. The baby on my mother's lap in the pictures never grew up. I took his place. Where was the grave? Did my mother ever visit it? Did she suffer the loss of that child in silence, so that I could be given his place in the family? Did she admonish the relatives never to tell me the truth about my past? She must have, but such choices were often made for adopted children in those days. It was considered best not to tell.

How many people knew?

Even as I considered the questions, looking at them from every angle, I was aware that, in my lifetime, I would most likely never know the answers. My mother's motivations had died with her, and there was no one else to ask.

When we carried our things upstairs, a consolation package of sorts lay atop my freshly made bed. Propped against the array of lacy pillows was a book, and not just any book.

The forbidden masterpiece of the elusive Mrs Mercy White lay waiting. On the cover, a sepia photograph of Mrs Mercy frowning pensively in her high school graduation photo had been partially covered with a Ward House Bed-and-Breakfast sticky note, which simply read, *Ssshhh.*

CHAPTER 20

Epiphany Jones

Mrs Mercy White's book changed everything. I could see why nobody in Groveland wanted it around, too. That woman told secrets about everybody and everyplace in town, and she knew a lot. Her daddy was the sheriff for twelve years, and her stepmom ran the phone exchange. J. Norm clued me in to the fact that, back in the day, a lady actually sat at a thing called a switchboard and plugged the phone lines together when people made a call. While she was doing it, she could listen to everything everybody said, and Mercy White's stepmom did. Mrs Mercy came right out and said so in the book.

Aunt Char passed through the upstairs parlor while J. Norm and me were reading. She gave a little smile that let me know she was the one who'd left the book for us. Then she said we should 'take everything in there with a grain of salt.'

I could tell that Aunt Char was dying to know what we were looking for in Mrs Mercy White's 'revenge rag,' as she called it. While J. Norm and me thumbed through the pages,

Aunt Char kept passing back and forth through the upstairs parlor with sheets and cleaning stuff, watching us from the corner of her eye.

It took us a minute to find the chapters about the Van-Draan house burning down, but once we did, J. Norm and me were side by side on the sofa, eating up those words like they were Blue Bell ice cream on a hot day. Mrs Mercy White (considering the stuff the book had in it, that name was what J. Norm would've called an oxymoron, by the way) served up enough dirt on old Luther VanDraan to bury him three times over, if he wasn't buried enough already. According to her, he was just about the most hateful person ever to show up in Groveland, Texas. He came to town after getting out of World War I, and he was drop-dead good-looking and had money. He was a gentleman type, always dressed up in a suit and a vest, with a gold pocket watch. Everybody in town couldn't get enough of him, at first. But he was as dark underneath the surface as he was fine on the outside. He was a player with the ladies, and he started buying up businesses and land around town, and not always in a nice way, either.

It wasn't long before Mrs Mercy White's daddy, the sheriff, got crosswise of Luther VanDraan, because he beat a black man to death. Mr VanDraan testified that the man had tried to steal a crate of apples out of a storage yard, but the sheriff knew the truth was that poor guy stumbled onto one of VanDraan's shipments of tax-free illegal liquor, and VanDraan didn't want any witnesses. There wasn't a thing her daddy could do about it, Mrs Mercy White said. VanDraan had a half dozen witnesses testify the man was a thief. All the witnesses worked for VanDraan.

By the time he'd been in Groveland a few years, VanDraan had bought up so much of the town that nobody could challenge him. He'd built the big house where the mini storage was now. Guess maybe he was lonely there, because one day, he caught sight of a schoolgirl named Fern Caufelt, an orphan who'd moved to Groveland to live with her spinster aunt. Fern walked by the bank on her way home from school one day, and that must've been the worst mistake of her life. Two months later, she'd quit school and married Luther VanDraan.

There were two or three more stories about terrible things VanDraan did to force people off their land, and then we came to the part about the fire. It was just a few pages, but if you could believe Mrs Mercy White, it said a lot.

. . . in 1941, on a Saturday. I remember waking in the middle of the night to the sound of the fire trucks leaving the station. I sat up and opened my window, pushed my face to the screen, and I could hear people yelling, 'The VanDraan house is on fire! The VanDraan house is ablaze!' Off to the south, the horizon was aglow from it, a big, bright circle of light against the starless night sky. I watched for a long time, and then finally the streets grew quiet. I pulled the window down and fell asleep at the foot of my bed. Sometime later, voices woke me, and I sneaked across my room, even though I knew that if my stepmother caught me, she'd blister my feet with a cane switch for being up. Sometimes . . .

Mrs Mercy White went on for a while then about how terrible her stepmother, the phone operator, was, and how little Mercy was so afraid to get out of bed at night that she'd wet herself, and then she'd get spanked for that, too. According to Mrs Mercy, her daddy never knew a thing about it. He was practically a saint, really, and wouldn't have let anybody treat her in a bad way.

J. Norm's finger swiveled back and forth down the page in a hurry, skimming over all that family stuff, until Mrs Mercy White got back to the point. It took two and a half pages, and then finally,

> . . . I tiptoed across my room, and I could hear my stepmother and Daddy arguing. 'Now, you listen to me!' she was saying. 'I won't hear of it; do you understand me, Caleb White? It's too much risk. We have our own family to think about. I have my position to consider. I have it on good authority that I'm to be invited into the Garden Club this year, for one thing. What do you suppose will happen if we're caught? Hmmm? Found sneaking behind everyone's backs? And on the word of some . . . some black girl? You know they can't be trusted.'
>
> My father's voice was low at first, and I couldn't hear. I got down on my knees and pushed my face close to the crack at the bottom of the door. '. . . on purpose,' he said.
>
> 'For heaven's sake, Caleb, you know that coloreds are habitual liars. They can't even help it. They're like children. They don't understand the difference. If what she says is true, then leave the matter to the courts, as is your job, Caleb White.'

Again my father was hard to hear. He paced the floor, away, then back. '. . . do something, Mora.'

'No!' My stepmother's voice was a harsh whisper, a hiss like a snake's. 'What will he do to you if he finds out? What would he do to us? You think he wouldn't do the same thing he did to that colored boy out behind his warehouse? You think he wouldn't do worse? And he'll find out. Why wouldn't he? This is his town, Caleb. He owns it, lock, stock, and barrel. Everything.'

'Just let me bring them in, Mora. Just for tonight. I'll figure something out in the morning.'

'Pah! The morning. You couldn't plan your way out of an apple crate. I will not have them in here, do you hear me? I will not be involved in this. Five children! Five, all with red hair. What, do you think no one would notice? Maybe they could live down on Hakey Creek with all those coloreds you're so fond of. Maybe you can shoe-polish their faces black and braid their hair and dress them up like pickaninnies. Maybe their little mammy can just raise them for her own. How about that? How about that for a plan? Shame on you, Caleb White! Shame on you for bringing this trouble to our home. The home where my children sleep! This is just your pride. This is just your way of getting revenge against Luther VanDraan, because you couldn't prosecute him after that trouble at his warehouse. And what does it matter? It was only a colored boy. Maybe he was stealing. They're all thieves. Did you ever think of that? Maybe he got what he deserved. I won't have you risking our family, our home, for your pride, for some tall tale. Now, you put them in that car, and you take them somewhere else. I don't want to see them again. I don't want to know anything about this; do you hear me?'

Mrs Mercy White hurried back across her room after that, and when she hopped into her bed, she looked out the window into the front yard, and as she put it,

There under the light of the gas lamp, huddled up against the holly berry bushes, was the VanDraans' colored mammy with those five little redheaded kids, all in their night-clothes, with soot and dirt all over them. I watched my daddy tuck them into the backseat of his patrol car and drive away down the dark street. The next day, when I heard that those kids and the maid had died in the flames as the VanDraan house burned to the ground, I knew it was a lie. We even went to the funeral and watched as the ladies in church cried about those little redheaded children and mourned pretty Mrs VanDraan. All the while I knew that whatever ashes were in those five little coffins, they didn't belong to the kids. I never knew if there was a casket full of ashes somewhere for the colored girl, too, or why my daddy did what he did, or where he took those kids. I never told a soul one thing about it, either. Not in my whole life. When I was little, I knew my stepmother would switch my feet until I limped and then tell everyone I'd gone out barefoot on the rocks again. Later, I knew enough to be fearful of Mr Luther VanDraan, especially after his second wife drowned in the river, and then his third wife died. Even when he sold his interests in Groveland and moved out of town, I knew I'd better keep quiet. My daddy could've gone to jail for what he did, and there were some men around who would have done even worse than that to him, if they'd known he took up the side of a colored girl against a white man.

Luther VanDraan lived quite a few more years down near Lufkin. I suppose many breathed easier after he left Groveland, but I sensed him out there, still lurking.

I never felt the same about the coloreds after that. I knew what it was like to be afraid, for one thing . . .

Mrs Mercy White talked on awhile about how things used to be between the black people and the white people who lived in Groveland. I read it for a minute, because I got interested, thinking about how life was then. Meanwhile, J. Norm kept scanning back over the page about the fire, his finger moving from side to side. He couldn't believe it, I guessed, but I did. There at the cemetery earlier, it was like I could feel that not only was the grave of little Willie VanDraan empty, but so were the other four of them. Somewhere out there, four more kids like J. Norm had lived their whole lives, maybe never even knowing who they really were. Since they were all younger than J. Norm, they probably didn't even remember the house with the seven chairs.

But what if somebody told them about it? What if some of them had parents who shared the truth, maybe when they got older, or after Luther VanDraan was dead and gone? What if not all the parents kept secrets like J. Norm's mother did, like my mother did?

Could there be people out there, a family, looking for J. Norm? Maybe they'd been looking for him for years, but they didn't know what his name was now, and they didn't have any idea how to find him.

Right after that thought came another one – an idea that had nothing to do with J. Norm, or the house with the seven chairs, but had everything to do with me. What if there were people looking for me? What if those women in the pictures hadn't decided they didn't want me? Maybe they hadn't tossed me out because my daddy died, or because they didn't want me around, or because they were embarrassed to have some little half-and-half baby in the family. Maybe my mama just took me away, and they didn't know where to find me. What if they'd been looking all along?

After a minute, the what-ifs started to hurt. They swelled like one of those surgery balloons they showed on a film in science class, small inside the vein at first, then pumping up and up, stretching a spot that'd been closed off for a long time. I knew if I let the balloon grow too big, something might bust, and I'd bleed all over the place, so I focused on J. Norm instead. The whole time we'd been trying to solve this mystery, maybe we'd been going about it all wrong. There was one thing we hadn't thought of. The most obvious thing of all.

'J. Norm,' I said, 'we've been looking up other people's names, but you know what we didn't do? We didn't look up *yours*. What if, all this time, somebody's been trying to find you?'

I was off the sofa and into J. Norm's room for the

computer before you could say *scat*. I brought it back and set it on the coffee table in front of the sofa. While we waited for it to boot up, J. Norm fingered the pages about the fire, then reached into our sack and pulled out the book with the pictures of the VanDraan family. He laid both on the table next to the computer.

The software came up. I plugged in the cell phone thing and connected to the Internet.

Aunt Char wandered by and took a peek, then went on down the hall, swatting a feather duster across picture frames, like she was trying to look busy.

I opened the browser and put in J. Norm's name. *J. Norman Alvord.* Then I thought better of it. 'What's the J. stand for, J. Norm? We should use the whole thing.'

'James,' he answered, and I typed in the word, then sent James Norman Alvord off into cyberspace to see what we'd find.

Not a lot, it turned out. There were some history things about the name Alvord, and then a few old articles about rockets and stuff that had J. Norm's name listed with a bunch of other names, something about a college reunion, and some genealogy pages done by some long-lost Alvord cousin who figured he and J. Norm were related. Man, was he wrong about that.

'Let's try the other name.' I tipped the book so I could look at the old picture and make sure I spelled it right. 'If someone didn't know what your name ended up being, they might look for you by the name you had before.'

I typed the names *Luther William VanDraan Willie* into the

browser bar and pushed RETURN. The stupid computer got hung up, and the little hourglass just spun and spun and spun, while J. Norm and me sat pressed together over the screen like two kids in front of the fish tank at the zoo.

'Hang on. It's stuck.' I tried to close the window, but nothing would work on the screen. 'Stupid computer. I'll have to shut it down and start it again.'

While we were waiting for the computer to reboot, J. Norm got to talking about back when they used big tape reels on computers, and sometimes the reader would eat the tape, and then you had a mess. He was right in the middle of the story when Sharla came up the stairs. She called out from the top step, 'Mr Alvord ... uhhh ... Norman? You've got a phone call.' Then she walked in with the cordless phone pressed against her chest. Leaning over the lamp table from behind, she snuck a quick look at the computer and the books on the table. 'I don't know what she wants,' she whispered. 'She called earlier today, too. She was very ... insistent.'

Norman's eyebrows humped up like caterpillars crawling down a log, and I knew he was thinking the same thing I was thinking. Who'd be calling us here?

The computer finished reloading, and I opened the Internet browser again, but I saw it only from the corner of my eye. I was watching J. Norm watch that phone. If he didn't do something pretty quick, Sharla was gonna think he'd blown a gasket. 'It's probably somebody calling about the book.' I nudged J. Norm down low, where Sharla wouldn't see. 'Remember, Grandpa, we told the people in that store to let us know if they found a copy.' That wasn't true at all, but it didn't sound too bad. When we were shopping for Mrs Mercy White's book, a few people had asked where we were staying.

J. Norm took the phone and then stood up with it. Sharla must've caught the look on his face, because she pulled back a little, her hand hanging limp-wristed in the air between them. 'Is something wrong?'

He straightened and shook his head, putting a hand over the receiver. 'Oh, no ... no, nothing. My mind was elsewhere, that's all. We've been doing genealogical research.' He waved toward the computer, and then headed off to the other side of the room to take the call. I was supposed to keep Sharla busy, I guessed.

'Oh, are you kin to the VanDraans?' Sharla's head twisted so she could get a look at the books open on the table.

I shrugged. 'Oh, I dunno. All the old records about our family ... got lost before I was born ... back when Grandpa was little, and Grandpa doesn't remember things so well anymore.' I tapped a finger to the side of my forehead and made a little pouty lip, like I was sad to tell her J. Norm's mind was going.

Sharla stopped trying to listen in on the phone call and leaned closer to me. 'I'm sorry,' she whispered.

I nodded and gave her another sad look, figuring at least I had her distracted. 'It's good that you're helping him get his family history together,' she said. 'A lot of kids wouldn't bother.' She sat down beside me and smiled like she was impressed, and then I felt bad for lying to her. She reminded me of Mrs Lora right then, and Mrs Lora reminded me of church, and church reminded me that I was a Christian, saved and everything, and I shouldn't have been lying. After the last couple days, I needed to repent like crazy. The preacher in church said that being saved didn't mean you were perfect, but it meant you'd try to be like Jesus. Lately, Jesus was probably shaking his head at me big-time.

'I don't mind.' That was the truth, actually. 'It's like an adventure. He remembers the store with the ice cream counter, the one with the VanDraans' name on it. That got us started looking up the VanDraans.' That wasn't a lie, either. It just wasn't all of the truth.

Sharla looked at J. Norm, but he didn't notice. He was hunched over the phone in the corner. That had me worried. He was arguing with someone, and even if he was keeping it to a whisper, I had a bad feeling I knew who he was talking to. That sharp sound in his voice usually meant one thing: Deborah.

There wasn't any way she could know we were here, though . . . was there?

The answer came to me as quick as one of those shocks you get when you grab the doorknob after you walk across the carpet in the wintertime. How did the police track people who came up missing, or wandered off, or all of a sudden weren't where they were supposed to be?

The credit card. J. Norm had been using it all along. It was like a trail. Deborah was into all of J. Norm's bank accounts. She paid his bills. As soon as she figured out he was gone, she probably knew right where to look. We might as well have been calling Deborah to give her updates.

I heard J. Norm say, 'It's my affair if I want to take a trip – to see some places I remember.' Then there was a pause, and Deborah was talking loud enough that I could hear the rhythm of her voice through the phone, like a drum beating somewhere far away, really fast. All the while, Sharla was talking in my other ear, going on about when she was a kid and they used to go to the soda fountain at the store – by then it was Mr Nelson's – to get strawberry Cokes, and milk shakes, and . . .

I heard J. Norm say, 'The school? What in the world for?' He was rubbing his forehead now, leaning against the bookcase.

I felt sick.

Sharla was talking about putting peanuts in Coke.

Sweat built up under my shirt and trickled down my back. What if Deborah had called the police? What if the school had? What if they'd talked to Mama? What if some sheriff was headed over here right now? He probably wasn't gonna just tuck J. Norm and me in the back of his car and help us get away, like Mrs Mercy White's daddy did.

Sharla touched me on the arm. 'Honey, are you all right? You look like you just saw a ghost. I'm sorry Chris got to poppin' off about ghost stories yesterday evening, by the way. He was only joking with you, and –'

'Preposterous!' J. Norm blurted out the word so loud that both Sharla and I turned his way, and she stopped talking.

'Grandpa!' I squealed, to try to remind him that I was sitting right there, *with* Sharla. I rolled my eyes and gave her a look, like she shouldn't worry about what he was saying, since he only had half his mind left, anyway. 'That's my aunt. She's nuts. They argue all the time.' Sharla didn't look convinced, so I figured I better lay it on thick. 'She tried to kick him out of his house and take all his money. It's a bad deal.' I sounded pretty convincing. Sometimes a theater class or two in summer enrichment really comes in handy. 'But don't tell him I told you, okay? It's embarrassing.'

Sharla's eyes were wide at first; then she softened up like butter in a pan. 'You poor thing. You're stuck in the middle of a mess, aren't you?' Her soft, slow Southern drawl made the words sound sticky sweet.

'It'll be all right. Grandpa won't let her take the house. It's been in the family forever. All my grandma's stuff is still there. She only died a few months ago.' For just a sec, I had the weirdest feeling of sadness. Grief, I guess you'd call it – like I was missing the pretty lady in the pictures on J. Norm's wall, like she really was my grandma, and I knew how it would be to go in her closet and play dress-up in all those beautiful clothes while she sat on the edge of the bed and told me I was her little princess.

It was a nice dream, really. Deborah didn't know how good she had it. I'd seen the mountain of scrapbooks Annalee made. Every little thing Deborah did in her life – every blue ribbon, every Girl Scout badge, every award-winning science fair paper – was pasted in a scrapbook with pictures, the date, and some kind of note, like, *Eighth-grade science fair. First place. So proud!*

If I had parents who cared enough to follow me around to the science fair and take pictures, I wouldn't thank them by trying to take the house and stick my daddy in a nursing home. Sometimes people needed to stop and take a look around and see how lucky they were – how different life could really be.

Sharla hugged me around the shoulders, and I wasn't ready for it. It felt good, though. I sank into it for a minute, while I watched J. Norm hang up the phone and punch the air. It was a slow, wimpy old-man punch, but I think if Deborah had been there, they would've been in a fistfight by now.

I could tell by his face that I needed to get rid of Sharla. J. Norm looked worried, and besides that, his face was washed-out and pasty. He took a step and swayed on his feet, like he might fall down; then he gripped the bookcase.

I scooted away from Sharla and moved the computer closer. 'I better get busy, I guess. Can we borrow the phone again? We'll probably need to call Aunt Deborah back in a minute, when everybody cools off.'

'Sure.' Sharla patted my knee, then used it to push herself to her feet. 'Y'all just take your time. I'm working on some strawberry shortcake downstairs. Y'all come down and . . .' Her eyelashes flew up, and the next thing I knew, she was beating it toward the door. 'Oh, mercy! I forgot I've got cakes in the oven!' She didn't even look at J. Norm on the way out, which was good, because he was sagging against the shelf, breathing like he'd just done the Ironman race.

'J. Norm.' I hurried over to him as Sharla squeaked off down the stairs in her white sneakers. Taking the phone, I slipped my hand under his arm. 'Are you okay?'

He scrubbed his fingers back and forth, fuzzing up his eyebrows. 'I only need to catch my breath.'

'Well, but come sit . . .'

He jerked his elbow out of my hand. 'Leave me be, Epiphany!'

I stumbled back, a bad feeling gathering somewhere in the middle of me, seeping outward the way sludge creeps into a clean river, covering the water, leaving an ugly coating over things that were normal a minute before. J. Norm hadn't talked to me like that since the two of us started being a team.

I was afraid he was going to tell me it was over – we were heading home. If the school and Deborah were on our tails, there was no telling how bad things might be. I wished I could've gotten hold of DeRon Lee right then, because I would've ripped his stupid head off. Sleaze. Liar. J. Norm was so right about him.

I left J. Norm alone and went back to the computer, figuring that if I let him be a minute or two, maybe things would turn normal again. I plugged the names *Luther William Van-Draan Willie* into the browser bar again and waited for the results to come through. When the listings flashed up, it was a mishmash – over one million entries, everything from stuff about the Van Daans in *The Diary of Anne Frank* to stuff about art. Then I remembered to put quotes around the name, and I sent the search through again, and came up with just one page. Right there in the third line was an adoption/reunion registry, and Luther William VanDraan's name was on it. A woman named Clara Culp was listed on www.lookingforlost.com, trying to find Luther William VanDraan. When I clicked on the link, there was the picture of the VanDraan family from the coffee table book, and a note Clara Culp's daughter, Amy, had written. *My mother, shown here at four years old with her siblings, who were separated and given different names. She is seeking information about any or all of her blood relatives.* Beside that was a work e-mail address for Clara Culp's daughter, and I didn't even have to look up the company to know where it was. I could tell by the e-mail address. J. Norm's niece, Amy Culp, worked for the Houston library system.

We were less than a hundred miles from Houston. There was a highway sign right outside of town that said so.

J. Norm's sister could be only a couple hours' drive away.

Just when I was about to tell him that, he turned away from the bookshelf, headed across the parlor toward his room, and said, 'It's time to go home, Epiphany.'

CHAPTER 21

J. Norman Alvord

We were on the lam again, rather than on the way home, and now that the decision had been made, I was secretly exhilarated, overflowing with anticipation, more alive than I had been in years. I once again felt like a young man in my prime, filled with power and vigor, traveling through my Camelot. Beside me, my copilot was quiet behind the wheel of the car. She seemed to have something on her mind as the air wafted through the window, stirring the dark curls over her shoulders.

'We've done it,' I remarked, wondering if she might be having regrets at this point, even though she was the one who had convinced me that we should send an e-mail to Clara and Amy Culp, and go on with our mission, rather than turn tail and drive back to Dallas. Perhaps, after sending the e-mail and hitting the road to Houston, Epiphany had stopped to consider the repercussions. I, on the other hand, had finally thrown caution to the wind. What could they do to me, really? I was an old man, practically at death's door. I could hire legal help to assist me in any battle that might arise, but for Epiphany, the realities were different. Perhaps she was mulling that over as we left Groveland behind. Epiphany was a child, a minor, at the mercy of the school administration, her mother, possibly even the legal system. What if the welfare authorities were to step in or some such? 'We can turn the other way,' I told her when we came to a highway intersection. Right toward Houston, left toward home.

She gaped at me as if I were daft. Apparently, she wasn't having second thoughts about our fugitive life. 'No way.'

'But *something* is wrong,' I pointed out. 'I can see it in your face. Something is on your mind.'

She puffed air, letting me know I was bothering her. 'I've got stuff to think about, that's all.'

'About school, or your mother?'

She rolled her eyes. 'No. Why would I be thinking about that?'

'But you *are* worried. Would you like to tell me what about? Grandfathers are old and wise and filled with sage advice, you know.'

She let her head fall against the headrest, her lips spreading into a reluctant smile. 'Man, this whole grandpa thing's gone to your head, seriously.'

I found myself laughing for no reason at all. Seeing my sister's name on the computer screen had been an exhilarating experience. Knowing that before the end of the day I might meet her filled me with anticipation. Erin or Emma, one of the twins who had held dandelions under my chin to see if I liked butter.

Did she remember that day?

Perhaps, on the way, I would stop alongside the road and pick a bouquet of dandelions to remind her.

Did she have any recollection of me? Had she always been aware that she was one of five children? How long had her posting been on the Internet? Had she found any of the others yet? Gazing out the window, I considered the missing pieces of my life, let myself sink into my own thoughts, questions spooling in my mind. If – no – *when* we found Clara Culp, would she be able to fill in the blanks about our family secrets? Had she learned more than I had? Less? How had she discovered her identity? Had someone told her, or had she tracked down the details by investigation, as Epiphany and I had?

'J. Norm.' Epiphany's voice broke into my thoughts. 'I got money with me. Cash. We can use it to get gas and pay for the hotel tonight and stuff. That way Deborah can't find out where we went by looking at the credit card charges.'

'You *have* money.' The grammatical correction was force of habit, and she sneered at it. 'And where would you have come up with money?'

'I brought it from home. I've been saving up my pay from Deborah. I had it stashed in the house where Mama and Russ wouldn't find it.'

A mild chill blew over my warm mood. 'You brought money from home? Why? You know I can afford to pay for anything we need.'

'I . . . maybe wasn't . . . *going* back home, okay?' She fluttered a hand up, then let it slap back to the steering wheel. 'I'm not going to that school again, and I'm not going back to that stupid house, and nobody'll care, anyway. They'll like it better when I'm not around.'

'Epiphany . . .' I soothed.

'It's true.' She swiped moisture from her eyes and sniffled, her lips trembling in a determined line that told me she'd given this decision some thought, probably quite a bit. 'Mama doesn't want me there. She can't wait till I'm gone.'

'I think you're mistaking your mother's intentions. Parents don't always . . .' *know how to show their feelings.* 'They think they're doing the right things, providing, protecting, guiding, but then they find out that it wasn't right. It wasn't enough.' *Your children grow up and you discover that while focusing on the work of parenthood, you've left all the important ties unbound.*

'She's embarrassed of me, okay! Her whole family is right up on Greenville Avenue. They own Tuscany Restaurant – the big Italian place with the guys in suits out front. They don't talk to my mama because of *me.* She hates me for ruining her life. Her family has a high-dollar restaurant, and we couldn't even afford to go in there for dinner. Because she got with my daddy. Because she had me. Who wants some little toffee baby in the family, right? It's better to keep it a secret.'

What was I to say to that? I had no idea how Epiphany's mother or her family felt. I could remember the days when something like this, a relationship between the races, a child, would have been a scandal to be hidden away, swept under the rug, kept quiet. Such things were only whispered about behind fingers cupped to contain the spread of sound.

But here in my car sat Epiphany – strong, clever, beautiful, bold. What family wouldn't be proud of her? What old man wouldn't want to hear the word 'grandpa' aimed his way? 'Have you ever confronted your mother with the question? Asked her about it? Listened to her explanation?'

She regarded me with the look that Deborah and Roy had employed when I complained that their teenage music sounded like a bad construction job performed by a pack of screaming hyenas. 'Uhhh, no. She doesn't want to talk about it, J. Norm. She never wants to talk about anything. She just wants me to stay out of her way, to quit costing her money and stop taking up space in her house.' Epiphany gesticulated along with the words, and the car drifted onto the shoulder, then back, careening along with the emotions of a sixteen-year-old girl.

'I doubt she feels that way,' I said, though I wasn't so certain. What sort of woman moved off with a man and left her child behind to be raised by some teacher from school? I pointed ahead. 'Pull off in that roadside park a moment. Let's stretch our legs and collect our –'

'I can drive. I'm okay.'

'Let's stop anyway. I think I see bluebonnets growing there. Bluebonnets were Annalee's favorite.'

For once, Epiphany did as she was told. We pulled off and sat in the car, the scent of bluebonnets wafting in through the window. Her head fell back against the seat and she closed her eyes, her long lashes squeezing tight, pressing out a tear. It trailed slowly down her cheek and dripped onto her T-shirt. 'Look, I just want to find my daddy's family, see what they're like, okay? You got the chance to come look for your people. Why can't I?'

'But I am not a teenager. You can't go off into the world alone, Epiphany. You can't blindly take off on a whim, hoping to find them.' The idea was unsettling in so many ways, and I realized that were she to decide to, she could disappear at any moment. I wouldn't be able to stop her. She was young and nimble, and I was old and slow. She could be gone in the blink of an eye.

What if, by giving her a way out of Dallas, I'd set something in motion that I couldn't control?

'I had *you* with me. I wasn't alone,' I reminded her, speaking gently, as you might to a skittish horse that was prone to bolting. 'We're a team, remember? A partnership. One of us can't just . . . make random decisions and set off without consulting the other.'

Another tear dripped from beneath her dark lashes and trailed along the velvet skin of her cheek. Letting out a sardonic hiss, she wiped the moisture with a clumsy swipe of her palm. 'Since when?'

'Well, since . . .' When, exactly? When had an *arrangement*, an unsteady truce based on blackmail and necessity, become something deeper – a friendship, a kinship? At this point in my life, I hadn't thought myself capable of such a rapid metamorphosis of feeling. I'd imagined myself old and stale, with the stiffness of weathered leather. Stuck in my ways. Not pliable. Yet this child had plied me without even intending to, just by listening to my stories, just by being herself.

If such a thing were possible with a stranger, with a young woman I'd met such a short time ago, what might be possible with Deborah, my own daughter?

The question was quickly opened and just as quickly closed. My daughter, who was trying to put me out of my house and warehouse me in some facility for the criminally old and intractable.

'When we've finished in Houston, after we've gone home and straightened out this mess involving DeRon and the school, then we'll find your father's family.' I offered the option like a hostage negotiator trying to talk a jumper off a cliff. 'We'll go on the lam again, if we have to, but I want you to promise me, Epiphany, that no matter what, you won't run away by yourself. It's a dangerous world for a young girl.' I recalled the day of her altercation with DeRon – pictured her scraped, bruised, shaken, her clothes torn. It could have been so much worse. The terrible possibilities in the wider world caused me to shudder. 'Promise me, Epiphany.'

'Yeah, whatever.'

'Promise, or we're going home now. Right now.' I'd sacrifice the quest to find my family this minute before I would allow myself to become a danger to Epiphany. 'We'll turn the car around, and we'll go back to Dallas.'

Her head swiveling in my direction, she wiped her eyes and studied me. 'You're gonna quit when your sister's, like, eighty miles away? You're just gonna turn around and go home?' Her chin dipped in punctuation, her hair clinging to the headrest.

'If it's a risk to your safety.' I met her gaze, paused because I wanted her to fully focus. 'You come first, Epiphany. You. Whether we find my family or not.'

Her eyes took on light, the realization seeming to dawn

slowly. 'Grandfather' wasn't just a camouflage, a pretend mask any longer. It was a word with meaning, a title that carried responsibility and commitment.

Sighing, she sat up and put her hands on the steering wheel again. 'Well, geez, I don't want that on my head. I'll be good.'

'So you promise, then? I have your word?' If I'd learned anything about Epiphany, it was that she could talk her way through a marble maze and back. 'You promise that you will not run away?'

'I promise.'

'Repeat the whole thing, please, and I want to see both hands. No crossed fingers.'

Her lips trembled into a smirk, and she lifted her fingers from the steering wheel, repeating mechanically, 'I promise I will not run away.' She blinked back the lingering tears, and the two of us sat collecting ourselves. After a few moments, she brought up a new subject. 'We're gonna have to get on the computer and see if the Culps answered our e-mail. We could also try looking for a home address or phone number for her daughter. We can't just start tracking down libraries and asking for Amy Culp. They have city libraries all over the place in big towns like Houston, and tomorrow's Sunday, anyway. They're probably not open. We'll have to find a place to stay tonight, too.'

I contemplated the problem. 'Well, fortunately for us, I know a bit about Houston. I spent part of my career at the Johnson Space Center.'

'Awesome.' Twisting around, she stretched into the backseat and came up with the computer bag. 'You want me to look for addresses, or do you want to do it while I drive? As long as we can get cell phone service, we can use the Internet.' She balanced the computer on the console, waiting for me to choose. 'I can tell you how to look stuff up.'

'I think I can manage it,' I told her. 'It's not rocket science.'

The corner of her mouth twitched upward. 'I guess if it was, we'd have it made, since you're the rocket man.'

I felt my lightness of spirit returning as she put the car in gear, and I took out the computer and set it on my knees. Epiphany guided me through the process of starting the software and connecting the hardware to the thumb-size Internet transmitter/receiver. When I didn't take instruction quickly enough, she reached across the console, pointing and trying to type.

The car swerved lazily onto the shoulder, then back. 'Hands on the wheel, eyes on the road,' I reprimanded. If I could be outpaced by a sixteen-year-old computer operator, at least I knew more about driving.

We continued along while the computer hummed and I studied the screen, taking in the tiny icons and trying to remember exactly which one was for the Internet. For a man who'd been in the consulting world not so long ago, I'd grown surprisingly rusty – proof that, after my heart trouble had led to a doctor's recommendation that I leave behind the stress of consulting, I'd spent far too much time sulking around the house, watching television and reading old books. Undoubtedly, I hadn't been much fun for Annalee to live with.

I selected an icon or two, and within moments I was

playing music and I'd managed to take a photo of myself. Another frame opened, revealing a live-action shot of a confused-looking old man peering at the computer, his eyes in a squint. Me, of course.

Epiphany craned sideways to see. 'What are you doing?' She reached for the computer again. I turned it away and scooted into the corner by the door.

'Hands on the wheel, eyes on the road.' I selected another picture, tapped the receiver pad, and opened yet another frame. I suspected I was recording myself. Or dialing China.

'Click the little red "X" to close the window,' Epiphany instructed, somewhat less than patiently. 'You want me to pull over and do it?'

'I have it under control.' I leaned even closer to the computer, so that the old man on the screen and I were almost nose-to-nose. 'I don't see an "X." '

'At the top corner on the window.'

'There is no "X." '

'There is, too. The top corner on the right. The red "X." '

'There is no "X," I tell you.'

She reached over from the driver's seat, and I pulled the computer away. The car drifted onto the shoulder again.

'Attend to the driving,' I barked, sounding more like the old Norman than the new kinder, gentler grandpa version.

Epiphany yanked the steering wheel, swerving and causing the two of us to wobble in our seats like the tines of a tuning fork. 'Well, bite my head o . . . Uhhh-oh.' She spotted the oncoming vehicle before I did – a white sedan with the telltale flashing light on top.

My pulse ratcheted up, and Epiphany drew a quick breath, then held it, her eyes wide, her face slack.

'What if he saw me swerve off the road? What do I *do*?' she hissed, her body frozen in place, her head stiff on her neck, as if she were afraid to move.

I found myself gripping the console on one side and the door on the other. 'Just keep driving at the same rate of speed. Not too slow, not too fast.' I noted her foot sliding off the gas pedal. 'Don't brake. It's a sign of nervousness.'

'I *am* nervous.' Her voice quavered, and suddenly she seemed very young, a little girl, all her bluster and bluff gone. 'Oh, man, what if we get stopped, J. Norm? What if he knows it's us? What if there's an APB out for this car, and –'

'Just be calm.' My mind sped ahead. Had Deborah continued to pay the insurance bills, now that the car wasn't being driven? Was there a proof of insurance in my glove box? I didn't dare look now. I was afraid to know the answer.

I pictured the two of us being hauled off to the pokey in whatever tiny town was ahead on the horizon. What did they do when they discovered an uninsured driver on the road? Certainly not give him a slap on the wrist and let him drive off to continue his offense.

'Steady behind the wheel,' I soothed, but the comfort rang hollow. Was it possible that we'd become the subjects of an all-points bulletin – one of those sad news reports about an addled senior who'd wandered off from his life, confused and disoriented? *Be on the lookout for a dark blue Cadillac driven by a man in his seventies. Family members report that J. Norman Alvord suffers from dementia . . .*

Ahead, the oncoming car swung toward the shoulder, no doubt preparing to U-turn and fall in behind us to make the collar.

'J. Norm . . .' Epiphany whimpered. 'I don't wanna drive anymore. I wanna get out.'

'Steady,' I advised. 'Just . . .' The cruiser pulled farther off the road, rolling slowly up to . . . a mailbox?

Epiphany leaned over the steering wheel, her mouth dropping open as we drew close enough to see the driver reaching across the front seat. An instant later, the lettering on the side of the car became visible. Epiphany's lips moved slowly as she whispered the words, 'U.S. Mail . . . J. Norm, that's the stupid mailman!'

I caught a breath, and a nervous snort pushed through after it.

Epiphany sank against her seat. 'Don't *even* laugh. I think I'm gonna pass out.'

Another chuckle escaped. I pictured the two of us, white knuckled in the front of the car. 'Frightened to death by the mailman. Some team of outlaws we are.'

'I still think I'm gonna pass out.' Epiphany wiped her forehead with shaking fingers.

'Let's find a place to pull off for a bit.' I pointed to the town ahead. 'I think a little break is in order.'

Epiphany nodded, sinking deeper into her seat. 'Yeah, I think so, too.'

We ended up at the Dairy Queen, exiting the car on shaky legs. Once inside, the two of us sagged against the ice cream counter side by side.

'Make mine a double,' Epiphany said.

'This calls for the whole banana split.'

The woman behind the counter gave us curious looks as she took our order. While she was ringing up the total, a commotion in the parking lot caught Epiphany's attention. A group of boys in high school baseball uniforms were on their way in, jostling and carrying on with one another as they went. It occurred to me that we'd left the computer in the car. 'Go on over by the front glass and watch the car. We left the windows open.'

Shrugging, Epiphany crossed to the front of the room, standing left of the trash can as the boys bulldozed through in a tangle. They noted her as they passed by, and she surreptitiously watched them, as well. Behind the counter, the clerk hurried to fill my order, calling out to the new customers, 'You boys just simmer down and make a line. Marvin's workin' on your order.'

After they were past her, Epiphany hurried back to the counter. She grabbed my arm and leaned close to my ear. 'J. Norm, look at their jerseys. Guess where we are.' She didn't wait for me to actually read the jerseys, but quickly added, 'Littlewood. Don't you remember? That's the place where the guy moved to after he got run out of Groveland for publishing Mercy White's book. Mr Nelson at the soda shop said he bought the newspaper. What if he still lives here? Maybe he could tell us about her – like, whether the things she said were true, and if she said stuff that wasn't in the book. We should look him up.'

Epiphany's quick mind never ceased to amaze me, and

like her mind, the rest of her was quick, as well. When the clerk returned with our food, Epiphany wasted no time in asking, 'Hey, can you tell me who owns the newspaper here now? My grandpa might know him.'

The clerk slid our frozen confections across the counter. 'Well, small world, isn't it? Leland Lowenstein runs the newspaper now, if that's who you were thinking of. His office is down on Main and Second.'

Epiphany cut a sideways look and arched a brow, undoubtedly thinking the same thing I was thinking. We'd heard that name before.

'He's probably at the feed store, hanging out with my dad, though,' one of the high school boys offered. 'That's where he gets most of his news.' A push-and-shove competition broke out in the back of the line, and he turned to yell at a smaller boy who'd bumped into him.

We quickly secured directions to the newspaper office and the feed store, thanked the clerk, collected our purchases, and hurried toward the door.

'Feed store, here we come,' Epiphany remarked on the way out. 'Good thing I had the idea to stop at the Dairy Queen, huh?' Shoving a bite of ice cream into her mouth, she smiled around the spoon. I opted for a sip of my ice water, rather than pointing out that the Dairy Queen was actually my idea.

Following our short ice cream break, we had no difficulty finding the newspaper office. It was closed, so we proceeded on to the feed store. The enormous grain silos, by far the tallest structures in town, would have clued us in nicely, even without directions. We found Leland Lowenstein perched on a stool in the office, just as we'd been promised. A friendly man of rather generous proportion, he was happy enough to make our acquaintance, until we mentioned Mercy White's book. His look turned decidedly sour at that point.

'Listen, I don't want anything more to do with that book. Or any book. That book and that publishing company nearly cost me everything I owned. I'm out of the publishing business, except for the newspaper, and we only print facts. No memoirs, no gossip column, no long, drawn-out stories from sweet little old ladies who swear it's the truth. You know that woman, Mercy White, had terminal cancer, and she was aware of it when she wrote the book? She knew she wouldn't be around to defend that thing, and I'd be left holding the bag. If you're here to try to sue me for defamation of character, don't bother. I dissolved the publishing corporation. It's done. It's over. There's no money to be had from me, and Mercy White donated all her estate to the American Cancer Society. So there.'

'We don't want your money.' Epiphany stepped forward, as if she felt the need to defend me. At the sales counter, the clerk and her customer paused, then politely tried to pretend they weren't listening in. 'All we want is to ask you some questions.'

Leland Lowenstein shifted backward on his stool. 'Listen, all I did was go through the stuff she wrote and try to condense it down to something readable, and' – he stabbed a stubby finger into the air, glaring at Epiphany and then at me – 'folks oughta have thanked me for that instead of running me out of business. There was a lot more dirt that I convinced her to take out of the book. A lot.'

My hopes rumbled like an Atlas/Centaur rocket making ignition, ready to lift off the ground. 'Was there anything more about the night of the VanDraan fire, about the children and what happened to them?'

Brows tightening, he licked his lips, tilting his head back and peering through his glasses, as if to get a better look at me. 'Why do you want to know? Because if you've got ideas of saying you're one of the long-lost VanDraan kids so you can get your hands on the family fortune, don't bother.'

His cool reception suddenly made more sense. 'I wasn't aware that there was a family fortune.'

'Well, there's not,' he snapped, and I decided he was quite an unlikable fellow. No wonder he was willing to print a book in which an embittered old woman sought revenge on her family members and the whole of the town. 'At least eighty-five people already tried it, after the book came out. A few even wanted to exhume old VanDraan's body, but anyone who knows about him knows he isn't buried under that headstone. The man fell off a fishing boat in the Gulf, drunk, or else somebody pushed him, but he was never seen again. There wasn't any kin, and he was pretty near broke by then, anyway. He was a drunk and a bad gambler. His ranch got sold for taxes, and any other readily available assets he had were dunned for debts. There was enough of his estate left to put the dates on his tombstone, and that was about it.'

My mind became a jumble, the pieces I had been putting together lying like a box of punch cards dropped on the

347

floor. The woman Epiphany and I were trying to track down, Clara Culp, could be nothing but a fraud. Mercy White's story could be a fabrication, and the truth, perhaps, was that my entire family had perished in the fire. I felt a loss that caused me to stagger slightly.

Epiphany caught my arm. 'Can we sit down?' She nodded toward the assortment of dusty chairs in the corner. 'My grandpa's got heart troubles.'

The mention of heart troubles either concerned the man or brought forth a dime's worth of sympathy, because he nodded grudgingly and slid off the stool. We moved to the corner of the room, to the obvious disappointment of the counter clerk, who'd stacked and restacked the same pamphlets several times as an excuse to remain within earshot.

Settled in the corner with us, Mr Lowenstein seemed slightly less defensive.

I thought again of the woman in Houston. 'Did anyone exhume the mother's body, or any of the children's? Was DNA testing ever performed regarding these people who claimed to be the VanDraan children?'

'There was a court case or two, but the judge ruled against it. Nobody even knew if there were enough body parts in those coffins to perform DNA tests. When a three-story house burns to the ground, especially back in those days, there's no telling what was or wasn't sifted out of the ashes.' His gaze darted downward and slid across the floor, as if there were more, but he chose not to share it. I considered how to best approach him further. If I told him why I was here, he'd likely assume I was another charlatan out for money or notoriety.

Folding a foot underneath herself in what looked like a most uncomfortable maneuver, Epiphany leaned closer to him. 'But if there wasn't any money in it, why'd people want to start lawsuits and stuff? Lawsuits *cost* money.' Clever girl. She'd hit the nail on the head.

Mr Lowenstein's discomfort seemed to increase twofold. He rubbed his hands back and forth on the chair arms. 'Listen, why do you want to know all this? I'm not looking to get in the middle of anything. I don't want to be called into any more lawsuits or tied up in anybody's mess, all right? I've washed my hands of Groveland, Texas, for as long as I live.'

'But how come someone would be making a lawsuit, if there's no money?' Epiphany pressed, blinking repeatedly, effecting the falsely innocent look of a teenager who knows exactly what she's doing.

Mr Lowenstein shifted my way, seeming to wait for me to shush her, but of course I had no intention of it. She was doing well.

Finally, Leland Lowenstein sank in his chair. 'Listen, the whole thing is a ball of wax that just needs to be left lie. My advice is, don't go poking into it.'

'Into what, though?' Epiphany's eyes were wide with fascination. She flashed an enthusiastic smile that didn't seem entirely lost on Mr Lowenstein.

'There was some dispute about the VanDraan holdings in Groveland, all right?' He spit the words out as if he were loath to. 'The man owned half the town, and a few years before he

349

took that fishing trip, he'd moved out of Groveland and sold off everything, most of it on terms of one kind or another – private contracts between him and the folks he sold to. After he died, his office burned, and all those private contracts were gone, you know? There were those who figured it was awful convenient, him happening to fall off a boat, and then his office burning down when a bunch of folks owed him a lot of money. Once he was out of the picture and the paperwork was gone, they were free to say they'd paid in full. The district attorney wanted to investigate at the time, but when he tried, he was out of office pretty quick. The county judge and a lot of those business owners were connected, you see? And who's going to get up in arms about debts owed to the most hated individual in town? VanDraan was a bad man. You didn't make your fortune in rum-running and buy up half of a town by being a saint. He practiced extortion, and he practiced brutality, both at home and in business.'

Painful memories haunted my mind – the terrible fighting upstairs, the bruises hidden underneath my clothes, my wrists tied together, bound to the iron lion's head that should have been for tying horses, a buggy whip splitting my skin. I'd been saved, spirited away from him, and I had to know what had taken place. 'Do you believe the Van-Draan children were alive after the fire?'

Mr Lowenstein considered me for a moment, his gaze connecting with mine, searching, until finally he nodded. 'Yes, sir, I do. I believe Mercy White was telling the truth – maybe not about everything in the book, but I think she was telling the truth about what happened in the VanDraan house. I think there were reasons her daddy kept it to himself until his daughter asked him about it on his deathbed. He finally told her the story, then. The truth was that the sheriff knew exactly what happened the night of the fire, because he ended up involved in it, too.'

Lowenstein paused for a moment, looking out the window as if he were conjuring up the essence of the past. 'VanDraan was a bad customer. He was drunk the night that house burned down, and he beat his wife either to death or close to it. Then he went into a rage, or a panic to cover up what he'd done, and he set the house on fire, with his kids and the maid, a black woman named Cecile, down in the nursery. He locked the door to the nursery and bolted the shutters so they couldn't get out, and then he set fire to the place. After that, he headed off to a club, where he could get his cronies to testify to his whereabouts for the entire night.

'Those old houses could go up like tinderboxes, but the kids and the housekeeper were on the first floor, so the smoke took longer to get there. As soon as VanDraan was gone, Cecile tried the doors and windows, but there was no way out. Fortunately, she was a smart woman, and resourceful, even though she probably wasn't but fifteen or sixteen herself. One thing a maid knows is the nooks and crannies of a house. There was a fireplace in the nursery, and it had a small iron ash hatch in back, so the fireplace could be cleaned from outside. That young girl, Cecile, got every one of those kids out through that little door, and she took them across town to the sheriffs house, on foot, in the dark, with the whole town in an uproar about the fire.

'That's the night Mercy White remembered. The part she didn't put in the book was that the housekeeper saved those children more than once. That night after the fire, the sheriff drove her and those kids down to black town, and she hid them out, and the sheriff took care of things with the undertaker – maybe he got some bones somewhere, or maybe they just put ash in the caskets and kept them closed, but he never told anyone those five kids weren't dead – especially not their daddy.'

'But what became of the children?' I imagined the story in my mind – horrific, terrible, triumphant as well.

'They were sent away, one at a time.' Mr Lowenstein studied me, and I had the sense that he knew why I wasn't surprised that the children hadn't perished in the fire. 'According to Mercy White, the maids arranged it. Back in those days – well, you probably remember how it was if you're from anyplace around here – every family of any stature had a maid or two, a black woman, who took care of the house and kept the kids, sometimes also a man who tended the garden or worked as a driver. If one moved on, or you needed new help, you didn't put an ad in the paper. You just asked the help you already had, or you asked a neighbor's maid, or gardener, or the man who swept up the theater. They all had aunts, uncles, cousins, friends, kids they'd grown up with who were looking for work. They knew one another. They knew where their relatives and their neighbors worked. They knew the families they worked for – which families could be trusted, whether they'd be sympathetic, whether they'd be inclined to take in a child, whether they could come up with the necessary paperwork to make the old names disappear and provide new birth records.'

Lowenstein's eyes curved upward slightly, as if he were admiring the handiwork involved in forming new identities. 'Back in those days, it wasn't so hard. No computers, no cross-references, no Social Security numbers for young children. You take a prominent family with connections, they could arrange it, especially in a town a distance away, where the child wouldn't be recognized.' Turning his hands palms up, he patted the air slightly, as if he were urging a reluctant little tyke into a new place. 'One redheaded child here. One there. Nobody would be suspicious. After all, no one was looking for them. They all died in the fire, right?' He offered a wide, slow smile, not particularly waiting for me to answer the question, but allowing me to think about it. 'Nobody was the wiser.'

I contemplated the story, trying to decide whether I remembered any of those events. Did I recall squeezing through the ash door, running along darkened yards, the winter air pressing needles through the thin fabric of my pajamas, my feet crunching into the frosty grass, falling snow muffling the sounds? 'Was it wintertime?' I asked. 'Was it snowing the night of the fire?'

He frowned at the question, then shrugged. 'That's the way Mercy told it. It was January, unusually cold for this part of Texas. The fire didn't spread to the houses nearby because there was a dusting of snow on the roofs.'

Epiphany's fingers squeezed my arm, a silent affirmation of the reality winding, threadlike, through my mind, gathering loose links into a chain. I was hearing the story of my life. For the first time.

'Were you ever able to talk with the housekeeper, Cecile?' The book was published almost twenty years ago, after all. Cecile could have been alive at that time, only ten years or so older than Mercy White, perhaps ten or twelve years older than myself. 'Did Mercy White ever talk with her? Did Mercy know where the children were taken? The names of the families who adopted them?'

Leland Lowenstein stroked his chin, seeming to note his need for a shave. 'Cecile was dead, remember? Just like the children. I imagine she moved away somewhere and found another life for herself, another name, another job. Mercy White thought she could have ended up in St Louis. Mercy's father took her to the big fair there when she was a teenager, and Mercy remembered being left at the hotel while her daddy went to visit someone. She couldn't imagine who, because they didn't have any relatives in St Louis, but when he came back, he had home-baked goods with him, like he'd been to someone's house to eat, and she thought that was odd. Whose house would he be visiting in a strange town? If you ask me, I think that sheriff paid a visit to Cecile.'

Disappointment settled heavily over me. Had I reached the end of the line of clues? I hadn't found what I needed. I still didn't know for certain where my siblings were, or whether this woman in Houston was one of them. 'Then Mercy White wasn't aware of the names – the families the children had been given to?'

Mr Lowenstein shook his head, seeming a bit regretful

354

now. 'Not that she told me, but with Mercy, it was always hard to tell. I figured that out the hard way. She'd spin out a tall tale as quickly as the truth, and just as convincingly. Believed her own version of history most of the time. I will say that after the book came out, when word got around and brought in the so-called VanDraan heirs, Mercy seemed to be able to rule most of them out with a question or two, so it's definitely possible that she knew where the kids had gone, what their histories should be, maybe even the names of the adoptive families. Whatever her reasons, though, she felt the need to keep mum about it, which for Mercy was saying something.'

Epiphany scooted forward in her chair. 'Did she ever talk about a Clara Culp? Did Mrs Mercy White know her? I mean, could she be one of the VanDraan kids?'

Leland shrugged. 'Couldn't say, young lady. That was a long time ago, and once things got so messy with the legalities, I figured the less I knew, the better. I just tried to stay out of it. Mrs Mercy was enjoying all the hoopla and the controversy and the people knocking on her door. She finally had every-one's attention, which was what she'd wanted all along. She was entertaining visitors and defending her side of the story right up until the cancer took her. Not how I'd want to spend my last days, but Mercy was a unique woman.' Shifting in his chair, he indicated to Epiphany that the conversation was over – there was nothing more to tell. 'Young lady, all I can say to you and your grandpa, here, is that if you're planning to poke around into what happened to the VanDraans and their money, you'd better be careful. There're still folks around who don't want to talk about it.'

CHAPTER 22

Epiphany Jones

I didn't ask if J. Norm wanted to keep on toward Houston or not. When we left Littlewood, I just turned south, grabbed some junk food, and tried to zone out. Beside me, J. Norm gazed through the car window while time passed, and I counted down the mileage signs to Houston. He didn't even seem to notice that we were getting closer and closer. He was off in his own world, probably thinking about all the things Mr Leland Lowenstein had said.

I wanted to check the e-mail to see if we'd heard back from Clara Culp, but I figured I'd better let things alone for now. J. Norm looked worried, and I was afraid he was thinking we should turn around and head back to Dallas. After what we'd learned in Littlewood, he was probably wondering whether Clara Culp was for real or not. Whether she was or whether she wasn't, I guessed our trip would be over once we found her.

Thinking about that sent a chill over me. The air from the window sat cold and clammy on my skin, even though it was still plenty warm outside. No matter what happened,

I couldn't go back to Dallas. I shouldn't have made that promise to J. Norm about not running away. From Houston, I could hop a bus and be out of Texas in no time. I'd figure out where Greg Nash Park was, and start there. I wanted to see the place where my first birthday pictures were taken, with all the family around. If I could find somewhere to stay for cheap, at a shelter maybe, I'd have enough money to last a little while. Maybe I could get a job – work during the days and keep my search going after work. How hard could it be to find my daddy's family? J. Norm hadn't seen his family in seventy years, and they were supposed to be dead, and we'd still found clues – enough clues to bring us here.

If I was going to do this, I'd need the computer . . .

I glanced at it on the floorboard. J. Norm's legs sagged over it, his bony knees stretching the brown polyester pants that it seemed like he wore about every other day. His hand jerked toward the computer, the kind of movement your body makes without you telling it to, and I knew he'd fallen asleep again. When I looked at him, he was out cold, his head drooping off to one side. He was probably worn-out after all the excitement. The little patch of hair he usually kept slicked across the top of his head was waving in the window breeze like a tiny flag. His glasses hung loose over his knee, where he might knock them onto the floor and step on them. Pinching them between two fingers, I set them on the console so they wouldn't get crushed; then I tried to think through my next move.

It wouldn't be too much longer before we started coming into the outskirts of Houston. I could pull the car over someplace where J. Norm would be safe, leave a little note to tell him I was sorry but I had to do what I had to do, and promise to get the computer back to him as soon as I had the chance. I could contact Deborah, let her know where he was. She might even be on her way to the bed-and-breakfast in Groveland by now. Aunt Char and Sharla had been snooping enough that they'd probably heard us talking about Houston. Once Deborah told them all the dirt on us, they'd probably share everything they knew.

You should leave. You should take off now, a voice inside me said. It was Epie's voice. I hadn't heard from her in a while. *You gotta look out for yourself, Epiphany. You don't owe nobody nothin'. You don't owe him one thing, that's for sure. You gotta take care of you.*

I didn't like how the words felt in my head. *Is that really who I am?* I wondered. *Am I Epie? Am I somebody who'd steal stuff from an old man, take off, leave him on the side of the road?*

J. Norm wouldn't be my grandpa after that. He wouldn't have anything to do with me ever again. Deborah would use it as one more way to prove that J. Norm was out of his mind, that he didn't have any sense about people. The principal at the school, Deborah, everybody would decide DeRon was right. I was a liar. I was a punk who took advantage of people, who stole things.

Mrs Lora would turn over in her grave. So would the preacher who put me under the water and turned me into a new person. I wasn't supposed to be like Mama, like Russ, like DeRon. I was supposed to be a new creation, something better. Mrs Lora always said I could be anything I wanted to be – that I didn't have to agree with the things my mama did, that I could pick myself out a whole different kind of life. A Godly life. She said I was smart, and I was good inside. She promised she'd help me all the way. *When something doesn't feel right, stop and ask yourself, Is this what God created me for?* she said. *Think about what kind of life you want, and then you set your feet on a path toward it. Don't let anyone or anything take your feet off that path, and . . .*

Something caught my eye in the rearview, and I glanced up and saw a police car behind us. 'J. Norm.' I grabbed J. Norm's arm and shook it. 'J. Norm, there's a cop behind us.' I tapped the brakes, and then I remembered that J. Norm had said not to do that. The cop closed in a little. 'J. Norm,' I hissed, and shook him until his head rolled off the headrest, and he snorted awake. 'There's a police car behind us for real this time!'

He blinked and looked around, confused.

'There's a cop, there's a cop, there's a *cop*,' I whispered, checking the side mirror, my heart pounding. The cop's lights went on, and he was coming up behind us fast. A bomb went off in my chest. 'What do I do? What do I do?' For a half a sec, I thought about stepping on the gas and outrunning the patrol car, action-movie-style.

J. Norm looked around and found his glasses. 'Pull off into that minimart ahead. Be careful to slow down and use your blinker.'

'Pull off? Really?' My voice wasn't much more than a squeak. My hands sweated on the steering wheel, but I did what J. Norm said. The car rolled to a stop at the edge of the minimart parking lot.

'Take out your driver's permit,' J. Norm told me. He was fishing through the glove compartment. 'You know where your driver's permit is, right?'

I nodded, because I couldn't talk; then I grabbed my purse and dug out my permit.

In the mirror, the officer was walking closer, his head tipped to one side like he was looking at the back of our car. Was he checking the license plate number? Had he heard a report about us?

'Be polite. No smart-mouthing.' J. Norm sat stiff in his seat, his back straight as a board, his fingers shaking a little when he dug through the cards and pictures in his wallet and pulled out his license.

'Okay . . . all right.'

Time seemed like it was moving in slow motion as I rolled down the window, and the cop asked for my license, and I handed it over.

J. Norm leaned across the seat and said, 'Here's the proof of insurance. Is there a problem, officer? My granddaughter and I are just on a little trip, practicing her driving. Was she doing something wrong?'

The patrolman wrote stuff from my permit on his great big pad of tickets. 'Wait here,' he said, and then he took our stuff and went back to his car. A minute later, he was on his radio.

'Oh, man, J. Norm, he's calling it in. We're toast. We're so busted.' I wanted to cry, and I wanted to make a run for it.

'Be calm.' But J. Norm didn't sound calm. He sounded like he was just as worried as I was. His voice was thin and watery, fake like the skim milk they started serving in the cafeteria after the state decided schoolkids were too fat. 'He's only checking the insurance and registration. He's following procedure.'

'What if they're *looking* for us? What if the police are in on it?'

'I don't think Deborah would go to those lengths.' But his face said that he did. 'Let's not worry ahead of ourselves. Remember that first moon landing. Confidence is half the battle. You have to believe things will go according to plan, until events prove otherwise.'

'What's this got to do with rockets?'

'Everything has to do with rockets. Launching a rocket is similar to any endeavor in life. You formulate your best plans prior to, but you must be aware that, at any moment, the unexpected may come along. Events can deviate from plan. If you wait until you can foresee everything, you'll never launch. The best you can do is to aim high and plan for contingencies.'

I looked in the rearview again, fear balling in my neck. 'What's our contingency plan?'

Pulling his lips between his teeth, so that his mouth was like the smile on a scarecrow, he lifted his shoulders. 'I couldn't come up with one.'

I slapped a hand over my eyes. This cop was gonna haul us in, and then we'd have to face Deborah, Mama, and Russ, and the school. Everything was crashing down around me. 'Oh, man.'

You could run. Right now, you could get out of the car and run.

The cop wasn't even watching us, because he was busy writing. I caught myself looking around. There was a patch of woods out behind the convenience store. I could disappear in there, go through the trees, come out the other side and find the way to a bus station . . .

My fingers touched the door handle, fiddled with it.

The cop got out of his car and made the decision for me. If I tried to take off now, he'd run me down before I cleared the parking lot. As soon as I knew I was trapped, I was glad, in a way. It went back to something Mrs Lora had told me: *What you do, you become.* I didn't want to be the kind of person who would bail on a friend.

I'd just have to stay here and face the music. Me and J. Norm together. We got into this together, after all.

'Sit up straight in your seat. Look confident,' he bossed.

For some reason – nerves, I guess – I laughed. 'I'm *not* confident.'

'Consider it an acting challenge.' He straightened in his seat, too, and we waited, stiff as a couple of store mannequins.

The cop stood beside the car, silent as he finished writing stuff on his pad.

J. Norm leaned across the console, and I saw his reflection beside mine in the policeman's glasses. 'Everything okay, Officer?'

'I wasn't speeding,' I said, and J. Norm pinched me on the arm.

We hung there on a string while the cop took his time finishing up. He had a little smirk down below his bad-boy glasses, like he could smell the fear and was enjoying it. If this guy took us off to jail, there was no telling what he'd do to us. He looked like the type who ended up on the news for slamming some grandma to the concrete and cuffing her after she turned the wrong way out of the church parking lot.

But he hadn't asked us to get out of the car yet. That was a good sign . . .

He stopped writing finally, then stared at us over the top of his ticket pad. *Just get it over with, already,* I thought. He kept looking around the inside of the car, like he was trolling for evidence, or trying to figure us out. Even through the sunglasses, I could see what he was thinking: *What's this little creamy caramel girl doing driving around with some old white guy in a car?* Bet if I was some cute little blonde-headed girl with big blue eyes, he wouldn't be holding us up.

'Where are you two headed, young lady?'

I swallowed hard, choked down the lump in my throat. This guy could tell something was fishy, and he was gonna sniff around till he could figure it out. 'We're on our way to Houston. Did I do something wrong? I wasn't speeding.'

J. Norm pinched me again.

I made myself give the jerky police officer a great big smile. 'My grandpa and me are going to see relatives . . . in Houston.'

The policeman tapped the back of his pencil against the pad, like he was deciding what else to write on the ticket. Could they just add stuff because they felt like it? 'Where at in Houston?'

'My grandpa knows.'

'Magnolia Estates,' J. Norm chimed in. How he came up

363

with that name, I had no clue, but he said it like he believed it. 'Afraid we're making a bit of a slow trip of it today, though. At this rate, we'll miss dinner at my sister's house. Surprised she hasn't started calling already to see where we are.'

I sat back and waited to see what else J. Norm would come up with.

'How far to her house?' The cop tapped his pencil some more.

J. Norm pretended to think about it. 'Oh . . . twenty miles or so. She's out past the loop.'

The cop nodded. Finally, he tore off the top sheet of his pad and handed it to me, along with our other stuff. I wanted to give it a big ol' kiss. Maybe we weren't about to get dragged out of the car, after all. 'Are you aware that your inspection sticker is five months out-of-date?'

'No, sir, I was not.' J. Norm gaped at the windshield, and my mouth hung open for a totally different reason. I wanted to say, *You stopped us and scared me to death for a sticker?*

'My wife passed away a few months ago. I haven't been driving,' J. Norm said.

The cop closed his pad. 'I'm going to give you a warning today. Take the car in for an inspection when you arrive at your sister's.'

I went from hating that cop to feeling like he was my best friend in the world. No ticket. No problem.

'Yes, sir!' J. Norm said, and I half expected him to give the guy an army salute.

'Drive carefully.' The policeman turned away and walked back to his car without another word.

J. Norm sagged, patting his chest, and I caught my breath. The two of us were panting like we'd just finished a marathon.

'Man,' I said.

'I think it's time for a soda,' J. Norm added. We pulled across the parking lot and went in the convenience store for snacks, taking our time and letting the cop get far, far away. Some guys inside told us about a place down the road where we could get the car inspected, so we went there next. Both of us breathed a sigh of relief when we hit the road with our new sticker on the window. No more cop stops for us.

After a while, I could tell by the billboards that we were getting closer to Houston. Finally we hit a serious traffic jam, and we inched along in a bumper-to-bumper mess for almost an hour, until we gave up and pulled off at a Pizza Hut so we could check e-mail and see if Clara Culp or her daughter, Amy, had answered us.

'I hope she doesn't think we're, like, a couple of crazy people,' I told J. Norm, while I was waiting for the computer to crank up and listening to my stomach rumble. The room smelled like pizza, and I was hungry for something besides junk food.

'They posted to the reunion Web site. They must expect to have answers.' He stirred his Coke with a straw, squeezed a lemon into it, then rested his chin on his fist, hunching over the table while I worked on the computer. A couple minutes later, he was staring out the window with his chin in his hand, his eyes a million miles away. It didn't matter, because I didn't find anything worth telling him about, anyway. No e-mail, and I found a bunch of addresses and phone numbers for Culp, but none for Clara or Amy. There wasn't any way to tell which of those addresses might be the right one, so I decided to focus on the city library angle. After doing some digging, I found Amy Culp listed with the staff at a library downtown. There were two problems with that – tomorrow was Sunday, and even if the libraries *were* open on Sunday, just looking at the map of how to get to that place scared me half to death.

J. Norm's attention came back to the table when the pizza got there, and I showed him what I'd found.

He picked a pepperoni off the top of his pizza and chewed it, slivers of evening light from the window blinds reflecting off his glasses while he thought about our problem. 'It would probably be best to get a hotel before we reach the loop and hope for an e-mail by morning. If we don't hear from them, perhaps we can start calling numbers.'

I didn't argue with him, but calling all those Culps in the phone book didn't sound too practical. I mean, what were the odds that we'd get the right number, they'd be at home, and they wouldn't hang up on us, thinking we were a couple crackpots? Stopping overnight and waiting for an e-mail did seem like the best idea, for now. It'd been a long, weird day, and I was ready for a shower and a bed. My body felt rubbery, like my bones were dissolving one by one, especially after I pigged out on pizza. On our way out, we asked the waitress if there was a hotel nearby that wasn't too expensive, and she pointed us down the road to one.

It turned out that the place wasn't anything fancy, but it

wasn't bad. J. Norm didn't have much cash on him, so I had to hand over a bunch of my stash to pay, which meant that something good needed to happen pretty soon. That was the end of my Florida plans, too, unless I wanted to take off with no money. But if we started using J. Norm's credit card, Deborah would find us. Somehow, some way, we had to hunt down Clara and Amy Culp tomorrow.

We hauled our stuff up to a room that the desk clerk called the 'family suite,' which was a bedroom, a little room with a pullout sofa and TV, and a minikitchen. Not bad digs, really. There was even a balcony outside. After showers, J. Norm and me took our leftover sodas from supper and sat on the balcony. It overlooked a drainage ditch, but with the sunset reflecting on it, it was actually kind of pretty. The breeze and the sun sinking behind the pines made it feel like we were in a Discovery Channel show about some river far away – the Nile or the Amazon. I even saw a log that looked like an alligator floating around in the water.

'Whoa, J. Norm, look at that,' I said, and pointed. The log started swimming, and I about freaked. 'Holy mackerel, that thing's real! You think we better tell the hotel people? What if it eats somebody?' *Like me*, I was thinking, and I wasn't sure I wanted to stay outside anymore.

'I imagine he's more afraid of you than you are of him.' J. Norm was kicked back in his chair, enjoying the sunset.

'I doubt it.' I sat up a little straighter, watching that gator come into shore. It was three feet long, at least. 'So they just, like, let alligators live in their ditches here? I mean, can't the police come get them or something?'

J. Norm chuckled, shaking his head at me. 'I imagine that would take more police than they have on the force. In the bayous, alligators are too numerous to count. You don't see most of them, but they see you.' He gave me a creepy look, like he was trying to scare me.

'Huh-uh,' I said, and laughed at him. 'I saw people out swimming today when we crossed over one of those creeks. Would they be swimming if there were alligators all over the place? Pppffff! I don't *think* so.'

He cocked back in his chair. 'I'll have you know that you are speaking to a man who once lived with alligators right out his back door. When –'

'Is this gonna be another "at the cape" story?' I asked.

'Humor me.'

'All right.' Pulling my legs up in my chair, I rested my chin on my knees and got comfortable. Off in the distance over the pine trees, the sky was turning dark velvet blue. A long-legged white bird landed at the edge of the water. It didn't seem worried about the gator.

J. Norm cleared his throat. 'When we lived on Switch Grass Island, *near* the cape, the cabin included an old aluminum boat that stayed in the water. On the occasions when I was home early enough, I would slip into my fishing clothes and paddle out onto the lake for an hour or so while Annalee was cooking dinner. In the summer, of course, it was sticky and hot, even in the evenings. One of those times, I decided I'd take a swim off the boat. I dived into the water, and when I came up, I was face-to-face with an alligator. I don't know who was more frightened, him or me.'

'Well, I could answer that question, if it was me in that water,' I said, and J. Norm laughed. 'How in the world could somebody live with those things around?'

He shrugged, his eyes going back and forth between the gator and the bird. 'You get used to them. Why, we even had alligators right by our launchpads at the cape. There was a pond at the end of pad thirty-six-A. One day we had to scrub a launch, and we were left with liquid oxygen to dispose of. So one of the guys says, "Hey, let's roll the tank over and dump it in the pond." So, as young men will do, we jumped on the idea, and the LOX went into the little pond. Liquid oxygen stores at negative one hundred eighteen degrees Celsius, so it made quite a splash in that warm water. The next thing we knew, an alligator was hightailing it out the other end of the pond, running for cover. I imagine he didn't know what had hit him. We never told our supervisors about our little lark with the LOX, of course.' He tipped his head back and laughed, and I thought about him being young and doing crazy things he probably wasn't supposed to do. I guess you forget, when people are old, that once upon a time they were pretty much like you.

While J. Norm told some more cape stories, I watched the first stars come out. A lopsided moon rose and glittered through the tops of the pines, too shy to be up in the sky on its own. I remembered how Mrs Lora used to sit outside with me on her old metal swing in the yard. Her house was on the edge of town, so we'd throw out food for the deer and watch them creep from the cedar brush, and we'd listen to the coyotes howling and yipping at the moon. I loved

369

those times with Mrs Lora. I loved the minutes when the last light of day was fading and a hush came over everything. I'd lay my head over on her shoulder and feel safe, even though my mama was someplace else – working, or out partying with her people from her job, or gone on a date with her latest guy. Sometimes I wasn't even sure where she was, but I was okay knowing that Mrs Lora and me would cook dinner and then sit in the swing together. Those were good nights. Safe nights.

Like this one.

I laid my head on J. Norm's shoulder, and he didn't seem to mind. He didn't braid my hair like Mrs Lora did – that would've been weird – but once he was finished with his story, we talked about the stars. He showed me how to find the constellations, and told me the Greek legends behind them, and how to measure distances by stretching out your arm and holding up your thumb. The moon rose with a big, bright star trailing from the tip. Venus, J. Norm said, and then he pointed out Saturn, and showed me how to find it in the constellation Virgo.

Venus and Saturn. I would've never known that, if it wasn't for J. Norm.

Without Mrs Lora, I'd never have learned how to snap a string bean or grow a tomato, or how good a batch of fresh purple hull peas tastes right after you shell them. Maybe that was the way things were supposed to be. Maybe not everyone got the mom who baked cupcakes and showed up at all the school parties. There weren't enough of those to go around, so maybe God used other people, like Mrs Lora and J. Norm, to make sure you learned how to shell a purple hull pea or find Saturn in the night sky.

It was all right for life not to be perfect. If you let it, if you didn't close yourself off from the chance for it, life could still be good. Better than good.

Tonight was pretty close to perfect.

J. Norm's voice turned into a soft hum, and after a while, I was only half listening. He was talking about the International Space Station and then something about living in Austria for a year while he was doing some kind of job over there. He lived in England, too, where he and his wife drove around on the wrong side of the road and visited castles.

'Someday, I want to have a job where I can go see castles on my day off,' I told him, and yawned. The day was starting to feel kind of long.

'I know you will.' The way he said it made me believe it. If J. Norm could come from a place like the house with the seven chairs and end up living all over the world and sending rockets to the moon, something amazing could happen in my life, too. Maybe something great was happening already, and this trip was only the beginning of it.

We went inside after that. J. Norm took the bedroom, and I took the sofa, because I wanted to watch TV.

I fell asleep sometime after midnight, and I dreamed about Cecile. I saw her in that big house, trapped behind a locked door when the smoke started coming in. She was smart, though. She plugged the bottom of the door with blankets, got the kids out of their beds, pushed them down low, and wrapped them in their quilts. I saw them huddled by the wall while she looked for a way out. Then she spotted the fireplace.

I smelled the ashes and the soot as she pulled the grate out of the way, opened the hatch door, whispered, 'Come on. Come on, now, babies.'

In the dream, I was one of the children. She was saving me, too.

She handed the baby through last – bundled him tight in his blanket and gave him to his big brother, who cuddled the baby close inside the puppy-dog quilt, while all the other kids huddled around him.

And then I *was* Cecile. My face was her face. I was looking at the hatch, wondering if it was big enough for me to pass through. I was hoping, praying. I didn't want to die there, so young still, never having a family of my own, never seeing much of the world. The smoke was thick, billowing toward the hole, clogging my nose and my mouth, choking me. The ash door was so small. I was afraid. I couldn't breathe. I couldn't think. I didn't want the children to watch me die here. 'You . . . go . . . on,' I coughed out. There was so much heat. So much smoke. I heard things falling overhead, glass breaking, dogs barking in the neighborhood. Someone would come soon. Surely someone would come.

'Come on, Cecile! Come on!' the children begged. The twins were crying, clutching their brother.

'Get . . . back. Get . . . away, now.' My heart pounded, filling every part of me with fear, with terror. I didn't want to burn to death. I could feel the heat now. So much heat. *Oh,*

Lord, I prayed. *Oh, Lord, Lord, help me. Make me strong enough, small enough . . .*

I started through the opening, pulling, pushing, wiggling, the rocks and the steel doorframe not giving way. I put my arms through, then my head, and a shoulder. I couldn't make it. The door was too small. My feet were burning, flames licking into the room.

I couldn't breathe. The children were crying. I screamed . . .

Air filled my lungs as I sat up on the hide-a-bed, my heart hammering, my throat burning, just like in the dream.

A dream. It was only a dream.

Lying back on the pillow, I saw the fire and the ash door and the kids like a movie in replay. Outside the window, light was pouring in, and when my eyes cleared up, I noticed that the alarm clock was blinking seven forty-five. Almost eight o'clock? I shucked off the covers and swung my feet around. Why hadn't J. Norm gotten me out of bed? He never slept past the crack of dawn, as far as I could tell.

An uneasy feeling circled inside me like leftover smoke from the dream as I got up and tiptoed toward the bedroom. The door swung open a little when I knocked on it. I tried to peek inside, to make sure J. Norm wasn't, like, standing there in his underwear or anything, but I could only see the wall and the edge of the bed. It was dark inside the room. No lights on.

I heard him breathing, then – raspy, short breaths, like he couldn't get enough air. Pushing the door open the rest of the way, I took a step into the room. J. Norm was in the middle of the big bed, flat on his back, cocooned in the covers.

'J. Norm? J. Norm, you awake? You all right?' He didn't answer or move around. The worry in me slithered a little higher, like a snake making its way up my spine. 'Hello-o . . . J. Norm? It's morning. We've gotta hit the road, Jack.'

He still didn't answer, and so I crossed the room to the bed, leaned over, and gave the covers a yank, rocking him back and forth. Maybe it was my dream or the mood it left behind, but I wanted to get out of this place. Something wasn't right this morning.

'J. Norm. Let's go.'

He moved finally, moaned, and turned his head away. A hand slid from under the sheet, the long, bony fingers stretching toward the ceiling. 'Annnna-leee, I'mmm not . . . not . . . I can't sss-see. You there?' he mumbled, struggling against the sheet like a mummy trying to get free, his arm reaching, every muscle tight.

'J. Norm!' I leaned over the bed, shaking him. 'J. Norm! Stop! Wake up.'

His breath came in a gush of air then, and he sat up, his chest rising first and his neck snapping up after. Blinking, he looked around the room, then at me, like he was trying to put everything together.

I backed away from the bed. 'Time to get moving, okay? We're gonna find the Culps today, right? We're looking for your sister, remember?'

'Yes . . .' J. Norm whispered, his voice thin. 'I'll . . . I'll be along . . .'

' 'Kay, well . . . ummm . . . I'll put some clothes on and run down to the lobby and grab us some of the continental

374

breakfast.' I started toward the door, the same uneasy feeling crackling over my skin.

He swung his legs over the edge of the bed, then sat rubbing his head. 'Where's Deborah?'

Where's Deborah? What? 'A long ways away, I hope.' The sooner we were out of here, the better. Maybe he was having a premonition or something. Maybe Deborah was nearby, tracking us down.

I tried not to think about it while I was hitting the breakfast bar downstairs. Just like Mrs Lora used to say, *You let a possibility into your mind, you let it into your life.* The only possibility I wanted today was that we'd find Clara Culp, and she'd be J. Norm's sister for real.

But all the same, as I was getting breakfast, I felt like the lady behind the desk was watching me, like she was trying to figure out if she'd seen me somewhere. The TV news announced that they had a report of a missing elderly man coming up after the commercial, and I didn't wait to see what it was about. I scooted out of there. That sounded way too close to home.

When I came back to the room, J. Norm was dressed and seemed better. He didn't argue about packing up and leaving the hotel, even though the smart thing would've been to stay around and check the e-mail and use the phone book. Instead, I stuck the phone book in my backpack and told J. Norm it was time to get in the car – we had places to go. He didn't ask *what* places, and I figured the sooner we were on the move toward Houston, the better. We could stop in a little while to check the e-mail.

When we got in the car, J. Norm smiled and asked, 'Did you see Roy's project?'

'Roy?' I started the car and backed out. 'What project?' What in the world was he talking about?

He had his face toward the window as we crossed the parking lot, so that all I could see was his wispy hair and the side of his cheek. The wrinkles around his eyes were deep, and he was concentrating on something off in the distance. 'For his history class. He did an oral report about the rockets.' He slid a hand under his collar and worked the back of his neck like he was trying to soften up dough.

'That wasn't Roy; that was me.' I glanced at him as a guy in a giant SUV stopped to let us into the wall-to-wall traffic creeping along on the road. 'That was me, J. Norm.'

'Did the rockets turn out all right? Roy's rockets?'

The question kind of pinched for a second. Why was he talking about Roy? Roy wasn't here. I was. 'Most of the stuff I took was Deborah's and yours. She wrote her name on the bottoms of the rockets she put together. Guess she wanted everybody to know which ones she built.'

He chuckled softly. 'Well, you know, sibling rivalry. I don't think it's anything to worry about. We'll just make sure to put the rockets back where they belong, and she'll be none the wiser.'

'J. Norm, are you all right?'

He shrugged, stretching his neck some more, then rubbing his chest, his forehead furrowing. 'I don't think I slept very well. Breakfast didn't agree with me.'

I frowned at the Styrofoam container on the console.

Breakfast was still in the box – two cinnamon rolls and a couple of boiled eggs. 'We haven't had breakfast yet.' I popped open the container, thinking maybe some food would fix him up. 'On today's gourmet menu, we got cinnamon rolls, served slightly dry, and eggs à la boiled. Which would you like, sir?'

He didn't laugh like I wanted him to, or tell me to keep both hands on the wheel. 'Nothing just now, I think. You know I could stand to lose a little weight.'

My speck of worry grew the way bacteria do on a science-lab Petri dish – invisible at first, but then morphing into a blob. J. Norm was thin as a rail fence. Deborah was always trying to get him to gain weight.

'You sure you're all right this morning?'

He glanced sideways at me, blinking. 'Splendid, actually.' Then he picked up a cinnamon roll and took a bite. After a minute, he set it down and rubbed his chest some more. 'I must have overdone last night at dinner. It's still with me, I'm afraid.'

'Eeewww.' I turned on the radio as some jerk squeezed into traffic ahead of me. 'That's TMI.'

'TMI?'

'Too much information.' We were getting close to the highway ramp now, and there were signs pointing every which way. Overhead, a gob of roads crisscrossed, a bazillion lanes of traffic whizzing different ways. I started to panic, and all of a sudden I couldn't remember any of the directions I'd looked up last night at Pizza Hut. If I got on the wrong road, I didn't know how I'd ever find a place to turn around. We could end up in Louisiana or somewhere. 'J. Norm, which way do I turn?'

He pulled a face and made an unhappy noise, a burp, I guess, but it sounded like it hurt. He must've been blown up like a balloon inside. His lips pulled tight across his teeth for a second, then relaxed. 'Where did you want to go? To Deborah's?'

Another car skidded in front of me, and I hit the brakes, rocking both of us in our seats. We were almost on top of the highway ramps now. 'Which way, J. Norm? Which way to Houston?' A sweat broke over my body. Cars were all around; signs were everywhere; people were honking, changing lanes, shaking fists and shooting the finger. A truck had stalled out in the intersection ahead. It looked like Russ's. I thought about Russ. I panicked. 'Which way? Which way to Houston? Which way?'

'Houston . . .' J. Norm muttered, like he didn't have a clue.

'Which way!' I squealed.

Finally, at the last minute, he pointed. 'Here, take the ramp here. Right here.'

I peeled off just in time to stop the guy behind me from cutting around. He laid on the horn, and I jumped in my seat, but then settled back down and let out the breath I'd been choking on. At least we were headed the way we needed to go. In another minute or two, we'd be . . .

At the end of the entrance ramp, the guy behind me cut into traffic, almost hit a truck, and whizzed by our car so fast, I thought he'd take our fender off. I screamed, clutching the steering wheel for dear life, as we ran out of entrance ramp and ended up cruising the shoulder. Luckily, the next guy let me in, but then he honked and whipped it around me, because sixty was my top speed, and he didn't want to go sixty.

'Oh, man,' I whispered. I'd really gotten myself into it this time. My hands were sweating so hard, the steering wheel felt like someone'd greased it. I'd never, ever been in any kind of traffic mess like this before. This was nuts.

Beside me, J. Norm must've been thinking the same thing. He sucked in a breath that sounded like it was coming through a pinched straw. I knew just how he felt. I couldn't breathe, either.

The radio got weirdly loud all of a sudden and crackled between a heavy-metal headbanger station and some kind of rap music. I was afraid to take my hand off the wheel to turn it down. Another lane joined from the right, and cars were rushing by on both sides, so fast they were blurs of color with little heads inside. 'Can you turn that down? J. Norm, can you . . .'

From the corner of my eye, I saw him jerk forward. He coughed and hacked until it sounded like a lung was coming up.

'Geez, take it easy.' I had the thought that maybe he was choking. What would I do if he was? We were trapped here. Cars were zooming past, ducking in and out of lanes, bouncing around like pinballs in a machine. I didn't dare do anything but drive straight ahead and try to make sure nobody hit me. 'You need help? You okay?'

Nodding, he pulled out a hankie and covered his mouth

with it, coughing and coughing, doubling forward over his knees. He coughed, then wheezed, then coughed, then wheezed. Cars raced by. Sweat broke over my skin, dripped down my back, circled around my ear, and made my hair wet. 'J. Norm? Hey . . . J. Norm?' A blue pickup truck zipped in front of us, then hit the brakes. I slammed on mine. Too hard. The tires squealed and the back end of our car fish-tailed. It wouldn't stop. We were gonna hit the guy. It was too . . .

Every drop of blood in my body froze.

A horn blared.

A guitar squealed high on the radio.

My heart hammered.

My mind rushed.

I wondered what would happen when we hit.

What if I died? What if I died right here on this highway?

Where would Mama bury me?

The pickup cut into another lane. I let off the brakes a little. Our car quit sliding, slowed down, rocked to a stop short of hitting the next car in front.

I sat there for a second, not moving, not doing anything, blood still pounding in my ears, air clogging my throat. The car behind us squealed its tires. I held my breath again. It stopped short of our bumper.

The radio fuzzed to static.

Everything got quiet, the cars packing in solid on all sides, the sounds of screaming brakes and squealing tires moving back, and back, and back. I heard the crackle and crash of a fender bender somewhere.

The van in front of us rolled forward, the line of traffic starting off again, like there was no reason to have stopped in the first place.

'J. Norm, did you see tha . . .'

Just before I let off the brakes, I looked to the side, and the words died in my mouth. J. Norm was twisted and crumpled halfway on his seat, halfway on the floorboard, his arm hanging back on the console, his head buried somewhere under the glove box.

'Hey!' I tugged on his shirt, shook him. 'J. Norm, hey!' His skin was cold and clammy, his body limp like a rag doll's. 'J. Norm, hey! What's wrong? What's the matter? Wake up! Sit up, okay?' My pulse went wild again. Panic came back like a brush fire sparking. 'J. Norm!' I screamed, then hollered his name again and again.

The thoughts in my head exploded, circled, rushed in all directions like cars on some wild freeway. What should I do? What could I do? Should I find a place to pull off? Look for a hospital sign? Stop and yell for help? I couldn't even get to the side of the road. I was stuck here, trapped.

The road, the cars, the sky, stores, hotels, buildings blurred behind tears. *Please, oh, please, oh, please,* I prayed. *Oh, please, God, I'm sorry for everything I ever did wrong. I'm sorry. I'm sorry . . .*

What do I do?

Tell me what to do!

Blinking hard, I looked for an exit sign, watched for something, anything ahead. *Please . . . something. A hospital, a police car, somebody . . .*

Somebody help . . .

A truck in the left lane backed off, and a gap opened. I watched it grow wider. I couldn't exit from there, but I could stop the car, try to get J. Norm out onto the grass in the middle of the road, yell for help.

Would somebody help? Would somebody stop?

Please, somebody. Please . . .

I turned the wheels, moved into the empty space, bumped over the line of reflectors onto the shoulder, stopped on the grass just before a bridge, my foot shaking so hard it would barely press the brake.

Grabbing my seat belt, I pulled and tugged, tried to push the button. My fingers were useless, numb. The seat belt came free. I opened the door, stumbled into the ditch, ran through the grass, the wildflowers pulling at my shoes.

'J. Norm, J. Norm!' My voice was high and raw, not loud enough for anyone to hear over the traffic as I yanked open the passenger-side door, leaned in to undo the seat belt, tried to pull J. Norm out. He was too heavy, wedged in too tight. Tears blurred everything. I ran to the side of the road, waving my arms, screaming, 'Somebody! Somebody help me!'

CHAPTER 23

J. Norman Alvord

There was a light nearby, so bright it was blinding. The light was beautiful, the beams radiating outward from a single center. Something was moving against its glow, crossing back and forth, but I couldn't make it out, couldn't see into the light.

I closed my eyes, opened them again, tried to clear my vision. My eyelids were stiff, swollen, grainy, but this place was warm, quiet, comfortable. White. Had I found my way to heaven, after all? Had grace brought me here, even though I'd allowed myself to become a bitter, irreverent old man? Had I been forgiven for all the ways in which I was a failure as a father, a husband, a human being?

I had a sense of someone female close by. A sigh hovered in the air, a soft, familiar sound, and then the clinking of jewelry. Was that Annalee? Was she here?

I tried to say her name, to call her to me, but my mouth was dry, my throat packed in cotton. I felt as if I were drifting, my body floating, then landing in a soft place, then floating again.

I swallowed hard, tried to say, *Annalee?* But the word was little more than a rough croak, a coarse bit of sound. The light shifted, and I could hear her coming closer, her clothes rustling. Instinctively, I was afraid. Where was I and who was out there?

I tried again to call her, but I produced nothing more than, 'Nnn-ul-eee.' I could see her now, silhouetted against the brightness. Annalee. The light behind her shifted, dots of shadow moving, swaying. Leaves. The shadows of leaves. Were there trees in heaven?

'Ssshhh,' she whispered. 'Everything's fine now.' And then just as quickly, she was gone, and I knew I was alone in the room.

I gave up trying to hold my eyes open, took in the sounds and scents instead. I was in a hospital. The room was strangely quiet, though – no beeping pulse oximeter. No blood-pressure cuff pumping up, then counting down.

I pushed my eyes open again, rolled my head to the other side, made out what I could. A wall, a closet, a door, a chair, a dresser. A room arranged for long-term occupancy, not a temporary stay.

A nursing home.

I was in a nursing home.

Fear splintered through me, a hail of broken glass. How had this happened? How had I come to be here? I tried to remember, struggled to drag together the bits and pieces of my mind, but all was scattered, flitting this way and that in a fog. The house with the seven chairs, the iron finial bearing a lion's head, a book . . . a book of some sort. An important book . . .

What did the book say?

Deborah. Deborah had threatened to take my house, to move me out of my home and into the Villas. *It's for your own good*, she'd said.

Had she done this to me? Had she brought me here, dumped me like an old hound left behind by a family that no longer wanted to bother?

I mustered my strength, called out. A voice answered, 'Hang on a minute, there, fella. You're all right.' The voice was a man's. 'Let me get on over there and push your button to call up a nurse.' Something clattered through the doorway, scraping the frame, then squeaked across the room. A head bobbed past, only slightly above the footboard as I struggled to blink the film from my eyes. I couldn't make out features – just gray hair, and as he came closer, a wheelchair. He made his way to the side of the bed, patted my arm, then stretched toward something. A soft electronic bell chimed once. He patted my arm again, left his hand there. 'Mary'll be here in a minute. She's one of the best nurses in all a' Dallas. You'll see. You been a model patient so far, but you don't talk much.' He chuckled at his own joke, and I felt him clasping my fingers, shaking my hand. 'Claude Fisher. Pleased to meet ya. I volunteer here Mondays, Wednesdays, and Fridays. Used to live here, but I met myself a hot chick, got married, and moved out. This is a good place, though. The nurses take fine care of folks.'

I pulled in a breath, swallowed past the drought in my mouth, tried to force my swollen tongue to conform to two words: 'How . . . h-howww l-l-long?'

'Oh, around two weeks,' Claude Fisher answered. 'Don't know how long you were in the hospital before that, though. They brung you here from someplace in Houston.'

'W-weeks?' *Weeks ... perhaps longer?* By now, Deborah might have sold my house, disposed of all my things, had her way.

The panic returned, stronger this time.

Another person entered the room, walked across it. A woman, blonde, young, pretty, I thought, though I couldn't see her clearly. She leaned over the bed, took my wrist, and measured my pulse.

'He's awake,' Claude said. 'Ain't that great?'

'How are you feeling, Mr Alvord?' The nurse spoke loudly, yet her voice was gentle, as if she spent much of her time soothing people.

'Irrr-ty.' Thirsty.

She left, went into the bathroom, ran water, came back and dripped some water from a straw into my mouth. I lapped at it like a man in the desert, but felt it escaping down the side of my face. The nurse wiped it with a tissue. 'Don't be in such a hurry. It's okay. I'm right here.'

It's okay. I'm right here. There was a girl. I remembered her saying that to me, her fingers intertwined with mine. *Epiphany.* I recalled her now. I closed my eyes, trying to piece together more.

'Claude, could you stay with him a minute while I go call Dr Barnhill to tell him Mr Alvord is awake?' She left without waiting for an answer.

Claude moved in again, patting my hand, then rubbing it

between his palms, as if to keep me from drifting away. 'You been in a coma. A real, live Sleepin' Beauty. You remember any of that?'

I shook my head slightly, but I was starting to remember, to pull the threads together a bit at a time. But for the weariness in my body and the strange, stale taste in my mouth, I would have said that the smattering of events I remembered had happened just a day ago, or two. But you don't land in a nursing home overnight. Time had passed . . . weeks, according to Claude Fisher. As he offered comfort and assurances, I tried to conjure a logical pattern of events. Epiphany, the trip, a hotel, a bite of cinnamon roll that seemed to sit on my chest with the heaviness of a cinder block . . .

A busy highway . . . so much traffic . . .

A car accident? Had I been in a car accident?

I worked to push the question past my lips, struggling to make Claude understand it. In the time it took, another question was brewing. If there had been an accident, where was Epiphany? Had she been injured? I remembered her being in the car, calling my name, and then darkness closing around me like the pinwheel shutter on a camera, narrowing from all directions.

Claude chuckled when he finally discerned the question I was working so hard to voice. 'No, friend, it wasn't a car accident. It was your ticker.' He patted his chest. 'Your heart. You had a heart attack. I been through one myself, few years back, so I know what that's like, but I woke up after mine. Some folks don't, though. You're lucky. They were gettin' worried you might not ever come to, but here you are. The nurses didn't tell me your private business, by the way. But you keep your ears open around here, you'll figure out things. I heard the doctor talking to your daughter when they brung you in.'

I heard the doctor talking to your daughter . . . I wanted to ask about the conversation, to question Claude as to exactly what Deborah had said, to see if I could read between the lines and discern my reality. Did Deborah come often? Had she mentioned my house? Where was Epiphany? Did Epiphany visit here and stand over my bed, wondering if I would awaken? How had we ended up on the highway together? Where were we going?

To a hospital . . . I remembered going to a hospital to visit a woman. Something about a blue dresser. And there was a house . . .

Bits and pieces returned, scraps of memory. My head throbbed, whirling and clicking, a phonograph too tightly wound. I closed my eyes, sank into the pillow.

'There's the doc,' Claude said. 'Must've been his day to make rounds. Hey, Doc! We got a live one here. Sleepin' Beauty just woke up.'

After that, the day passed in a muddle of medical jargon, and waking, and sleeping, whispered conversations about recovery, therapy, and deprivation of the brain during the heart attack. They wondered how completely I was able to understand them and how completely I would recover. In the afternoon, a therapist attempted to test my cognitive abilities. She cheered every task I was able to complete and pronounced me a star patient for being able to muster a modicum of words. She seemed to indicate that my future looked promising. In all the hoopla, one thing was missing. There was no indication of Deborah rushing to my bedside, euphoric at the idea that I'd finally awakened.

The nurse made repeated promises that my daughter would be arriving soon, but Deborah did not come. Nor was there any sign of Epiphany, which concerned me even more, particularly as I began reconstructing the details of our trip. We'd been partners, cohorts, amateur sleuths, and fugitives on the lam together. She wouldn't have abandoned me here in this nursing home unless something was very wrong.

Unless she had no choice . . . or she wasn't near here.

Had she run away?

Was she all right?

I attempted to ask the questions as the day went on, but I couldn't pronounce Epiphany's name correctly, and no one seemed to recognize it. I tried not to think the worst. Between waking and sleeping and working to control spongy, uncooperative muscles, I watched the door and thought alternately of Epiphany and of Deborah.

As evening began closing in, the nurse, Mary, became flustered by my continual attempt at questions. 'Your daughter's out of town,' she said, settling her fingers tenderly over mine and giving an apologetic squeeze. 'Her office couldn't reach her, but they've left a voice mail on her cell. I'm sure she'll pick up the message soon. She'll be so thrilled. She's been really worried about you.' Her kind blue eyes flitted away, betraying a caution she didn't want me to see. Undoubtedly, it is unhealthy for a coma patient to discover on his first day back that no one cares if he wakes up.

'I want . . . to sss-see . . . mmm-my . . .' The fog was thickening in my brain this evening, making the words more difficult to find and to form. I sounded like a drunk on a park bench. I had the drunk's headache, as well. 'M-my law-yer.' If I could have dredged up the name, I would have given it to her, insisted that she write it down and look up the number. Even a prisoner in jail is given the right to one phone call. Surely a patient in the nursing home deserved that much.

In the hall, an old woman was pacing and raving like a lunatic, crying out that someone had stolen her china and silver, and then alternately calling for someone named Felix. Perhaps Deborah had deposited me in the dementia ward.

Mary cocked an ear to the sound, then turned back to me. 'I'm sorry about Mrs Klemp. She's having a tough time, and we haven't had the heart to move her to the Alzheimer's wing. She's been here six years.'

Six years . . . Something inside me clenched. I'd be better off never having awakened.

'I'm going off duty now.' Mary adjusted my sheets. 'Ifeoma will be coming on. She'll take good care of you. As soon as we hear from your daughter, she'll let you know. Would you like the TV on for a while?'

'*H-oh-gan's Heroes*,' I answered bleakly, but the words were slurred. I ended up with *Extreme Home Makeover* on the TV.

I watched two and a half episodes before sinking into sleep.

When I awoke, it was morning. I knew this without looking. Pink light filtered against my eyelids. I opened them and scanned the room, uncertain at first where I was, and then remembering. The recollection was a blow. I closed my eyes again, but I wasn't sleepy. Just weary. Weary in mind, and body, and spirit.

An old hymn ran through my mind. One of the women sang it in the kitchen of the VanDraan house, 'I'll Fly Away.'

I wanted to fly away. I wanted to fly away like a rocket, streaking through the atmosphere, from the known to what is beyond. I'd always been a man to lean on science more than faith, to rely on what could be plotted, and predicted, and explained with the proper equation.

But science was of no use to me now. It could not bring me from this place to the next, from Earth to heaven.

Lean not on thine own understanding. Perhaps this was my mistake – the casual forgetting of that one little verse, repeated so often as I sat in catechism classes, drawing diagrams in the corners of my papers. Perhaps I'd been stubborn, shortsighted, arrogant. But lying here in this bed, I had no way to help myself. I had little choice but to make contact with God, to rely on prayer.

Seems like that's a bad time to start ... Epiphany had said when I'd flippantly espoused my intention not to return to church until I arrived there in a coffin.

Out of the mouths of babes.

In my pain and my arrogance, I'd left myself alone in this little room.

So completely alone ...

Closing my eyes again, I attempted to consider, perhaps with not as much determination as I should have afforded, how a fitting prayer would be worded at this point. What should I pray for? My health, my recovery, so that I could continue to fight for my home? My freedom, so that I could find Epiphany and attempt to undo whatever damage I had done? Answers, so that I could solve the mysteries of my past?

A miracle?

Should I pray for a miracle?

Such was probably too much to expect for a man in my position. Miracles involved faith and supplication – two qualities in which I had never excelled.

But then again, there was no other viable contingency plan at this juncture, and so I made an attempt at prayer, in the way a catechism student might, when given it for an assignment.

Father in heaven,

Please take up this struggle where I have failed in it. Please do not let this journey have been for naught. I need to know the truth before I die, and I need to leave things well with Deborah and with Epiphany. If I've lacked in anything in life, it has been in the asking for help when I needed it and in the believing of things I could not prove.

I'm asking now, which ultimately means that I do believe.

And perhaps that I'm at the point of desperation.

You accept prayers from both perspectives, I suspect. Thank you for accepting this one.

The end . . .

I mean . . . Amen.

I waited then, through the nurse's morning rounds and breakfast and a meeting with an occupational therapist. The staff changed, the third shift leaving and Mary returning. 'Your daughter called,' she announced. 'She's trapped in a storm in Kansas City, but she'll be here as soon as she can get a flight out.'

Deborah arrived later that day, rushing in the door, haggard and breathless, travel-weary. She stopped at the sight of me sitting up in bed, blinked, and dropped her chin a bit, as if she hadn't really expected to find me functioning. In that instant when she was off guard, I tried to read her emotions. What lay beyond her obvious surprise? Disappointment? Happiness? Reservation?

Was she mulling through the eventualities, thinking, *What do I do with him now that he's back among the living?* The doctor and the occupational therapist had given me reason to hope that I could expect a fairly full recovery, with some continuing therapy. An emergency surgery after the heart attack had opened the blocked coronary arteries and placed two stents. Deborah must have consented to the procedure when I was unable to consent to it myself. Why would she have done that if she only wanted to put me away?

I thought of the prayer earlier. I needed to leave things well with Deborah . . .

Only a fool prays in one direction and walks in another.

I put on a smile – sort of a slow, clumsy, lopsided thing, as my muscles were slack from lack of use. I lifted a hand toward her. It had a bit of a shriveled look, but it could have been holding an olive branch.

Deborah stood frozen in place, seeming uncertain, afraid to come closer. Her lips pursed, she swallowed, took a pair of sunglasses dangling from her fingers, and hooked them over her purse strap without looking at it. 'They called me ...' The sentence seemed unfinished, as if she didn't know what else to add. She took a tiny step, then halted.

A lifetime passed through my mind, the memories pungent and sweet and painful. Deborah as a baby, our firstborn. Deborah as a toddler, independent, curious, persnickety in her choices of food and playthings. Deborah as a teenager, stubborn, smart, difficult. Deborah as a young woman, opinionated, obstinate, accomplished. Deborah as a bride, beautiful on the beach in a simple white cotton dress. And now *this* Deborah, a woman in the middle of her life, still watching me from a distance. How many times had she taken a step in my direction only to find me brushing on by? How many times had I failed to see it, failed to see her? Failed at the most important thing of all?

I'd come so close to being only a regret in her life. A person dead and gone, with whom amends could never be made.

'It'sss all right –' The words formed a bit more easily now. 'I'm n-n-not going ...' *Anywhere.* Anywhere was the final word, but I couldn't force it out. My lips trembled, and of all things, tears pushed into my eyes. The image of my daughter blurred.

'Dad,' she said softly.

'I'm h-here.'

She crossed the room, opened her arms, and leaned over the bed, her sob dying against my chest. I encircled her clumsily, the movement feeling awkward, but any affection between us would have been, after so long a time. We were in uncharted territory. Like *Surveyor* landing on the dry seas of Oceanus, Mission Control uncertain what would lie beneath the surface.

For a while, there were only tears, Deborah's and mine. I held her and thought of all the missed moments, the missed connections, all the things I'd waited too long to say. Perhaps there had always been, inside me, the little boy from the house with the seven chairs – afraid, alone, trying to hide the bruises by keeping anyone from getting close enough to touch him.

Emotions so many years in the making take time to vent. Nearly an hour had passed before Deborah slid into a chair beside the bed and mopped her face with a Kleenex from the dispenser on the night table. She looked a wreck, and now somewhat embarrassed, perhaps even a bit wary of broaching the next step in the conversation.

I rested against the pillow, my body filled with lead. I wanted to sleep, but I couldn't allow myself. So much territory needed to be covered yet.

Deborah discarded one Kleenex and reached for another. 'The h-house?'

I formed the words carefully, cast them out into the empty space between us.

Deborah dabbed at mascara stains and wiped her nose. 'The house is fine. Terrence has been looking after things. His daughter, Dell, and her husband were down for a visit last week, so they stayed in the house.'

I felt a sense of relief disproportionate to an inanimate object. Terrence was looking after my house. Everything was fine there. Everything was as I left it.

Deborah looked away, as if there were more, but she was reluctant to share it. Her eyes hid beneath lowered lashes, then turned my way again. 'I read the letter you wrote to me ... on the notepad from the bed-and-breakfast in Groveland.'

'G-good,' I whispered. If she'd read my letter, then she knew. She knew that I loved her. She knew that I regretted the sort of father I'd been, the things I hadn't taken the time to say. I reached for her, held her hand. 'I'm s-sorry.'

Squeezing my fingers, she nodded, sniffled, dried another tear. 'Dad, why did you do ... Why did you take off like that? And with Epiphany? With a sixteen-year-old girl? What were you thinking? Why would you help a teenager to run away from home?'

'R-r-run ...' What was she talking about? Hadn't Epiphany told her? Hadn't Epiphany explained why we'd gone to Houston, what we'd found? Why would Epiphany have kept that secret after I was in the hospital? Unless ...

Unless Epiphany wasn't there. Unless she'd run away when I was rushed to the emergency room in Houston. Had Epiphany left before Deborah came, before anyone could stop her? 'Epie ... di-d-didn't te ... tell ... you?'

A fan of wrinkles formed around Deborah's nose. 'Tell me what? Dad, her parents had turned her in as a runaway. By the time I got to the hospital in Houston, the police had her in custody. I haven't seen her, and I'm sure that's for the best.' Deborah sneered a little, her eyes hardening. 'Why would you let her talk you into taking off for Houston? I mean, I guess I'm partly to blame for getting the whole thing started, with her working at your house. I should have known that a kid from her sort of background might . . . take advantage, but, Dad, you shouldn't have . . .'

I lifted a hand to quiet her. Suddenly the effort seemed astronomical. If I let my eyelids touch, I'd be asleep in an instant. 'Where isss . . . she?'

Deborah drew back, straightened her neck, irritated. 'I don't know, and I haven't asked. After what she did, I'm not inclined to try to find out. I trusted her. I trusted her with you, with the house, and she took advantage. It's just fortunate that this whole thing didn't turn out worse. Her parents don't seem inclined to press any charges, thank goodness.'

'Char-ges?' My eyes fell shut, and I pushed them open again. My thoughts were starting to blur now.

'Yes, *charges*,' Deborah snapped, and then seemed to catch herself. She paused, as if she were silently counting to ten. 'You can't just take off with someone's child . . . a minor . . . a young girl, without permission. Given the type of family she comes from, we're lucky they haven't spied a gravy train and decided to . . . make something of it.' She hooded her eyes, embarrassed by the idea.

'Epiph-any wouldn't . . .'

'Of course she would, Dad. Don't be naive.' She clipped the last word, catching herself again, closing her lips tightly and swallowing something bitter before continuing. 'She's

397

run away before. Did you know that? And she's in all sorts of trouble with the school. This isn't some innocent sixteen-year-old kid.'

'No.' I shook my head, my scalp scratching against the stiff institutional sheets. 'We . . .'

Deborah didn't wait for me to put together the rest of the sentence. 'I'm not trying to be critical of you, all right? I blame myself. I should have checked things out more carefully. Her mother isn't even a regular employee with the university cleaning service. She's just a temp. I shouldn't have let either of them in the house. Thank goodness something worse didn't happen.'

The fog swirled through my mind, pulled me under. Images flashed by – the hotel, the dime store, the lion's head, tombstones, the picture of the VanDraan family, Cecile's face, my father's . . .

Deborah smoothed a hand over my shoulder. 'It's all right, Dad. Just rest now, okay?'

Just rest . . . I wanted to rest, to let myself tumble into sleep, to tackle this another day, but another day might be too long. What if I drifted off and didn't wake again and the truth never came to light?

'No,' I whispered, then took Deborah's hand and pulled her close. 'Listen.' Opening my eyes, I took a breath and began as best I could to tell the story of the house with the seven chairs.

CHAPTER 24

Epiphany Jones

After a couple weeks, I finally got to move from my bedroom to the porch. I could sit out there after Russ picked me up from school and dragged me home, where he could keep an eye on me while Mama was at work. She'd told everyone, including Russ, I was a runaway, and that I'd done it before, and she didn't have a clue what my problem was or why I liked to take off. She'd even told the school counselor and two different social workers that.

'Epie's just trying for attention,' she'd said, and really I think it was her that liked the attention. She liked having people sit there and listen while she griped about me and acted like she was the model mother. 'It's been just me and her for a long time, and she's having some trouble with there being a man in the house now. I think that's her problem, mostly.'

The counselor and the social worker ate that up whole, even though none of it was true. It'd never been just me and Mama. There was always some man with her, or a friend who took us in after she broke up with a guy, or somebody we met by showing up a few times at some church, or an older lady like Mrs Lora. There was always somebody who got talked into feeling sorry for Mama and helping her out.

I don't know why I thought the school would be any different. Really, the principal just wanted to get the problem off his desk by letting me finish the year in the in-school suspension room, where you got watched all day, like you were in prison. You couldn't even go to the bathroom unless it was time for the whole group to go. During bathroom breaks, some teacher hung around outside the door. That was fine with me, though. It kept DeRon and the rest of them away from me, and I got my classwork done without having to worry about being jumped during the school day.

Some of the worry about getting jumped went away after Russ and his buddies caught DeRon's crew at the convenience store. Russ let them know what would happen if they ever messed with me again. When Russ picked me up from school that day, we dropped by basketball practice, too, and Russ had a little talk with the coach. I could hear him telling the coach that if he didn't teach his star player some manners, there wasn't gonna be enough of DeRon left to play basketball. I stood over in the corner, and DeRon never even so much as looked in my direction. On the way home, Russ told me I wouldn't have any more trouble with those punks, only 'punks' wasn't the word he used. The next day at school, DeRon changed his story about J. Norm and me. He said he didn't know what'd happened between us – he was just assuming stuff. He probably choked on the words. That was some satisfaction, anyway. Weird as it was, I had

Russ to thank for clearing my name. It crossed my mind that I would've been a whole lot better off if I'd told him about my problems with DeRon and the trouble with the other kids at school in the first place. If I hadn't tried to handle it on my own, maybe J. Norm and me wouldn't have gone on the run, and the heart attack never would've happened. It's funny how mistakes are so much clearer after you've already made them.

Russ wasn't so bad, really – as Mama's men went, that was. He'd picked me up after the whole runaway thing, and he hadn't asked me a whole bunch of questions, which was good because I didn't figure anybody would believe the truth. I could see myself trying to explain about the Van-Draan house, and the fire, and Cecile, and Mr Lowenstein in the feed store. They'd think I was so full of it. Next thing, Mama'd be trying to send me away to a loony bin. The day the police picked me up in Houston, she'd warned me that if I kept giving her trouble, she could get me *committed* someplace, and the state would pay for it.

Russ didn't make threats like that. He'd just told me that first day I came home that he'd had a little sister who ran away when she was sixteen and got killed. 'She was a real pretty girl. Had a whole life to live yet, you know?' There were tears in his eyes when he said it. 'You gotta take your time, Epiphany. I know you and your mama don't get along good, but you're not ready to be out on your own. You gotta hang on a couple more years and get your school finished up, and then figure out what you want to do, all right?'

I said, 'All right, Russ.' And I guess I meant it. The idea of taking off for Florida was out, anyway. My money stash was gone. Besides, I couldn't leave without knowing what was happening with J. Norm.

It took me a while to come up with a way to find out about J. Norm, but finally I did. I looked up the number for the guy who lived in J. Norm's garage apartment, Terrence Clay, and I called him from Russ's cell phone while Russ was outside working on his Harley, which was about all Russ did since the wreck. Russ was hoping for a big insurance check and maybe some disability money, too.

When I called Terrence Clay, he told me where J. Norm was and how he was doing. The word 'coma' hit me like a brick to the head.

'But for how long?' I asked, peeking between the blinds to make sure Russ was still outside. 'He's gonna wake up, right?' By then, it'd been almost three weeks – a long time to still be unconscious. It was my fault. Terrence had said the coma was due to lack of oxygen to the brain during the heart attack. If I'd been smarter that day in Houston – if I'd paid more attention, taken J. Norm to a doctor when he wasn't feeling good that morning, everything would be different.

'They don't know how long it might be before he wakes up, or what shape he'll be in when he does,' Terrence told me. 'His daughter has him in the nursing home here, at least for now.' He sighed, like he didn't see anything good coming, and then we got off the phone.

After that, I called Terrence whenever I could get a chance at Russ's phone. It wasn't as good as being able to go visit J. Norm, but it was something.

The third time I called, Terrence told me that J. Norm had woken up. I was so happy, I almost squealed out loud. Terrence was out of town right then, so he didn't know many details. He just knew that J. Norm was awake and talking a little. 'He's got you to thank for that, Epiphany. If you and that truck driver hadn't gotten him out of the car and started CPR, he wouldn't be here.'

I felt pure joy for the first time since J. Norm and me were on the road.

'When you see him, can you tell him I asked about him? Tell him I'm okay. He doesn't need to worry about me.'

Russ was on his way in, then, and I had to hang up. I put the phone back on the end table with Russ's wallet. I hoped he wouldn't notice I'd used it, but if he did, I could probably make him understand. Russ listened, at least. He was even starting to like me all right. Most days, I helped him out with his projects, or fetched beers and sodas out of the fridge when his buddies came to hang out. Russ was kind of weirdly parental about it, though. If anybody looked at me the wrong way or said something rude, he gave them a dirty look and said, 'Hey. She's a kid, okay?'

I decided that, somehow, he'd started to think about me like the little sister who ran off and never came back. Maybe even a guy like Russ wanted to make up for the things he'd done wrong in the past. I guess he wished he'd looked after that little sister while she was around.

Once I knew that J. Norm was awake, I started working on Russ. I tried to make him see, little by little, that I wasn't going to end up like his sister who ran away. If I could convince him of that, maybe I could convince him to take me to visit J. Norm.

Russ didn't have a clue that I had something in mind, of course. He was just happy I'd listened to him about the runaway thing, and after school finally let out for the summer, he was glad to have somebody out on the front porch every day, watching for cars to go by. 'Now that I got this disability claim goin' on,' he said, 'I can't be havin' some investigator from the insurance company drive up and see me putting an engine on the hoist, or running the grinder on some motorcycle part.' He grinned at me, like he was pretty proud of himself for thinking it through. 'You keep an eye on the road while you're sitting out there, okay? Holler at me if you see any cars that look like they don't belong in the neighborhood.'

'All right, Russ.' I gave him a smile and a wink to butter him up. 'I got your back.' Just like that, Russ and me were the best of friends.

Things were going so well between Russ and me by the second week of summer vacation that I got the courage to ask him to take me to see J. Norm at the nursing home. Russ had downed a few beers that morning, and he was just hanging out on a stool in the carport, tinkering with a carburetor, so I figured it was a good time to bring up my big question. When I asked, he gave me the same look he used on his buddies if they tried to check me out. That look said, *You just crossed the line, and you better get back on your own side.* 'You're gonna have to talk to your mama about that.' He picked up a spark plug and blew on it, like the conversation was over.

'You know what she'll say,' I pushed. I hadn't been able to get ahold of Russ's cell phone for a week. He'd started keeping it in his pocket. I wondered if he'd figured out I was using it. 'You and I could just go, Russ – while she's at work. We can run over there, and she won't know anything about it.'

For a minute, I thought he was considering it, but really he was just looking for the little piece of sandpaper that'd blown off the cable spool he used for a workbench. I picked it up and handed it to him. 'I'm not gettin' involved in that. I'm not gettin' in the middle between you and your mama. That man's daughter . . . what's her name . . . Deborah? She's called twice in the last couple weeks, and your mama wouldn't even talk to her on the phone. That tell you anything?'

I stomped a foot, frustrated after six and a half weeks of being trapped here in jail. 'Come on, Russ. Mama doesn't even have to know. It'd just be between you and me.'

He looked me square in the eye then, his mustache crinkling on one side, like he had a bad taste in his mouth. 'I'm not your daddy.' I took a step back, felt like he'd hit me. *I'm not your daddy.*

Russ looked away again, sanding the contacts on the plug. 'I can be your friend, Ep, and I can take you by Wal-Mart for the grocery shopping, and keep watch over you now that it's summer break, and make sure that DeRon kid knows what happens to little boys who jerk a girl around, but I'm not gonna get into it with your mom. Her and me are good together, you know?'

I gave up then and went back to the porch to watch for cars and read *To Kill a Mockingbird*. It'd been an English assignment to begin with, but I'd missed taking the test on it while I was stuck at home after all the hoopla about the runaway thing. The teacher made me keep the book after the end of school, because I had to write the paper before she'd release my semester grade. I was bored enough that I'd read the story more than once. It made me think about Cecile and the women in the baby pictures with me. They lived in times like that, in places like that. If anybody'd caught Cecile taking off with those five little redheaded kids, she'd have been dead, and nobody would've done a thing about it. Everybody who helped her hide those kids would've been dead, too.

Did Cecile and the sheriff argue about whether to go through with it? Did they worry about what might happen to their own families? How did they know who they could trust? How did they find people like J. Norm's mother, who would take in a little child and keep the secret? Did the maids really arrange it all, like Mr Lowenstein said?

I still needed to know the rest the story – as much of it as there was left to find, anyway. J. Norm did, too. Some way or other, I had to get back to see him again.

I tried to leave off wondering and think about *To Kill a Mockingbird*. Even though I'd read the book three times, I couldn't come up with the right thing to say about it in a paper. Maybe I didn't care if that English teacher flunked me for not making up the assignment. What was the point, anyway? So many people had written about that book, anything I said would be a repeat of stuff somebody else already came up with.

Some days, I just wanted to walk out of this whole, stupid

life – skip writing about *To Kill a Mockingbird* and get a job and my own place. J. Norm would be all over me for even thinking about it if he found out, though. He'd probably get right up out of that hospital bed, and . . .

'Russ, there's a car coming,' I hollered over my shoulder. A high-dollar ride was melting out of the heat waves a couple blocks down. It was silver, something expensive, like a Beamer or an Acura. A new one. Nothing like people from our neighborhood would drive. 'Russ, there's a car!' But Russ couldn't hear me. He'd started the grinder, and he was busy running the wire brush on a rusty gun barrel. I set my notebook down and started toward the carport. If Russ didn't get the big insurance settlement he was counting on, it would be my fault, since I was the lookout. Russ and Mama had plans for that money. Russ wanted to find a bigger, better trailer for his business, and they were gonna buy a house and fix it up. There was a new program through the Blue Sky Hill homeowners' association, where low-income homeowners could get matching money for a down payment. The only problem was, you had to have some money to match, which Mama and Russ didn't.

While the silver car was waiting at the stop sign, I jogged around the corner and got Russ away from the grinder. The wire brush was still spinning to a stop when he took off his goggles and moved to his lawn chair behind the holly bushes. He picked up a hot-rod magazine, trying to look like he'd been there all day.

The car pulled up to our curb, and I thought, *Well, maybe I really did guess right. It could be a lawyer in that nice car.*

Someone from the insurance company, coming to offer Russ a bunch of money for not suing in court. If that happened, I wanted to watch. Russ taking on some slick lawyer would be better than getting ringside seats at WWF wrestling. A battle of the rip-off artists. Atticus Finch may have been a lawyer with principles in *To Kill a Mockingbird*, but so far the people from the insurance company were as oily as the pavement on a used-car lot. I halfway hoped Russ won, even though he was scamming. When you're picking between two wrongs, it's tough to know where to fall, but lately, Russ was the closest thing I had to a friend.

I couldn't see past the holly bushes, but I heard car doors open and shut, and then the trunk. Russ leaned forward and rubbed his back, practicing while he tried to see through the hedge and figure out who was here. I picked up the screwdrivers from around the grinder so it wouldn't look like somebody'd been working.

'Go see who it is,' he whispered, trying to catch a glimpse through the bushes.

'No.' If it really was somebody official, and they asked me any questions, I didn't want to get caught up in Russ's lies. I was in enough trouble already, and I wasn't going to jail for insurance fraud.

I stood there fingering the screwdrivers, waiting for someone to come up the sidewalk, but it took forever. Keys jingled, and something metal rattled and clattered. I heard a soft, high squeal, like wheels turning. Maybe it was an insurance company doctor with a case of medical stuff, here to check Russ out.

'Go see,' Russ whispered again.

'All right, all right.' I couldn't stand it anyway. The curiosity was killing me.

I poked my head around the end of the holly bushes, the screwdrivers still in my hand. Whoever it was had made it almost halfway up the front walk. I caught sight of his T-shirt and pants before he disappeared behind the corner of the house. He wasn't dressed like a lawyer or anything, but he was a big guy. He had a lady with him, too. I could hear high heels – not, like, I-serve-drinks-at-a-club high heels, but the kind of sensible pumps that ladies wear to someplace official.

A feather of fear tickled my shoulders. Maybe this wasn't about Russ at all. Maybe it was about me. I'd thought the whole thing with me running away was settled once we had the big powwow with the police and social workers and the counselor from school. What if it wasn't?

I waited until the woman clonked up the front steps, and then I moved carefully down the driveway, leaning over so that I could get a look at them before they got a look at me. I could see the man's leg now – a tennis shoe, khaki pants, kind of wrinkled. Definitely not a uniform. His shirttail was hanging out. The shirt was blue, the kind that tells you his name is probably sewed on the front somewhere. He had a T-shirt underneath, stretched tight over some love handles, a little skin showing. *You're probably scaring yourself to death for no reason. He's probably here to check the gas lines or something.* Some lady on the news had her house blow up after a gas leak last week. It'd crossed my mind that if our house blew up, I was in trouble. There were burglar bars on all my bedroom windows, and as far as I knew none of us had the key.

The man's hand was resting on a rubber grip . . . a handle, like you push something with . . .

I took two more steps, and all of a sudden, I knew who the guy in the denim shirt was. Teddy, the sweet, slow-minded guy who lived next door to J. Norm and grew all the flowers. What was he doing here?

Another step, and I figured out what he was pushing. A wheelchair. The screwdrivers slipped from my hand and clattered against the cement, and a second later, I was running through the scrappy grass Russ never mowed. It was just six or eight steps, but it felt like I couldn't get there fast enough. By the time I made it across the yard, tears were spilling from my eyes, and I was calling his name: 'J. Norm! J. Norm, you're here!' I tripped on the edge of the cement and half knelt, half fell over J. Norm's chair, tackling him with a great, big hug I couldn't have stopped anyway. 'You're here! You're here!' I kept saying. All I could think was that everything would be all right now.

J. Norm patted me between the shoulder blades and whispered exactly the same thing that was going through my mind. 'It's all right. It's all right now . . .'

We hung on like that for a minute. In the background, I could hear the woman coming back down the steps, and Teddy saying, 'Don' cry. Don' cry, 'kay? It's gon' be ohhh-kay. Mr Al-verd goin' home from the hop-sital. He just gotta use wheelchairs jus' a little bit. Jus' little while. He gon' be all right. Them wheelchair's heavy, too! Them wheelchair's heavy, huh, Miss Deb-ah?'

'Yes, Teddy, it's heavy. Good thing we had you along, and your mom loaned us her car, so we could get Daddy in and out.'

I pulled away when I heard Deborah's voice. What was *she* doing here? When the police had me down in Houston, she didn't even call to see where I was, or let me know what was happening with J. Norm, or ask me what'd happened. She just decided everything was my fault.

J. Norm caught my hand before I could get away. He hung on, squinting up at me. 'You're all right.'

I couldn't tell if it was a question or not. 'I tried to come see you, but I couldn't get there.' I leaned close, thinking in the back of my mind that Russ would be walking around the corner any minute, and then there was no telling what might happen. Teddy was a big guy, but as far as I could tell, he was gentle as a kitten, and Russ was . . . well . . . Russ. He might not like it that they'd shown up here. 'Mama won't let me go anyplace, and I finished the year in the ISS room at school. It's like jail, so I couldn't come see you. I called Terrence, though. He told me you were a lot better. I didn't know you were, like, getting out, though. I haven't been able to call in a while.' I looked over my shoulder, checking for Russ. Deborah looked, too, and tugged her suit jacket, crossing her arms over it like she was worried about who else might be here.

'Deborah sprung me,' J. Norm said, and he looked at her in a way I hadn't ever seen before – like he was actually happy she was there.

411

For about a half sec, I was jealous. The feeling burned off quick as a paper fire, and then I was nothing but ashes inside. If he had Deborah, he didn't need me. The good times of me and J. Norm being partners in crime were over. We didn't have anybody to fight against. 'So you're, like, going home now?'

'I'll be staying at Deborah's for a while.'

I wanted to cry, except these weren't the happy kind of tears. J. Norm was here to say good-bye, same as everybody always did. He was moving across town to live with Deborah. Once that happened, he wouldn't be back. 'Oh,' was all I could think to say. I stood up, pulled my hands away, and stuck them in my jeans pockets.

He cleared his throat, the way he always did when he was about to say something I wouldn't like to hear.

Here it came – the big good-bye. I looked down at my shoes, saw a ladybug crossing the cement, thought about how easy it'd be to squish it. The little thing was just out there all by itself in the middle of the concrete, fragile, trusting for some stupid reason that it could cross the sidewalk between four people and nothing bad would happen. Then I realized what a lousy thought it was – squishing it. The ladybug was just trying to find a safe place to be.

'I was hoping to speak with your mother,' J. Norm said.

It took me a minute to hear him. 'You're . . . wha . . . ?'

He cleared his throat again, and Deborah shifted from one foot to the other, looking at their car like she really wanted to leave. She didn't head for the curb, though, which surprised me. Normally, she wanted to be the boss of everything.

J. Norm was still looking at me. 'I was hoping, if we talked things out, that you might take the job of looking after my gardens and watering the yard until I'm back in my house. I don't want everything to die while I'm away. You could come for a few hours in the afternoon – turn on the sprinklers and give everything a good soaking.'

A big, prickly lump came up in my chest. Man, he didn't know how much I wanted that. He didn't need me at his house, of course. Teddy or Terrence could turn on the sprinklers, but at least J. Norm wasn't trying to leave me high and dry. 'Oh, hey, I . . .'

Russ picked right then to walk around the corner. 'What the . . .' he said, and then added a few fill-in-the-blanks. 'What's goin' on out here?'

Like an idiot, I introduced everybody, like Russ couldn't figure it out for himself. Maybe it was a good thing to do, though, because Russ must've thought he needed to show some manners. He shook everyone's hands, and then listened while J. Norm told him why they were here.

Russ heard the words 'pay her' in there, and he quit standing with his arms flexed like he was about to headlock somebody. 'Sounds like a deal to me,' he said, and then offered everybody a beer. When they said no, thanks, he put on a worried frown and added, 'But you'd have to talk to her mama.' He looked disappointed then. No doubt the idea of having me tied to the strings of his combat boots all summer was a drag, even for Russ. 'Her mama's pretty upset about what happened – Epiphany running off and all. Her mama says Ep's done it before. More than one time.'

Deborah glanced at the car again, ready to quit right there. Teddy wandered off to look at an overgrown rose-bush by the porch, and I wanted to shrink down to flea size and hitch a ride on the ladybug's back. None of what Russ said about me was true, but nobody would believe me if I told them. The only time I'd ever left Mama's place with my stuff was when she was dating some creepy guy who was way too into ten-year-old girls. I took my clothes and went next door to the neighbors' place. They told Mama that if she didn't get rid of the guy, they'd call somebody official. Mama never did forgive me for that.

'Is her mother home?' J. Norm had that look in his eye, like he was ready to take somebody on and he wouldn't be giving up anytime soon. In a battle between J. Norm and Mama . . . well . . . it was hard to say how things might turn out.

Russ shook his head. 'Nah. She's working.'

J. Norm kept on. I guess he figured Russ was a good place to start. 'I'd like to straighten out this misunderstanding. To begin with, it was never Epiphany's intention to run away. The trip to Groveland and then on to Houston was my idea and for my purposes. You see . . .' He went ahead and told Russ about the VanDraan mystery – standing right there in our driveway.

Russ's mouth dropped open, and his eyes were getting wider and wider. Every once in a while, he'd rub his chin and spit into the grass and say something like, 'Man, well, don't that beat all?' or, 'That sounds like it oughta be on TV.' I wondered if Russ was really listening, or just playing along and enjoying the story. Would he do anything about it, even

414

if he did believe J. Norm? Mostly, Russ wasn't into causing himself any extra trouble, and Mama had been nice to him lately to make up for the fact that he was having to keep me in jail. She hadn't even been griping at him about money.

When J. Norm was finished, I held my breath. Russ spit into the grass again, then rubbed his chin, thinking.

'Come on, Russ, please?' I begged.

He gave me that I'm-not-your-daddy look.

'I can come back when her mother is home,' J. Norm suggested. 'I'd like to talk with her about returning to her job cleaning my house, as well.'

Russ softened up a little more, letting his hand drop off his chin, then nodding. He'd heard Mama say more than once that those big houses on Blue Sky Hill were easy money. She got paid a lot for cleaning them, and most of the time there weren't even any kids to mess up the place. 'Let me talk to her about it,' Russ said.

J. Norm thanked him, and they shook hands like they were old friends. Then Russ gave J. Norm his phone number and said, 'Give me a call tomorrow, and I'll let you know how it goes with her mama.'

And that was that. I said good-bye to J. Norm without getting all gushy about it. I didn't want Russ to have the idea I cared too much. I just hoped he really would talk to Mama. He'd have a lot better chance with her than I would, especially right now, while they needed to make up for the money they lost after the accident.

At suppertime, I fixed burgers for Russ and me, just to be nice, and then cleaned all the dishes, while Russ hung out with his buddies in the carport. The later it got, and the more beer they drank, the more worried I was. Mama wouldn't be happy if she came home and he was partying it up. He wouldn't be in any shape to talk to her, either. *Please, God, let them run out of beer,* didn't seem like much of a prayer, but I tried it, anyway. It must've worked, because they did, and Russ came inside and fell asleep on the sofa.

I went to bed, figuring I'd hear when Mama came in – if Russ talked to her, anyway. They were never quiet when they talked.

I slept all night, though, and when I woke, it was almost ten in the morning. Russ was still on the sofa, and Mama was out cold in bed. She didn't get up until almost noon, and by then Russ was outside. I was afraid he'd forgotten about his promise to J. Norm. I fixed some grilled cheese sandwiches for lunch, figuring I could get everybody in one place that way. Eating and talking was probably a good idea. It might slow down the reactions a little.

Russ had grease up to his elbows when he came in from the carport. He washed in the kitchen sink, which Mama never liked much, but she didn't say anything about it. She was slicing some leftover birthday cake she'd brought home from the break room in a building she'd cleaned. 'Dessert,' she said, and set it on the table. She seemed in a pretty good mood.

Russ decided to bring up the deal about J. Norm while he was right in the middle of using the dishrag to scrub grease off his elbows. He didn't even get the story halfway out before Mama slammed a butter knife down on the table. 'You let him step foot in this yard? In my yard?'

Usually, once she ramped into an argument, Russ would ramp it up, too. This time, he was calm, though. 'If you'll just hold on and listen to me a minute . . .'

'I don't want to listen,' Mama snapped. 'I'm tired of all this trouble with her. I'm tired of all her lies!'

'Mama, I didn't . . .' I said, but Russ held up a big, meaty hand dripping soapy grease.

'Everybody just chill down, now.' Leave it to Russ to make a family argument sound like a beer commercial. 'We can talk about this without gettin' in a great big fight.'

I stepped back and took a breath. For once, Russ was the smartest one in the room. 'I'm sorry. I just want Mama to know what really happened.'

Russ gave me a hush-up look, and so I did. I just stood there while he told Mama everything J. Norm had said.

When he was done, she sneered at him. 'I don't *care*. I don't want *anything* more to do with that old man. Thinks he's so important, with his big house and all his college degrees on the wall. Thinks he can treat people any way he wants – take off with somebody's kid, and then throw a little money our way, and we're just gonna say, Oh, yes, *sir*, anything you want, *sir*. Well, he can forget it. Epiphany's *my* kid, not his. *I'm* her mama.' She spun toward me. 'And you can forget it, too. That old man doesn't have anything we need.'

'But, Mama, I *want* to go work there.' I was torn between pleading and getting hostile, but I knew where hostile would end up. We'd land in a big fight, Russ would give up and walk out of the house, and I'd never get what I needed.

If only I could make Mama see. If only, for once, she'd do something that was good for me. 'I like it there. He teaches me things, and helps me with reports for school, and he knows stuff. He landed rockets on the moon, and . . .'

'And *what*?' Mama's lip curled, and she faked a smile, tipping her head from side to side. '*What*? You think you're gonna go make you a rocket and fly off to someplace? You think you're too good for this house – for all the stuff I worked for?' She slapped a hand to her chest. '*I* work for it. *Me.* And you think you're too good. You think you're gonna run off to someplace else. You're nothing but his *little housemaid*, Epiphany. That's all you are. He doesn't *care* about you. Nobody wants –'

'Hey!' Russ stepped between us, his palms going out like stop signs, his eyes flashing wide. 'Hey! Now, I said we're not gonna fight.'

Taking a step back, Mama threw a hand over her eyes, fingers trembling. She sniffled, pushed her lips together, and swallowed hard. 'Tell *her* that,' she said finally, her voice shaking, her shoulders stiff. She dropped her hand, and her eyes were hard and cold. 'What do you want from me, Epie? Why can't you ever just leave it alone? Why does it always have to be like this?' Her arms flew out, her hands fanning the air, as she screamed, 'What do you want!'

Something broke loose inside me, rushed forward like a wild animal kept caged too long, finally seeing open ground. 'I want you to stop being mad at me! I want you to stop hating me for who I am. I want you to tell me I'm smart, and I'm pretty, and I can do things. I want you to be

418

my *mama*. I want you to stop *lying* to me. I want to know about my father.'

Mama let out a gasp, gritting her teeth, but I kept on before she could say anything. It was now or never. If she kicked me out, I'd go to J. Norm's house, grab the hidden key, and let myself in. Either way, I'd get at least some of what I wanted. 'I want to know who my father was. I want the *truth*! I know he has people out there. I saw the pictures – the ones you keep hidden in that shoe box. They loved me. They wanted me, and you took me away, didn't you? Didn't you?'

'Ffff!' Mama spat. 'They wouldn't even help us when we needed it. Want you? They were ready to let us starve on the street. That's how much they wanted you.' Yanking open a kitchen drawer, she started digging through scissors, old notepads, dried-up ink pens, twist ties, rubber bands, and other junk. Finally, she pulled something from the bottom of the drawer, spun around, and flung it at me. It hit my knee and landed on the ground by my feet. A little book, not much bigger than a credit card, tattered and yellowed, the kind you get free from the bank or an insurance company. 'There! There, you happy now? You ready to get off my back, to quit making me out like the terrible mother? Mean, horrible Mama. You've even turned Russ against me. All you *ever* do is try to *screw* it up for me. You never think of *anybody* but yourself, Epiphany. Just go ahead and try calling your daddy's family. See how far it gets you. See how much help you get out of that self-righteous bunch of witches!' She turned around and stomped out of the kitchen. Her bedroom door slammed a few seconds later.

I picked up the book. Inside, there were addresses and phone numbers, the ink faded, the names written a long time ago. They were notes from another life – places in Tampa, Florida. A bank, a church, a dentist, an entry marked *Epiphany's pediatrician*, and then in the 'J' section, a half dozen people with the same name as my father, Jones, including one that just said, *Nana Jones*. I stood there looking at it, trying to get my mind around the idea that, after all this time, their names, my history, were right there in my hands. It'd been stuffed in the junk drawer all this time. They were just a phone call away.

Now that the truth was so close, I was scared. What if Mama was right? What if they didn't want me? What if there was something horrible in my past, just like we'd found in J. Norm's? Maybe I was better off not knowing.

Russ sighed and started for the door. 'I better go talk your mama down.' He sounded tired. On the way past, he stuck his hand in his pocket, then pulled out his phone and handed it to me. 'You can use it if you want.'

I didn't, though. I wasn't sure why, but I put Russ's phone and the book in my pocket, and I just kept them there. In the bedroom, I heard Mama sobbing, and I felt bad, because I knew that, whether she'd ever say it or not, I'd hurt her. She cried all the while I was cleaning up the dishes from the lunch we never ate. The three slices of cake were still on the table. I stared at them for a minute, remembering that she'd been excited about the free dessert.

When Mama came out of the bedroom again, we didn't talk. She had a couple hours until she needed to go to work, and we sat in the living room, watching old reruns on TV and eating our slices of cake, while Russ disappeared outside.

Mama didn't ask about the book, and I didn't tell her where it was. When she left for work, she stood in the door for a minute, then grabbed her keys off the table and said, 'It's a short night. I won't be so late.'

"Kay,' I whispered, and I wondered why sometimes the people you wish you could understand the most are the ones you can't understand at all.

After Mama left, I went back to the bedroom and got out the box, then laid the pictures on the bed and looked hard at them. I looked into the eyes of those women, and I saw pieces of myself. I looked into Mama's eyes, and I saw myself there, too.

And I saw Cecile. I saw her in those beautiful black women, in their fancy church hats and their Jackie Kennedy dresses. In my mind, I decided that Cecile had moved far away from the house with the seven chairs. She'd moved to St Louis after she made sure all those little redheaded children had a place. She'd made a whole new life for herself, a happy life. And maybe, because she'd done something good for them, those rich families who got the children had kept sending her a little money over the years, just to make sure she was taken care of. On Sundays, she put on a big hat, and a beautiful dress, and clean white gloves, and sang praises louder than anybody else.

That's what I'd say in my essay about *To Kill a Mockingbird*, I decided. I'd make sure the English teacher knew that the story of Jem and Scout and Atticus Finch wasn't just words someone made up in a book. There were people who lived it – people of all different colors. They were brave, and they were strong, and even though it was hard, they did what they knew was right.

I'd tell her about Cecile, because a story like that ought to be told.

And I'd tell her my story. I'd tell her how, after I looked at those pictures long enough, and opened and closed the address book a half dozen times, and picked up the phone and set it down over and over, I finally thought about Cecile. She was just some girl who cleaned the house, but she saved those five little kids when everyone else in town was afraid to.

Sooner or later, if you want to do what's never been done, you have to find the courage to take the first step. Just like J. Norm said, *Only impossible journeys achieve the impossible.*

That's what I'd tell the English teacher.

And then I'd tell her that I picked up the phone, and I dialed the number for Nana Jones. My hands were shaking when I pressed the phone to my ear. I held my breath, waited through one ring, two, three, almost hung up in between each. My heart was pounding so hard, I couldn't think. I wouldn't know what to say if someone answered . . .

And then someone did – an old woman. She had a nice voice. 'Hello?' she said once, and then again, after I didn't speak.

I pushed a hand to my chest, tried to hold my heart inside. 'Hello . . . is this . . . is this Mrs Jones?'

'Yes, it is. May I help you?' she said in a way that wasn't rude really, but told me to get to the point.

'Hi.' My throat clutched the word, like a fist squeezing so tight the muscles trembled. I felt myself breaking open, thinking, *Just hang up the phone.*

I heard Mama's voice saying, *Want you? They were ready to let us starve on the street. That's how much they wanted you.*

Tears pushed into my eyes.

'Hello? Is somethin' wrong? Is ever-body okay?' The woman on the phone sounded old-fashioned and Southern, like Aunt Char at the bed-and-breakfast.

Just hang up the phone.

And again I thought of Cecile. I saw the smoke billowing all around her, the heat licking at her skin as she squeezed through the ash door.

I thought of J. Norm, sending his rockets to the moon, past the Russian trawlers with their signal jammers, and all the people who said the moon was covered in five feet of dust, everyone who said it couldn't be done. Maybe, even though J. Norm didn't know it, when the rocket left Earth, he was hearing Cecile's voice, too. Maybe she was telling him never to let other people tell you when to give up hope.

I swallowed hard, took a breath. 'Hello.' The word was faint at first, then stronger. 'This is Epiphany. Epiphany Jones . . .'

CHAPTER 25

J. Norman Alvord

A midsummer rain had just stopped falling. It shone against the grass and glimmered on the pavement, giving the world a freshly washed look as Terrence's car turned into the drive. Evening sunlight streamed beneath the shelf of clouds, reflecting against the vehicle's sleek metal skin.

I watched from the parlor window as Epiphany stepped out, slinging her backpack onto her shoulder. She stopped to say thank-you to Terrence, and to Terrence's daughter, Dell, as they exited the front seats, and then, impulsively, she gave each of them a hug. Terrence and his daughter smiled at each other and then started up the stairs to his apartment, Terrence keeping a hand under Dell's elbow as she balanced the weight of a pregnancy. Watching them, I remembered the house on Switch Grass Island, where the swelter of summer days left Annalee, then round with life, exhausted after strolls along the shore. I held her arm as we walked up the stairs to our porch above the water, and she huffed and puffed, laboring with each step.

I'd probably never shared that story with Deborah. Tonight, when all the festivities were over, I would ask Deborah and Lloyd to stay over a little while before they headed home. I'd make some coffee – decaf, of course, because a man with much to do must look after his health. Over coffee later, I'd share the stories of Switch Grass Island with my daughter. It was as much her story as mine, after all.

It was also our story.

I moved to the door and opened it as Epiphany stepped onto the porch. Blinking, she registered surprise, then frowned at my comfortable clothing – the old brown polyester pants and a striped button-up shirt that, for some reason, women found distasteful. 'You're going in *that*?'

'Hello to you, too.' I did my best to appear offended, but on a day like this one, smiles pull from the inside, making a curmudgeonly countenance difficult to maintain. 'You don't appear to be ready, either.' I pointed at her jeans and a T-shirt with some hideous rock star on the front.

Slipping through the door, she dropped her backpack in the hall. 'I brought all my stuff so I could get ready here. I figured if I hung around home too much, Mama would change her mind and tell me I couldn't go.'

'Oh, I don't think so,' I said, trying to smooth things, but Epiphany could be right. Her mother was a difficult woman, filled with her own jealousies and resentments. Even though I'd been much more cooperative since she'd returned to keeping house for me, I'd been unable to warm her up very much. The breach between her and Epiphany might never be fully healed, but who could say? Deborah and I stood as a testament to the fact that what is broken can sometimes be mended a bit at a time.

'You didn't see the mood she's in. I had to clean the whole stupid house to get out of there,' Epiphany complained, and then offered a one-sided smirk that reminded me she was still a teenager.

'Did you help to create the mess in the house?' I asked.

She narrowed her eyes. 'Don't *even* take her side, J. Norm.'

'It was just an observation. Stirring up the waters is hardly a help in building a bridge, now, is it?'

'Look who's talking.' Incredulous eyes regarded me from beneath lowered lashes. 'You been using the walker, like Deborah told you to? Because I don't see it around here.' She made a show of peering into the front parlor and checking behind my back, as if that insidious four-wheeled rabbit cage might be there. Deborah was overreacting in her fear that I wasn't yet steady enough on my feet.

'I'm fit as a fiddle.' I patted my plumper stomach. Those lunches out with Deborah and Epiphany's dinners four days a week were starting to add up. Deborah was pleased, of course. 'This new pacemaker has me in such good shape that I even went out and filled the bird feeders yesterday.' Afterward, I'd sat on the patio and watched the songbirds come in, and felt as if Annalee were there in the chair beside me.

Epiphany drew a breath, scandalized. 'J. Norm! Teddy could've come over and done that, or Terrence.'

'Terrence has company, and besides, I wanted to do it myself. It's my house, after all.'

Grabbing the backpack again, Epiphany rolled her eyes.

426

'Geez, J. Norm. Somebody needs to be here to keep you out of trouble twenty-four/seven. Next time, let me do the bird feeders, or Deborah.'

It occurred to me then that if Deborah found out I'd been filling the feeders, we'd end up having a discussion over it. 'If she notices them next time she comes, tell her you filled them.'

My request was answered with the measured look of a poker player gauging bids across the table. 'Only if you promise to let me do it next time. You have to get on a ladder to reach those things, J. Norm.'

'Only one step.'

'Do you promise or not? Because I told you I wasn't helping you hide stuff from Deborah anymore.'

'All right. I promise.' Too many women in a house makes misery for a man. Misery, or perhaps a lively challenge to the power of old age and treachery.

Moving to the end of the hall, Epiphany looked both ways. 'Where is Deborah, anyway? I thought she'd be here by now. Sorry I'm so late, by the way. When Dell and Terrence picked me up, Russ dragged them to the carport to show them his Harley, and then him and Terrence got to talking bikes. I thought poor Dell was gonna have her baby right there on the street before they got done. Mama wouldn't even come out and say hi, of course.'

'Let's not complain about Mother today, all right?' I urged gently. Perhaps Epiphany's mother had come as far as she was willing, or as far as she could at this juncture. One thing that discovering my own history had taught me is that we must learn not to whip ourselves for the failures of others. When a mother cannot love and protect her children, it is not the children who are defective. I had a sense that if I could help Epiphany to understand at least that much, I'd be adequately fulfilling this late-in-life task I'd been given. 'Deborah and Lloyd will meet us at the dinner. They had to go to the airport.'

Epiphany's eyes sparkled with enthusiasm. 'You mean I get to drive? Just you and me?'

'Just like old times.'

She wiggled in place like an overwound toy, and I felt like jittering along with her. I thought better of it, however. Given my luck, I'd fall and prove Deborah right about the walker.

'Cool!' Her high-pitched squeal vibrated through the entry hall and might have shattered the crystal in the dining room. Suddenly in a rush, Epiphany headed for the stairs. 'I gotta go get ready.'

'Hold on,' I said, and then felt the need to correct her. 'You *have* to go get ready.'

'Right. I have to.' She turned toward the stairs again.

'I've moved my things to the powder room off the kitchen,' I told her before she could flit off. 'You can use the bathroom in the master suite. Annalee always loved her vanity area and the full-length mirrors in there. She left some paraphernalia in the closet you might want to use.'

Spinning around with her mouth agape, Epiphany staggered off the bottom step. 'You mean ... the ... I can ... Like ... the shoes ... and ...' She caught my gaze with intensity, waiting for me to explain myself.

'We are going to the sort of place where one *dresses* for dinner. Take anything you like from Annalee's closet.'

Epiphany looked down at her clothing, smoothing the front of her T-shirt self-consciously. I could only imagine what she had in the backpack. 'Meaning more than just changing into jeans *without* holes and a clean pair of flip-flops,' I added.

Looking down at her feet, she wiggled her toes. 'Where are we going, anyway?'

'Someplace . . . fitting the occasion. It's a big night.'

A dark brow arched upward. 'Not someplace over by the airport, I hope. Because I'm scared of the airport.'

Standing there, she seemed so young. Too young to be flying off to Florida for a monthlong visit with family members she'd never met. I'd made a few arrangements to be certain she was looked after, though. I still had friends in Florida from my days at the cape. 'You'd best get used to it, if you're to be flying out next week.'

'I'm not scared to fly. I'm just scared of the trip to the airport. Russ's taking me. Actually, me driving might be safer than riding with Russ.'

'Highly unlikely.'

'Thanks a lot.' She gave a sardonic smirk, then hitched up the backpack and darted off, her voice echoing behind her. 'I gotta get dressed! This'll take a while!' She disappeared down the hall with the speed reserved for the young and nimble.

Despite being old and far from nimble, I proceeded on to my designated bathroom, and was dressed and ready long before Epiphany. I paced the living room, turned on the television, flipped through the channels, tried to watch, but my mind was rumbling like a rocket on the launchpad just before liftoff. I couldn't remember the last time I'd felt such anticipation – perhaps in the moments after *Surveyor* left for the moon, or when the astronauts of *Apollo 13* splashed down, alive and well. Yet perhaps even those days didn't compare to this one. This day was not of my own making, but an act of God, the sort that cannot be questioned or denied, but only observed with a profound sense of awe.

When I heard Epiphany's steps in the south hall, I rose and met her in the entryway, near the bottom of the stairs. She paused in the shadows of the corridor, shrinking into herself, lifting her hands palms up, her nose crinkling. 'Is it okay, do you think?'

I smiled as she stepped into the light, slightly unsteady in a pair of sequined silk sandals Annalee had purchased at a market in Morocco. To go with the shoes, Epiphany had chosen a cocktail dress in red satin and black lace, something Annalee had worn with a sweater at Christmas, when Roy played with a jazz quartet at a charity ball. I couldn't remember anything else about the dress except that Annalee wore it on that happiest of happy nights, one of our last holidays with Roy. 'I think it is perfect,' I said to Epiphany. 'Annalee would be so pleased.'

Epiphany's lips lifted into a smile; then she spun around and hurried unsteadily back to the bedroom, returning with her flip-flops dangling from her fingers. 'No way I can drive in these things, though.' The sandals were a hair too

430

small, perhaps, but passable. Balancing on one foot, she removed Annalee's Moroccan sandals and then slipped into her flip-flops.

'As long as you change when we reach the restaurant. No flip-flops tonight,' I said, and then held out my arm. She put a hand under my elbow, as if to support me, and I paused to show her the manner in which a lady should expect to be escorted by a proper gentleman. 'Just catch me if I fall,' I said.

'No problem, J. Norm.'

As we proceeded up the hallway, I took a walking cane from the umbrella stand, so as to pacify Deborah. Under no circumstances did I intend to be seen toddling around behind the rabbit cage tonight. A man does have his pride, after all.

I was relieved when Epiphany chose not to kibitz about leaving the walker behind. She merely strolled with me to the car, helped me in, then settled herself into the driver's seat, and we were off on another of our little adventures.

When we were just a block from our destination, I asked her to pull over in a parking area.

'What for?' she questioned, letting the car drift to a halt in an empty commuter lot. 'You getting cold feet or something?'

'No, no. Nothing like that.' Although, at this juncture, every nerve in my body had come alive, as if I were filled with electrical circuits and someone had just thrown the switch. 'I want to drive.'

Epiphany's mouth dropped open. 'You want to *what*?' Her

fingers tightened around the steering wheel. 'No way. You're not supposed to drive. Deborah doesn't even really like it when I drive you.'

I pointed toward tall brick walls that formed the back of a series of buildings ahead. 'We're almost there. It's just around the corner and up the block a bit.' I was deliberately vague, so as not to give away all of my secrets, even though I was about to share at least one. 'I believe I can be trusted to pilot my vehicle that far. It won't do for the inaugural recipient of the Annalee Evans Alvord Memorial Scholarship to pull into a swanky joint and be seen changing out of her flip-flops, now, will it? I'll drive and you change your shoes.'

'I can change . . .' As usual, Epiphany argued first, then processed. 'The . . . what? Scholarship . . .' Putting the car in park, she turned to me, her hand falling off the steering wheel and landing on the console with a slap. 'J. Norm, what are you talking about?'

I couldn't contain my smile. It was pressing through from the inside again. 'Deborah and I discussed it. We want to provide a scholarship for an exceptional high school student to attend St Clare's. It's now an academy focusing on math and science, and an outstanding school. Small classes, opportunities for enrichment, a curriculum tailored to the needs of the individual. Almost all of their students are awarded funding for college. If Annalee were here, she'd want you to be the first to receive a scholarship in her name. She would be so pleased, Epiphany, so proud of the type of young lady you are.'

432

Epiphany looked at me for a long while, then sniffled and blinked, dabbing underneath her eyes. 'Man, J. Norm. You're ruining my makeup.'

'My apologies,' I said, then slipped a hankie from my pocket and gave it to her, our gazes holding fast again. 'You deserve this, Epiphany. You'll change the world someday.'

She swallowed and wrung the hankie in her hands, looking down at it and slowly shaking her head. 'No, I don't. I mean, but . . . Deborah thinks it's okay? She's not mad or anything? I bet St Clare's costs some serious money.'

'A bit,' I agreed. 'But worth every penny. You'll have to work very hard there, of course. It's no cakewalk.' My thoughts ran ahead, filling me with a sense of anticipation. I couldn't wait to see Epiphany removed from the school in which she was surrounded by negative influences, faced with bullying and intimidation, and moved to an environment in which she could thrive. 'I can help you with math and science, of course, but in literature, English, and public speaking, you'd be on your own.'

'Uh-oh.' She laughed and sniffed again, still looking down at the hankie, thinking it through. Her mouth pulled into a frown. 'Mama won't ever let me do it, J. Norm. You know she won't. As soon as she hears "St Clare's" and "private school," she'll have nine million reasons why I can't go there.'

Smiling to myself, I reached for my door handle. If we didn't proceed, dinner would happen without us. Deborah and Lloyd were probably in the restaurant already, Deborah checking her watch. 'Have a little faith, Epiphany. I have the rest of the summer to charm your mother into it.'

The comment won a soft, if slightly rueful chuckle. 'Oh, well, if *you're* gonna charm her, then we got nothing to worry about.'

'You'd be surprised what I am capable of.' Opening my door, I swung my legs around and stood up. In that moment, I felt ten feet tall, capable of anything, a man still in the prime of his usefulness, if not in the prime of his life. There were yet worlds for me to conquer, mysteries left to solve, bridges to be built. 'Now switch places with me and change your shoes.'

For once, Epiphany did as she was told. We traded seats, and she slid her feet into Annalee's sandals, then freshened her makeup. Occupied with looking in the visor mirror, she didn't see where we were until we'd pulled into the portico and the valet came out.

Gasping, she took in the valet stand, the building, the sign painted in antique letters over the door: TUSCANY RIS-TORANTE. 'J. Norm . . .' she whispered, her breath rising and falling as she pressed a hand to her chest, her skin a soft, golden brown against the black lace of the dress. 'We're . . . we're going here?'

Her reaction was exactly what I'd been hoping for. 'It's a special night,' I said. 'I think they should meet the lovely, charming young woman they've missed out on, but it's up to you. I didn't tell them who you were when I arranged to have dinner here, and I won't, if you don't want me to. But I think you should consider it, and tonight's as good a night as any. There's always time for people to change, Epiphany. As long as there's life, there's hope.'

The valet opened the door, and we exited the car. Forgoing the walking cane, I waited for Epiphany on the curb, then held out my elbow. 'Make sure I don't fall and embarrass myself on the way to the table.'

'I will,' she answered, and hooked her arm with mine. 'Don't worry, J. Norm. I got ya.'

'I'm depending on it.' We walked up the long red carpet, and the doormen opened the doors.

'You nervous?' Epiphany asked softly, looking around the candlelit interior as somewhere in the dining room a string quartet played 'Sentimental Journey.'

'Somewhat.' I doubt I would have admitted that to anyone other than Epiphany, but in truth, she already knew.

'Me, too,' she whispered, trying to peer around the corner as we stopped at the maître d's stand. Behind a privacy wall, the dining room and a central dance floor were only partially visible. 'You think they're in there?'

'One way to find out.' Leaning over the stand, I gave my name.

The maître d', a young man with a Mediterranean look about him, stopped writing immediately. 'Oh, yes. Yes, sir! We have your party waiting. It is a special night for you, I am told. *Una riunione di famiglia.*'

A reunion of family. 'Yes, it is.' Perhaps tonight would be a family reunion in many ways. One could always hope.

'Follow me, please,' the maître d' offered with a flourish. As he guided us toward the dining room, Epiphany's hands compressed my arm, as if she were dangling off a cliff, clinging to the rope. I laid my fingers over hers to draw

435

comfort as much as to offer it. We were on a journey again, Epiphany and I, traveling an unknown country.

My heart pulsed in my throat, the beat strong and measured, heavy with anticipation as we rounded the privacy partition and started through the dining room, past a large wall with an old brick fireplace, past diners seated at cloth-covered tables beneath black-and-white photos that detailed the history of Tuscany Ristorante, past the grand piano and the string quartet that reminded me of the black-tie celebrations Annalee and I attended during our days at the cape, past the dance floor where couples spun 'round and 'round to a Viennese waltz. We strolled slowly toward a table in the corner where, finally, I spied my daughter and son-in-law. Deborah was laughing just then, her head tipped back, her smile radiant, so like her mother's. The chairs at the table were filled, except for the two reserved for Epiphany and myself.

Noticing our approach, Deborah touched the hand of the person across from her, a tall woman with soft red curls piled loosely atop her head. Next to her, a woman with a face that seemed too young for her gray hair turned to look, and then the whole group paused, hanging as if in suspended animation. No one needed to tell me which were my sisters and my brother. It was as if I knew them still, as if they had been inside my mind all this time, waiting to become real. I could see bits of myself in each of them. There were seven at the table in all: Deborah and her husband, my two sisters, two spouses, and a brother – the baby whom Cecile had bounced on her knee. Perhaps someday we would discover what had become of Johnny, the little boy who toddled through the yard after the twins, scattering dandelion seeds to the wind.

For now, there were the four of us, and the people with whom we had lived our separate lives, made our own families. As they rose to meet me, all else fell away. In the arms of my sisters and my brother, their tears wet on my skin, I felt the pieces of myself coming home. All that had been broken and lost and scattered on that day we were last together had finally been brought together again.

I understood that Annalee was right, after all, in something she'd told me as we studied the stars over the college lawn long ago. *Nothing happens by accident, Norman,* she'd said. *It's all part of a larger plan.*

I'd scoffed playfully at the time, asked how it could be the plan for someone like her to end up with someone like me. But now I knew that she was the wise one, the one who'd been right all along. We do not live in this world at random, bodies drifting through empty space, forming and colliding by mere chance; nor are we the masters of our own destinies, as much as we may desire to be. Rather, we are like the dandelion seeds my brother cast into the summer sky, ferried along by He who guides the winds and stills the waters, our journeys a mystery to us, except in hindsight. Along the way, we find those we are meant to love and those who are meant to love us. We fashion our lives according to what we have known and what we have yet to learn. At times, each of us is the child in a burning house, escaping through tiny doors, dependent upon the grace of God and the kindness of strangers.

Wherever our journeys may take us, whatever struggles they bring, one solid truth underlies all that is. Not a drop of water falls from heaven unintended. We are, each of us, meant to change the ocean and to be changed by it, to become new creations as we travel our paths, and answer our challenges, and live and relive our Camelots.

ACKNOWLEDGEMENTS

Writing a book is, in some ways, similar to engineering those early missions to the moon. You find yourself making plans to travel into the unknown – to go to a place no one has ever been. Success in such an endeavor depends upon the generous contributions and expertise of many people. *Dandelion Summer* would never have safely soft-landed in the bookstores without the help of some wonderful, amazing, and thoroughly inspiring contributors. As the head of mission control for this project, I'd like to take a moment to give credit where credit is due.

To begin with, fathomless gratitude goes to former Hughes Aircraft engineer and treasured friend Ed Stevens for invaluable help, advice, encouragement, and the many, many shared stories over the past several years that inspired the creation of Norman. Thank you for answering countless questions, for sharing photos and documents, and for bringing the early years of America's space program to life. Thank you for your help with technical projects over the years, and for the wisdom you've shared. I love hearing your stories, and I treasure your friendship.

I would also like to pay homage to the men and women of Cape Canaveral's early years, who worked tirelessly in many capacities with NASA, JPL, and Hughes Aircraft, and whose innovation and hard work led to an era of shining moments for America. We have always been the sort of country that does what has never been done. It's worth noting that the names of those who said Surveyor's mission to the moon was impossible have long since passed into history, but those who believed it was possible *made* history. As my friend and adviser on this mission, Ed, once told me, 'No one ever erected a statue to a critic.'

My gratitude goes out to my family for being wonderful, supportive, and amazing in general. Thank you to my mother, Sharon, for editing, hashing over plotlines, proof-reading, and helping with all things book related. Thank you to my mother-in-law, Janice, for helping with address lists and for being such a sweet grandmother to my boys. Thanks also to relatives and friends far and near for encouraging, supporting, hosting us on book trips, sharing stories, and always asking at family gatherings, 'So, what are you writing now?' Everyone should have such a loving, encouraging, and fun family. I'm incredibly grateful to Teresa Loman (yes, I now know there is no 'H' in either of your names) for heading up the Facebook readers' group and often making me laugh like a crazy woman. I'm grateful also to my friends and fellow Southern gal bloggers at www.SouthernBelleView.

com. What a hoot to be sharing a cyber-porch with you and blogging about books, good food, and life in general.

On the print-and-paper side of things, I'm grateful to the dedicated professionals at New American Library and Penguin Group. Thank you, Kara Welsh and Claire Zion, for your support of this book, and my appreciation also goes to the hardworking folks in marketing, sales, and publicity, who bring the books to the stores. A measure of deep gratitude goes to my editor, Ellen Edwards, for believing in this book from the first time we talked about it on the phone. Thank you for your encouragement and guidance in this project and in so many others. It's hard to believe it has been ten years since we started this journey with the publication of *Tending Roses*! To my agent, Claudia Cross at Sterling Lord Literistic, thanks again for all that you do.

Last, but not least, gratitude beyond measure once again goes out to reader friends far and near. Without you, Epiphany and Norman's little dandelion parachutes would have no place to land. Thank you for sharing this story circle with me and for sharing the books with friends, recommending them to book clubs, and taking time to send little notes of encouragement my way via e-mail and Facebook. I cannot imagine that any storyteller, anywhere, has ever been blessed with a more wonderful, enthusiastic, and supportive group of listeners. I hope this latest journey into the unknown brings some pleasant reading hours and that this little batch of dandelion seeds leaves behind even a fraction of the happiness you've given me.